PRAISE FOR THE INDENTURED QUEEN

I love Carol Moncado's royal stories. Her fans have waited a while now to read King Benjamin's story. He was not a very nice fellow in the snippets from previous books, so you'll just have to wait and see what she does with him. The story was delightful and I devoured it. Loved it.

— SUSAN S

I've run out of words to describe Carol's books. I have loved them all. But The Indentured Queen has just joined my short list of Favorite Books of all Time!

— MARIE P

I love her characters. They have some real depth to them but she also writes with such a great sense of humor. The story line flows smoothly from one book to the next and I love how her different series are connected throughout!

— ESTHER G

Carol Moncado has done it again, bringing us a beautiful royal romance showing God's love and guidance. I loved the amazing characters. My favorite character was the sassy, snarky, Katrin, who always had a positive attitude regardless of her circumstances.

— LINDA R

The Indentured Queen

Crowns & Courtships
Book 4: Royals of Eyjania

Carol Moncado
USA Today Bestselling Author

CANDID
Publications

Copyright © 2018 Carol Moncado

All rights reserved. No part of this publication may be reproduced, stored in a retrieval system, or transmitted in any form or by any means — for example, electronic, photocopy, recording, for personal or commercial purposes — without written permission of the author(s). The only exception is for brief quotations in printed or electronic reviews.

This is a work of fiction set in a fictionalized southwest Missouri and a redrawn, fictionalized Europe & Atlantic Ocean. Any resemblance to real events or to actual persons, living or dead, is coincidental. Any reference to historical figures, places, or events, whether fictional or actual, is a fictional representation.

Tamara Schmanski (writing as Tamara Leigh), holds all rights to the Wulfen Castle, the Wulfrith family, and the Wulfrith dagger of the Age of Faith series referenced in this novel and are used with the author's permission.

Crown Prince Theodore of Valdoria and Princess Alexandra of Litiania are property of Julia Keanini and used with permission.

Cover photos: Copyright: Sonyachny/DepositPhotos
    Author photo: Captivating by Keli, 2010
    First edition, CANDID Publications, 2018

For Allen
The original Wheelchair Preacher
My second cousin
No matter how distant the relationship, we are family.
I am so incredibly thankful for the invention of Facebook and the connection we made over the last few years. I am eternally grateful for the family reunion in Baton Rouge and for the hours we spent together in Tyler, even if you were in the hospital.
I loved every minute of getting to know you and your exuberant spirit.
Your love for your friends, your family, and, most importantly, your Savior
was infectious and inspiring.
I wanted to do you justice and know I didn't even come close.

10/22/85-1/25/18
They say it's all about how you live your dash.
You lived yours to the fullest.
We miss you but rejoice that you've been made whole.
You ran your race.
You finished your course.
I can only imagine the joy on your face when you heard
"Well done, my good and faithful servant."
I love you, cuz. Now and always.
This one's for you.

1

In forty-eight hours, King Benjamin James Timothy would be in complete control of his household for the first time.

He strode through the wide hallways of the Eyjanian palace toward his uncle's quarters.

The quarters that Isaiah should be in the process of vacating.

It had only been a few hours since he'd stood up to his uncle for the first time at the Mevendian Founders' Ball held at the Eyjanian home of Prince William and Princess Margaret of Mevendia. Benjamin's security team knew the instructions he'd given Isaiah. Benjamin also knew Isaiah likely wouldn't follow them without force.

A maid he didn't recognize scurried down the hall, stopping just long enough for a quick curtsy. Benjamin barely noticed. Staff members, outside of senior staff members, were to be seen and not heard, and not seen whenever possible.

Someone else, just out of Benjamin's line of sight, ducked through an open door. Good. He didn't like to be disturbed. Most of the staff knew to get of the way before he was close enough to see them.

"Is he packing?" One of Benjamin's most trusted guards stood outside the door.

"Unlikely, sir." Thor bowed slightly at the waist. "I haven't heard any noise coming from inside his quarters."

"And the tunnels are sealed off?"

"I have a man inside each of the tunnels leading from these quarters, and another at the exits. They report in every fifteen minutes. He won't be able to get anything out of here those ways." Thor knew Benjamin would hold him personally responsible if Isaiah did make off with anything.

"Good." Benjamin stared at the door and wondered about going in. No. Not now. Tomorrow, if there were no indications of movement, he would enter and remove his uncle from the premises. Rather, he would have Isaiah removed. He had people to do that.

He retraced his steps until he reached the Rainbow Reception Room. Across the room, in front of a wall between the floor-to-ceiling windows, a dagger sat encased in a glass cube.

The knight's dagger belonging to King Alfred the First.

Sent to train at Wulfen Castle in England, Alfred had obtained what many aspired to, but few ever achieved - knighthood from the Wulfriths, the most esteemed family to ever bestow knighthood. The story had been handed down for nearly a millennia in the form of legend. The ruby at the cross between the hilt and the guard, winked in the dim lighting. His ancestor was the stuff of legend himself, but even he didn't compare to those who trained him.

Would Benjamin have been found worthy of such a dagger?

He'd known this dagger existed, was in this room, for as long as he could remember, but it wasn't until after Christmas that he started to come stare at it. Not until King Edward of San Majoria had lectured him at Christmas had Benjamin spent time wondering if he would be worthy.

If he was a worthy successor to both King Alfred the First *and* King Alfred the Second.

Benjamin's father.

The first note of music didn't surprise him. Neither did the second. Or the crescendo that built. By turns, the sounds of excitement, danger, happiness, anger, despair, and finally joy filled not only the room but Benjamin's soul.

King Alfred's Overture had been written by an Eyjanian composer several hundred years earlier.

Eventually, the resolution trailed away to nothing.

This time Benjamin heard the scraping of the piano bench and footsteps walking away.

"Halt!"

The gasp from the pianist, whoever it was, said his suspicions were correct. His presence had been undetected.

He turned to see a young woman across the room. Her back was to him, but based on her uniform, she worked in one of the industrial kitchens. "Turn around."

She did, but didn't raise her head.

A few steps brought him closer to her. "Do you know who I am?"

"Yes, sir." She dropped into a deep curtsy. "My apologies for disturbing your time, sir."

"Do you have permission to play in here?" He already knew the answer. No one did outside of rare special events.

"No, sir."

"Is this the first time?"

Her hesitation told him the answer before her word. "No."

"You work in the kitchen?"

"Yes, sir."

Something about her drew him closer, and he took a step into her personal space. "Look at me," he commanded.

She finally raised her chin and met his gaze. Her eyes, the color of chocolate, were guarded.

"What's your name?"

"Katrín."

"Do you know where my office is, Katrín?"

Her face tilted downward. "Yes, sir." Her voice sounded resigned.

To what?

Crooking his finger under her chin, he tipped her face back up. "I have some business to take care of. Be waiting for me when I return, and we'll forget this ever happened."

Before she could say anything, he kissed her, his hand sliding around to the back of her neck as his other arm slipped around her waist. Her hands clutched his jacket, holding him to her as much as he held her to him.

He'd long been told that, as king, he could request this kind of thing from his female staff members and expect their acquiescence, but he'd never availed himself of it before. Something about this girl drew him, though, differently than any one before.

Benjamin pulled her more tightly against him before letting his lips leave hers, brushing kisses lightly along her jawline toward her ear.

"Come to my office in an hour. We'll forget all about this."

He felt her fingers tighten on the sides of his jacket. Unsure what it meant, he loosened his hold.

"No."

"Pardon?"

She pushed him away. "My terms of indenture do not extend to *that*."

Benjamin straightened his jacket. "Then I will have to speak with Mr. Bond and see that your services are terminated."

The look in her eyes changed to icy flames, as she laughed, dousing any attraction he might have felt. "I'm afraid not. Short of attempting to kill your royal self, I cannot be terminated for at least a decade."

He crossed his arms over his chest as his eyes narrowed. "Why is that?"

"My family owes yours a debt. My services fulfill our end of the deal until the debt is paid." She spun on her heel. "But I don't have to acquiesce to those kinds of demands."

He watched her leave, then went to Mr. Bond's office. The head of kitchen staff confirmed what the girl said.

"Demote her as far as you can," Benjamin ordered.

"I cannot, sir. I would, but she's already the lowest member of my staff, likely the lowest member of all staff in the palace. The only way she could not be would be someone else with an indenture greater than hers."

"And a transfer somewhere else? The stables? Mucking out stalls?" Even he'd done that a time or two when he'd gotten in trouble before he became king.

"A promotion. Caring for the royal horses is an honor."

It irritated Benjamin, but it didn't appear he could do anything about it.

He left the kitchen offices and went to the executive wing. Though he'd spent the evening at the Mevendian Founders' Ball, he did have work to do, especially to make sure Isaiah didn't have access to anything he shouldn't.

It was not the time to dwell on the embers long stoked but fanned by that kiss. His ability to compartmentalize was learned, but necessary. It would be more difficult than ever.

Time to work.

KATRÍN SANK against the door of her room as she locked it behind her.

She'd seen the king from a distance before, but had never actually spoken with him. Certainly she'd never kissed him. Or turned down his advances. She'd never heard of anyone else who had.

If she thought long enough, she'd never heard stories of other female members of the staff being summoned to his office for anything other than actual business, and that rarely enough. But Katrín was mostly an outcast, even among the lowest of the kitchen staff. Seldom did anyone speak to her when they didn't have to.

She didn't have much experience, but that kiss told her he clearly had more - or he was really good at faking confidence at something as intimate as kissing. The desire that had unexpectedly coursed through her had shocked her even as she knew she wouldn't acquiesce to his demand.

His request.

As infuriated as it was, he hadn't actually *demanded* anything of her.

Temptation had been too much. The red grand piano called to her far too often. It really had only been a matter of time before someone found out. She'd gotten too complacent. Before she'd always carefully looked around the room to make sure she was alone. This time, she'd assumed. The king was gone for the evening. Everyone's attention had been drawn to the other end of the palace for one reason or another. She'd thought it was safe.

Her gaze settled on the keyboard on the other side of the room. Found cheap by her mother at an estate sale, the keys weren't weighted. They didn't feel the same as a real piano. The only good thing that could be said for it was that the speakers didn't work. She could plug a headset in, but she couldn't accidentally make too much noise and get in trouble for disturbing her neighbors.

Not many people lived down here, though. Mostly, they lived in other parts of the servants' quarters or in the city. Her mother had lived in the city when she worked for the palace. She still did, along with Katrín's sister and brother. Her sister had recently taken a job at a new house, for the Crown Prince of Mevendia. Katrín didn't know what the position was, but knew the job was a good one.

For actual money.

As terms of her indenture, Katrín made little money, but received room and board and two half days off a month. Or was supposed to. She rarely did. When had she had a full day off? Ever?

Five years since she came to the palace to live, hugged her mother goodbye, and walked away without looking back. She hadn't seen any of them since. They wrote old fashioned letters, mailing them once or twice a week. Katrín tended to get them every few weeks, though she mailed them more often than that. If she didn't know any better, she'd think someone in the mail room was out to get her and didn't deliver her mail as soon as it arrived. She rarely ventured to the upper basement where a whole town existed. A post office, ATM, security station manned by both local police and palace security forces, a theater, even a commissary for those who lived on property. Katrín could shop there, but anything she spent was subtracted before her bi-weekly pay was deducted from what her mother owed.

What she owed.

After about ten minutes, she picked herself up and got ready for bed. At least she had a small washroom of her own. The shower fit her, though she wouldn't fit if her hard work didn't ensure she remained slender.

The windowless, soulless room had been her refuge, her haven, the last five years, but tonight the walls seemed to close in on her.

Two days went by and the walls didn't come crumbling down. Mr. Bond didn't glare at her any more than usual, though he glared constantly so it wasn't saying much.

Tuesday, four days after she turned down the king's advances, whispers around the kitchen caught her attention. No one talked to her, though not many people did with any regularity.

"Katrín!"

She looked up from the sink where she was up to her elbows

in soap suds. "Yes, sir?"

"Your presence is required in the executive offices." Mr. Bond's hard stare told her he likely knew about her piano excursions and wished she could be demoted. Too bad she was already the lowest rung on the totem pole of the palace.

Katrín shook the suds off her hands then wiped them on the apron. They weren't dry, but they seldom were. With a tug of the strings, she took it off and hung it on the hook reserved for her apron.

A severe looking security guard escorted her from the industrial kitchen toward the stairs. She knew the layout of most of the palace, but he took the lead. As they reached the top of the first set of stairs, another guard fell in place behind her. Did they think she was going to steal something? Run off?

The next set of stairs were the tallest in the palace - and most intimidating - and led to the royal offices.

The guard in front held the door to the executive office wing open and let her walk in on her own. A severe looking man stood up from behind a desk. Slender with a dark gray mustache to counterbalance his white hair, his eyes were nearly ice blue. "This way, please." His unexpectedly deep voice caught her off-guard.

A door, one that extended from the floor nearly to the sixteen-foot ceiling, opened when the assistant leaned his entire weight against it, the royal crest splitting in half as it did.

It took all of Katrín's self-control not to gape at the opulent scene in front of her. Her room could fit inside the office a dozen times, maybe more. The desk, situated a few feet from the center of the wall opposite the door, was bigger than the bed she slept on.

King Benjamin didn't stand, didn't even look up, as she walked in. With no other instructions, she just stood and waited for him to notice her arrival.

Katrín looked at the wall of windows to her left, with an impressive view of Akushla beyond. While she waited, she studied the paintings, including one of his parents' wedding and one of his official coronation after he turned eighteen.

"Are you planning to stand there all day?" He made a note on the piece of paper in front of him.

"I'm not sure what else to do, sir."

Finally, he looked up, his face impassive, and she did as expected, and curtsied.

"Have a seat."

Perched on the edge of the chair, she waited for him to finish reading whatever paperwork was in front of him.

"I have a proposition for you."

Her heart thudded in her chest. "If it's anything like the proposition you made the other night, my answer remains the same." He couldn't have her beheaded or anything, but he could make her life completely miserable.

"No. There will be none of that sort of thing." He turned the papers around so she could read them if she'd been closer. "This proposition ends your indenture in about a year."

Somewhere deep inside, hope began to blossom. "Okay."

"You don't know what the terms are."

"Are they so horrible that I'd say no?"

"Unlikely." He leaned back in his chair and crossed his arms over his chest. "In approximately a year, you will disappear. As far as anyone knows, you'll be deceased."

The bloom of hope wilted. "Why would I do that?"

"The debt you owe will be forgiven, and your brother will be taken care of for the rest of his life."

The man knew how to put someone over a barrel. He had to know how much her family meant to her and how much she worried about her brother when her mother passed someday. "And in return?"

His eyes reminded her of the ocean in the dim light before he kissed her a few nights earlier. Now, they were insipid cesspools. "In return, you will marry me."

2

Benjamin watched Katrín, his fiancée, walk out of the room and return to work.

Chamberlain returned to his usual seat across the desk from Benjamin. "She agreed."

"Yes. She did." Benjamin stared at the contract she'd signed. "Do we know where the announcement came from?"

"No. Best guess is Prince Isaiah before he left Monday morning, but no one knows how he managed it."

Benjamin reached for the printed copy of the press release announcing his engagement to Katrín Jónsson. No one in the palace knew about it until the phone started ringing off the hook a few hours earlier. "His access to the palace network, along with unrestricted access to the family network, was cut off after I returned from the Mevendians' house the other night."

"Best guess is that he managed to do it before then or has help from someone still working for the palace."

"Find out."

"We're working on it."

"I want a report every morning until it's figured out."

"Yes, sir."

The door opened without an announcement of anyone's arrival. Benjamin's aunt, Princess Louise who had served as his regent until he was of age, entered. "What is all this in the news?"

"I'm getting married," Benjamin told her, the grim lines of her face mirroring his tone. "We're not sure why or how, but the announcement was made this morning, and it was all over the news and Internet before we could stop it."

"And who is this girl?"

"She works in one of the industrial kitchens," Chamberlain told Louise.

"That is completely unacceptable." Aunt Louise sat in the other chair, her back ramrod straight and ankles to the side. Benjamin couldn't help but compare her to how Katrín sat. Katrín sat primly, but clearly didn't have the ease Aunt Louise did. "The King of Eyjania will not marry a commoner who works in the lowest portion of the palace." He could hear Louise's unspoken comparison to his father's choice of a commoner. His father never stood for anyone belittling his wife, Benjamin's mother, and Louise knew it had always been off-limits. But at least his mother had several years to learn how things worked before she became queen.

"It's going to happen, Aunt Louise. To back out after the publicity already this morning would destroy the public's perception of the family." Or so he'd been told. The PR office insisted their already shaky popularity would take a further nosedive.

"Then you shall never have children. One of your sisters will have to provide your heir, the next monarch."

Benjamin closed his eyes. He knew his aunt's perspective was somewhat skewed, and Benjamin didn't necessarily agree with her assessment that Katrín, or someone like her, would be unacceptable as his queen and mother of his heir, but this wasn't the time or place to delve into it. If he'd found a young woman from that social strata and still somehow fallen in love with her, he would take up the fight, but that wasn't the case here.

"We'll deal with that later," he told her.

Chamberlain frowned, but Benjamin ignored him. No one could know the situation with Katrín was temporary. He needed to remember to tell her that. Not even Chamberlain knew about the plan for Katrín to disappear. Benjamin's right hand man only reluctantly approved of the plan to marry Katrín, but Chamberlain took the marriage vows seriously. Once they were made, they were meant to be for life. Not for "until her death was faked."

"Don't give her one of the heirloom rings." Aunt Louise's warning tone caught Benjamin's attention.

What could be behind that attitude? "You think she'd try to sell it?" She'd be crazy to even consider it.

"Do you know why she's indentured?" Aunt Louise sat even straighter, if that were possible.

"No." The practice wasn't common anymore, but Benjamin knew there were a few people who were working off a debt to the crown.

"It was one of the first real decisions you made on your own as king."

Benjamin leaned back in his chair and tried to remember. He'd been so young and distraught after the death of his father. "I need more than that."

"Her mother was caught stealing a priceless hand mirror, in the family for generations."

It started to come back to him. He remembered a stoic woman, likely in her thirties, standing before this very desk. "Her son was in a wheelchair." Spina bifida. He knew that now, though he hadn't then. "He needed an operation. She never said a word in her own defense, just let us presume her guilt. However, her husband had left them, and she was the sole wage earner. It was agreed that she could work off a fine rather than prison time, but it wouldn't take more than ten percent of her income until her children were grown." Isaiah had been livid.

Louise didn't smile, but he could see the approval in her eyes. She'd believed he'd made the right decision. "Correct."

"What does that have to do with Katrín?" Another memory niggled the outskirts of his mind. "She came to us a few years later and requested she be allowed to work off her mother's debt in her place." Isaiah hadn't liked that either, but Benjamin hadn't cared much one way or the other. He'd never met Katrín, just had the proposal submitted for his approval since he was the one who'd imposed the sentence in the first place.

"Also correct."

"And you believe she would try to sell an heirloom ring for money for her family."

"Since she'll no longer be working, they won't have income."

"And she shouldn't ever have access to some of the family funds to help support her family?" Benjamin hadn't thought that far ahead, but under normal circumstances, it would make sense. If he and Katrín had fallen in love and he'd proposed as any normal boyfriend would, it seemed likely that he would make sure her family was taken care of from the beginning. He'd already insinuated to her that he would. "Or I shouldn't take care of them because they're my in-laws? If we're concerned about how the country sees our family, wouldn't taking care of my invalid in-laws move us up a few notches?"

Louise sniffed. "I suppose you have a point. However, my reservations remain."

Benjamin stifled a sigh. This wasn't going to be as easy as he'd hoped. "I'll take it under consideration." And, at some point, figure out whether to give Katrín a family ring.

THE NEXT AFTERNOON, it still hadn't sunk in when Katrín dropped into a deep curtsy as the Queen Mother and Princess Genevieve walked into the Queen Akushla Sitting Room.

"Good afternoon, dear." The Queen Mother looked every bit as genteel and kind as she did in her pictures, but she also looked every bit the queen that, in many ways, she still was. "Please, call me Eliana."

Katrín nodded, but knew she'd never find the nerve.

The Queen Mother turned slightly. "And this is my daughter, Genevieve."

Katrín curtsied slightly again, though it probably wasn't strictly necessary. "A pleasure to meet you, Your Royal Highness."

The corners of the princess's lips twitched. "Likewise, Katrín. Please call me Genevieve. Would you care to join us for tea and a snack?"

Butterflies in Katrín's stomach wouldn't let her eat, but she wouldn't tell them that.

The Queen Mother motioned toward a small table. "Please, have a seat."

Katrín waited for the other two women to be seated, then took the third chair.

Princess Genevieve took the silver dome off the tray as the Queen Mother poured tea. "Esther has developed a love of cookies since she's lived in America. She shared it with us when we visited."

Who was Esther?

"These are her favorites," the princess continued. "Mother and I quite enjoy them as well. Do you like oatmeal raisin cookies?" The princess looked at Katrín expectantly.

"They're fine." Katrín took a bite of the oatmeal raisin cookie. "I love oatmeal. I love raisins." Therefore, she must love oatmeal raisin cookies.

But what she really wanted was chocolate chip cookies. Her very favorite. Because something about oatmeal raisin cookies made her nauseous.

The Queen Mother took four cookies off the tray and wrapped them in the cloth napkin. "Take them with you then. Cook will make more."

Princess Genevieve smirked at Katrín, though she wasn't sure Princess Genevieve understood the undertones. How could she? No one, not even her mother, knew how Katrín felt about oatmeal raisin cookies. The queen's assistant entered the room and whispered with her, but Katrín couldn't hear what it was about.

"How long have you lived at the palace?" Princess Genevieve asked her, while her mother was distracted.

"About five years." Katrín nibbled on the cookie in her hand.

"And where do you live?"

"Downstairs." Vague was good. What would the Queen Mother and the current heir presumptive think if they knew she lived in the sub-subbasement? Surely, they could find out with a well-placed question or two, but Katrín saw no reason to point it out to them.

Princess Genevieve munched on her cookie. "There's a kitchen down there for you to use, isn't there? I haven't been down there in years, but I seem to remember there being a community kitchen."

"There is," Katrín confirmed. She'd used it. Once. Not long after she moved in, she'd bought everything she needed, made her mother's famous chocolate chip cookies to alleviate a bit of her longing for home, cleaned up very well, but missed a measuring spoon that had fallen on the floor. She'd been yelled at, berated, by at least five other members of the staff, so she avoided it at all costs. When she didn't eat in the staff dining hall, she ate in her room. Nothing that needed cooking, but snacks of questionable nutritional value. She didn't even do that often, because the cost of the food took away from paying off her indenture.

It was one reason why she didn't mind having so little time off. At least when she worked all day, she got fed three meals. Fortunately, the Queen Mother had asked Katrín to meet when she wasn't supposed to be working.

"You should make some of your favorites." Genevieve sipped her tea.

"Yes, ma'am." No point in getting further into the discussion.

"They don't even have to be oatmeal raisin," Genevieve went on. "Peanut butter, sugar cookies, shortbread, snickerdoodles. Any of those would be wonderful." She shrugged. "Even boring chocolate chip."

Katrín didn't reply. She didn't know how to. Something about the way Princess Genevieve said it made Katrín think she knew more than she was letting on.

"Oh, leave the poor girl alone, darling." The Queen Mother sipped on her tea. "She won't want to do anything as mundane as baking, not when she has a wedding to plan, especially since Eyjania has the ridiculous custom of the monarch or heir marrying so quickly after the announcement is made. Mine was the same way, though Alfred proposed a couple of months before the announcement, so plans were already well under way. I do wish Benjamin had talked to me first, so I could let him know the best way to do things." She sighed. "But such is life. And after the wedding, Katrín will have a household to learn how to run."

Unlikely.

King Benjamin seemed to imply that nothing would change.

Katrín, the new queen, would remain in her windowless sub-subbasement quarters, wash dishes, scrub pots, clean fryers, and occasionally, in her copious amounts of time off, get fitted for dresses for the fancy galas and balls that she would sometimes be required to attend as the wife of the king.

She wouldn't be able to consider herself the queen. She wasn't going to be his wife. She was a means to an end. A way to keep the royal family from declining further in the eyes of the general public. A feel-good story for the press.

But never truly queen. She likely wouldn't have any more

conversation with King Benjamin than she had the first five years she lived in the palace. He wouldn't need her except to occasionally remind the people that he was "happily" married before he became the "grieving" widower in less than eighteen months.

She certainly wouldn't have access to the family's kitchen in the private quarters portion of the palace.

Or did they each have their own kitchens? Were there multiple kitchens so they didn't have to share?

What did she know?

It was a portion of the palace she'd never had been, and never would be, welcome.

3

"Benjamin."

He looked up from the paperwork on his desk at the sound of his mother's voice to see the disapproval he heard evident on her face. "Good evening, Mother." He set his pen down. "Have a seat?"

"No." She crossed her arms over her chest. "I just came from tea with your intended."

"Katrín?" A ball of lead formed in his stomach.

"Yes. She's a lovely girl."

"But?" Clearly she had something on her mind.

Her hands shifted to her hips. "You haven't officially proposed to her? When the news came out the other day, you told us the two of you had kept things quiet, but she told me there was no official proposal."

Benjamin swallowed his sigh. "No. I never got on one knee, if that's what you're asking." Kings didn't do that sort of thing. So Isaiah had tried to ingrain in him.

But maybe Isaiah had been wrong about that, just as Benjamin was learning he'd been wrong about other things.

"And you haven't given her a ring, either."

His mother's frown was almost too much. "I didn't know what ring to give her," he answered honestly. "I'm not sure a family heirloom is the right way to go. I feel like those should be saved for my sisters." He had enough sisters, and few enough rings with that kind of significance for the royal family. At least, engagement rings.

"Oh, fiddlesticks." He'd done a double take the first time his mother said that, but Esther had picked it up while living in the States and his mother quite enjoyed the phrase. "There are plenty of heirloom rings, even if some of them have never been used as engagement rings before."

"If you say so. Crown jewels have never been a source of fascination for me." That was Genevieve's department.

"Your sister thinks something odd is going on because there's no ring and no proposal story." His mother's gentle tone would convict him if he let it.

"Nothing odd." Benjamin leaned forward, resting his forearms on his desk. "I just don't know anything about rings and didn't want to talk to anyone until Katrín said yes."

He closed his eyes and when he opened them a jeweler's box sat in front of him.

"Give her that one."

Benjamin glanced up at his mother to see tears shimmering in her eyes. He popped open the box, then shook his head when he saw the ring. "I can't, Mother." He snapped it closed and held it out. "This is your ring."

She nodded, the tears spilling over. "The one your father gave me when he took a knee in front of everyone at the Festival and asked me to be his bride." After a deep breath, his mother smiled. "And I want your bride to have it, if you think she'll like it."

"Who wouldn't like it?"

"Then propose properly and give it to her."

He didn't see a way out of it without telling her more than he should. "I'll ask her."

"Good." She came around the desk. He stood and let her wrap her arms around his waist. Embracing her, he wondered what his father would say. Benjamin wouldn't be in this situation if his father had lived. The royal family had been quite popular before his father's death and his mother's depression following the loss.

His mother moved away. "She's going to be good for you, Benjamin. She already has been."

He sat back down as she started for the door. "What do you mean?" It had been less than two days since the news broke.

She hesitated then looked him in the eye from across the room. "Isaiah is your uncle, and your father's brother, but he needed to be removed from a position of power a long time ago."

He picked up his pen and twirled it between his fingers. "Why didn't you say something?"

"I tried a few times, but you weren't ready to listen. Now that you have Katrín, you stood up to him. He wouldn't have approved of you marrying someone indentured to the family, but you made sure he wasn't here to tell you not to marry the woman you love." She smiled as she swiped at her cheeks. "I'm proud of you."

Before he could respond, she left the room.

She thought Katrín was the reason he'd finally stood up to Isaiah? He'd let her continue to believe that. In reality, he'd heard what his uncle said to Princess Margaret of Mevendia. He'd seen his uncle bring his fist up to strike her with his backhand.

And he'd put himself in between his uncle and the future queen of one of their most important trading partners.

He hadn't thought about it in quite those terms, of course. He'd just known he couldn't let Isaiah hit her. When he'd seen the look on Isaiah's face, Benjamin knew it was time.

For years, his uncle had been telling him he was due certain things, like respect, because of his title. Because he had been crowned King Benjamin the First, he could expect things like what he'd requested of Katrín the first time they met. But the look in his uncle's eyes as Benjamin stood up to him for the first time was something he'd not soon forget.

"Get out." Benjamin had never heard his own voice quite so low or dangerous.

"Let go of me." Isaiah's tone matched Benjamin's. "I am your uncle. Show some respect."

Benjamin didn't let go, but held on tighter as he forced Isaiah to move away from Princess Margaret.

Prince William, future king of Mevendia, put himself between his wife and the confrontation.

"I. Am. Your. Uncle!" Prince Isaiah bellowed. "You. Will. Respect. Me!"

Benjamin didn't back down. It had finally come to this. "And I am your king." His tone was far more controlled, but no less menacing. "Tonight, you have disrespected your country, your king, and yourself. I am through with your behavior. I am under no obligation to allow you to live under my roof, or to represent me in any business dealings. I am certainly under no obligation to allow you to represent my people. You have seventy-two hours to get your things out of the palace, or you will be arrested for trespassing unless you have specific permission from me. Not my mother. Not your sister. No one but me. If you want to come see any of them, you come through me. Do. I. Make. Myself. Clear?"

Isaiah stared into Benjamin's eyes and must have decided his nephew was far more capable than he previously believed. "Crystal," Isaiah finally said.

Within two hours, all of Isaiah's access had been revoked. There was still no indication of who sent the press release or when.

Benjamin reached for the phone and pressed the intercom button. "Please have Katrín sent to my office immediately."

"Yes, sir." Chamberlain was already gone for the night. The afterhours clerk would have to do.

And Benjamin would have to at least sort of officially propose to the woman he was going to marry in just a few weeks.

He wouldn't be ready. Would she?

KATRÍN WONDERED if she should have changed before going to the executive offices again. Pajamas and fuzzy slippers didn't exactly scream "I'm meeting with the king." She had a hard time bringing herself to care, though. After sitting through an evening tea with the Queen Mother and Princess Genevieve, she'd changed into comfortable clothes, plugged her headphones into her keyboard, and started playing.

She'd been so engrossed in her music that she'd nearly jumped out of her skin when the knock on the door came. The messenger told her the king required her presence. When she'd glared at him, he'd stammered the clarification that the king required her presence in his office immediately.

"Immediately" meant she didn't have time to change.

The man sitting at the small desk off to the side, looked her up and down, unable to hide his disdain. "The king will see you now."

Katrín bit back the snarky remark that threatened to roll off the tip of her tongue. Instead, she put her full weight into opening the gigantic door.

King Benjamin stood staring out the wall of windows on the far side of his office. She didn't know what he could be looking at with days still being fairly short this time of year.

"You wanted to see me?" she asked, foregoing pleasantries and formalities, including an attempt to curtsy in her pajamas. He hadn't turned, but surely he could see her in the window-turned-mirror.

"There's a box on the desk. It's my mother's engagement ring. It is yours for the duration of our marriage."

Katrín blinked. The Queen Mother's ring? "Sure you don't

want to get one out of a box of Cracker Jacks? That would be more suited for this farce of a thing."

"My mother insisted."

Great. Indebted to the Queen Mother.

"She will also want to know about the proposal and how I asked you to marry me."

Katrín crossed her arms over her chest. "She did seem a bit appalled when I said I didn't have good proposal story. She told me how your father proposed to her."

"One knee and everything."

And there it was. "But a king isn't supposed to kneel before anyone? Is that it?" She half-snorted and shook her head. "Don't worry. I'll make up some good story about how we met accidentally and that you gave me every girl's dream proposal tonight, in your office. The only place more suitable would be the throne room, though everyone knows this is where business is actually conducted and therefore the seat of power around here."

"If she asks, that would be a good story to tell."

"Don't worry. I'm sure your mother has far more important things to do than hang out with the palace dishwasher. But if it ever comes up in conversation, I'll make it sound good. I'll make *you* sound as impressive as a king should."

He didn't turn around.

"Am I dismissed?" she asked, barely concealing the snark.

He turned, hands still clasped behind his back. "No one knows the nature of our engagement and marriage. My family, especially my mother, is not to ever find out."

"So leave the ring behind when I die. Got it. Which means everyone will think I left you and offed myself, right?"

He shook his head. "I wouldn't ask you to let your family think you committed suicide."

"Just that I disappeared, accidentally not wearing my mother-in-law's priceless engagement ring, and am presumed dead. Much cooler."

His icy stare made her want to back out. "You knew the terms when you agreed."

Instead she stared right back. "Yes. I did. And I'll go through with it, exactly as we discussed. That doesn't mean I have to be happy about my family thinking I'm dead, even in exchange for them being comfortable financially after my *death*." A thought came to her, a bit diabolical for sure, but if she could find a way to have a conversation with the Queen Mother, possibly with the *king* in earshot, she might be able to make it work. "Maybe we should go tell your mother all about it right now."

He raised a brow. "Dressed like that? You do not go see the queen in your pajamas."

"I came to see the king in them, didn't I?"

"I haven't worn pajamas in front of my mother since I turned five."

It took everything in Katrín to retain her composure. "Not even on Christmas morning?"

"No. Only if I was sick in bed, then she came to visit my rooms to check on me. I was not required to dress for the occasion if I was ill."

Could that be pity Katrín felt? The Queen Mother seemed to care deeply for her children, but to always have to be "on" even in front of your parents? With a sigh, she walked to the desk and picked up the box, sliding the ring onto the correct finger.

Romantic.

"I'll leave you to your work." She started to turn.

"Thank you."

Katrín looked back at King Benjamin. "Pardon?" Had he actually just thanked her?

"I said..." He stopped and looked behind her.

"Benjamin..."

The voice behind her made Katrín's heart thud to a stop.

What was the Queen Mother doing there? She took a deep

breath and turned, pasting a smile on her face. "Your Majesty." She dropped into a curtsy, something she hadn't done for the king.

The older woman studied Katrín with a half-smile on her face. "I thought I told you to call me Eliana, but I understand how difficult that transition can be. I made it myself once. After the wedding, there will be no need for such formalities. I will be your mother-in-law." She smirked - the Queen Mother actually smirked! - in the general direction of her son. "I never curtsied to my husband in private. He actually forbade it. In public is different, of course."

"Of course, Mother." King Benjamin's voice startled Katrín. She looked up to see him standing far closer to her than he'd ever been, even the night they met, except when he was kissing her.

Time to put on a bit of a show. "Thank you so much for the use of your ring, ma'am." Katrín held out her hand then glanced up at the king with what she hoped was an adoring smile. "Your son is so kind. He was actually just telling me how he's going to make sure my mother is taken care of as soon as the wedding's over. She won't have to work anymore so she won't have to find someone else to look after my brother." She fluttered her eyelashes at the king whose expression hadn't changed. "He already knows me so well, to know that's a huge weight off my shoulders."

4

Had Katrín really just said what he thought she did? Benjamin tried not to let his irritation show. She'd backed him into a corner, and she knew it.

He pasted a smile on his face, but kept looking at Katrín in hopes his mother might not notice. "Of course I want to take care of your family. They'll be my family, too, after all. I know you and your mother both stress about making sure there's someone competent and reliable taking care of your brother. Who is more competent and reliable than your mother?"

"I know she will appreciate it. I can't wait to see her and tell her all about it." If he didn't know better, he would buy Katrín's lovesick grin. Hopefully, his mother did.

"You haven't seen your mother since the announcement?" His mother frowned. "She didn't know about the two of you either?"

Katrín turned to look more directly at him. "Oh, no. No one knew until Benji sent out the announcement the other day."

Benji?! "We thought it better to keep it close to the vest. We didn't want anyone to know and harass her family until we knew for certain this was going to last." He kept his eyes on Katrín. What was her end game?

"I do hope you've sent security to her family's house, Benjamin." His mother's worried tone made him look away from Katrín's dark eyes.

"Of course. Security was dispatched about the time the news came out." Thor had seen to that, or so Chamberlain had reported.

"My sister works for Princess Margaret of Mevendia, so I'm certain they've made sure she's taken care of."

Benjamin couldn't let his mother know he wasn't aware of her sister's employment. Had he met her sister when he visited the Mevendian home? Unlikely. He hadn't really interacted with any members of their staff.

"Benjamin, you need to make sure she isn't so busy wedding planning to spend plenty of time with her family before then. If history is any indication, the first few months as the wife of a member of the royal family are bound to be a whirlwind."

He clasped his hands behind him. "I'm afraid the wedding planning is going to be a whirlwind in itself. We didn't want to wait any longer than necessary."

"I know. Three weeks. That's less than I had with your father, though we didn't make the announcement until several months after he proposed. You don't have long and many of the dignitaries from other countries are not pleased at the lack of notice. My office has received several calls already from those who anticipate being invited."

"The invitations will go out tomorrow," he promised.

"Good."

"And speaking of tomorrow." Katrín seemed to practically bounce in those ridiculous pajamas of hers. "I have a busy day and need to get to sleep." She took a step away from him. "Thank you again for the ring. I will cherish it until death us do part, and then some."

His mother smiled. "As I have. Perhaps one day you will pass it on to your child or grandchild to use."

"Perhaps, but in the meantime, I'm afraid I must take my leave. Good night." She turned and kissed her fingertips before blowing the kiss his direction and wiggling her fingers as she walked to the door. "Goodnight, love. It won't be long until we don't have to say that anymore."

He managed to wave his fingers the same way she did, just a bit of a wiggle. "Goodnight."

As soon as the door closed behind her, his mother turned and arched an eyebrow his direction. "Seriously, Benjamin? You can give the poor girl a kiss goodnight. She is your fiancée after all. And I know I told you to propose to her as soon as possible, but in her pajamas?" Both of her eyebrows lowered in unison as she frowned. "She lives here?"

What could possibly concern her about that. "Yes, she does."

"The two of you haven't been sneaking off together to..." She didn't finish the sentence.

Benjamin wasn't in the mood for his mother's riddles. "To what, Mother?" As soon as he said it, he knew that was the wrong tone to use with her.

"To practice making an heir. I taught you better than that. That is for after the wedding."

"No, Mother. We have spent absolutely no time alone together in any location where we weren't fully aware that someone could walk in at any time." To be honest, the possibility that he'd be expected to produce an heir with Katrín hadn't crossed his mind outside of the conversation with Aunt Louise.

He'd have to explain to his aunt why he'd given his mother's ring to Katrín. Or maybe he wouldn't. Though he was beginning to understand that his aunt had his best interests in mind the whole time she acted as his regent, unlike his uncle since the day Benjamin's father died, he didn't *owe* her anything but gratitude and what was due her as a former regent.

His mother's hand on his arm brought him back to the conversation at hand. "Good. I hope the two of you have the kind of marriage I had with your father. It wasn't always easy, especially the first year after he ascended the throne when his father died, but I always knew how much he loved me."

"*Everyone* knew how much the two of you loved each other, Mother. One only has to look at any picture with you both in it or at the number of siblings I have." He was fairly certain that irritated Isaiah, despite one of them being named for him. The more children Benjamin's parents had, the further down the line of succession Isaiah was sent.

The smile she gave him was the sad one, the one that meant she was missing his father more than usual. Swallowing his exhale, he embraced his mother.

"It doesn't matter if everyone else knows you love her, Benji." His mother hadn't called him that since he was a boy. No one had, until Katrín a few minutes earlier. "It only matters that Katrín knows."

"I've never made a secret of how much I love her." Benjamin hated that his mother would get the wrong impression, but she could never know the deal he'd struck with Katrín. It would break her already fragile heart. "Just like you always knew how much Father loved you."

She stepped away. "I hope you love her far longer than your father loved me, Benji. I pray neither one of you go through what I did when he left this earth. That kind of heartache should be reserved for after you've lived a lifetime together, not only a few years."

Conviction rolled over Benjamin in waves. He would have to fake that kind of grief sooner than he cared to think about, but if his mother knew the truth, it would break her heart even further.

He had to make sure she never found out.

KATRÍN HAD no one to walk her down the aisle.

Benjamin hadn't asked. Neither had the event planner.

What Katrín wanted had nothing to do with how the wedding would go. Her dress, her hairstyle, the veil, the shoes that pinched her feet and made her want to cry.

There were no flower girls or pageboys in the bride's room with her.

Just Katrín.

No maid or matron of honor, though she'd been told one of the princesses would stand up for her. Prince Josiah would stand with King Benjamin. No mention had been made about why Prince Darius, the next oldest of Benjamin's brothers, wouldn't be there.

The clear sliver of the stained-glass window showed her person after person, couple after couple, walking into the cathedral.

There had been no response to her letter to her mother. Or her sister, though the Mevendian Crown Prince and his family no longer made Akushla their home. Was Nína even still in Eyjania? And Katrín had no access to a phone in the palace. Was her family even in attendance?

Did they know she was the one marrying the king? Or would they find out on television with everyone else? Surely, they'd seen the press release, but would King Benjamin, or more likely the event planner, have considered them acceptable to end up on the invitation list? Katrín was inclined to believe the Queen Mother would throw a fit, in her regal, queen mother, sort of way, if she discovered Katrín's family wasn't in attendance for anything other than medical reasons.

The small room, with its colored light filtering in, and its small sliver of clear glass seemed familiar to Katrín. A little bigger than her quarters in the palace, she didn't feel claustrophobic like she might have expected, but rather she felt safe. Comfortable.

And she felt that way until the door opened and someone told her it was time.

She would walk down the hall, take a deep breath, and, in front of hundreds of people and on television in front of millions, marry a man she'd spoken with exactly three times.

Her existence wouldn't change. The ring wouldn't stay on her finger. The dishwater would still ruin her hands now hidden by elbow length gloves. She wouldn't share quarters, much less a bed, with the man she would speak vows to. Her in-laws wouldn't hug her or laugh and share confidences or accept her as one of their own.

Why would they?

When one of their own, the monarch, her husband, didn't accept her or cherish her or even want to get to know anything about her.

The only thing he'd wanted from her was help saving face - and her presence in his office for his own pleasure that one time. If that was all he wanted, why would his family want anything more?

"Are you ready?"

Katrín turned to see Princess Genevieve - at least she thought that's who it was rather than Princess Evangeline - waiting for her. "As ready as one can ever be when marrying a king, I suppose."

A sad smile crossed the princess's face. "That's one way to look at it. Another way would be that you're marrying the man of your dreams."

"That would be another way to look at it," Katrín admitted, without actually saying that was how she felt. "But even if Benjamin is the man of my dreams, he's also the king. With that comes a whole host of other issues and pressures and responsibilities that I'm not certain I'm ready for."

"I would tell you that we'll help in any way possible, but my brother informed me earlier today that he wanted you all to himself for a while. Since he's unable to leave right now for an official honeymoon, he's sending the rest of us on an extended vacation to the St... an extended vacation."

Katrín hadn't thought about a honeymoon, or how she'd explain her absence to Mr. Bond. He was already going to be annoyed she missed today, though she turned in the proper paperwork for a day off.

"I appreciate the thought, regardless, Your Royal Highness."

The princess frowned at the title. "I thought my mother told you none of that was necessary in private. In fact, in about an hour, once my brother signs the order, all of us will defer to you as the Queen Consort. The only one you fall under in the Orders of Precedence is Benjamin and perhaps my mother, as the former queen, depending on how the order is worded."

"That won't be awkward for any of you, will it?" Despite the weariness in her tone, Katrín hoped the princess also heard the absurdity of it.

"Most likely, my brother won't enforce it in private." Her face took on a hard look, one so fleeting Katrín thought she might have misunderstood. "Unless you insist."

Katrín shook her head. "I don't see why I would. I am not a member of your family. I'm just me."

Princess Genevieve seemed to shake herself out of whatever funk she was in. "We're all just me." She started to say something else, but a throat cleared behind her. "It's time."

Katrín followed her down the hall, someone she didn't know taking care of her train for her. As they walked, she caught a glimpse of herself in a mirror.

Her hair was pulled back in a severe bun, nothing like how she normally wore it when she wasn't working. Her eye makeup was far darker and more dramatic than anything Katrín would have attempted on her own. The lipstick was such a dark red, it was nearly maroon.

None of that struck her hardest.

Instead, it was the nearly vacant look in her eyes that concerned her the most.

Could she manage to make this look convincing rather than like she was being forced into this?

The argument could be made that she was doing this against her will, but she wasn't being forced.

She needed to smile, to take a deep breath, and make herself relax. Even if she wasn't going to get a happily ever after in the traditional sense, this was still the first day of the rest of her life.

Princess Genevieve looked at her and smiled before taking a left turn and entering through the double doors.

The music changed. The event planner motioned her forward.

Time to go.

5

Benjamin signed his name with a flourish borne of years of practice. He didn't always, but for this kind of official, ceremonial document, it was almost a necessity.

Katrín stood at his side, having already signed the marriage document. This one solidified her spot in the Orders of Precedence. He remained at the top. His mother retained her spot as the second in the order in deference to her position as both his mother and the former queen. Then Katrín, as the wife of the king, took third place as the queen consort. His family knew he wouldn't enforce the strict hierarchy in private. His immediate family, except Isaiah, never had.

Isaiah, despite his position so close to the end of the hierarchy that he would soon fall off it all together, had often tried to insist that everyone except Benjamin, and perhaps Louise, should defer to him.

Benjamin signed his name to several more documents securing Katrín's position as Queen Consort. He placed the quill back in its stand then offered his arm to the woman who was now his wife. An unexpected jolt worked its way through his system as she slid her gloved hand into the crook of his elbow.

The bellow of someone unseen could be heard throughout the cathedral, announcing that King Benjamin had named Katrín Jønsson as his consort. As custom dictated, he'd stood with his back to the crowd as Katrín walked down the aisle. He'd yet to get a good look at her. He had not gotten a look at the crowd until now.

On one side stood his mother, tears running freely down her cheeks, with the rest of his siblings lined up next to her. Darius, and his wife, Princess Esther of San Majoria, being the notable exceptions. He wasn't sure how his brother's absence would be explained.

Across the aisle sat a teenager in a motorized wheelchair. Next to him stood a woman so similar to the one at Benjamin's side that there was no mistaking their relationship. Tears ran down her cheeks as well. The young man wore a grin unlike any Benjamin had ever seen. His face practically glowed.

The man continued to yell something about Benjamin and his bride. The assembled crowd all bowed or curtsied. He waited for half a beat then gave a slight nod of acknowledgment. Everyone returned to their standing position.

It was one of the few times Katrín wouldn't be expected to curtsy as well.

Did he expect her to in private? Benjamin shoved the thought out of his mind as music began to play. That was the cue for them to leave. He made certain to walk slowly down the stairs so she wouldn't trip. When he thought about it long enough, he knew Katrín wasn't used to formal clothes and the heels she had to be wearing. She was several inches too tall.

Benjamin knew he had a reputation for being stoic and that served him well as he walked back up the aisle with Katrín next to him. He did his best to hint at a smile.

"That's over," Katrín whispered as they exited the cathedral proper into the narthex.

"You did well," he told her. "I know being in front of so many people the first time can be intimidating."

"You grew up doing this."

His mind flashed to the first time he'd stood in the front of the cathedral, as he took the scepter and wore the crown for the first time. "It's still overwhelming." Six months after the death of his father and still too soon.

"Now what?"

The outer doors opened in front of them as they continued to walk. "Now we take a carriage ride back to the palace along a very winding parade route through Akushla." The carriage was only a few steps from the door. They weren't expected to acknowledge the crowd just yet.

"Fabulous." The word was barely breathed, so Benjamin could hardly hear it. Someone wrapped a cloak around her.

"Just remember to smile and wave. Did you see the photos of Jessabelle, wife of Malachi in Mevendia a couple years ago?" Whatever happened next, they couldn't have that.

"Yes."

"Do better than she did, and you'll be fine."

"Perhaps more like Princess Yvette did after her wedding in Ravenzario last summer when her fiancé turned out not to be dead?"

He stood to the side to allow Katrín to enter the carriage first. Taking his offered hand, she stepped up. "Precisely."

"I can offer you somewhere in the middle," she told him as she sat down, maneuvering her dress so he would have enough room. Fortunately, the fabric took up enough space that he wouldn't be expected to sit too close.

"Very well."

The driver called to the horses and the carriage began to move. As it rounded the corner, the din of the crowd went from background noise to quite noticeable.

Katrín reached over and rested her gloved hand on his. She didn't say anything, but gripped it lightly as she began to wave then blow kisses.

Cameras.

She was holding his hand for the cameras.

Benjamin pasted on the best smile he could and began to wave, though he didn't have the easy grace Katrín seemed to project.

"And after this?" she asked.

"A reception at the palace." More waving. "We will have dinner on our own." Just the two of them in an intimate alcove overlooking the city. "Then the wedding ball will last well into the night."

"Fantastic."

She continued to wave out her side as he did his best to alternate sides, whispering to her that she should as well. When she turned, he noticed her wide smile. She put on a good show, even if it didn't quite reach her eyes.

As an actress playing the part, she was doing quite well.

"You never told me what we're doing for our honeymoon." Her smile didn't falter, but Benjamin felt his slip.

"We're not going on one," he told her. Had she expected a vacation? That wasn't part of the deal. "I have work that can't be put off or given to anyone else to do, so here we'll stay."

"I know. I just wanted to hear it from you." She turned to wave out her side again.

She already knew? What game was she playing?

For whatever his other faults, King Benjamin was polite, if a bit entitled. Though Katrín understood the protocol of it, she wasn't crazy about always being expected to walk a step or two behind.

In the last couple of weeks, when she had time, she went to the computer area available to off-duty employees. She'd searched for modern consorts to see what kind of protocol she might need to follow. What she'd found, in general, was that prince consorts tended to walk a step or two behind. Prince Philip was often cited as an example. But he was also a good foot or so taller than Queen Elizabeth. If they walked side by side, someone wouldn't be able to see the queen. Same with Queen Christiana and Duke Alexander in Ravenzario and Queen Adeline and Prince Charlemagne in Montevaro.

The queens consort though... The ones Katrín looked at, including her new in-laws tended to be a bit more equal. Maybe a half-step behind. Of course, all of those women were significantly shorter than their husbands, so they weren't obstructing any view. Katrín was nearly a foot shorter than her new husband. She wouldn't be obstructing anything.

Maybe it was just ingrained in him, and he really didn't notice. If anything, on her wedding day, a bride was supposed to be in the spotlight. Katrín had no desire to steal it from him, but she wouldn't mind sharing a little bit either.

She stayed a full step behind him as they walked through the palace, and he took long steps, so she had to scurry to stay even that close.

They'd taken pictures. Smiled appropriately - she hoped - as the photographer clicked away. Fortunately, they were limited to what they expected to release to the public and not anything more than that, though she did at least get to sit at the red piano again, though she didn't play.

Katrín followed him through an arched entryway to an alcove with floor to ceiling windows overlooking the city of Akushla. A small table for two sat in front of the windows.

A staff member Katrín didn't recognize pulled her seat out for her. "Thank you," she murmured.

"My pleasure, ma'am." He then removed the silver domes off both plates with a flourish. "Enjoy your meal, Your Majesties."

Majesties? He was including her?

Katrín bowed her head and prayed to herself, blessing the food and asking for strength to get through the rest of the day, the year, her life as presumed dead.

"Won't there be dinner at the ball this evening?" she asked King Benjamin as he took a bite. No. Not King Benjamin. The man was her husband. At least in her mind, she should be able to refer to him by just his name.

Benjamin frowned. "No."

"Really? A whole ball and no food?"

He didn't look at her, but cut another bite of food. "There will be food. The guests are eating right now, but in a banquet hall."

"And we're not with them... why exactly? It's a bit odd for the bride and groom not to show up for their own wedding feast, isn't it?"

"Perhaps in many places, but here, it is customary for the monarch and the new spouse to have a meal alone."

"I see." She didn't. Not really. She'd much rather be in the banquet hall with her family sitting at the same table. No one would guess the tears in her eyes as she walked down the aisle weren't because the love of her life waited at the other end.

Not in the traditional wedding sense.

No, she'd seen her little brother spin his wheelchair around and watch her. His grin had always been able to light up the room, and this time it lit up the whole cathedral. On the other side of him, their mother. She also looked tearful, though more of a happy or possibly bittersweet tearful than Katrín felt.

It was the closest she'd been to her family in years and all she'd been able to do was give a watery smile.

The food looked and smelled delicious, but Katrín barely tasted the little she ate.

"I don't believe we discussed what happens after this." Benjamin took another bite, his plate nearly clean.

Great. One thing she'd learned in her research was that when

Benjamin finished eating, the meal was over. If the way he currently devoured his food was any indication, she'd have to find a lot of snacks when she ate with him. But he'd asked her a question. "No. We didn't."

"For the time being, I expect no changes in your arrangements."

Why would there be? She'd just become queen of his country. What else would she be expected to do? He didn't seem to be waiting for an answer, but she nodded anyway. Just as well. She didn't belong in the world she imagined the royal family occupied. If they'd eaten in the banquet hall, she probably would have made a fool of herself and the family by using the wrong fork or drinking at the wrong time. Kind of like Mia in *Princess Diaries* at her first state dinner.

"How long is this thing tonight? Are we expected to dance or what?"

"Word has been circulated that you've injured one of your ankles, and you are unable to dance this evening."

"Just as well. I'd hate for you to have to pretend you like me any more than you absolutely have to. It wouldn't do for the general public to discover that an already not-very-popular king seriously dislikes his new bride."

"I don't dislike you." He didn't even look at her as he said it.

"You clearly don't actually *like* me so the point remains the same." She took a deep breath. "But, for your mother's sake at least, I'm sure it would be better if no one realized we're not an actual thing. At least if we're not dancing, the general public will write off our lack of open affection to the reticence you've already exhibited for the last decade."

He didn't say anything as she speared a bite of food.

"I mean, no one expects us to be like your parents. Everyone knows you're nothing like your father."

6

Benjamin didn't care what this woman thought of him, so why did it hurt when she said he wasn't anything like his father?

"I mean," she went on, "your father was an outgoing, gregarious man. You're not. Everyone knows you have a much more reserved personality by nature."

The ache eased a bit. She didn't mean he wasn't the kind of man his father was, just that they had different personalities.

Wasn't that a big part of the reason why the country didn't like him, though? As Katrín mentioned, his father was beloved by all, and the only thing he loved doing as much as spending time with his family was spending time with his people. Benjamin could honestly say he'd never have the same kind of magnetism his father did. That was part of the problem when it came to his lack of popularity. He didn't know how to fix that.

Maybe if, after his time as a "grieving widower" he found someone the people adored, someone who could be like that on his behalf, make the people love him through her, as they loved his father.

The thought of his father convicted him. He probably shouldn't be thinking about his next wife when he'd been married to his current wife for just a couple of hours.

"You're probably right. It's better if we don't give the media any ammunition. Except for the dance with my mother, you'll stay right by my side, but since everyone has already been told your ankle is bothering you, we'll stay seated on the dais."

She simply nodded.

For the first time, Benjamin took a good look at her. This was their fourth meeting. She looked quite different than she had the first three. The first two times, she'd clearly come from work. Her hair had been pulled back, but less severely than now. When she'd come to his office for the engagement ring, her hair had been loose around her shoulders. She hadn't worn make-up any of those times, or at least nothing like she wore for the wedding.

The most noticeable part of her face was the lipstick. Some sort of very dark red that nearly matched his shirt and the rest of his glass of wine.

"Your Majesties."

Benjamin turned to see Chamberlain standing in the entry to the alcove. He pushed his plate away slightly. "Yes?"

"You will be introduced to your guests in approximately fifteen minutes." He bowed slightly at the waist then left.

"I'm not finished."

Benjamin looked at Katrín to see her glaring at a member of the staff. His own plate had already been removed.

The waiter looked to Benjamin who gave a slight nod. He left Katrín's plate.

Benjamin frowned. "You haven't eaten much."

"You may be used to all the pomp and circumstance and having everyone scrutinize your every move, but I'm sure not. It's messing with my appetite."

"Then it's probably just as well you won't be dancing. If you haven't eaten, you may not have the energy."

"And I wouldn't want to embarrass you or the family by passing out at the wedding ball."

"Precisely." Did he detect a hint of sarcasm in her tone? No one was ever sarcastic with him except occasionally Genevieve. "You have time for a few more bites then you'll be able to freshen up quickly before we have to walk over to the banquet hall."

"And no one will think it's weird that I can walk around this place but not dance?"

"For all they know you're only walking when in sight of people."

She pushed a bit of food around with her fork. "At least my family will be there."

She might not be his favorite person, but he didn't relish telling her. "Your family has already left. Your mother and brother both weren't feeling well and went home."

Benjamin watched as she tried to hide the emotions playing across her face. "Oh."

"Sir? It's time."

The voice behind him wasn't one he recognized but he knew no one would dare interrupt if it wasn't actually time. He moved back from the table as someone else held Katrín's chair for her.

"This way, ma'am."

Katrín glanced at him then followed the woman who had appeared from nowhere. Benjamin knew where he was going, with Chamberlain walking next to him toward the anteroom near the banquet hall.

"Any other directions for me this evening, sir?" Chamberlain asked.

"See I'm not disturbed once I leave the ball. I'll say goodbye to my family in the morning before they leave." A comment from Josiah about wanting to get to know his soon-to-be sister-in-law after Benjamin and Katrín returned from their honeymoon reminded Benjamin that others would expect them to go on a wedding trip as well. Since there was no actual reason for one, he'd decided to send his family on a trip to see Darius and Esther, ostensibly giving himself and Katrín time alone without actually leaving town.

In reality, he expected to see little of his wife.

"Shall I have the queen's belongings moved to the consort's quarters, sir?"

It took Benjamin a few seconds to remember Chamberlain was talking about Katrín and not his mother, the former queen. No one else had used the title since Benjamin's grandmother died when he was a child.

"Not immediately."

"There's nothing the queen will need before then?"

Normally, Benjamin was pretty good at reading Chamberlain's tone of voice, but his assistant seemed to be doing a very good job of hiding whatever it was he felt.

"I'll have her tell you if she does."

"Nothing else you need me to take care of?"

Even with Chamberlain's carefully modulated tone, Benjamin knew there must be something he'd missed. "If you think of anything else, feel free to take care of it."

"I wouldn't dare to presume that I knew better than you what needs taken care, sire."

Sire? Chamberlain never called him that. Your Majesty in formal settings or first thing in the morning, sir the rest of the time, but rarely sire. And his assistant presumed all the time, though he generally couched it in such a way that it sounded like it was Benjamin's idea in the first place.

Chamberlain didn't seem to be so inclined this time, so Benjamin let it drop. He quickly brushed his teeth then emerged back into the anteroom.

Katrín already waited there. Her head was bowed and her shoulders slumped, but then she straightened and held her head higher. She turned. "Are we ready to do this?"

WITH A SMILE PASTED on her face, Katrín slid her hand into the king's elbow. Despite her earlier determination not to think of him as King Benjamin, she doubted she'd ever be able to think of him as *just* Benjamin.

An unseen announcer's voice boomed through the ballroom.

"King Benjamin and Queen Katrín."

Everyone in the room was on their feet with polite applause filling the air.

Was she supposed to limp?

They had emerged onto the dais so there wasn't far to walk. Since they weren't eating dinner, they didn't sit at a table. Instead, two not-un-throne-like chairs were waiting for them. Set at a slight angle, they were only close enough to hold hands. No other physical contact was even possible.

Benjamin stopped in front of the chairs and stood there for a moment. Finally, he leaned down and spoke quietly. "I am going to dance with my mother." From the angle, anyone else might think he kissed her cheek.

She took her seat, watching as he walked to his mother's side, bowing slightly and extending his hand to her.

As they danced, Katrín remained perched on the edge of her seat. That wasn't going to work for the rest of the night. She gathered her dress to the front then tried to scoot back, but doubted it looked as elegant as a queen was supposed to. Once in position, it was better.

The music ended. Katrín expected Benjamin to return to her side. Instead, he danced with one of his sisters as others joined them on the dance floor.

A young woman came to stand next to her. Katrín's chair was close enough to the edge of the dais that when the woman stood on the next step, her head was about the same level as Katrín's. "Many of those present would like to extend their congratulations. Given your inability to circulate they will come to you. I'll tell you who is who."

That was a weight off Katrín's shoulders. She'd never remember even the people she was supposed to already know. "Thank you."

For the next half hour, people came to see her. They stopped, bowed or curtsied, made one of several congratulatory comments, then moved on.

"Crown Prince Theodore Kane of Valdoria and his wife, Princess Alexandra Torre, previously of Litiana," the woman's voice said softly.

The striking couple didn't bow or curtsy. They were the first members of royalty to stop to talk to her.

Katrín inclined her head in as much of a bow she could muster. "Thank you for coming, Your Royal Highnesses." How exactly was she supposed to address them?

"Congratulations, Your Majesty." Princess Alexandra leaned closer. "Your dress is gorgeous, but I can imagine you're grateful you don't have to dance in those heels."

Katrín managed a weak smile. "I wish I'd been able to have a first dance with the king this evening, but such is life." If she was dancing, at least she wouldn't have this receiving line.

Alexandra glanced around then lifted the hem of her dress to show sparkly tennis shoes. "If my mother and mother-in-law aren't around, I can get away with it." She smiled at Katrín, one of the few truly genuine smiles from this line. "If you ever want to talk, give me a call. I'm sure I can give some pointers on royal life if you need them. When the time comes, a long time from now, I'm sure I'll welcome talking to someone who's been a queen consort for a while."

The way Prince Theo's arm slid around Princess Alexandra's waist and the way she smiled up at him, Katrín suddenly realized they were a couple and not just friends attending together. Somehow, she knew those two would go the distance.

They moved on, though Katrín kept an eye on them as the night went on. Benjamin continued to dance and circulate. The only other royalty to come through the line was Princess Jacqueline Grace of San Majoria. There hadn't been much notice after all. Not even a representative of the Auverignonian royal family had made it - unless they just didn't stop to add their congratulations. She wondered if Princess Jacqueline Grace or Princess Alexandra, or any of her new in-laws for that matter, noticed that she didn't wear a tiara.

Maybe it was another odd Eyjanian tradition...

"They will cut the cake shortly, ma'am," the young woman told her as the line petered out.

"Could I get some water please?" she asked.

The woman gasped. "Of course! My apologies for not asking earlier, ma'am. Please let me know if there's anything else I can do to serve you."

Words Katrín's mother had likely said to the king when she was his server. At least King Alfred had never taken advantage of a woman. Never, in the five years Katrín had been in the palace, had she heard whispers of the late king doing those sorts of things. Prince Isaiah? Everyone knew he did. The rumors even said he'd fathered at least one child.

Which reminded Katrín of what was supposed to happen later. The very thing Benjamin had propositioned her with when they met.

She accepted a goblet of water from the woman who'd been standing next to her as a chill swept down her arms. "Is it possible to get the cloak I was wearing in the carriage? It's a little chilly up here."

An odd look crossed the woman's face for a split second. "Of course."

Katrín looked around. Some of the lights were focused directly on the dais. She should probably be warmer, but she hadn't been moving around, dancing, like much of the rest of those gathered.

A moment later, she hugged the cloak around her. The outside matched her dress, but the inside was dark, nearly black.

Benjamin came to stand in front of her and held out his hand. "I believe it is time to cut the cake."

She slid her hand into his and let him help her down the stairs. At least while she'd been seated her feet weren't subjected to quite as much torture.

It took all of her willpower to force a smile to her face. That wouldn't leave much willpower left.

Not when all she really wanted to do was smash frosting into the blasted beard.

7

Who created the ridiculous custom of feeding each other cake? Benjamin had fully intended to return to the dais and sit next to Katrín, but his sister commandeered a dance, followed by one woman after another.

Now he had to pretend to smile, eat one of his least favorite flavors of cake, and probably give her a kiss for the crowd.

He'd been watching the married couples in the crowd for how they acted, especially those who came in close contact with royal families regularly, but there weren't many. Most were unable to attend. Robert and Lizbeth Padovano were the representatives from Mevendia. They reminded him of his parents. Theodore and Alexandra of Valdoria were the same, but even more laid back.

Benjamin didn't do laid back.

Even as a child, he was more serious than his siblings, or so he'd been told.

The photographer gave them directions on where and how to stand, how to hold the knife - a replica of King Alfred the First's Wulfrith dagger - and then talked them through the actual process. He noticed she'd removed the cloak she'd worn in the carriage.

"Queen Katrín, you go first. Feed a bite to the king."

Katrín looked up at him, her dark eyes wary. She picked up a piece of the cake with one hand and cupped her other underneath it to catch the crumbs.

The lemon cake didn't taste as bad as he expected, but he still swallowed it as quickly as possible.

"Your Majesty." The photographer clearly meant for him to give Katrín a bite.

Carefully, Benjamin followed the instruction.

"Now, pull her close and give her a kiss. Hold it until I tell you to stop."

Katrín's eyes closed, but he imagined everyone else thought it romantic. He guessed she just wanted to get this over with, like he did.

But he had to put on a good show. And so he slipped his arm around her waist then leaned down, closed his eyes, and pressed his lips to hers until the photographer told him he had the picture.

Her lips clung briefly to his before he moved away.

They returned to the dais where a small table had been set in front of their chairs. The first two slices of cake were on plates. Benjamin breathed a sigh of relief when his appeared to be plain white cake rather than the lemon of the first bite.

"Now the champagne toast." The photographer directed them to sort of link their arms then sip from their own glasses while looking deep into each other's eyes.

In Katrín's, he saw not only wariness but weariness.

Then the photographer finished. Benjamin turned back to the cake. "You need to eat the whole piece," Benjamin told her quietly.

"What if I hate it?"

"Doesn't matter. If you don't, it will be reported and significantly hurt the reputation of the baker."

"I see." She took a bite. "Fortunately, it's delicious."

"Of course it is. The pastry chef made it."

"I've met him a couple of times. He's very kind."

Benjamin had never noticed. He wasn't sure he'd ever met the man.

After he finished his cake, the photographer staged a first dance picture.

Chamberlain nodded at him.

Benjamin offered Katrín his arm. Just another moment or two, and they'd be done with this farce. She picked the cloak up off the chair and tried to put it on, but couldn't quite get it right. He took it from her, draped it over his other arm, then extended his elbow again.

She slid her hand inside and that same jolt he'd felt several times shot through him.

"You can put it on in a minute where no one will see you struggle with it."

"I see."

They went back out the same door and down the wide hallway until they turned a couple of corners. There, they would be out of sight of the guests. He dropped his arm and handed her the cloak as Thor emerged from a side door.

Benjamin started for a staircase at the other end of the hall. A few things had come to mind over the course of the evening, and he needed to make some notes while they were fresh in his memory.

After trotting up the stairs and into his office, he sat behind the desk to jot them down. Several minutes passed before he realized he wasn't alone.

He looked up to see Katrín standing there, her cloak still in her arms. "What?"

"Just figured everyone would think I was spending my wedding night with my husband, so I went where you did. I didn't expect it to be your office, though this is where you told me to meet you that first night."

"I needed to write some things down." Like a thought about how to make Darius's marriage legal. He suspected his brother had remarried Princess Esther of San Majoria again already, though Darius had never said so during their weekly phone calls. Keeping Benjamin in the dark meant Darius wouldn't be exiled. The whole thing had been a disaster.

Benjamin knew it was his own fault for letting Isaiah influence him, but fixing it was proving difficult.

"Am I on my own tonight?"

"Sure."

"I'll be sleeping alone?" she clarified. "In my quarters."

Why was it so hard for her to understand? "Yes." He looked back up at her. "You made it quite clear what your indenture did and did not include."

"Well, at the time, my indenture also didn't include marrying you." She shrugged. "How am I supposed to know what's changed?"

"Do you need me to dismiss you?" He waved the hand holding his pen toward her. "You're dismissed."

Katrín dropped into a deep curtsy until he could only see the top of her head. "Thank you, Your Majesty. You are too kind."

Her biting sarcasm made him want to engage in a war of words with her, for fun, but not tonight. It had been a long day. He didn't have the energy.

His only response was to tell her good night and return to his notes.

When he looked up again, she was gone.

OUTSIDE BENJAMIN'S OFFICE, Katrín took stock of her situation.

Married.

Kicked out of her new husband's office.

Not entirely certain how to get to her quarters.

And wearing a wedding dress. Not exactly incognito.

What exactly was a girl to do?

With a sigh, she shook out the cloak. Could she wear it inside out? The dark wouldn't draw as much attention as the bright white, would it?

Once she got it situated, she flipped it around her shoulders only to have it catch on the veil she still wore.

Looking around the outer office, Katrín found a mirror and used it to guide her as she took out the clips holding the filmy material in place. She laid it on the chair at her side. At least she didn't have to worry about a tiara.

With the cloak in place, dark side out, she seemed a little less conspicuous. Could she pull the hood up? Or did that make her look like a hooligan?

She left it down and started for the staircase. If she wandered around long enough, she'd either find her way downstairs or, more likely, have security come across her and escort her down.

By the time she reached the bottom of the giant staircase leading up to the executive offices, Katrín knew she needed to take her shoes off if she wanted to survive. She worked on her feet, all day every day, but these heels were too much.

Leaning against a wall that had to be nearly a thousand years old, she managed to take both of them off and let them dangle from her fingers as she decided which way to turn. With her eyes closed, she tried to picture the palace layout.

Right. She needed to go right. If not, she could figure it out once she got to the first basement.

As Katrín approached the next intersection of hallways, she heard voices. Frantically, she glanced around until she found a recessed doorway she could hide in.

"That's done." Was that the Queen Mother?

"She seems nice." One of the twin sisters, though Katrín wasn't sure which, said the right words, but her tone held doubt.

"I'm sure she's lovely, or she wouldn't have married Benjamin."

"I don't love that he's making us all leave for a month." A third, younger, female voice enter the conversation.

"You love Darius and Esther," the Queen Mother's voice held a slight reprimand. "The Midwestern United States are lovely this time of year."

Darius? The missing prince? All she'd heard was that he hadn't been seen in ages, a year or so by now. Who was Esther?

"Esther has to be getting big pregnant by now. Her doctor was even talking about the possibility of bed rest because of the twins." That was the other twin sister as the voices began to trail off.

Katrín waited a moment then emerged from her hiding spot. She breathed a sigh of relief when she was alone. Hurrying, she made her way the direction she thought she needed to go.

As she did, she turned the conversation she'd heard over in her head. Prince Darius was living in the States with a woman named Esther who was expecting twins soon, but not soon enough if she might have to go on bed rest. Was Darius married to the woman? Had she ever heard of an Esther in connection with the royal family?

Wasn't there a Princess Esther in San Majoria? Could the two countries be expecting their first mutual heirs in centuries?

After two wrong turns, Katrín finally made it to the sub-basement. Quick glances around corners helped her stay out of sight until she reached the narrow staircase to the sub-sub-basement.

Staff members scurried about, though most were still upstairs dealing with the aftermath of the wedding and ball. Only a few others even lived on her hallway, and she doubted she'd see any of them.

Katrín stopped in front of her door and wanted to cry. Her key was in her purse. The one she'd left in the room where she'd gone to get ready for the wedding ceremony. Who knew where it was at this point. Probably in Benjamin's quarters where everyone presumed she was at this moment.

Think!

The day had been too long for her to take her own advice quickly, but after a moment she remembered something. One of the stones near her door was loose, and she'd hidden a key in it not long after she moved in.

In a moment, she was in her room with the door secured behind her. The shoes were dropped unceremoniously to the floor, but she laid the cloak carefully over her desk chair.

At least she had a hanger for the dress. Not the fancy kind of hanger, but good enough. Whoever picked the dress out hadn't asked Katrín what she would like, but at least it was easy enough to get off. It didn't have an impossibly long row of tiny buttons. The zipper could present a bit of a problem since the dress restricted the motion of her arms some.

In her desk drawer, she found a thing of dental floss. After pulling out a couple of arm lengths worth, she twisted it into a tiny, mint-flavored rope. It took some contortions, but she was able to feed it through the hole in the zipper pull and tie it off. Once she unzipped it as far as she could, she let the floss-rope dangle and reached around the other way to pull it from there.

Foregoing the much needed shower, Katrín hung the dress up as carefully as she could, threw on some sweats and declared herself ready for bed without even brushing her teeth. Tonight, that took more energy than she had.

Once she flipped off the light, she settled under the covers of her tiny bed and, despite her exhaustion, her mind wandered.

Had King Benjamin always planned to sleep alone on their wedding night? Or was he alone? Had he found a willing, discreet, female to share his bed?

A tear streaked down her temple and onto the pillow.

She didn't want to be in Benjamin's bed.

She'd gone into his office expecting rejection.

So why did it hurt so much?

8

"You're late." Mr. Bond glared at Katrín. She tried to look appropriately contrite, but she was too tired to care. "I'm sorry. I was up late last night."

"You also weren't here yesterday."

"I turned in the paperwork for the day off."

"And it was denied." He leaned back in his desk chair.

It was? She hadn't bothered to check. "I was at the wedding and the ball. As the... a guest." She didn't want to deal with his questions and derision if she tried to tell him she was the new queen.

"No one had the day off yesterday except anyone who had an actual invitation to the wedding and presented it to their supervisor. You did no such thing."

Katrín stifled a sigh. "Fine. Add a couple months to my indenture, and we'll call it good."

"I already have." He glared again. "Get to work."

At least she wouldn't have to worry about working out the couple extra months. In a year, more or less, it wouldn't matter.

She went into the kitchen, with its study in contrasts - modern and ancient all mixed together. The fireplace where some food was still cooked was part of the original building, but most of the stone walls had been covered with more modern, cleanable, materials. The counters, storage, and refrigeration were all twenty-first century.

So was the dishwasher.

She had three sinks she used to rinse and prewash some of the dishes or to wash the few that couldn't go through the actual dishwasher. Several plastic racks were already waiting. She powered up the machine, knowing it would be several minutes before she could run the first rack through. As she waited for the water to heat up, she scrubbed the first pot.

Someone had oatmeal for breakfast.

Her husband? It was well-known to be a favorite of the family. At least she'd remembered to take the Queen Mother's engagement ring off. Without a jewelry box, or a safe guarded by Knights of the Round Table, she hoped the top drawer of her small nightstand would be safe enough. No one should be in her room. No one had a key except herself and probably security. It would make sense that security would have access to all parts of the palace.

Pot after pot. Pan after pan. Tray of drinking glasses after tray of drinking glasses.

It never ended.

At least she didn't have to put most of it away.

When she took her short lunch break, Mr. Bond informed her she would need to work two hours late to make up for being late in the morning.

Katrín actually didn't mind that, not too much. It gave her less time sitting in her room, and she rarely left until the last lunch or afternoon tea dish was done anyway. Supper was served out of another kitchen with its own dishwasher. She wouldn't have to worry about working with the hot machine for the last couple hours. She'd get to do something easy.

Like scrub grout.

Hours later, Katrín finished the wiping down the last counter. No one else remained. If only it could be like this more often. She swiped her badge through the time clock to let the system know she was off-duty. If she hurried she'd make it to the employee dining area before they stopped serving dinner. She knew the fastest ways and as long as it was less than an hour since she'd clocked out, the cost wouldn't be taken out of her earnings.

She smiled at the few people she passed in the hallways, but didn't talk to anyone. After filling a tray, she swiped her card again at the end of the counter, then found a seat by herself. She sat with a few different people from time to time, making inane chitchat with them, but had no one she'd really call a friend.

"There you are."

Katrín looked up to see an acquaintance walking over. "Hi, Laurie." Her relationship with the other woman was the closest thing Katrín had to a friend. "It has been a while, hasn't it?" The last few weeks she'd eaten quickly or chose food she could take with her.

Laurie didn't have a tray, but sat across from Katrín and leaned forward. "Rumor has it 'the dishwasher' wasn't at work yesterday because she claims she was at the wedding."

Katrín pushed a bit of meat around on her plate. "True." She wouldn't outright lie to the closest thing she had to a friend, but she wouldn't offer any extra information either.

"So?" Laurie leaned even closer. "Tell me everything."

Katrín shrugged. "There's not much to tell. I couldn't see much of anything from where I was." That was the truth. "I never got a good look at the king during the wedding." She hadn't looked directly at him until they were outside. "And I only got a glimpse of the bride." In the mirror on her way to the doors. "I didn't even get to eat at the dinner or dance at the ball." She had eaten most of her piece of cake as she sat on the dais.

"Still." The grin on Laurie's face. "That's better than most of us who were slaving away here all day."

"Maybe."

"How did you get an invitation?"

Very good question. "I haven't seen them in years, but I know the bride's family. I went to school at King Alfred the First. The new queen went there. Same age and almost the same name thing." Almost everyone she knew in the palace thought her name was Katrina.

"It is almost the same, isn't it?"

"And the same last name," she confirmed.

"Excuse me."

They both looked up to see an imposing man standing there with a tray. "Yes?" Katrín asked, trying to figure out where she knew him from.

"Do you mind if I join you?"

She glanced around at the room that had emptied out significantly since she arrived.

"I'd prefer not to sit alone. If I wanted to do that, I'd go back to my office in security."

That's how she knew him. He'd followed them around the day before. Did he know who she was?

"Sure." Katrín nodded to the seat next to Laurie. "We'd love to have you join us."

He set his tray down then held out his hand to Laurie. "It's a pleasure to meet you." He turned to Katrín and inclined his head. "And you as well. In fact, you remind me of the wife of a... friend."

Katrín and the security guard both ate their dinner while Laurie chattered on about the people she'd seen the day before.

As she pushed back from the table, the security guard did as well.

He stared at Katrín. "Perhaps I'll run into you ladies again sometime. It's been a pleasure."

"You never told us your name." Laurie gave him a coy smile.

He didn't smile back. "Thor. I'm widowed with three sons and a member of the palace security team, which precludes me from having any sort of relationship with anyone employed by the palace." He nodded at both of them. "But pleasant conversation is always nice over dinner."

Thor waited for Katrín to go first. She put her dishes away, grateful she wouldn't be the one washing them.

"I'll see you soon." Thor's voice caused her to turn. "In fact, I believe I'll take most of my meals down here from now on."

Katrín gave him a wobbly smile. "I only eat dinner here. Breakfast and lunch are whatever I can grab real quick in the kitchen."

He didn't frown, but she sensed he wanted to. "Very well. Then I will see you at dinner." He inclined his head again. "Until tomorrow, ma'am."

She knew he was waiting for her to walk away, so she did. He wasn't going to formally acknowledge who she was, but he knew, and had been sent to make sure she was okay.

The only question that remained... who sent him?

BENJAMIN GLARED at anyone or anything in his way. He had been in the middle of an intense conversation with Queen Christiana of Ravenzario regarding trade between the two countries when Chamberlain interrupted him, despite Benjamin's instructions that he wasn't to be disturbed.

All his private secretary would say was that his presence was required immediately in the security office.

He hurried down three flights of stairs and stalked through another corridor. The security official on duty outside the office stood, saluted and pressed the buzzer to unlock the door. Benjamin gave him a half-nod as he twisted the knob. He didn't speak to the deputy head of security but just glared.

"We're sorry to bother you, sir, but..." The man glared back.

"Not sorry enough to keep from bothering me," Benjamin

snapped. "I was in the middle of a very important phone summit and left instructions not to be disturbed. What was so urgent that those instructions were disregarded?"

The deputy - was his name Thor? - nodded his head toward the wall behind Benjamin. "She was found in the family's portion of the palace, sir. She says she's your wife."

Benjamin turned to see Katrín sitting there, leaning forward with her arms twisted behind her back. "She is my wife." Such as their relationship was. Technically, the truth.

The look on the Thor's face came close to another glare and not the surprise Benjamin expected. He removed Katrín from the handcuffs. "My apologies, ma'am, sir. Her name is not on the list of those allowed to be in the private portions of the building, nor is her fingerprint on record."

Why hadn't Benjamin thought of that? Or more accurately, why hadn't Chamberlain reminded him? Wasn't that part of his job? "See that it's taken care of."

"Yes, sir." Thor returned to the desk. "Ma'am, if you could come over here?"

Katrín glared at Benjamin, then rubbed her wrists as she stood.

What did he do?

A minute later, she was in the system as able to access all portions of the palace, save personal areas prohibited to anyone without invitation, such as the family's individual private quarters. No one entered his room without his permission, and he was the only one allowed to enter any portion of the palace without an invitation from the resident or a security reason.

Once back in the hall and far enough away from the officer stationed outside, he asked a question of the woman walking at his side. "Why were you in that portion of the palace unaccompanied?"

"Since half of my stuff disappeared out of my room, and since I am, technically, your wife, I thought I would come find you and ask where it all went. I was told you weren't in your office. The next logical choice was your quarters. So I went to your quarters. Or tried to. I was arrested - handcuffed - before I got there. So your security works."

Even Benjamin, with his relative inexperience with women outside his family, could read between the lines of snark. "That's good to know."

"You'd think they'd know not to arrest your wife."

"You weren't actually arrested." He knew that wasn't the point.

"Detained. Handcuffed. Whatever." She stopped next to a narrow staircase. "I don't expect to actually be your wife, or live in the opulence you and your family do. I do expect to be consulted before my belongings are taken out of my room and disposed of."

Without waiting for him to respond, she turned and went down the winding stairs. Benjamin bit back a groan and followed her. Had he ever been down this far? Did he even know there was a basement below the subbasement?

The sub-subbasement hallway was narrow, though not too narrow. "Katrín..."

She didn't even slow. Not until she reached a door near the end of the hall. The key she pulled out of her pocket went into the lock but wouldn't turn.

"Seriously?" she muttered before glaring at him. "Would you tell your goons to let me in my room?"

"I don't have goons, and that's not your room anymore." Though he was suddenly curious to see it. To that end, he pulled his own set of keys out of his pocket. He rarely carried them, but today he'd grabbed them when he put on his signet ring. "This should be a master key." He fit it in the lock and it turned easily.

She glared, though there wasn't quite as much animosity behind the look. "Do you mind?"

Benjamin leaned against the wall opposite her door. "I'll wait."

"I'm not planning to leave anytime soon. My shift in the kitchen ended early today. It's my half-day off."

"Half-day?" Was that a thing?

"I get two half-days off a month." She pushed the door open.

"How many full days?"

"None."

Benjamin frowned, but didn't say anything as she walked into her room. He didn't follow her in but did move to lean against the door frame. It took half a second to completely sweep the room and categorize its contents.

A small bed, barely worth the name, stood bare in one corner next to a small side table. A desk and chair along with a narrow dresser lined the opposite wall.

Katrín turned in a circle. "Where's the rest of my stuff? Most of it was still here earlier." She opened a door he didn't think he could fit through. "Even my toothbrush is gone."

"That's because it isn't your room anymore." Chamberlain had done his order-disguised-as-a-request-or-suggestion thing and encouraged Benjamin to move her to the consort's quarters as people would begin talking soon if she wasn't seen in the area.

Something besides anger flashed out of her eyes, but Benjamin couldn't tell what it was. "Did you bother to ask me if I wanted to move? Or at least tell me ahead of time?"

Benjamin didn't reply. As king, his decisions were rarely questioned by others.

"Where am I going to be living?" The resigned set of Katrín's shoulders told him she'd come to grips with the thought of moving to another part of the palace.

"The consort's quarters."

"I suppose that's in part of the palace I'm allowed to roam now?"

"Next to my quarters," he confirmed.

"Ah." The knowing nod of her head annoyed him somehow. "To make conjugal visits easier. Couldn't have the queen too far away when the king wanted a visit."

"I suppose." He moved out of the way as she closed the door

behind her. For once, he waited for someone else to precede him. As he started to follow Katrín, he glanced back at the door. It finally hit him what bothered him most about the room besides its postage stamp size.

There was no window.

9

It was all Katrín could do to control her emotions as she actually walked in front of King Benjamin toward the family's living quarters - a place she never expected to visit much less live, even temporarily.

No one walked in front of the king.

Ever.

Except maybe his mother, but she had too much class to do so in front of anyone else. Truth be told, it would surprise Katrín if she did in private either.

She wasn't stopped as she neared the cordoned off section. Though few people roamed the palace without good reason to be there and knew better than to go beyond their personal boundaries, the cordon remained.

This time when she unhooked the velvet rope, no one stopped her.

The young guard standing there even had the grace to avoid looking at her.

She pushed through the door, easily as large as the one going into the king's office and stopped. How was she to know where the king's suite was, much less the consort?

Besides, she'd had no idea what lay beyond that door.

Her eyes swept across the room, hoping she'd be able to keep moving rather than follow King Benjamin's lead.

The large area reminded her of an elegant hotel lobby with potted plants and small groupings of fancy chairs.

Hallways extended off the room on either side, but directly in front of her were doors that made the others seem normal by comparison.

So that was where she headed.

Of course the monarch would live in the most ostentatious portion of the palace.

Darting one way then the other around the groupings of chairs and indigenous plants, Katrín reached the doors and pushed.

Nothing.

Pulled.

Still nothing.

Not even a budge to tell her which one was right but she was too weak.

"This way." King Benjamin's voice caused her to turn but couldn't see where he was coming from.

She started toward his voice.

A panel in the wall stood open.

"So secret entrance. Noted."

His glare told Katrín her tone annoyed him. She didn't care.

"There's another entrance that's less hidden, but you didn't wait for me."

She went through the panel and stopped as it closed behind her.

It wasn't what she expected. Not his room, like she expected or even a sitting room.

Instead, it was more of another foyer.

King Benjamin pointed toward one nondescript door. "That's mine." Then a more ornate one. "Yours."

"So if the palace is overrun by invaders, they come for me first?"

He shrugged. "I suppose."

"Isn't that the same thing you said about the purpose of the proximity of the two sets of quarters? Do you know anything?"

The king shot her another glare. "The building is hundreds of years old. I don't know what the rationale for every choice the builders or designers made."

A throat cleared behind them. Katrín turned to see the king's assistant standing there. "Sir, ma'am." He gave a slight bow.

"Why wasn't she in the system, Chamberlain?"

Katrín glanced at Benjamin. He'd been mad earlier, likely at being interrupted, but now seemed more annoyed or irritated.

She looked back at Chamberlain. "Because you never told me to, sire."

Was there subtext she was missing out on?

"I asked you to take care of whatever needed taking care of, didn't I?"

"And I told you I would never presume to know what you need doing until you request it of me, sir." How did he keep a straight face while actually retorting to the king? She needed to learn how to do that.

"You may presume anything you need to in order to make sure Katrín has what she needs."

How about a new job? Or no job? Should the queen actually be working a regular job? Shouldn't she be doing charity events and visiting sick kids in the hospital? It had been years since she'd done that and missed it.

She wasn't about to say anything though. Better that she be forgotten in their little power play.

"Perhaps the queen should be given a tour of her new quarters and told the best way to get to them, as well as how to tell where the passages are, should she ever have the need to find a secure location quickly."

"I'm sure you're much more qualified for that than I am, Chamberlain. I need to call Christiana back and finish our summit."

"I spoke with the queen. She sends her regrets but needed to end the call anyway. She and Duke Alexander have an engagement this evening, family dinner with their son, and it was time. Besides, I can imagine no one better to show the new queen around her sleeping quarters than her husband, the king."

Katrín glanced at Benjamin, who didn't look pleased. Because he couldn't be bothered with her? Because he had more pressing things to do? Because he didn't want to be in any sleeping quarters with her at all?

Chamberlain bowed a bit more deeply. "Have a pleasant evening, Your Majesties. I will be going home now."

He left out a door Katrín hadn't noticed before.

"That's the best entrance," Benjamin told her. "It's down the hallway to the left of the main seating area. The door we came in is actually a secret panel. Please don't use it unless there's an emergency."

"Noted." She looked at the doors to her quarters. "Is there some super-secret entrance to my room too?"

"Yes, but those doors are the main one." He walked back toward the wall where they'd come in. "See these four rosettes?"

Katrín stood next to him and ran her fingers lightly over the ornate wall. "What about them? There's rosettes throughout the palace."

"Correct. In different numbers and patterns. However, the clusters of four indicate a secret door." He showed her the ten-step pattern. "That will open any of the doors. However, they are not to be used when anyone else is around unless it is a dire emergency and the alarms are sounding."

"What if I'm being chased by someone who wants to kidnap me?" A likely situation.

"You will be briefed by security on what to do in different circumstances. Generally, if you're in danger and can safely get into one of the secret doors, do it, but not if those after you can see what you're doing. That puts everyone in danger." He pointed to a tapestry hanging off the wall. "You'll see these all over the palace. "If it goes floor to ceiling and has a knight with his dagger drawn, there's a small alcove behind it. The knight is protecting the one hiding behind him. If he has a sword drawn, there's access to the tunnels from the alcove. If he has both drawn the corridor has a safe room. There's alcoves cut into the walls of the corridors. The safe rooms are three alcoves down on the right, so be sure to note which knight has what weapon still sheathed and keep track as you go."

He pivoted on one heel. "I'm sure you know how doors work and can show yourself around your new quarters. You don't need me to do so."

Katrín watched him walk away, until the door to his private quarters closed behind him. She turned toward the door to her new rooms.

With a deep breath, she started toward them.

Here went nothing.

BENJAMIN PULLED on a tank top as he walked toward the wall with the rosettes. He'd told Katrín they were only for emergency use, but he didn't like walking through the halls, even of the residence portion of the palace when his family was out of town, when he was in workout clothes.

He just didn't feel he could justify converting one of the rooms in the suite where the monarch had lived for the better part of a millennium into a workout room when there was a whole gym downstairs. This particular hidden corridor went where he needed to go, and faster than if he went the regular way, so he used it often.

His trainer waited in the outer room so he wouldn't know how or where Benjamin entered the main training room.

"Sir." He bowed slightly. It was the only time he'd be nice until the workout ended. "What kind of workout do you require today?"

"A hard one."

One that left him so tired he couldn't think when he went to bed. Between the trainer, the nutritionist who worked with the palace chef, and Chamberlain, Benjamin ate well, worked out well, and got enough sleep. He hadn't worked out in several days and hadn't slept well either.

When he didn't fall right asleep, he had too much time to think. And when he had too much time to think, he didn't tend to like himself much. He compared himself to his father and always came up lacking.

"We'll do two HIIT rounds then?" The high-intensity interval training workouts were certain to leave Benjamin so exhausted he couldn't think.

"Sure."

"Start with forty-five mountain climbers."

Benjamin knew each workout well. He didn't need the trainer to tell him what to do next, but to make sure he did the workout as intensely as he could. To drive him.

The man, a former drill sergeant, could yell with the best of them.

And he did.

Benjamin knew his form was a little off. His shoulders didn't quite maintain their position, his arms didn't want to stay straight, and his glutes weren't cooperating, but it wasn't as bad as the yelling would indicate.

"Have you never done these before, *Your Majesty*? Tighten

that core!"

Benjamin lost track of his count, but the countdown his trainer provided helped.

"You get sixty seconds to rest."

He wanted to collapse but couldn't. Getting back up would be too hard.

"Plank."

Benjamin held perfect form in his plank for nearly all of the two minutes.

"It's a good thing you were never in the military, son! You'd never get away with such sloppy form!"

The first time such things had been yelled at him during his workout, Benjamin almost quit and fired the man, but it angered him, and he'd stuck with it. Before he left the fifth day, the trainer had smacked him on the arm, smiled, and said, "I knew you could do it."

Even though he understood the rationale behind the yelling, Benjamin couldn't slack off. He pushed himself until he could do it right.

"How long has it been since you worked out?"

"The last time you were here," Benjamin groaned.

"Six days! Why?"

"I've been busy."

The man chuckled. "Getting married. Too busy working out with the queen to get to the weight room."

Before he realized what he was doing, Benjamin had backed the man against the wall, his forearm against the other man's chest.

The trainer didn't look scared. Amused maybe.

But Benjamin was seeing red. "I let you get away with a lot of things in here, but talking about your queen that way is unacceptable. Do I make myself clear?" That the insinuations were wrong didn't matter. Holding a plank left him with the time to think that he so desperately avoided.

And when he'd said something about the queen, Benjamin knew his father wouldn't have stood for it.

He'd reacted accordingly.

The only thing preventing Benjamin from ending up on the floor with his arm twisted behind his back and a knee on his spine was the other man's acquiescence.

Finally, a nod. "My apologies, sir. Comments about your wife, the queen, are off limits. It won't happen again." And a smile. "Nice to see you capable of catching me even a bit off-guard though. You might be able to hold your own in a fight against a lesser opponent."

Benjamin took a step back. "I don't intend to be in any fights. I have security with me at all times. That's enough to get someone to back off."

"True, but things happen. I can think of two instances in the last year or so alone where members of royal families were kidnapped or assaulted."

It took a second for Benjamin to remember. "Princess Yvette of Mevendia was kidnapped not long after she married Prince Nicklaus of Ravenzario."

"And her sister-in-law?"

"Christiana was nearly killed by the man she thought was her uncle."

"Both were able to use cunning to escape, but that's not always the case. They both had the best security and both were reached on palace grounds. There is no guarantee." He put his hands on his hips. "And didn't you have a run-in with your own uncle not too long ago?"

Benjamin had long ago learned not to question his trainer's sources. They were impeccable.

"All we had was a stare-down."

"Are you one hundred percent certain it would never be more than that?"

After a moment's thought, Benjamin shook his head. "Ninety

percent, maybe."

"Then next week we'll add some self-defense and even a bit of offense to your workouts." He pointed to the floor. "Push-ups. Now."

Four rounds of workouts, circuit training on the weights machines, and an hour and a half later, Benjamin stepped under the hot water in his private shower.

Normally, he was so tired he couldn't think and just let the water sluice over him. But tonight he wondered what had possessed him to jump up and confront his trainer.

It couldn't be feelings for Katrín or even real indignation at the insinuations.

No, it was a gut feeling that his father would have done the same. Because his father never would stand for anyone demeaning his family, any of them, but especially his wife. The one person in the world he loved more than anything.

It would have killed him if she'd died first. It nearly did kill her.

Benjamin admitted to himself that he might be overdramatizing it a little bit, but few people had seen his mother for nearly a year. Even when they were together, she was a shell of her former self. Only after Alfred was born did she even began to smile again, and not until after the first anniversary of his father's death that anyone heard her laugh.

Once dressed in his pajama pants, he went into his bedroom and stared at the bed. He'd never thought about it before, and he knew furniture could be changed out with new pieces or those in storage, but was this where his parents had slept every night?

Had his mother ever lived in the consort's quarters before his father's death when she did live there?

And now that he was, technically, a married man, did he feel the need to find out?

Rather than worrying about it any further, he collapsed onto the turned down covers and willed himself to sleep.

10

Katrín spent two hours slowly working her way through her new home, took a shower, then decided she needed to play her keyboard. It had been too long since her last session. With everything going on, she hadn't played since the night she met the king.

For twenty minutes, she looked for it through every nook and cranny of the consort's quarters and came up empty handed. Where could it be?

Her eyes narrowed, and she left through the same door she'd entered. When she reached the plain door on the other side, she banged hard with her fist. "Open up!" Every thirty seconds or so she did it again until finally the door opened.

Her mouth dropped open, but she snapped it closed. She wouldn't allow the shirtless and adorably rumpled king to derail her train of thought. "Where is it?"

"Where is what?" King Benjamin ran a hand through his hair causing it to stick up even more. Even his annoying beard seemed bedraggled.

Focus on that. Not the six-pack. She glared at him. Better than staring. "My keyboard."

"I didn't know you had a computer."

"I don't, you numbskull. It's like a piano. But electronic. Where is it?"

He shrugged. "I have no idea." Then turned. "Come on in. I'll see what I can find out. Of course, it is the middle of the night so it's possible I won't find out anything."

Heart racing, she followed him into the monarch's quarters. Even more opulent than the rooms she was supposed to occupy, though that shouldn't have come as a surprise to her. "It's not the middle of the night. It's ten."

"For those of us who have to be up early, it's the middle of the night. And why didn't you just call?"

"You really think I know anyone's phone numbers? Besides, I don't have a phone, unless there's one hidden in the consort's quarters."

He glanced at her over his shoulder. "Why don't you have a phone? Everyone has a phone."

"Not when every dime you make goes to paying back the royal family. Then you survive without one. It's not hard when you spend 24/7 either in the kitchen scrubbing dishes or in a 10x12 room with nothing but your music to keep you company."

He tapped on the laptop sitting on the table in the middle of the sitting area. "Your things were inventoried when they moved them from your room," he told her by way of explanation. He tapped a few more times. "Looks like it was disposed of because it didn't work."

Katrín expected anger. She got tears.

"It's a keyboard. Just get a new one."

She didn't want to deal with him. Or this. Or any of it.

Katrín spun on her heel. "I'll just use the piano downstairs," she shot back. "Looks like you finally got me in your room." She let the door slam behind her. Despite her marital status, the red piano was off limits. Technically, she was now allowed anywhere in the palace, but she wasn't about to take advantage of that. Too much chance for embarrassment.

Instead, she went back to her new quarters. Was there anywhere she wouldn't feel out of place?

"What's your problem?"

Katrín gasped and clutched her stomach. "What are you doing in here?"

At least he wore a t-shirt now, though it appeared a size too small and did little to hide his broad shoulders and muscular arms. "I am allowed to enter any portion of the palace I want." He shrugged. "Privilege of being king."

"Stay out of my quarters. I don't care if you're allowed. I don't want you here."

"Too bad. You don't get to tell me what to do."

She turned and glared at the same time. "You sound like a petulant toddler."

"You're the one with the no boys allowed sign," he shot back.

"It's not no boys. It's now my room which means I get to say who can come in and who can't, and you're on the no list. So is everyone else."

"That's not how it works."

"I don't care if you think that's how it works or not. Get out." Katrín was close enough, barely, to push against his chest. "Get. Out." She pushed harder.

The stupid mountain didn't move.

He crossed his arms over his chest, and Katrín had to stop herself from staring at his upper arms. "I'm a good foot taller than you and weigh probably twice as much. I'm exhausted after my first good workout in over a week, but you're still not going to get me to move."

"Fine, you big tree, get out of my room." Sitting room. Whatever. "I'm not going to get to play tonight. I'll get over it, but I do need to get some sleep. You may have to get up early, but I have to be up earlier. Get out."

He chuckled and turned. "Fine. I'll get out. You might contact security tomorrow. They'll know who actually moved your things and may be able to find out if it's actually been disposed of or still sitting somewhere."

"I'll ask Thor tomorrow."

Benjamin stopped and turned back around. "You know Thor?"

She nodded. "He's had dinner with me every night since the day after the wedding. He's kind of hinted it's because he's security, and I'm the queen and all, even though no one knows that."

"Then why did he detain you today?"

"He wasn't the one who arrested me. I didn't see him until I got to the office. He didn't acknowledge that he knew who I was so I didn't say anything. He probably didn't want to be seen as countermanding any sort of order you had or hadn't given. Now, if you don't mind, I need to get some sleep."

She glared at him until he left.

With the door closed behind him, Katrín turned. The consort's bedroom, the huge one with the Furniture of Historical Significance, was out of the question. There had been another room, maybe belonging to a lady-in-waiting or something, that was more her speed.

She opened two wrong doors, but found it on the third try. Still easily three times the size of the room she'd slept in the night before, it was much cozier.

Despite her exhaustion, sleep didn't come easily, but eventually it came. Her dreams were filled with longing to be held in those arms and being loved.

Katrín awoke almost more tired than she had been in the first place, but she didn't have time to worry about it. She needed to get out of this part of the palace before anyone else saw her and questioned why a dishwasher was hanging out in the king's quarters.

Accusations of an affair were just what she needed to get this farce of a marriage off on the right foot.

"You wanted to see me, sir?"

Benjamin looked up from the paperwork he had read four times and still not comprehended. "Thor, right?"

The security team member was familiar, but not one Benjamin worked with closely on a regular basis. "Yes, sir."

"Have a seat."

Thor hesitated then sat across the desk from Benjamin. "What can I help you with, sir?"

"You were there when Katrín was brought in yesterday."

"Yes, sir," he confirmed.

"But you've been eating dinner with her for several days. You know who she is. Why didn't you take care of it?"

Thor stared at him in the same way Chamberlain did. The way Benjamin felt his father would have when he was displeased. "To be quite frank, sir, it's not my job to make sure your wife is in the system until you tell me it is. In fact, I could lose my job, my pension, and even be imprisoned for adding someone to that database without express orders from your office."

The barb struck where it was likely intended to. "You left her in handcuffs."

"I received no official information on who the new queen is. Until I did, I must act reasonably while still protecting the crown. That is my primary responsibility, not whether or not a woman I believed to be the new queen was uncomfortable without confirmation of her identity. Since the new queen, whoever she was, hadn't been added to the system yet, I had no way to know for certain if she was really the queen or someone claiming to be."

It infuriated Benjamin that this man, like Chamberlain, could do his job to the letter and still make Benjamin out to be the bad guy.

Maybe he was.

No. He was the king. He couldn't be the bad guy unless he did something truly terrible. He'd told Chamberlain to take care of everything necessary. Chamberlain hadn't done these things, saying he wouldn't presume to know what Benjamin wanted even though he did just that all the time.

Thor was cut from that same cloth. Ostensibly protecting and deferring to Benjamin while at the same time giving him a lesson in being a man as his father would have done.

"Is there anything else you can think of that I should have done that I haven't? Clearly, I should have made sure Katrín had the access and protection a queen needs, but what else have I missed?" The question surprised him. It certainly wasn't the one he would have expected to ask when he sent for Thor.

Thor looked like he wanted to say something but didn't.

"You have permission to speak freely, within reason."

"Very well. Your wife shouldn't be working in the kitchen."

"But that's her job."

Thor shook his head, which Benjamin realized was suspiciously absent of any hair, the opposite of his movie counterpart. "No, sir. Her indenture was to the crown, to pay off the debt her mother owed. If she ever came into any money, she could buy out the rest of her indenture. Most spouses of the family are given access to at least some of the accounts your family holds. I know how much her indenture is. Paying it off, for your royal self, sir, is about like me picking up Chinese food on the way home. A drop in the bucket. If she were given access like one would anticipate your wife would be given, the indenture would go away."

The man had a point, one Benjamin didn't want to discuss. "Then what is her *job*?"

"Her job is to be your wife, and all that entails. To be the *queen*, like your mother was your father's queen, and still is to some degree. Like your older siblings have the job of Prince or Princess of Eyjania. Before long, her job is likely to be the mother of your children. Until then, and even after, her role is to be your help meet. And, at the risk of sounding impudent, you need her."

This should be interesting.

"Your father was an immensely popular king. Your mother was very popular. There's no timetable on grief, but 'the people' don't always see it that way. She hid out. I was there when they met. I watched them fall in love. I know how hard it was for her. I'm not saying it was the wrong move because forcing herself into the public would have been detrimental to *her* well-being but doing what she needed to do for herself made the family much less popular. Your aunt isn't the most personable, but she did her best to be the public face of the crown until you turned eighteen. Then your uncle began to exert even more influence on you."

Benjamin's stomach began to sink.

"You told me I could speak freely, so here it is. Your uncle is an entitled..." Thor stopped himself. "Jerk. He's self-centered and has an inflated view of his own importance which he's passed on to you. You may be king, but you're a man, just like the rest of us. The people have noticed your attitude and compared it, unfavorably, to your father. I worked for him for many years. He was king, but he knew he was blessed, that he didn't deserve any of this anymore than anyone else, and it was simply the luck of the genetic draw. You don't have the natural charisma your father did, but that doesn't mean you can't make your people fall in love with you, too. Your wife can be a big part of that."

Benjamin leaned back in his chair as he considered Thor's words. "You've given me a lot to think about." He didn't want to think about any of it. Not now. Possibly not ever. "That's all for now."

Thor stood. "It's my pleasure to serve you, sir. I know the man you could be, the man I hope you become." He hesitated again. "This may be too far out of line, but I'll say it anyway. I hope you become half the man your brother-in-law is."

He left before Benjamin could ask him to elaborate.

His brother-in-law? Wasn't his name Allen and still a teenager, with a paralyzed, broken body? What could he have that Benjamin could have to live up to?

Dismissing the thought, he decided to get back to work.

Katrín sat a table by herself, knowing Thor would be along momentarily. She glanced up to see him leaving the line. Weary to the bone, she just wanted to eat and go to bed. The person who covered dishes on Katrín's half-day off never did a good job, and she had to clean up the mess.

Thor sat across from her, but didn't ask how her day had been. It must have shown on her face.

Finally, she broke the silence. "How was your day?"

He took a bite and didn't look at her. "I met with my... big boss about an incident yesterday."

That was a creative way to talk about it. "Are you in any sort of trouble?"

"No. I was able to give my assessment of the situation honestly without fear of repercussions."

"I'm glad."

"I'm just glad the other party involved understood that my hands were tied."

Katrín couldn't stop the snort. She covered her mouth with her hand. "Sorry. That was funny."

He gave her a wry grin. "It kind of was."

She wanted to ask what Benjamin said, if he'd said anything about her or... she didn't know what she wanted to know. Mostly she just wanted to go to bed.

"I understand you've moved out of your quarters into new ones?" he asked.

"There was something I wanted to ask you about that. Something went missing when my things were moved. Something that doesn't work properly but holds great sentimental value."

Thor smiled at her. "The keyboard is in my office."

Katrín closed her eyes and breathed a sigh of relief. "Thank you."

"I know it holds great meaning for you. It's already been taken to your new room."

Tears filled her eyes. "Thank you, Thor."

He smiled. "My pleasure, ma'am."

Now she had to figure out how to word her next question. "I'm not very familiar with the part of the facility where my new residence is. Do you know the quickest, most..."

"Discreet?" he offered.

"That works. The best way to get there."

He didn't answer immediately. After a couple of bites, Thor asked another question. "I suppose that depends on several factors, including how many entrances there are from the hall to the sitting room."

She tried to think what that could mean in the code they seemed to be using. "Well, there's one main one and another one kind of off to the side. It's trickier though. It sticks." That should work.

"In that case, I'm sure we can find a way." He took another bite then pushed his chair away from the table. "If you're finished, I do have some paperwork I need you to look over for your new residence."

Katrín took her tray and put it up. Since Thor had started eating with her, she'd gotten more sideways glances. It turned out, he was well-known in the palace, and they were likely wondering why he'd taken such a sudden interest in her.

A few minutes later, they were in his private office.

"You have an actual Thor hammer?" she exclaimed as she spotted it.

He chuckled. "My niece gave it to me two Christmases ago. She said I needed it. My son decided that since his name is Thor, too, he should get to run around with it so I brought it in here."

"How'd you get the name Thor anyway? It's unusual for an Eyjanian to be named after the Norse god."

"My mother is Icelandic. Her father was *Thorbjørn*. She shortened it to Thor for me."

"It is a curious name for a senior member of the security team at the palace."

"Quite."

He picked up a folder and carried it with him, motioning her to go ahead of him into a conference room across the hall. Closing the door, he put the folder on the table. "No one can hear what we're saying in here, but the windows mean we can be seen, and no one could ever accuse either of us of anything untoward."

Katrín nodded, trusting her new friend. "None of that kind of thing ever occurs to me."

"It has to, Your Majesty. It's one of the downsides of being in the public eye."

"I'll try."

He flipped the folder open. "Now, to be a bit less circumspect, you'd like to find a way to get from the consort's quarters to the general area where you work without being seen walking through certain portions of the palace in your uniform."

She could tell by his tone what he thought about her still working in the kitchen.

"Yes."

"Unfortunately, the ones that would be the most direct have their other end in conspicuous areas, like a hallway and there's always the chance someone could see you exit."

Katrín deflated. "That won't work."

"No, it won't, but I have a thought. It's not shorter, but it is much more circumspect."

"What's that?"

"The room across the hall from your old room was once used for the king's mistress. Many, many years ago, but it does have a secret entrance. For all anyone needs to know, you've simply moved across the hall because it has a window. We can move some random belongings in there so should anyone happen to see you walk in or out, it won't look odd. You could even have Laurie over for a girl's night or something to help the illusion."

Katrín shook her head. "I already feel bad about not being completely honest with her, though I've been very careful not to lie."

"Understood. I'll get you a key. There are no rosettes in there, but a set of small stones amid larger ones." He tapped a spot on the map as she studied the familiar hallway. "Right here. The pattern is the same. At the end of a short hallway, there's a winding staircase. It's very tight. Are you claustrophobic?"

"I don't think so."

"If it's too much let me know, and we'll see what else we can work out. There are several exits, but you want to go all the way to the top. It's a full four or five stories worth of stairs," he warned. "It won't be easy at the end of a long day to walk back to your old room then climb all of them. When you get to the top, there's another short hallway. The door to the left goes into the king's quarters. The door to the right goes into yours."

"Why does the secret hallway to the king's mistress's quarters have an exit in the consort's quarters?"

Thor raised a brow.

"Oh. For the prince consort when there was a queen."

"Exactly. At the entrance in your quarters, you'll also notice there's no rosettes, but the same smaller stones. It actually lets out in the lady-in-waiting room."

Katrín nodded. Perfect. "Thank you. Can I get a key and get moving? I'd like to shower and collapse."

Thor closed the folder. "Of course, Your Majesty. It's my pleasure to be of service to the crown."

11

Benjamin found himself wanting to talk to his wife, but he couldn't quite put his finger on why. Maybe it was Thor's comments earlier about needing Katrín to get the people back on his family's side.

He sat in one of the chairs between the entrances to their quarters and waited for her to arrive. A glance at his watch told him it shouldn't be long, but when he'd finished reading the eighteen page document in front of him, she still hadn't arrived.

Could he have missed her? No, he didn't believe that. More likely he had misjudged the time she would return. He walked to her door and reached for the handle.

She'd told him he wasn't welcome, though he had the right to walk in anywhere he wanted. Instead, he knocked, waited a full minute and a half, then knocked again. After the third round, the door finally opened.

Katrín looked rumpled. Something he'd never seen before, even when she'd come to his office in her pajamas. "What?"

Benjamin frowned. "Were you sleeping?"

She shot him an icy glare. "I was until someone started pounding on my door. What do you want?"

"When did you get back here?"

"Nearly an hour ago. I took a shower and went to bed. I'm tired."

He set his papers on a nearby table. "I've been sitting out here the whole time, and I didn't see you."

Her shoulders slumped. "Thor showed me another way to get here. I didn't think you'd want someone in my uniform walking through the main portion of the palace to get here."

"One of the passages?" he asked with a frown. He thought he knew all of the ones that led from either one of these quarters and, except for the one that went to the workout room, none ended in locations conducive to Katrín getting to and from the kitchen unseen.

"An extra secret one. It goes to the room across the hall from my old one. The kings and prince consorts of the past used to keep their mistresses there." She leaned against the door. "It's perfect. I can say I moved across the hall because it has a window. He's even going to have it set up so it looks like I actually live there."

That had bothered him since he saw her room. "Why did you live in a room with no window before?"

"You have no idea how the palace really works do you?" She shook her head. "Of course you don't."

"Enlighten me."

Katrín turned and walked into her sitting room, leaving the door open as she took a seat on a lounge chair. "If your job comes with room and board, there's a minimum standard that is included. If you want more than that, it affects your salary. All of my salary goes to paying off my indenture. That room is legally the base room for someone indentured to the palace."

He sat down across from her, intrigued.

"If I want to live across the hall where the room is basically identical except for the window, it comes out of my wages. Not much, but I needed every cent I could get so I lived with it. I get my breakfast and lunch paid for on my breaks, and if I eat dinner in the employee dining hall within an hour of clocking out, I get that paid for, too."

"And on your days off?"

"Half days off. I can eat in the same hall, but it's taken out of my wages."

The way she discussed it so matter-of-factly bothered him. He thought it seemed a little unfair, but what did he know about how this kind of thing worked? And apparently it met the legal guidelines.

It wasn't the only thing he needed to mention to her. "I will be leaving town for a couple of days tomorrow morning."

"Okay. I'll miss you." Her sarcasm actually hurt a bit.

"Chamberlain thinks you should go with me. Your first official public appearance, but away from Akushla where the spotlight shouldn't be quite as bad."

"Can I get a note to get out of work? I got written up for missing work the day of the wedding."

He frowned. "You were at the wedding."

"That's what I told Mr. Bond. I even filled out the form to have the day off, but since I didn't actually have an invitation, the request was declined. No one got the day off unless they could show their supervisor an invitation."

Had he ever thought about how many unseen people it took to keep the palace and the governmental offices in it running smoothly? Clearly far more than he realized.

"Were there consequences?"

She shrugged. "None that really matter. I overslept the next morning so I had to work late, but I don't mind that because it's so much quieter when I stay late. He also added two months to my indenture because it was my third and fourth write up. Since I'll be dead before my indenture ends, I figured it didn't matter too much." She stood. "Now, what do I need for this little road trip?"

"We're not driving, but I'll make certain Mr. Bond extends no consequences for missing work."

"Aw, thanks." Her tone and expression was gratitude, but exaggerated somehow. "I'm so glad I won't get in trouble for accompanying my husband the king on his trip."

He glared back at her. "I'll tell Chamberlain to make sure you have what you need. We'll leave around noon tomorrow. Our first stop will be a local restaurant for lunch, then a short plane ride to the northern part of the country. I have meetings there."

"And while you do your whole meeting thing, what do I get to do?"

Benjamin shrugged. "I have no idea. Take a nap at the hotel? My sisters would probably shop, but that doesn't really seem like your thing."

"Not really. Not when I have no money."

She had a good point. "Very well. I'll see you in the morning."

"Do I need to go to work for a couple hours?"

Benjamin stood as he shook his head. "No. Sleep in. Someone will make sure you're awake in time and have everything you need." He did something he'd never done to anyone but his parents.

He inclined his head in as close to a bow as he ever came in private. "Sleep well."

KATRÍN WAS GOING to screw this up.

She sat in a chair in the consort's quarters with one person doing something to her feet, another one giving her a manicure, and cucumbers kept her eyes closed while a warm towel wrapped around her face.

It took all of her concentration not to twitch as the pedicurist did whatever pedicurists did. If she wasn't careful, she'd kick someone. Eventually, they finished, but she was left with a hair stylist who was talking about cutting her hair.

"Uh, excuse me?" she asked. "I really don't want to cut my hair."

"Not much," the woman told her. "Just a bit of a trim and spruce it up. You have lovely hair."

"Okay." Surely the woman wouldn't lie to the queen. Katrín could probably make it so she never worked again - if she were really queen, but the woman didn't know she wasn't.

Half an hour of snips and combs later, she spun Katrín around to look in the mirror.

Katrín gasped. The woman hadn't been wrong. "I love it."

"Just a bit of a trim and a few long layers. It will look better with the shape of your face like this."

"I wear it pulled back a lot for work." She winced. "Or I did before the wedding anyway. A lot's changed in the last few weeks."

The woman smiled. "I can't imagine, but at least you're with the man of your dreams who just happens to be the king." She stepped back and began to gather her things. "The head family stylist will be here in a few minutes. She'll have your clothes and the staff stylist who will go with you."

"Thank you."

"My pleasure, Your Majesty." She curtsied then left.

A minute later, there was another knock. "Come in," she called.

Another woman, this one in her forties or fifties came in along with another woman in her thirties. The older one introduced herself as the head family stylist. She apparently coordinated everyone's outfits for family pictures or something. Katrín didn't really understand what she said.

"And this is Rosalie. She did your make-up for the wedding and will be traveling with you."

Katrín smiled at Rosalie. "I remember. Thank you."

The younger woman curtsied. "My pleasure, Your Majesty."

Good grief. Everyone was so polite. It was refreshing to a point, but not when you couldn't be sure who was just trying to butter you up.

"We have about an hour before you leave. Your new wardrobe is packed and an outfit is in your dressing room for you. I'm going to finish your hair and make-up before you change."

Katrín just nodded. She wasn't even sure where the dressing room was. She *had* noticed her bed was never made so maybe no one really came in here without her knowledge.

It took Rosalie about half an hour to do the hair and make-up. Katrín was pleasantly surprised when she looked in the mirror.

"No wine-colored lipstick?" she asked.

Rosalie shook her head. "That was just to match the king's shirt and your wedding colors, ma'am."

Good to know.

"If you need any assistance getting dressed, please let me know."

"I'm sure I can manage."

Rosalie smiled. "Occasionally, there's a zipper or button or something that doesn't cooperate. That's why I'm here."

Katrín just smiled at her and headed into the main bedroom and through it to the closet. She'd guessed right. An outfit was hanging on a hook and clearly meant for her to put on.

But it wasn't quite what she expected. Rosalie's outfit was sleek and modern and stylish, but this... It seemed older and more matronly. Maybe the other woman had chosen it. Katrín just prayed all the new clothes weren't like this.

She didn't need any help and was back out in the sitting room in a few minutes.

Something Katrín didn't catch frittered across Rosalie's face. Did she approve or not?

"You look just like a queen should," the other woman declared.

That's what it was. The outfit looked like something the Queen Mother would wear, not one of the princesses. While it might be fine for a widowed mother of ten, it didn't exactly suit Katrín.

This wasn't the time to complain. There likely wouldn't be a time to, not when she wouldn't be doing this sort of thing very often.

The head stylist glanced at her phone. "The king is ready to leave."

Katrín nodded to both of them. "Thank you again."

Rosalie gave a longer nod back. "I will see you this evening, ma'am."

Before Katrín could thank her, they'd both disappeared. She went into the external sitting area to see Benjamin walking out of his quarters.

"Are you ready to go?" he asked as he fiddled with his cuff link.

"If you are, I kind of have to be."

He looked up and frowned.

"What?"

"I like the hair and make-up or whatever, but I'm not sure about the outfit."

She shrugged. "This is what the stylists gave me."

"Then I guess I must not know enough about women's fashion." He started for the main door, expecting her to follow. The heels were going to make it difficult, but she did her best.

Staff members scurried out of sight as they approached. Only a few held their ground and bowed or curtsied as Benjamin walked by. They watched Katrín with varying degrees of open curiosity. In a few minutes, they reached a portico with a car waiting underneath it. Benjamin had stopped for her to catch up before walking out the door.

He entered the car and situated himself on the far side of the back seat. A liveried footman-type guy motioned for her to follow. As soon as her seatbelt was fastened, the car began to move. Were they watching for her to do that?

"Where are we going for lunch?" she asked.

"A bistro not far from here. The owner is friends with my mother's family. It is tradition to stop there on the way to the northern part of the country."

"I see."

Katrín stared out the window as the city whisked by. Except for the wedding, how long had it been since she'd been out of the palace?

Years.

"There will likely be photographers. This trip has been planned for a while, and they all know where we'll be eating."

"So smile and pretend like I want to be here. Got it."

He wasn't wrong. The car glided to a stop in front of a small restaurant. The streets were crowded with news personnel as well as a bunch of ordinary people.

The door on Benjamin's side opened, and he climbed out. She couldn't see him, but imagined him smiling and nodding at the crowd. Not a big, crowd-pleasing smile, but the reserved one he always used.

"Ma'am?" A member of the security team held out a hand to assist Katrín out of the car. With a deep breath, she took his hand.

As long as she didn't fall flat on her face, it would all be okay.

12

Benjamin turned to watch one of the security team help Katrín from the car. Should he have done that? Too late now, but he did offer his arm for her to take.

Katrín slid her hand into his elbow but still stayed slightly behind him. On purpose?

The reporters called questions as cameras clicked.

"Just smile," he whispered as he stopped in the middle of the sidewalk facing the reporters. "Just for a few seconds."

He waited for a thirty count then turned her the other way for a few more seconds. Those gathered would feel cheated if they didn't get a picture, or so he was told. After a few more seconds, he started walking the four more steps into the building.

"King Benjamin!" The proprietor's wife came toward him with her arms outstretched. "It has been far too long." It was as though she realized he wasn't alone because she suddenly stopped and curtsied. "We're happy to have you here, Your Majesties."

Benjamin dropped his arm so Katrín's hand slipped out and closed the distance to the woman. "It is good to see you, Celeste."

He took her hands and kissed her cheek. "Mother would love to have you and Cornelius come for dinner sometime soon. After she returns from holiday, of course."

"We would love that."

Benjamin turned. "Celeste, this is my wife, Katrín. Katrín, Celeste's mother was my grandmother's best friend when they were children."

Katrín held out a hand. "It's a pleasure to meet you, ma'am."

A minute later, they were seated at a table near a window overlooking a park.

"Do we have menus?" Katrín asked softly once Celeste was out of earshot.

"No. She'll bring us Cornelius's special of the day. Whatever it is will be fabulous."

On the other wall was a television set, turned to one of the local stations. The lunchtime news was on, and Benjamin wasn't surprised to see himself. He read the closed captioning.

King Benjamin and his new wife, Queen Katrín, left the palace for the first time since the wedding. The picture shifted and said "moments ago" on the top. *The king has never been comfortable in front of cameras, often looking like he'd rather be just about anywhere else. The new queen looked even less comfortable, though it is her first real foray into the public eye. Her hair and make-up are an improvement over the wedding, though the consensus was that she matched the tone of the day, even if the styles didn't seem to suit her. Here, she's freshly styled, but seems to have stolen something from the Queen Mother's closet to wear.*

Benjamin looked at the video of the two of them. He looked like he always did, but Katrín looked almost scared and pale, a shaky smile appearing and disappearing on her face.

Then the story was over.

"Am I actually going to interact with the public on this trip?" the real Katrín asked him. "Or am I staying in some hotel room the whole time?"

"That's up to you. I'll be working during the two days we're there. We have a dinner with the mayor tonight, but it's a small event with only a dozen people or so. Tomorrow night, we'll have dinner with a local charitable organization. The next night we have no specific plans. We'll return after lunch the next day. You can sleep in and order room service, or whatever you prefer."

"Sleeping sounds nice," she murmured, staring out the window.

"Here we are!" Celeste and Cornelius set bowls of steaming soup in front of them.

"Thank you," he and Katrín said in unison.

After a minute of small talk about the wedding, they were left alone.

"Have you ever been up north?"

"No. We went to Lake Akushla a few times when I was younger, but that's it. My mother rarely took time off, except for the weekends and not even then if there was an event at the palace."

He'd forgotten. "She worked for my father?"

"She was his official server. Any meal outside of the family quarters and sometimes inside, she served him and occasionally visiting dignitaries. She wasn't the head server, yet, but she was the best."

"Then why did she quit?"

Katrín shrugged. "When they think you are stealing, you often lose your job or get demoted. A few years later, when I took over the indenture, she quit her new job and went to work closer to home with fewer hours so she could be with my brother more. My sister was working and helping pay the bills by then so she could afford to take the pay cut."

Something about what she said bothered Benjamin but he couldn't quite put his finger on what. "I'm going to make arrangements so she doesn't have to work anymore."

"Thank you."

"That was your goal, wasn't it? With the comments in front of my mother. That your mother wouldn't have to wait a year to have financial security."

"I didn't think you'd actually do it." She took a spoonful of soup.

"Did you think I actually would next year?"

Katrín didn't look at him but shrugged as she ate another spoonful of soup.

"I'm a man of my word," he told her, suddenly angry at the thought she didn't believe him.

"If you say so. I barely know you. How would I know if you are?"

He didn't answer, but ate his soup instead. A second course followed that with dessert at the end.

"Will the crowd be gone when we leave?" Katrín pushed her dessert plate away.

"Normally, most of them would, but since this is your first public outing, I don't know." He took a couple more bites, then wiped his mouth on a napkin before standing.

Celeste and Cornelius emerged from the kitchen to say goodbye.

"Just relax and smile," he told Katrín as they approached the outer door. "They won't hurt you, just take your picture."

Maybe he should make more of an effort to smile, too. They didn't expect it from him, but that didn't mean he couldn't change their perceptions. Wasn't that the whole point of this wedding in the first place?

KATRÍN STAYED a stair step behind Benjamin as they walked to the tarmac. The flight had been short and quiet, with Benjamin going over paperwork with Chamberlain. As it was Katrín's first flight, she spent most of it staring out the window and trying not to look nervous.

Now back on solid ground, she wondered if she'd ever get as used to it as Benjamin clearly was.

They were met by the mayor of the town, though Katrín couldn't remember the name of it or his name. She needed to get better about that.

A car took them to a fancy hotel. The crowd was bigger than at the restaurant, but comprised mostly of people and less of media. The walk was longer, but they didn't stop. Grateful the king had offered her his arm, she gripped the inside of his elbow like a lifeline, and refused to think about the warmth that spread through her from that point of contact. If she dwelt on it, she might realize it meant she found him somewhat attractive, despite his perpetual resting grumpy face.

They were taken directly to an elevator, which went straight to the top floor after their escort swiped a key card. The elevator opened into a suite. It wasn't as nice as the suites at the palace, but other than that, the nicest place Katrín had ever been.

Benjamin dropped his arm and let her hand slide out as he walked toward a conference table on the far side of the room. Katrín moved a bit further in and away as the rest of their entourage poured out of the other elevator.

What exactly was she supposed to do?

"Ma'am?"

A sigh of relief escaped before she could stop it. "Thor? I didn't know you were coming with us."

"This way, ma'am." He motioned with one hand.

So when it wasn't just the two of them, he would be stiff and formal. Great.

She went over to a group of chairs out of the way and took a seat. Thor sat in the chair next to her.

"This is for you." He handed her a thin box. "Keep the phone with you at all times."

"A phone?" She shook the box open. Inside were several electronic devices. A phone, a tablet, what looked to be an ereader, and a very thin laptop. "All of this is for me?"

"Yes, ma'am. You *should* have an assistant before long who would help you set all of it up, but since you don't have one yet, I'll help you."

"Thank you. And thank you for the keyboard. I haven't had a chance to play it yet, but I appreciate it."

"My pleasure, ma'am." For the next half hour, Thor walked her through how each one worked. Her phone held precious few numbers, though Benjamin's private line was in there. Her family's numbers were in there, as were the numbers of several members of Benjamin's family.

"Is it really okay for me to have the king's private number?" she asked.

"You are his wife." Thor didn't look at her and his voice was emotionless, which told her enough about what he thought about their situation. "Just don't give it out to anyone."

"Of course not."

"These devices are set up to require both a thumbprint and a code to get in. There are also emergency overrides on them. Only the king and security can override them. You are never to turn off your location services. In fact, you can't. And it stays with you at all times."

"Even at work? I'm not allowed to have a phone in the kitchen."

"Then keep it in your pocket and don't take it out, but it stays with you. Even in your suite."

"Okay. But what about the rest of his family? They don't care that I have their numbers?"

"You are his wife. Some of them may think it odd they didn't have your number until now."

Right. Because normal would be very different.

Thor showed her how the laptop worked and the ereader. "My niece listed some books she thought you might like. They've been preloaded. There's some by a Kimberley Woodhouse." He pointed to a folder, then to two others. "Melanie Dickerson's novels are Medieval fairy tale retellings. Tamara Leigh's are about Medieval knights and apparently quite good. My niece gushed on and on about them. Karen Witemeyer and Mary Connealy write about Texas and the American West. Bethany Turner's is apparently quite funny, as is Mikal Dawn's." He glanced up. "There's a few dozen others on there, and you can purchase any other's you might like to read. You can also log onto the website on the tablet or laptop and order covers for them that you like."

"Thank you, and thank your niece for me."

"She's with the Queen Mother right now, but will be home in a week or so if you'd like to thank her in person."

"I would like that." Maybe she would be a friend. Katrín could use more of those. Laurie was friendly and nice to hang out with, but Katrín wouldn't really call her a true friend. There was too much Katrín wouldn't share with her - or anyone.

She stared at the ereader in her hands. "What should I expect the next couple of days? I have no idea."

Thor sighed. She thought he wanted to say more, to commiserate with her, but didn't dare. "In about an hour you'll change into your clothes for dinner this evening." He glanced away from her. "You'll be in the master suite over there tonight. Both of you."

Katrín closed her eyes. It hadn't even occurred to her that they'd be expected to share a room while away from home.

"I know about the first time you met," Thor said softly. "I know what he asked of you, and I know how you responded. I'm proud of you, but I also want you to know that, to my knowledge, he'd never done anything like that before. Just because you're in the same room tonight doesn't mean he'll expect more. And even if he did, and you didn't, I have no doubt that you'd be able to take care of yourself and the king might be explaining how he 'tripped' and got a black eye."

The snort of laughter caused Katrín's shoulders to relax a bit.

What she knew of Benjamin in the last few weeks didn't fit with her first impression of him that night. It was good to know it had been wrong, because she had a feeling this night could be interesting.

13

"My wife is an accomplished pianist," Benjamin told the mayor over dinner. "Though I don't have the pleasure of listening nearly as often as I'd like." He smiled at Katrín who suddenly looked petrified. "In fact, the first time we met, she was playing at the palace."

Katrín shook her head. "I'm afraid my husband is mistaken, or perhaps besotted. I play well enough, and I love it, but I'm not accomplished." Her cheeks had turned a new shade of pink, though Benjamin wasn't sure why. Embarrassment didn't seem quite right.

"Would you let us be the judge of that, Your Majesty?" the mayor asked her.

Katrín glanced at him. She clearly didn't want to, but didn't want to disappoint him either.

"Perhaps another time." Benjamin nodded towards Katrín. "I do know my wife hasn't had a chance to sit at a piano in a while, and I put her on the spot a bit. I can tell you her version of *King Alfred's Overture* is inspiring."

This time the pink creeping up her neck and into her cheeks had to be embarrassment.

"You're just saying that because it's the first time we met." She took a bite of her meal.

Benjamin held back a chuckle. "It did take me a little by surprise."

The topic shifted to how the mayor and his wife met, but Benjamin had a hard time paying attention. He needed to talk with Katrín. Until Chamberlain mentioned it to him, Benjamin hadn't realized they were expected to share a room. This was the same suite he'd stayed in many times, but never with a significant other - or even an insignificant other like he'd insinuated to Katrín the first night they met.

He mentally shook himself to clear his head and paid attention to the conversation. An hour later, they were alone in the elevator. He wasn't sure how to broach the subject.

"So I hear we're sharing a room tonight." Katrín stared straight ahead as she spoke.

"Who told you that?"

"Thor when he showed me all the new tech I get to play with sometimes."

"What kind of tech?"

"Laptop, tablet, ereader, and phone."

"You told me you didn't have a phone before. Did you not have any of the others?"

"No. There's a computer lab of sorts for employees to use. I used it sometimes, including to research what I needed to know for when we are together in public and what my role should be when I'm not working, but I haven't use them much since I moved to the palace."

"What kind of books are you going to read?" He found himself curious about her.

"Thor's niece gave him a bunch of recommendations. I guess she works for your mother."

That made Benjamin frown. "Thor's niece works for my mother?" he clarified.

"That's what he said. Something about social media."

It bothered Benjamin that he didn't know this, though he couldn't define why. Maybe because the mayor had once worked for Benjamin's father and had gushed about how wonderful he'd been to work for.

The doors to the elevator slid open. The staff members were waiting for them. "I have some work to do before retiring, but if you'd like to get comfortable in the other room, you're welcome to."

Katrín didn't move toward the open door.

He clarified. "I don't mean anything by that except to change into something actually comfortable and read a book or watch a movie. Nothing else."

"Thank you."

This time when he walked forward, she followed. He went to the conference table. Katrín headed for the double doors leading to the master suite. He followed her with his eyes until the door closed behind her.

Nearly two hours later, he closed his last folder for the night and sent Chamberlain to his own quarters. Maybe Katrín would already be asleep. Instead, he walked through the door to find the room still lit by a fire, with Katrín curled up in a chair completely engrossed in what appeared to be the ereader.

"Good book?" he asked.

She jumped. "I didn't hear you come in."

He hid a smile. "What are you reading?"

"It's this book by an American. Bethany Turner. It's called *The Secret Life of Sarah Hollenbeck*. Not what I was expecting, but hilarious and an interesting look at life in the States."

"I'm glad you're enjoying it."

"Immensely."

"I'm going to take a shower. Do you need in there before I do?"

She shook her head. "I'm ready for bed."

"Very well." He started for the bathroom. "Take whichever side you'd like. I generally sprawl all over so it doesn't really matter."

Katrín didn't reply but went back to her book. Benjamin gave a mental shrug, then went through his own nightly routine, wishing he could get a good HIIT workout in, but it wasn't really possible here. When he returned to the bedroom, Katrín hadn't moved.

"Go ahead," she told him. "I've got about half an hour left in this book, and I don't want to stop."

"Good night."

"Night." Her distracted tone told him what he needed to know. She was in a different world. Two of his sisters were the same way. They'd probably enjoy talking about books. He needed to remember to mention that to Evangeline when they returned.

What was he thinking? Katrín would still be working. She likely wouldn't have much time for reading or having long conversations with his sisters. As he settled into the unfamiliar bed, that idea bothered him. He'd seen Katrín once during the middle of her work day. Closing his eyes, he tried to recall what she'd looked like. Hot, sweaty, and tired looking, though not so tired she didn't give as good as she got.

Maybe continuing to work in the kitchen wasn't the best idea. Could he have Chamberlain find something else for her to do that wouldn't seem quite as odd for the woman everyone believed to be the queen he married for love to do?

That would take some thinking on.

KATRÍN SLOWLY CAME TO WAKEFULNESS, covered by a weight and warmth she didn't recognize. How was that possible?

She blinked a couple of times to see Benjamin walking out of the bathroom as he slipped his suit coat on.

"Good morning. You didn't have to sleep on the couch."

Yes, she did. "How did I get over here? I didn't want to bother you."

"I moved you when I woke up and saw you over there. That was about an hour ago. I already ate breakfast and am leaving for the day. I'll be back in time to dress for dinner. We're meeting with a charity of some kind. I don't remember what."

Katrín pushed herself into a seated position. "And what can I do?"

"Whatever you want. But if you leave the suite, make sure Thor is with you. He'll handle your security."

"Wouldn't do to have the new queen accidentally die too soon?" she asked, too tired to give it her full dose of snark.

Benjamin stared at her with that look he always seemed to have. "I don't want you dead."

Just pretend dead.

"I'll make sure I have Thor with me if I go anywhere. I might just read all day."

"Chamberlain will make sure your assistant knows what time you need to be ready for tonight." He walked to the door and left without a goodbye.

Katrín stared after him then swung her feet over the edge. It didn't take long for her to get ready for the day, but after breakfast and reading most of *Count Me In* by Mikal Dawn - which was also funny - she decided she needed to get out.

"Thor?" she called walking into the main sitting room.

"Yes, ma'am?" He stood up from his spot at the conference table.

"I was told to let you know if I wanted to go anywhere."

"Where would you like to go?"

She shrugged. "A walk? I don't really know. I just know I don't want to sit here all day if I don't have to."

"Give me half an hour, and I'll make it happen."

Katrín started to thank him, but he was already on the phone.

She scrounged through the clothes Rosalie had packed for her. After managing to find a pair of skinny jeans and blousy top, she found a pair of boots that far exceeded anything she'd ever dreamed of owning. They fit perfectly. A coat, hat, scarf, and gloves were also available for her.

By the time she emerged into the sitting area, Thor and two other men were waiting for her.

"There's a marketplace nearby," he told her.

"I don't plan to buy anything."

"You don't have to, but if you see something you like, we can make a note of it and send someone back."

She wouldn't, but the thought was nice. "What about lunch?"

Thor glanced at one of the other men. "Since it's unannounced, we can stop for lunch if you'd like."

"You mean no one would know I'm coming so they could poison my food?"

"Something like that."

This was a whole new world, so different from her old one - the one she still kept one foot in.

Once outside, it surprised her to see a few photographers waiting for her.

"Ma'am."

She looked to see Thor handing her a pair of sunglasses, though they probably weren't strictly necessary. She took them, but only slipped them on and then up into her hair like a headband. It didn't make sense, but she was more comfortable without Benjamin to make her nervous.

"Good afternoon," she called and waved at them, but stayed right between her security detail as they walked toward the marketplace. The photographers dogged their steps, though she didn't acknowledge them again.

Instead, she beelined for what appeared to be a popular restaurant. In line was someone she definitely wanted to talk to.

"Thor," she said softly. "I can buy my own lunch, right?"

"Yes, ma'am."

"Can I buy another family's?"

"I suppose."

"I don't actually have any money though."

"I'll take care of it."

Fortunately, the people she wanted to talk with were at the end of the line. "Excuse me?" she asked the woman who appeared to be the mother of the bunch.

She barely glanced at Katrín, her full attention on her children. "Yes?"

"I'm here all alone today. Would you mind if I joined you for lunch? My treat."

The woman's head snapped around. "What?"

Katrín repeated her offer.

"Why would you do that?"

She couldn't keep the tears from her eyes. "Because your little man here reminds me of my brother, and I miss him. I really am all alone for lunch. I would appreciate it if you would let me treat you."

If this woman was anything like her mother, and Katrín suspected she was, even a stranger buying lunch at a marketplace stand would be a blessing.

"Um, sure." The woman glanced behind Katrín. "But you don't exactly seem alone."

"Yeah. I have some security goons with me." She winked at the mom. "They're great guys, but not exactly company."

"And photographers." The mother's tone grew wary. "I don't know who you are but is this some kind of publicity stunt?"

Katrín shook her head. "Not at all." She pulled her phone out of her pocket. "Let me see if I can work this. Believe it or not, I just got my first smart phone. My mom has Facebook and pictures of my brother." It took a minute, and they were nearly to the front of the line, by the time she managed to find her mother's profile picture. "I look a lot like my mom, and that's my little brother." She held it up for the other woman to see. "It's been forever since I got to talk with him or have lunch together. Please, let me do this?"

The mom nodded then swiped at the phone. "Wait. What's your name?"

She'd hoped to avoid that part. "Katrín."

The other woman gasped and pointed. "As in the new queen?"

Katrín wrinkled her nose. "I was kind of hoping that wouldn't come up. I just want to have lunch." The woman started to curtsy, but Katrín stopped her with a shake of her head. "Please? I'm just a young woman who misses her family and wants to buy your lunch."

The woman held out her hand. "I'm Alyssa. It's a pleasure to meet you. This is my son, Liam."

Katrín took the offered hand. "It's a pleasure to meet you."

"Next!"

They turned toward the counter. Katrín smiled. "Order whatever you want. It's on my security detail today."

"You should see this, sir." Chamberlain held out his tablet.

"What is it?" Benjamin asked, taking it from him.

"Just watch."

On the screen, Benjamin saw Katrín emerge from the hotel and wave at the paparazzi. With that smile on her face, he almost didn't recognize her. "Where did they go?"

"Lunch apparently. Watch the next video."

Katrín shook hands with a woman a few years older than herself, maybe even closer to mid or late-30s. They ordered food. Thor paid for it. Katrín helped carry the tray of food to a wheelchair accessible table. She moved a chair out of the way.

A boy, maybe twelve, wheeled himself into the spot where the chair had been. Katrín sat next to him and across from his mother. They were talking and laughing in a way he'd never seen her, except maybe the night she'd shown up in his office in her pajamas.

"What's the press saying?" he asked, handing the tablet back.

"That they understand why you married her, but that the wedding itself didn't do much for either one of you. They also pointed out that she seems much more comfortable in her own skin when you're not around, at least based on what they've seen the last couple of days. One reminded them that she's not used to the official business and likely felt overwhelmed in your shadow, but today she was free of official expectations."

Made sense. "Where is she?"

"They're walking back in now."

"I'd like to ride up with her by myself." Maybe see why she couldn't be like this in public with him.

Three minutes later, they were alone in the elevator. "I saw the videos from today."

She smiled up at him. "I had a great time. Liam reminded me so much of my brother, though he's paralyzed after an auto accident when he was five. He remembers being able to run and play."

"You looked happy."

Her smile softened. "I was. I had a great afternoon."

A clang and clank startled him before the lights went out and the car shuddered.

Before Benjamin realized what was happening, his arms were around Katrín as she stumbled into him. The jolt he felt wasn't only from the elevator's sudden stop.

"Sorry," Katrín muttered, pushing away from him and leaning against the far wall, as the emergency lights came on.

The conversation they'd been having fled, replaced by incoherent mutterings filling his mind. Elevators just weren't his thing. Not enough room to pace.

But he tried anyway. His phone buzzed. He ignored it. Two

steps along the back wall, two on the side, two by the door, two more on the other side. Two and a half corner to corner.

And his wife, in the best mood he'd seen her in, scurrying to get out of his way the whole time.

Until she didn't.

Leaning against the corner, Katrín glared at him. "Go around." She answered a call on her phone.

He glared right back, but spun on his heel and went the other way until he reached her again. This time he went back to the last corner then across. By the time he made it back to her side, she'd slid down to the floor, with her legs stretched out in front of her, blocking his path when he wanted to go through the middle.

"Do you mind?"

"Nope. If you want to pace, go right ahead. That was Thor, by the way. An auto accident around the corner took out the power to the whole block. They're trying to get to us."

His mind raced. He needed out. Running a hand through his hair, he looked up.

"No."

"No what?"

"You're not going to try to climb out the top. Thor said they'll be here soon. If they tell you to, then you can. Otherwise, stay put."

"You don't get to tell me what I can't do, Katrín."

"No, I suppose I don't, but I'm going to when you're being an idiot." She had pulled her ereader out of her bag and turned up a light on it. "And if you try to climb out, you're an idiot."

"I can have you imprisoned for that." He walked from one side to the other again.

"For telling you the truth? Go for it. See how well that goes over when the country finds out you put your wife in prison because she told you not to do something moronic. That'll do wonders for your popularity."

"Is that why you bought that kid lunch? The crippled one? To make me look good?"

Katrín actually threw back her head and laughed. "I, quite literally, could not have cared less how my buying them lunch made you look. I did it because it seemed like a nice thing to do for a nice family who probably struggle to make ends meet. That's all. If I could have done it without the photographers, I would have in a heartbeat. And don't call him a crippled kid. He's anything but. Liam is smart as a whip. He could probably school you on Eyjanian history or any other subject you'd like to choose."

"So a random ten-year-old in a wheelchair is smarter than me?"

"What does the wheelchair have to do with how smart he is? I'll answer for you." She glared at him. "Nothing at all, so ditch that whole line of thinking right now."

Whatever.

More pacing two steps one way, turn, two steps, about face, reverse.

"You know, if you wanted to be more popular, you might work on your resting grumpy face."

"What are you talking about?" he growled.

"Just that. Some people have rather pleasant faces when they're not actively making one expression or another, but you're not one of them. You look perpetually grumpy. I'm not sure if that's because you are always grumpy or if you just have a grumpy resting face. Maybe you can find a face coach or something to help you with it. Now, would you mind sitting down? You're driving me crazy. Probably driving yourself crazy too."

"I'd rather pace." He glared at her.

She glared back. "Sit. Before I make you."

14

Whatever Benjamin's problem was, it wouldn't be solved by pacing in the elevator. Katrín also didn't want to have to trip him to get him to stop, because he was driving her bonkers.

"So tell me the truth," she started. "Why did you really send your family away for a while? Ashamed of me?"

The glare returned, but he did sit down as far away from her as he could. "No."

"Then why?"

"Figured neither one of us wanted to answer their questions until we were a bit more settled in our routine."

"I see."

"I really don't see my family as often as you'd think living on the same floor of the same building."

"Because it's more like you have your own apartments rather than just your own bedrooms in a house."

"That's one way to look at it, I suppose."

"Why do you think you don't see your family more? I would imagine they'd like to, especially your mother."

"Maybe."

He seemed to be calming down. She needed to distract him further. "When did you move into your current residence? As soon as you became king?" That seemed a better way to word it.

He shook his head. "No. My mother had never used the consort's quarters that I'm aware of, though all of us children lived in there when we were younger. As we grew up, we moved further down the hall. Mother moved in there with my youngest siblings - Josiah down, I think. I was thirteen, my twin sisters would have been eleven or so, and Darius was ten. Josiah would have been seven I think."

"So Darius and Josiah are the furthest apart of any of you, aren't they?" She'd done the math once. Most of the children were somewhere between about eighteen months and two years or so apart.

"Yes. I think Mother had a miscarriage in between, but I'm not sure." He closed his eyes and rested his head behind him.

"So she moved into the consort's quarters with like seven kids?" *Keep him talking.*

"Five until Alfie was born."

Katrín had to stop herself from gasping. "Alfie? You call your little brother Alfie?"

"He's starting to get a bit old for it, but yes. The twins don't really have nicknames. I never did either, probably because I was the heir, I guess. Mother called me Benji sometimes, but not often. Darius and Josiah don't have nicknames either. Everyone else still does, but may not as they get older, I guess."

"What are they? Isaiah and Isaac are the twins, right?" She knew this as well as any other Eyjanian, but if he was talking about his family, he wasn't pacing and trying to break out.

"Zay is older by five minutes. Zach gives him a hard time about it. They're almost eighteen. They finish their schooling in a couple months. Angie's fifteen and dying to learn how to drive. She comes to my office every couple weeks to beg me to let her."

"Why don't you?"

"She's my little sister and a princess. She'll never need to drive and I don't want her to get hurt."

"You do know women, and even members of royal families can drive, right? Have you ever seen Queen Elizabeth behind the wheel? She always has a smile on her face. Haven't you heard the story about her and the king of Saudi Arabia?"

"Can't say that I have."

"They were at her Balmoral Estate, I think it was. She was taking the king on a tour of the grounds. He sat in the passenger seat with his translator in the back. She climbed in the driver's seat and peeled out. Women weren't allowed to drive in Saudi Arabia at the time. She's apparently quite proud, and rightfully so, of her driving abilities, learned during the Second World War. If she can drive, why can't your sister?"

"I can't." Something vulnerable had appeared. "None of my other siblings can either. She'll be fine." There it went. "Gabby hit her teens a few months ago. Alfie is ten."

"So your mom lived with six kids in the consort's quarters? No one lived in the monarch's?"

"Not until I turned eighteen. Mother insisted I move then. My uncle had been trying to convince me to for a quite a while. Louise wanted me to, but for different reasons, I think."

Melancholy wasn't what she'd been trying for but if it calmed him down, it worked. "What reasons?"

"I think they both wanted me to move in there because I was king, even at thirteen. My aunt because it was just what the king did. He lives in the monarch's quarters. For my uncle, I think it was more about the power that goes along with it all."

That's what had always bothered her about his uncle. "He wanted to be king."

"I think so." He seemed to be thinking something over. "I'm also pretty sure he's the one who set up the press release about the wedding."

"You kicked him out, didn't you? So he set it up so that you would marry the lowest person in the palace."

His eyes were still closed. "I don't think you're the lowest person in the palace."

"You know what I mean."

With another jolt, the lights came back on and the elevator began to move. Katrín stood up and held a hand out to Benjamin. "Come on."

He reached up and took her hand. She leaned her weight back to keep from tumbling onto him, but he didn't let go once he was upright.

She looked up, way up, straight into his sky blue eyes.

"Thank you." The look in his eyes was softer than she'd seen from him before.

"For what?"

"For keeping me from freaking out."

Katrín tried to keep her shock from showing. "A little claustrophobic?"

He dropped her hand and looked away. "Something like that." He sighed. "I'd appreciate it if you wouldn't mention it to anyone, though. I'm not sure anyone knows."

"Not even your mother? Or Chamberlain?" That surprised her.

"No one." Another pause. "Only my wife."

SEVERAL DAYS after returning to Akushla, Benjamin climbed out of the car and turned to offer a hand to Katrín. She took it and emerged with a smile plastered on her face. Even he knew it wasn't real.

There were a few photographers waiting. How did they know? This wasn't a scheduled event. In fact, it had only been decided a few hours earlier when a text from his mother asked him what he was doing for Katrín's birthday.

Chamberlain made reservations at one of the most exclusive restaurants in Akushla about four hours earlier. Unless Chamberlain had made them sooner and planned to do his suggestion-that-isn't-really-a-suggestion thing.

Benjamin tucked Katrín's hand into his elbow and gave a small, reluctant wave to the press, just a lift of his hand.

"What are you celebrating?" one of them yelled.

Benjamin smiled but didn't answer as they walked through the door held open by a restaurant employee.

"Good evening, Your Majesties." The maître d' bowed at the waist. "Your table is waiting."

He led them past a dance floor to a secluded table with Akushla Park glittering outside the window.

"Thank you," Katrín said softly as the maître d' held her chair for her.

"My pleasure, ma'am. Happiest of birthdays to you."

Her smile became more genuine. "Thank you."

A second later they were alone. Benjamin leaned in a little closer across the table. "I don't believe I've said happy birthday yet. I do hope you're having a lovely day."

Katrín raised a single brow as she took a sip of her water. "I worked most of the day. I got off work just in time to get dressed and come here. I'd much rather be soaking in a tub or reading a book than on display for the entire country to criticize."

The waiter arrived before Benjamin could respond. Grateful he didn't have to decide how to, he gave the man his order without looking at the menu first. Katrín hesitated then said she would have the same.

Before he could say anything else, their wine appeared. When they were alone again, he spoke. "You didn't look at the menu."

"What you ordered sounded fine."

Something else lurked behind her words. "There's more to it." It wasn't a question.

She leaned forward. "Look. I haven't spent more than the

absolute minimum on a meal in years. The lunch last week? Just my food cost twice as much as I usually spend. If I look at the menu here, I won't order anything but water because that probably costs money too."

He took a sip of his wine. "There are no prices on the menu at a place like this. If you need to know how much it costs, you can't afford it."

"Exactly. But you can hardly be annoyed at me for spending too much if I get the same thing you do."

"I won't see the bill. It will be sent to my office to pay at the end of the month."

"Then Chamberlain can't get annoyed with me." She glanced at the restaurant. "You know people are sneaking pictures of us, right? Even among the upper echelons of Askushlan society, you out for dinner with a woman is enough of an anomaly for them to take pictures with their phones as surreptitiously as they can. You might want to look a little more enamored with your wife. We are newlyweds after all."

She had a point. Benjamin stood and moved his chair to his right so they were closer together and he faced the window. All anyone would see from behind was a blurry reflection and him reaching for Katrín's hand occasionally.

Maybe he should ask her to dance. That would be a very birthday celebration thing to do. Weren't there photos of his parents dancing as they celebrated a birthday or two at this restaurant?

He pushed away from the table again and stood holding out a hand. "May I have this dance?"

"I don't dance." She looked up at him, a smile frozen on her face.

"I think you can handle this one."

Her smaller hand slid into his as she stood. "Fine."

She walked almost directly behind him as they skirted several tables to reach the dance floor, which cleared as they arrived. The band leader bowed then turned and whispered to the rest of the band.

They started to play *Everything I Do*. Benjamin slid his arm around her waist and pulled her closer then leaned down to whisper. "Everyone's watching."

"I know." She rested her hand on his shoulder. This time her smile was soft. "Thank you for dinner tonight."

"You haven't eaten it yet."

"No, but I'm sure it'll be great. And even if the food isn't, I don't get the chance to dress up like this very often."

"You'll get to do so more in the next few months. Do you like this dress better than the outfit from last week?"

"Much."

"You look amazing." The color was nearly the same as his shirt at the wedding.

"Thanks."

He didn't know what the material was, but knew the shiny, smooth fabric showed off her curves, but wasn't so formfitting that she should draw criticism for it.

"Did you hear from your family today?"

She shook her head. "No. I haven't given them my new number yet. I'll probably have mail waiting for me, though. Whenever I get it."

It bothered him that her family didn't know how to get in touch with her, then her last sentence sunk in. "What do you mean 'whenever you get it'."

She shrugged, the motion shifting her a little closer to him. "I mean that my mail isn't always delivered in a timely manner. Generally, I get a pile of mail once or twice a month, maybe every three weeks or so."

"Do you know why that is?"

Another shrug. "I have no idea. It's been that way since I arrived. I'm able to drop letters in the mail, and they seem to get delivered like normal, but I don't get them like I should."

Could it have something to do with her position in the palace? Between this information and what he'd learned from her about living quarters, he needed to discover more about how employment in the palace actually worked.

Focus on anything but Benjamin. The words ran through Katrín's mind, but did little good. His cologne. His breath near her temple thanks to heels so tall they might as well be stilts. The warmth of his nearness.

Why did he affect her so much? She barely liked him, didn't really.

But on a purely physical level, he definitely affected her.

She'd said he didn't have the charismatic, magnetic personality his father did, but maybe she needed to rethink that assessment. His was just more understated, or perhaps hidden due to their very different life circumstances. If he let that side of him shine in public, opinion would turn on a dime.

Shifting even closer to him, to the strength he exuded, wouldn't help her attraction, but would hide it from him a little better.

As the song ended, Katrín started to move away, but Benjamin held her in place with the palm of his hand on the small of her back. "One more?"

Her eyes closed as they moved slowly on the dance floor to the next song.

Focus on anything else. It worked. And then she'd breath or he'd rub his thumb on hers.

"This song sounds familiar," he said softly, for her ears only.

"*When a Man Loves a Woman* by Michael Bolton."

"Right."

"Don't worry. I won't get any ideas. Any more than you should have from the last song."

"What was it?"

"*Everything I Do* by Bryan Adams from *Prince of Thieves*."

"Prince of what?"

"*Prince of Thieves*. It's a Kevin Costner movie from the 90s. Robin Hood. Merry men. Maid Marian. Sheriff of Nottingham. All that good stuff plus Morgan Freeman and Christian Slater."

"I literally have no idea what any of that was, except the Robin Hood part."

Katrín leaned back to see amusement in his blue eyes. "Really?"

"Not a clue."

"We're going to work on your 90s movies sometime soon."

"I have a feeling it wasn't quite in my preferred genre."

"There are sword fights."

Suddenly interested, he swung her around. "I might be able to get on board with this after all."

"There's also a brief view of Kevin Costner's bare tush. We can skip that part, though. From a plot perspective, it does nothing."

"As long as we leave in the sword fights."

"Absolutely." There were sword fights, weren't there? It was during the Crusades. They had to have sword fights. "Tell Chamberlain to schedule a movie date for us."

"You know we have a theater in the palace. We can watch there."

Of course they did. "Works for me."

The song came to an end, and her hand automatically slipped into his as he led the way back to the table. A smattering of applause came from around the room. For what? Not tripping?

Benjamin held her seat for her this time. Someone had moved his tableware so it was in front of his new seat location.

She was very aware that every eye was on them. This night couldn't be over soon enough. Being on display after a long day at work, and before another one, would get old fast.

Waiters appeared with their first course, followed quickly by their second, then third. They didn't talk much, but that was fine with Katrín. Benjamin did ask if she was enjoying the food.

"It's all new to me, but yes, it's delicious."

"I'm glad." He wiped his mouth on his napkin. How did he never get any food stuck in his beard? She'd always wondered how that worked. Would anyone tell him if he did? Which was worse - letting the king be embarrassed by food in his beard or telling him he didn't eat as impeccably as he thought?

Thor held her car door as she climbed in. By the time they reached the palace, she'd nearly nodded off. Benjamin shook her back to wakefulness.

"What does your week look like?" he asked as they walked back toward their shared common area.

"I work every day, but only half a day Thursday."

"How about plans for a movie night then? You've got me curious."

"As long as I can wear comfortable clothes and shoes with no heel." Her feet were killing her.

"Of course. We won't even leave the family's private quarters."

"Then it's a date."

The words reverberated through Katrín's mind until Thursday when she got off work after lunch. Laurie asked if she wanted to grab dinner later, but she had to tell her friend she already had plans. Someday soon she needed to tell Laurie the truth.

She rummaged through her clothes and finally dug up a pair of old sweat pants and a t-shirt left over from high school. Soft and faded and perfect. At least it hadn't been thrown away in the move.

Benjamin waited for her outside their rooms when she emerged to look for him. "Ready?" he asked, looking up from the tablet he seemed to have with him almost all of the time.

"Do you ever stop working?" she asked, falling into place half a step behind him as he started for the hall.

"I wasn't working, not really."

"Then what were you doing?"

"The public relations office sent me a report earlier today, and I didn't have time to look at the links."

"What links?"

"Stories about our dinner the other night. Apparently, the public loved it."

"Of course they did." She shrugged. "You were behaving like an actual human. Out for dinner with your wife, dancing to romantic songs of the 80s and 90s."

He didn't reply.

"What? The actual human comment bothered you, didn't it?"

"I know how people see me."

"How?"

"Stern. Cold. Unfeeling."

"Perpetually grumpy."

"Yes."

"Wouldn't you like to change that?"

He stopped in the middle of the hallway then turned to look at her.

Was that pain in his eyes? Whatever it was, it fled as quickly as she noticed it.

"I'd give just about anything to change it. I'd even give up my crown if it meant the public would approve of my family again."

15

Benjamin joined Katrín, grateful she didn't push him to talk more about his family's popularity with the people - or worse, his own abysmal approval rating.

"Have you been to the screening room?" Changing the subject seemed like the best bet.

The look on her face told him he hadn't succeeded in distracting her but she let it go. "What do you think?"

He managed to give her a half smile. "That you've never explored the private quarters."

"Exactly."

"Except the screening room isn't up here. It's on the floor above your old one."

"I knew there was a movie theater there, but I never went. I didn't know it was for the private use of the family. I thought it held showings every weekend."

"It does, unless one of us has reserved it."

"So the king of Eyjania shares his theater with the plebes."

Benjamin wasn't sure what to make of her matter-of-fact

statement. "I'm not sure the last time I watched a movie in here. Almost certainly before my father..." He didn't finish the sentence.

"So it's been a while."

The rest of the walk to the screening room was completed in silence. Once inside, he led Katrín to their seats.

A member of his staff had set it up so there were two recliners, with no arm rest between them, near the back with tabletops covering the seats next to them. On the tabletops were silver domed trays containing their dinner. His server would make sure they had refills on their drinks and dessert later. Chamberlain told him the meal was one of Katrín's favorites, though Benjamin had no idea what it would be.

"Thank you," she said softly as another server lifted the dome on her tray. "I'd like a Coke to drink, if you don't mind."

"Yes, Your Majesty," the aide replied.

Katrín stared at her hands in her lap.

Benjamin leaned closer to her and spoke softly. "I grew up being addressed much more formally than most people, but it took me a long time to get used to being addressed that way."

She nodded and adjusted the seat so her legs were stretched in front of her then picked the cheeseburger off the plate and took a big bite. "Mm. This is delicious," she mumbled around a mouthful of food.

He turned to his own plate, recently uncovered by the server. "I'm glad you like it."

"And maybe the evening dishwasher will do the job correctly, and I won't even have to wash these tomorrow."

Benjamin watched her out of the corner of his eye. She didn't seem to be making any kind of commentary on her job, just making a statement.

"When does the movie start?" she asked before taking another bite.

"Whenever we're ready. They can leave the lights up a bit until we're done eating." He motioned to the aide in the back of the room.

A minute later, the picture filled the screen as the lights went down.

As they finished their burgers - Benjamin's with a salad and Katrín's served with what she called "the best fries ever" - the plates were removed quietly and their drinks refilled.

The lights were lowered the rest of the way, with just a few small lights on the floor in case of emergency.

Benjamin remembered why he didn't come in here to watch movies. He didn't feel quite as closed in as expected during the outdoor scenes, but when the screen showed tightly enclosed spaces, he found himself starting to hyperventilate. Though he was able to control it by focusing on his breathing, it did inhibit his enjoyment of the movie.

Until he realized Katrín was holding his hand and her head rested on his shoulder. Then it wasn't as bad.

"What did you think?" Katrín didn't move her head when it ended.

"I would have preferred a few more sword fights."

"And a little less gushy love stuff?" It sounded like she was smiling.

It made him smile a little more. "Maybe."

"So *Princess Bride* is probably out. It has a princess, but also a giant and a pirate and Rodents of Unusual Size."

"Does it have sword fights?"

"Yep."

"It might not be too bad then." He hesitated. "Maybe we could make this a weekly thing?"

She didn't answer for a few seconds, then, "I'd like that."

Benjamin rested his head on hers. "We could even watch that rodent movie sometime, but I get to pick sometimes, too."

"Have you seen that many movies?"

"Not really, but I can at least pick the genre and you or Chamberlain or someone can pick the actual movie."

She nodded against him. "Okay, but none with too much cursing or gore. I can't stand that."

"Agreed, but this is probably about as romance-y as I'd prefer. Surely we can find plenty that we'd both enjoy."

"I would think so." Katrín yawned. "As much as I've enjoyed this, it's time for me to get some sleep. I have to be at work early in the morning."

Conviction settled over him as she moved away. She was the queen. She shouldn't be working in the kitchen anymore.

No.

She was his *wife*.

He could pay off the indenture in half a heartbeat if he wanted to, or even forgive it all together, though that would be entered in the public record.

Benjamin stood and offered Katrín a hand. She grasped it. He didn't let go as they walked toward the door. A glance around told him the staff members had left as soon as dinner was done, leaving them alone together.

As they went up the stairs to the back of the room, Katrín tripped into him. He turned and helped her up. "Are you all right?"

"Yeah. Just missed the step."

In the dim light, he found himself staring into her eyes. What would it be like to kiss her?

For real.

Not like the kiss the night they met.

Benjamin reached out and brushed a bit of hair off her forehead. "I enjoyed this."

She smiled. "I did, too." Her voice was soft and made him wonder if she was thinking the same thing.

Taking a chance, he leaned down and brushed his lips against hers before coming back to linger. Before it could intensify, he backed away.

Katrín's eyes remained closed for a moment. "That was..." she whispered.

"Nice," he finished for her.

"Very," she answered with a nod.

The DVD went back to the menu screen and music blared, ending the moment.

So that's what it was like to kiss his wife. Benjamin thought he might like to do that a little more often.

KATRÍN TOOK HALF a step back and cleared her throat. "Why don't you go back upstairs? I need to see if I have any mail while they're still open." The outer room where the boxes were never closed, but she didn't think he probably realized that.

Benjamin put more distance between them. "Sounds good. I'll see you later." He held the door open to let her out into the mostly vacant square around which the virtual town was situated.

He closed the door behind them and looked at her before he walked toward a staircase.

Katrín watched him until he disappeared up the steps then turned toward the mail offices.

"Katrina!"

A feeling of dread swept over her as she heard Laurie's voice. She turned. "Hi."

"Were you coming out of the theater?" The other woman fell into step beside Katrín as she started for other side of the square.

"Uh, yeah. I watched a movie." She shoved her hands in her pockets and walked faster.

Laurie kept pace. "I thought there was a notice posted that the king was watching a movie in there tonight."

"I didn't see that anywhere." There had been a notice on the door, but Katrín hadn't read it.

"I thought for sure I saw King Benjamin walking upstairs right before I saw you." Laurie stopped Katrín with a hand on her arm. "You came out of there together."

Laurie's eyes went wide, and she leaned closer. "Are you having an affair with the king?" she hissed.

Katrín wrenched her arm away. "No. He's been married for less than a month. Do you really think he'd be having an affair already? Do you really think I'd have an affair with him, regardless of how long he's been married?"

"What's going on?"

Katrín closed her eyes and took a deep breath. "Listen, it's a whole thing. There's legal issues to be dealt with that haven't yet, so *no one* knows this, not really." Except Thor and Chamberlain. That was about it. "My name isn't Katrina. It's Katrín. No one ever gets it right so I just don't say anything."

"Katrín?" Realization then shock crossed Laurie's face. "Like *Queen Katrín? That Katrín?*"

With a nod, Katrín grasped Laurie's wrist. "Seriously. My contract with the palace was signed a long time ago, and it can't just go away. It's got to be done a certain way to be legal, and it takes time. So we're kind of keeping it quiet that I'm still working." Tears filled her eyes, though probably not for the reasons Laurie would imagine. "Please promise you won't say anything."

"What kind of contract can't the king just cancel?"

Katrín could see the wheels turning in Laurie's head.

"An indenture?" There weren't many, but a few existed.

"My mother was accused of stealing something. She didn't, but couldn't prove it. She had to pay off a fine. When I turned eighteen, I took it over so she could stay home with my brother who has health challenges. It's got all kind of legalities that complicate things."

"And the king can't just pay it off for you?" Laurie looked understandably skeptical. "He's the king. He has plenty of money."

Katrín started for the mail center again. "It's not that simple." Maybe it could be. She didn't know. "But I need you not to say anything."

Laurie gasped. "That's why you weren't here the day of the wedding! You were in it! You said you didn't get a good look at the king!"

"Have you seen the footage? The way Eyjanian royal weddings are, we didn't actually look at each other until we were back outside." She used her key to open her box and took out a stack of envelopes. "I didn't lie about any of it, just left some of it open to creative interpretations."

"Is that why the guy from the security office started eating dinner with us?"

Katrín nodded as they went back out into the square. "Because no one knows, I don't need a ton of security, but yeah. That's why Thor comes down for dinner now."

"But as soon as you get the legalities worked out, you won't be down there anymore. You haven't been in a while."

"We finally got everything moved upstairs, so I eat up there when he's not working late." Or grabbed something in the kitchenette in her quarters, but Laurie didn't need to know that.

They reached the staircase Benjamin had disappeared up earlier. Laurie stayed a step behind as they ascended. "I won't say anything," she promised, but Katrín heard a hint of something in her voice.

Distaste? Resentment?

They reached the top and Katrín started toward her next staircase, the one that led closer to the family's quarters.

"Yeah. I'm not allowed up there," Laurie told her, walking backward toward a staff hallway. "But I'll see ya around. Maybe." She bobbed a curtsy then turned and hurried off.

Great. Her one kind of friend wouldn't be anymore.

It hung over her like a cloud for the next week. She had a half day off on their next movie day. After taking a shower and dressing in something more comfortable, but presentable, Katrín went to Benjamin's office. He'd left a message for her to come by at her convenience.

Ninety minutes after clocking out, she sat across his desk from him. "What's going on?" she asked.

He held up a finger as he scribbled a note. "You work in the kitchen so you might have a better idea." He explained about a cooking show that was going to air in the Quad-Countries, an informal name sometimes used for Eyjania, Auverignon, San Majoria, and Islas del Sargasso. Each palace was sending a chef, but not one of the actual palace chefs, someone else to compete on their behalf.

"Laurie," she told him without hesitation. "She's an excellent home chef, if you will. I've had some of her creations, and they're excellent. She's talked about wanting to be a pastry chef someday."

He made a note. "Done. Now, I have a little bit more work to do before our movie tonight."

She wandered toward the window. "Okay. I think I'm going to take a nap so I won't be so tired." Something caught her eye in a park some distance away. "Is that the Festival?" The annual celebration was held to commemorate the city's founding, but wasn't the more formal occasion celebrating King Alfred the First and his wife, Queen Akushla.

"I think so. I'm not certain. I've never been."

Katrín gasped as she turned. "You've never been to the Festival?"

"No."

"You should go!"

He actually snorted. "I'm the king. I can't just go to the Festival."

She crossed her arms. "Why not?"

16

"So why don't you just do it?"

Benjamin just blinked and stared at Katrín. "Why don't I just what?"

"Go to the Festival. Wear a baseball hat and sunglasses. Make your bodyguards stay in the background and go hang out."

"I can't do that." Could he?

"Why not? You said you want the people to like you better. It seems like something your father might have done. He was always out talking to people. Even if they don't know it's you, it'll give you insight into how you can do better at that."

She might have a point. That didn't mean Benjamin was going to do it. He and his father weren't the same. Never had been. He wished he was more like his father, but that didn't mean he wanted to do everything the way his father had. She might be right in this case though.

Benjamin pressed the button on his desk phone. "Chamberlain, can you come in here?" He waited for the other man to enter his office. "Katrín and I have plans this afternoon. I need you to make sure it happens."

He gave Chamberlain the details and told him to do whatever necessary. Chamberlain seemed skeptical but didn't argue. That was a good sign.

Katrín left and went back to work, he guessed. He didn't really know where she went. It could be one of her half days off, for all he knew. She had said she would meet him at four, though, because she had gone in early so she could get off early. The longer they were married, the better he got to know her, the more awkward he felt that she still held the same job. Should he try to get her something else? Or maybe she should do whatever it was a queen was supposed to do, at least for the next eleven months or so.

His family would be back soon. What was it Thor told him? Thor's niece, who worked for Benjamin's mother, was expecting her first child and the doctors had some concerns. Nothing too scary, but she might need to cut back on her work and only work remotely. Benjamin thought that wouldn't go over well with his mother. Not because she didn't like Clari but because she preferred her staff be present and not commute.

Benjamin didn't have time to dwell on it at the moment. Instead, he had to turn his focus to the business at hand.

"Good afternoon." Christiana's voice came through his headset. He preferred it to holding the phone between his ear and shoulder. "I trust everything is all right in Eyjania?"

"Of course. Why wouldn't it be?" He leaned back in his chair and wished he dared put his feet up on his desk.

"You had to go so suddenly a couple of weeks ago, I was worried something else was going on with your uncle." He heard hints of vulnerability in her voice. It had only been about a year since her own run in with the man she'd believed to be her uncle.

"No. It was a misunderstanding with security, but everything's fine. It always was." If one considered the new queen handcuffed and detained "fine."

THE INDENTURED QUEEN

For the next two hours they discussed a variety of topics pertaining to the two countries and their trade.

As they wrapped up, Christiana issued an invitation. "Alexander and I would love to have you and Katrín for a visit. We would love to come there sometime, but we would rather not leave Baby Nicklaus just yet and don't really want to travel with him at this age either."

"I'll talk it over with Katrín and see what we can work out." He remained noncommittal. "Is there anything else we need to discuss?"

"Nothing in my notes."

"Then I'll talk to you sometime soon, I'm sure."

"Big plans?"

There was no harm in telling her. "Katrín and I are going to attempt to go to the Festival this afternoon, while remaining *incognito*."

"Oo! That sounds like fun! I should like to do that someday. You should shave your beard. That would help no one recognize you," Christiana told him thoughtfully. "How long would it take you to regrow it? If you could have a reasonable one in a week or so, you could stay out of the public eye until it's regrown enough that no one knows and keep the secret."

Maybe she had a point, but Benjamin wasn't going to try it now. Instead, he said goodbye to Christiana and headed upstairs. By the time four o'clock rolled around, he wore a pair of blue jeans and hiking boots, the baseball hat Darius gave him at Christmas in the States and held a pair of over-sized sunglasses.

"You know, if you really didn't want anyone to recognize you for a few days, you'd shave your beard."

Benjamin looked up to see Katrín walking out of her quarters.

"Christiana suggested the same thing." He rubbed a hand against his beard. "You don't like it?"

She shrugged. "Not my favorite. But Christiana who? I thought

133

we weren't telling anyone we were going this evening. But she's right."

"The queen of Ravenzario. She won't tell anyone. How do you know I don't have some hideous birthmark underneath here?" he asked with a smirk.

"We would have seen it before you were old enough to grow that thing."

Why did he have a beard? His father never had. They never been customary for Eyjanian kings to have beards. His uncle had one. Could that be why? Some sort of subconscious desire to please Isaiah? To make Isaiah think Benjamin was worthy of being king? The longer he'd been gone, the more Benjamin realized Isaiah had sought to undermine or minimize Benjamin's abilities. Since spending more time with Chamberlain and Thor, he was beginning to see the subtle ways Isaiah had manipulated him for years.

"Regardless, I'm not shaving my beard."

"Fine. Are you ready to go?"

He finally took a good look at her. She wore the same skinny jeans she had to lunch when they got stuck in the elevator but a different shirt. He was pretty sure she wore the same dark brown knee boots. Her hair was also pulled up into a cap, but hers was simply solid black with no sports emblems on it like his had. His was Navy blue with a stylized S, T, and L and a red bird on it. He had no idea what team that was. He didn't even know what sport.

"I'm ready."

Katrin smiled at him in a way he'd never seen her smile at him before. "Then let's go."

IF NO ONE knew who they were, maybe it would be easier for Katrín to relax and be herself. Maybe Benjamin could, too. She kind of liked the man she'd seen in the elevator. The one who wasn't a completely cold fish.

The car took them to a hotel parking garage near the Festival. They emerged into the lobby through a side door and merged with the crowd. Thor and the rest of the security team stayed back a bit until they knew if the disguises would work.

No one gave them a second glance, so she decided it must be working. Once outside, the crowd thickened, so she grasped his hand to make sure they didn't get separated.

Fortunately, Benjamin just curled his fingers around hers and didn't make a big deal of her staying directly at his side. At times, she was forced so close, she practically hugged his arm.

"Where do you want to go first?" she asked him.

He looked down at her, though she couldn't see his eyes behind the mirrored sunglasses. "I have no idea. I've never been before. What's your favorite part?"

"The food, but it's a bit early to eat. The good stuff doesn't come out until later." She looked around. "There's shopping and rides."

"How about a ride?"

Katrín winced. "These aren't the kinds of rides your *friends* would be okay with you going on. They're taken down and put up every few days. While I'm sure they're reputable, they're probably also a bit too rickety to be really safe."

"I'm sure my friends appreciate your attention to my safety. What else is there?"

"Carnival games." She actually hugged his arm, surprising herself with her own forwardness. "You can win me a prize."

"I'd be happy to try."

Katrín steered them toward the midway. "I want a giant stuffed panda if they have them still." One year she'd managed to win one for her brother. He'd loved it, but it had gotten ruined when the car window had been left open and it rained.

"What game should we try?" he asked.

She looked around. "How's your aim? There's a ball toss thing over there."

"We'll find out." He let go of her hand and stepped up to the counter. "I'd like to try."

The barker had a gleam in his eye that Katrín wasn't crazy about. He named a price which startled Benjamin.

She jumped in and pulled some cash out of her pocket. "I got money from the bank, sweetheart. I knew you wouldn't have time after work."

He looked relieved. "Thanks. I had a business call to Ravenzario that took a lot longer than expected."

Katrín wasn't sure she believed him, but it sounded plausible enough.

The barker handed him the first ball. Benjamin turned it over in his hands a few times, then threw. He hit the bowling pins and knocked four of them over.

"One more try." The barker handed another ball over.

Benjamin threw it again and got the last two to fall.

Katrín jumped up and down clapping. "You did it."

With a grin, Benjamin pointed at the prizes. "Which one do you want?"

The barker made sure to point out that she could only pick from the smallest of the prizes. Katrín picked a small penguin. This booth didn't have the pandas anyway.

For the next half hour, they wandered along the stalls, with Benjamin playing one game after another. Katrín waited for one that she wanted to try, but none appeared.

"This is fun." Benjamin handed her the most recent prize. He reached for her hand, intertwining their fingers as he'd done a few times before as they walked between games.

"I'm glad you're enjoying it."

"Of course I am. It's just the two of us and not my... friends or family."

That wasn't strictly accurate. Katrín could see two members of the security teams from where she stood and others were around. She'd bought an oversized bag from a San Majorian vendor. The Caribbean colors made her happy and her prizes all fit inside.

"Is it time to eat yet?"

"We can."

"Let's go that way then." Benjamin let go of her hand, but slid his arm around her waist. "What's your favorite food?"

"They usually have traditional Eyjanian food. That's my favorite."

"Then let's go find it."

A few minutes later, they were in line at one of the vendors. Benjamin moved slightly behind her, something she was certain he'd never done in his life, and leaned down to whisper in her ear.

"I have to admit, I'm not crazy about the standing in line part."

Katrín grinned. "You'll be fine."

"I know, but I still like the part where I don't have to." His arm slid further around her waist, his breath still warm on her ear. "But if it's part of doing this then I'm okay with it."

They shuffled forward a few steps and started discussing the menu. Once they had their food, Katrín looked around at the nearly full eating area.

"A place to sit would be a bonus."

"That's not how it works here. Come on." She started for a table with a couple of empty seats. "Hi," she said as they reached it. "Can we join you?"

"Of course." One of the young women scooted her chair over a bit. "Have a seat." The two couples looked to be in their early or mid-twenties, just like Katrín and Benjamin.

"Are you certain?" Benjamin asked. "We wouldn't want to intrude."

Katrín joined the others laughing as she set her plate down. "He's never been to the Festival before. This is how it works, sweetheart. You find empty seats and make new friends."

Benjamin shrugged. "All right." He set his own plate down.

"Then it's nice to meet all of you. I'm James." One of his middle names. "And this lovely lady is my wife, Kat."

Close enough.

The other four introduced themselves but the girl next to Katrín narrowed her eyes then pointed her fork at Benjamin. "Has anyone ever told you how much you resemble the king?"

17

Benjamin froze at the woman's words, but Katrín just laughed.

"He gets that *all the time*. And since I have a passing resemblance to the new queen *and* my name is similar, you wouldn't believe the comments." She took a sip of her water. "I think we should talk about doing those look-alike appearances where they say the king is going to be there, but really it's someone who's five-foot-two, has the same color hair and no other resemblance."

Relief washed over him. The girl was quick on her feet.

She leaned in closer. "Besides, I can't imagine the king actually wandering around here without eighty-four security guards. And I happen to think my guy is a lot cuter than the TV king."

The girl with the fork stared at him in a way that unnerved Benjamin like few other things ever had. "I think you're right. He is cuter than the king."

Benjamin wasn't sure if he should be insulted or flattered.

"You definitely look like the new queen though. Not from the wedding or on the way to that trip they took, but when she was out by herself that day."

"I never saw the video from it."

"I did." Benjamin jumped in. "She looked great, but I think you look better."

Katrín turned three shades of red and their new friends laughed.

"How long have you two been married?" one of them asked.

"Just a few weeks," he told them.

"So newlyweds." One of the men nodded knowingly. "We've all been there."

"You should totally do the look-alike thing. You both look close enough that you'd do really well." She studied Benjamin. "Except the king doesn't smile nearly as much. He's always so serious, almost grumpy. I guess losing a parent so young and then having so much responsibility will do that to someone."

Benjamin forced a smile on his face. "I would imagine so." Was that really how the people saw him?

"You know..." One of the men turned to the group as a whole. "I think that's part of why the family isn't nearly as popular. I remember the former king and queen being out and part of life for a long time, even with their kids. But after Benjamin became king, there was really nothing for years. I get he was a young teenager and the Queen Mother was grieving, but out of sight out of mind, right?"

His wife nodded. "Prince Isaiah the Elder was the only one really around when I was in high school, and I always thought he was slimy. If the king and his new queen really want to get back in the good graces of the people, they should look at how his parents were."

"Princess Genevieve has done better, somewhat."

Benjamin listened as the other four, with occasional input from Katrín dissected his family and their public image. Everyone liked the charity work and visits to hospitals and such that his next younger siblings had started doing as they turned eighteen. They wanted to see more of him, even if not in the same capacity, and all of the family to at least seem more accessible.

"Who is that on your hat?" one of the men asked Benjamin.

He took it off and looked, trying to remember the design. "Honestly? I have no idea. My brother gave it to me when I went to see him in the States where he's attending university."

Katrín reached up and ruffled his hair. "I kind of love your hair all messy."

Was that her way of reassuring him taking the hat off wouldn't lead to being truly recognized? He tugged it back on. "Thanks, I think."

"Would you two like to join us wandering around? We're going to play some games."

Everyone stood up and began clearing their plates. Benjamin followed their lead and looked at Katrín. "What do you think?"

"I think I still want a giant panda, and I haven't seen one yet. All of the prizes seemed pretty small this year, but I haven't been in a while."

"It's this way."

Benjamin berated himself for already forgetting the woman's name.

"They have two sections this year. The kid-slash-small-prize-cheaper-games section and one with slightly higher stakes."

He held Katrín's hand as they walked with the small crowd. As they did, he caught sight of Thor glaring at him, but more of a warning to keep an eye out than of doing anything wrong. Unless he was very mistaken, all four of their new companions had already been checked out by security.

They reached the first booth and Katrín was nearly giddy to realize there were pandas. He needed to win her one.

But as he played and spent time with the not-quite-strangers, Benjamin found himself feeling differently than he ever had before. Included and accepted for himself rather than because of the titles he'd been born to. It was different. Intriguing.

Katrín told them he was an executive, having inherited the business from his father a few years earlier. Not an outright lie, but not quite accurate either.

"And what about you, Kat? If he's the owner of a successful business, you must be able to do whatever you want." The woman sounded envious.

"Actually, I have the same job I've had for a few years. I promised I'd stay for a while longer."

"What do you do?"

Katrín glanced up at him. "I'm a dishwasher in a family business. My mother worked for them for years, but needed to take care of my brother. They gave me a job, with compensation I couldn't say no to. I promised to stay for another year. After that, we'll see."

"Like you hand wash dishes?" one of the guys asked.

Katrín shook her head. "Some, but mostly I use one of the giant conveyor belt dishwashers."

One of the men winced. "That's a hot, miserable job," he said.

Benjamin had never really thought about that aspect of it.

"What do you want to do when you're done there?" his wife asked.

"I don't know. I still haven't really thought about it." She sighed and a dreamy look crossed her face. "Maybe I'll go to San Majoria or Islas del Sargossa and sit on one of the beaches and stay there until everyone who knows me, except this guy of course..." She pointed at Benjamin. "...thinks I've been gone so long I must have died."

KATRÍN BEGAN MENTALLY BEATING herself up as soon as she said it. She felt Benjamin tense at her side.

"That sounds heavenly." Elise sighed, a far off look crossing her face. "Just the beach, the sun, the waves, and Marty."

"We're coming, too!" Marissa jumped in. As best Katrín could tell, she was Marty's sister. "Harry and I want to sit on the beach. At least during the winter."

The conversation changed to the best vacations they'd ever taken. Katrín stayed quiet, as did Benjamin. He still held her hand, but remained stiff.

"James aren't you going to win that panda for Kat?" Marty asked tossing Benjamin a ball. "You're almost there."

"Sure." He dropped her hand and went back to the game.

Three rounds later, she held the giant panda, but the moment wasn't quite what she'd hoped for a few minutes earlier.

"I need a bun." Elise looked around. "Where are the snack vendors?"

"We just had dinner." Benjamin looked confused. "How can you be hungry again?"

Katrín slipped her hand through his arm as the rest gaped at him. "He's never been, remember?" She smiled up at him. "There's always room for buns, sweetheart."

He shrugged. "Okay, then. Lead on to the buns."

In just a few minutes they were seated at an impossibly small table. So small, it had only three chairs, but it was the only one they could find, and their food wouldn't take up much room.

She could see Benjamin waffle about what to do. As king, he would expect to be given his own chair. As a gentleman, he was expected to not take one so his wife could.

Marty solved it for all of them, but sitting down and pulling Elise to sit on his leg.

Katrín had half hoped the men would stand.

Harry and Marissa bought two plates piled high with the sticky buns. Benjamin sat down and looked up at Katrín. She sat tentatively on his leg, as far away from his torso as she could. It didn't look very newlywed-ish, but she didn't care.

Benjamin didn't let her stay too far away, though. His arms

went around both sides of her as he leaned forward. "Are these the same buns they serve before Lent?"

Katrín picked one up. "Similar." Like Iceland, Eyjania officially celebrated three days leading up to Lent and the Easter season. The first one, everyone ate all the buns they could. Light and fluffy and filled with cream, it didn't take many to get sick on them. The second day, Eyjania departed from Iceland in their traditions, but it consisted of meals filled with meat before giving it up for Lent. Ash Wednesday, like Iceland, saw children dress up and visit businesses and homes to sing for candy.

As they ate, they talked. Elise told a joke about King Alfred the First.

They all laughed, but something sounded off.

Katrín turned to see Benjamin's face turning red, and his eyes bugging out. He pounded on his chest.

"What is it?" Katrín stood up.

His eyes stayed wide as he tried to gag.

"Get up, James." Marty's voice rang with authority.

Marissa grabbed Benjamin's arm and pulled him up as Marty climbed on the chair.

His face was beet red.

Tears had begun streaking down Katrín's face as she wondered where Thor was.

Marty wrapped his arms around Benjamin's abdomen and heaved. Benjamin gagged then Marty did it again.

This time a bite of bun popped out and landed on the ground. Benjamin drew in a deep breath.

Before anyone could say anything else, they were surrounded by security, who rushed them through a nearby gate.

"What's all this?" Elise asked, her arm grasped by one of the men Katrín barely recognized.

"Look at me." Thor stood in front of Benjamin, his face grim. "Talk to me."

"I'm fine." Benjamin still seemed to be gasping for air, but his color had already become more normal. "Really. I'll be fine. Thanks to Marty and Marissa." He looked over at Katrín as she realized tears were still streaking down her face. "I promise."

"What is all this?" Marty demanded.

Benjamin took his hat off and ran his hand through his hair. "You weren't wrong, though we'd appreciate it if you'd keep it to yourselves."

Marty's eyes went wide, followed one by one by the rest. "You really are...?"

Benjamin nodded. "Katrín and I wanted to get out without everyone knowing who we were."

The four of them practically fell over themselves to bow or curtsy.

Elise gasped and covered her mouth with her hands. "What we said about you and your family..."

Benjamin shook his head. "Were all things I've needed to hear. How can I know what the country thinks if no one will talk honestly with me?"

Before anyone else could say anything, medics arrived. Benjamin tried to shake them off. "I'm fine, Thor."

"Too bad." He gave a glare that would have made the Norse god proud.

While Benjamin sat down and let the medics check him over, Katrín, along with their four new friends were guided away.

"I will need all of you to come with us and give a statement," one of the guards told them. "It's just a formality, but since His Majesty needed medical intervention, it's required. All of you will be taken in separate vehicles to prevent you from influencing each other." His look softened. "I'll need your phones. It's protocol."

The four of them just looked kind of shell-shocked, but they handed over their phones, complete with selfies the six of them had taken.

"Wait." Katrín held up a hand. "You're not going to do anything with the phones are you?"

He shook his head. "Just hold onto them until the statements have been made."

She turned to the couples. "Look. I get it. Believe me, but could you do me a favor?"

They all shared a look, but no one said anything or even nodded.

"I don't want them to take any of the pictures off or anything, but we do ask that if you share them with anyone, you laugh about the king's look-alike and the wife with a similar name, just like you would have done if you'd never found out. Can you do that?"

After another glance, they all nodded. "We can." Marty spoke for all of them and handed his phone to the guard. "At least for a few years. Then maybe we'll tell the truth."

A wave of relief washed over her. "Thank you."

In two minutes, they were all in separate security or police vehicles beginning the trek back to the palace.

That's when it hit her.

The thought of something happening to Benjamin had rocked Katrín to her core, though she'd barely had time to give the thoughts space to form.

What did that mean, and what, if anything was she going to do about it?

18

"The piano is *red*." Benjamin heard Marissa make the exclamation as he walked into the room.

"It's a red grand piano," he confirmed.

They all turned and bowed or curtsied. It felt far more normal, but at the same time, he thought he would miss being "James." "We have several others in black and white throughout the palace." He smiled in Katrín's general direction. "This is where we first met."

She hung back, uncertainty all over her face.

"You can go hug him, kiss him even," Marissa whispered loudly. "We won't tell."

Katrín moved hesitantly to his side and wrapped an arm around his waist. "I'm glad you're okay."

He put his arm around her shoulders and tugged her closer, glad she was there.

"Wait."

They turned to look at Elise.

"The family business you inherited? You mean the throne?" He could see it all starting to register.

Benjamin nodded. "Yes. I do a lot of executive type work

including negotiations with companies and other countries. In many ways, it is like a business."

Marissa looked at Katrín. "You're a dishwasher, though? Really? That has to all be part of the act, right?"

Katrín moved away from him. "I've been a dishwasher, and I've worked for the palace since I turned eighteen. I do have a contract that is technically still in place, though it's enforcement is not what it used to be. There's a clause that specifically says it's still applicable in case I get married. I think most of the contracts with the palace are like that."

"So you're not actually still a dishwasher?" Marissa seemed as confused as Benjamin was starting to be by the whole thing.

Katrín laughed. "Can you imagine the headlines? *Eyjania's New Queen Works As Dishwasher In Palace Kitchen.*"

She didn't lie, but the truth behind it bothered Benjamin.

Everyone else laughed with her, but not Benjamin.

Harry raised a brow at him. "I hope you don't take this the wrong way, sir, but I think I liked you better as James. You weren't nearly as uptight."

Benjamin just nodded as Thor came and told everyone they were free to leave. Thor escorted the six of them toward the portico where a car waited to take the other two couples back to the Festival.

"Thank you again," he told Marty and Marissa. "I appreciate your help."

They grinned at each other. "We've worked together before. We used to be lifeguards. You wouldn't believe how many kids choke on snacks." Marissa told him. "And we were glad to do it. It was a privilege to be of service."

After another minute of idle discussion, the other four climbed into the car and drove off.

By the time Benjamin turned around, Katrín had already started to walk back up the stairs toward the residential section.

"Wait," he called after her.

She stopped three stairs up and turned. "I'm glad you're all right."

He searched her expression for a hint of whether it was anything more than concern for a fellow human being. "It scared me."

"I can imagine."

Benjamin stood in front of her, their eyes nearly level. "Are you okay?"

A sheen of tears covered her eyes. "Why wouldn't I be?"

Maybe there wasn't anything else behind her concern. "Because you were right there."

Katrín reached out and rested a hand on his shoulder before letting it drop to his upper arm. He found himself wanting to reach out and take her in his arms.

"It was scary, but I'm fine." Her hand fell to her side. "I have to be up early in the morning, so I'm going to turn in unless there's anything else you need from me?"

Benjamin found himself wondering what it would be like to kiss her, but didn't say anything and just shook his head. "No. Sleep well."

He went back to the Rainbow Reception Room and walked across it until he reached the case. He stared at the dagger. One day, he wanted to take it out, hold it, turn it over in his hands, and imagine what it would be like to have it handed to him after being knighted.

But no. Even the king of Eyjania wasn't to take such an ancient piece of weaponry and art from its protective case except on extremely special occasions.

He couldn't explain it. Something about the story of King Alfred called to him. Not just the daring knight's adventures that made up any Medieval story, but something about Alfred specifically. By all accounts, he was head over heels for his wife - a scullery maid traveling with a larger contingent, including the lady Alfred's brother was to have married. When vagabonds ambushed their group, the lady and most of the others had been killed and the treasure stolen. Only Alfred and this maid survived.

Though no one particularly cared about the reputation of such a lowly servant - Alfred did. As the story went, he behaved completely honorably during the week or so they traveled alone together, the message for his father secreted on his person. But when they finally reached a town where it was safe for them to reveal their identities, one of the first things Alfred did was marry her, banns or not.

When he returned to Eyjania a couple of weeks later, Alfred discovered that his father and all three of his older brothers had been killed when their ships collided in a storm. At the time of his marriage, he was already king.

Conscience pricked Benjamin. Since he was young, he'd wanted to be worthy of Alfred's dagger.

Yet, he was planning to arrange the alleged death of his wife in a year. Play the grieving widower. Eventually, remarry and have children with a woman of higher breeding.

All while his current wife's family believed her to be dead.

It wasn't a very knight thing to do.

He'd vowed before God and country to lead his people to the best of his ability. He'd been thirteen. Had little choice in the matter, though he still took that oath seriously.

He'd vowed before God and country to love, honor, and cherish Katrín for as long as they both shall live. He'd been twenty-six. Felt he had little choice in the matter, but the reality was he could have found a way around it. It wouldn't have been easy, but he could have.

"Staring at that dagger again?" His mother's voice didn't surprise him.

He didn't turn around. "Wondering if King Alfred would be proud of me, of the man I've become - am still becoming."

"That's a question only you can answer."

Which meant she wasn't sure. Didn't know if her oldest child was the kind of honorable man his father had been.

And that meant he probably wasn't.

Benjamin needed to figure out where he was deficient. It couldn't just be not meaning his wedding vows. It had to be something else. Something... more.

He turned away from the case holding the dagger to find his mother already gone. Had she ever even been there? His family wasn't supposed to return for several days. His gaze passed over the red piano.

Katrín played beautifully. She knew *King Alfred's Overture* by heart. But he'd never heard her play except the once. Never asked her how she learned. Why she loved it.

He'd even dismissed the loss of her keyboard, belittled her feelings when it clearly upset her, though he didn't see a reason for such an old instrument that didn't work to mean so much.

Benjamin knew he wasn't worthy of King Alfred's dagger.

And maybe he never would be.

KATRÍN WANDERED AROUND HER QUARTERS, still shaken from Benjamin's near-near-death experience. She'd lived there for weeks now, but still hadn't slept in the consort's bed. She still far preferred the lady-in-waiting's room with its more normal size and Furniture-of-Historical-Insignificance.

She leaned against the doorframe and stared into the bedroom. Had the Queen Mother slept here? Had she slept with her husband? Given the number of children they had, and the pictures of the two of them together, Katrín suspected the latter. Katrín's own mother had told her stories about the late monarch and his wife. Or hadn't Benjamin said the younger kids lived in this suite while his parents lived in the other one?

Well, Katrín wouldn't spoil this room for Benjamin's permanent wife. She wouldn't sleep in here at any time before her alleged death.

But it still called to her. She wandered around the room, running her fingers lightly over the wood tops of the tables, desks, and dressers.

Some of the wall panels held ornate carvings like parts of the rest of the palace did. One held rosettes.

Where did this passage go? Likely an escape tunnel should they be under attack.

She pressed them in sequence, and the panel swung in. As she expected, a tunnel went off both directions. To the left, a set of stairs told her it was the exit route. She went to the right, just to explore a little bit.

A minute later, she found another exit, this one on her left. It likely went into the consort's sitting room, though she was a bit turned around. It might lead to the giant foyer area.

She pressed the release and moved out of the way of the door as it opened inward.

Katrín blinked and her jaw dropped.

"Sorry," she gasped as King Benjamin turned, his eyes as wide as hers likely were.

"What are you doing here?" he asked, his expression turning into a smirk instead of the shock it had been.

"I was just exploring the tunnel." She looked anywhere but at him. His bathroom was even nicer than hers. "I thought this door went to my sitting room."

"Not even a little bit." He walked toward her, that annoyingly smug expression she hated seated semi-permanently on his face.

He reached for the towel wrapped around his waist.

Katrín gasped and turned. "Really?"

"Relax. I'm just making sure it's secure. I wouldn't do that to you."

It shocked Katrín to realize that she believed him. The night she'd first met him, she would have felt differently.

"You don't believe me." It wasn't a question.

Katrín stared at the ground. "I'm not sure I know you well enough to believe you."

"The towel won't come off, literally or metaphorically, until you take it off." She heard him walking toward her stopping when his feet were in her line of sight.

"Good to know."

When his finger crooked under her chin and raised her face until she could see his. "What?" she whispered.

King Benjamin shrugged. "Wanted to look you in the eyes while we talk."

Katrín found herself very aware of her loose fitting, but fairly low cut, pajama shirt - and her husband's lack of shirt all together. "What are we going to talk about?"

"For starters, how you probably shouldn't just walk through random hidden doors unless you're prepared to get an eyeful of someone you didn't expect to see. This tunnel also has exits in several other sets of quarters."

"Duly noted." She didn't want to notice the amusement lurking in his dark eyes. "But shouldn't you have some code in the hallways to tell you where each door goes? Nothing as obvious as the king's bathroom or the consort's bedroom, but something."

"Also duly noted." His finger left its spot under her chin and found a new one near her temple before tracing a line down the side of her face and along her neck.

Katrín swallowed as something unfamiliar fluttered deep inside. "What are you doing?" she managed to whisper.

"Wondering what it would be like to kiss you." His voice sounded husky to her ears.

"Why would you wonder that?"

In her peripheral vision, she saw his shoulders lift. "You're my wife. Isn't it natural to wonder what it would be like to kiss you again? To wonder what it might be like for more?"

He knew far more about what "more" would be like than she

did. He'd made it quite clear to her that he could have any woman he wanted, though he had promised he wouldn't cheat on her for the duration of their short marriage. Thor had told her he wasn't really like that, but she didn't know what she believed.

"Don't try to tell me it hasn't at least crossed your mind."

Katrín took a step back. She needed away from him, away from his magnetism. "Just because it's crossed my mind doesn't mean it's a good idea. I wanted to try to fly off my roof as a child, but it wouldn't have ended well if I did. No matter how much either of us might want to, neither would this."

She turned and fled back down the tunnel until she reached the door to the consort's bedroom.

With one hand on the post of the four-poster bed, she closed her eyes and tried to breathe.

"Why would it be a bad idea? You are my wife. We are legally married." His voice in her quarters didn't startle her like it probably should have.

"Temporarily," she reminded him. "Both of us will likely have future spouses and do we really want to explain this to them? If we sleep together, it's one more complication when I set up a new life."

The reality was she didn't think she'd marry in her new life. More likely she would have a life as a spinster. Too complicated otherwise.

"And you don't think my next wife will expect that we would have slept together?"

She spun to look at him. "I suppose that depends. Are you going to tell her the truth about your first wife? That it was all a revenge plot from your uncle to force you to marry the most unsuitable person in the palace?"

"That hasn't been proven."

She rolled her eyes. "You and I both know that's what happened."

"Most likely." He took another step toward her.

Katrín tried to step back but found her spine against the post of the bed.

"One kiss," King Benjamin whispered. "Just one."

She found herself nodding even as her breath caught in her throat.

His hands framed her face as he leaned down. Katrín's eyes fluttered closed, and she waited.

Benjamin wanted to sit in his desk chair, slouch down, and prop his feet up on something. Instead, he stood in front of one of the floor to ceiling windows, feet shoulder width apart, hands clasped behind his back. Really, he found himself wishing he was back in the consort's bedroom, but not waking up alone.

The massive door whispered open. It didn't dare groan or squeak, not when Chamberlain was around.

"Her Majesty, the Queen." Chamberlain's condescending tone was directed at Benjamin. He knew that.

But Benjamin didn't turn, even after the door closed. He waited for Katrín to say something, but she didn't. Finally, he turned to see her standing in front of his desk.

She glared at him as she curtsied. "You summoned, Your Majesty."

He'd never resented the title more than when she laced it with sarcasm.

What was he supposed to say to her? Why had he summoned her in the first place? *Wondering why I woke up alone* didn't seem quite right.

He motioned to one of the chairs across from the desk and sat down in his chair. "You were up early." That seemed safer.

"I'm always up early. I have to be at work early." She sat but the glare didn't dissipate. "Besides, I didn't sleep well. Unfamiliar bed and all."

"We slept in your room," he pointed out.

"No. You slept in the consort's room. I stared at the wall of it. I've never slept in there before, and I didn't actually sleep."

"Why on earth not? It's your room."

"No. It's the suite I'm borrowing temporarily. I stay in one of the other rooms because that one is too big, too ostentatious, for me. I'd planned to leave it as something your next wife could enjoy with the knowledge I rarely stepped foot in there."

Benjamin studied her and her dark brown eyes. Something more lurked behind her words. Pain? Resignation? He didn't know how to respond to that, so he didn't.

Instead, he went to the next order of business. He could have let Chamberlain take care of it, but decided to do it himself. "You won't have to be up so early anymore. You're not going to be working in the kitchen."

She didn't say anything, though the glare lessened. "I won't be?" Did she sound almost hopeful?

Benjamin shuffled the paperwork on his desk. "No. You'll be working for my mother instead."

The silence lasted for several seconds. "I see."

"She's in need of a temporary Social Media Manager."

"For Thor's niece?"

He nodded.

"I see. When do I start?"

"You'll need to see the palace personnel office. They'll make sure you know what you need to."

He looked up as she brushed her hair back and frowned. "Where's your ring?"

She looked down at her finger. "The engagement ring?"

"My mother's engagement ring. The one my father had made especially for her." The one he hadn't wanted to use for this marriage. He hadn't wanted to use it at all. Benjamin didn't believe he'd ever find someone who meant as much to him as his parents meant to each other.

"It's in my room." She crossed her arms over her chest. "I didn't think you'd want me wearing it to wash dishes."

She had a point. "And you've taken it off every day since?"

"I've washed dishes every day, haven't I? Except when we went out of town."

Benjamin realized he had no idea. "It wasn't on the list of things removed from your apartment," he pointed out.

"Because I put it back on as soon as I get back to my quarters, wherever they are. That was a half day off. I worked, went back and took a shower, put it on, then went to mail a letter at the post office on the floor above mine. By the time I got back, half my things were gone. I went to find you, and got arrested."

"You weren't arrested," he reminded her.

"Whatever. Just be sure to let the personnel office of my change in employment status, would you? I'd hate to get reprimanded for not being somewhere I'm not supposed to be."

Something about that didn't sit well. "Has that happened before?"

"I have four reprimands in my file for missing work."

"When?"

"Once when I was sick. I got one a couple years ago when some flowers were delivered to me by mistake. It took all of an hour to convince the florist I wasn't the intended recipient. His delivery guy sorted it out, but it didn't matter."

"And the other two?"

She stared straight into his eyes. It disconcerted him. "The day of the wedding and the morning after when I overslept because the ball ran so late. I almost got written up again because of the trip out of town, but Chamberlain managed to get that off my record."

"You were reprimanded for missing work on the day we got married?" He still found that hard to believe, but hadn't she mentioned that once before? "They didn't know where you were?"

"I told my boss I was at the wedding. He didn't believe me without an invitation. Wrote me up anyway."

"You didn't tell him you were the bride? That's why you didn't have an invitation," he pointed out.

She snorted. "Why? So they could give me a hard time about being the new queen while still working as a slightly modernized scullery maid? Please. They can't fire me. It was better to just take the reprimand." Katrín stood and started for the door. "At least your mother might understand if I need to miss work occasionally for some fancy shindig where you need to pretend this is a real marriage."

Her cavalier attitude toward him and his authority irritated Benjamin. He stood, his hands on the desk with his weight resting on them. "I haven't dismissed you yet."

"You didn't dismiss me this morning either," she called over her shoulder.

"You haven't been given permission to leave."

With a mighty tug, she pulled the door open, and walked through, leaving Benjamin to stare after her as she called back.

"Then exile me."

19

Katrín went to her fake room and started to press the stones to open the corridor back to the consort's suite, but she stopped before completing the sequence. Instead, she went to stare out the window.

The city spread below her with the Festival lights still visible off in the distance. The evening before had been everything she'd hoped for when she finally finished her indenture and found a guy. He'd even won her the giant panda she'd wanted for so long.

What had happened to it? And all of the other prizes Benjamin had won for her?

She needed to accept that they were likely long gone. Maybe she'd ask Thor if someone had grabbed them.

It had been at least ten minutes of staring and trying to quiet her tumultuous thoughts, and avoiding going back to her suite where she'd spent the night with her husband, when an unfamiliar buzz sounded in her pocket.

The caller ID said it was the security offices. "Hello?"

"Your Majesty?" the voice asked.

Yeah. That was her. "Yes?"

"There's someone at the gate claiming to know you, ma'am. She has a giant panda she says belongs to you."

Hope began to blossom. "Who is it?"

"Elise."

"Yes, I know her."

"Would you like to meet her in the conference room in the security offices? She hasn't been cleared for the rest of the palace."

"Of course." Katrín hung up and left the room, walking up the narrow staircase to the security offices.

Thor met her at the door and handed her a long coat. "You might want to put this on."

Katrín glanced down. She still wore her uniform. With the coat buckled around her, she went into the conference room where Elise waited.

"Good afternoon."

Elise bobbed into a curtsy, something Katrín doubted she'd ever get used to. "Good afternoon, Your Majesty. I brought something for you, but they confiscated it to check it out, I guess."

"Probably." She motioned to one of the chairs. "Please, have a seat."

They both sat down. Katrín stared at her hands. "I'm sorry about yesterday."

"What about it?" Elise looked concerned. "None of us are upset about being detained at the *palace*."

Katrín shook her head. "Not that. I know you understand why we did it, but we really skated the line on lying to all of you and that bothers me, even though there were excellent reasons to do so."

"Hey."

The compassion in Elise's voice made Katrín look up to see concern on her new friend's face.

"You guys didn't date very long before announcing the wedding, did you?"

Katrín managed not to snort. "No."

"You didn't have time to figure out what it's like to be in the public eye before the wedding, so you're going to have to figure it out afterward. I don't blame you for not wanting to go to the Festival publicly. It wouldn't be near as much fun that way. And, if I had to guess, you and King Benjamin are still getting to know each other. For whatever reason, you knew there was something between you. You knew you wanted to spend your lives together, but you didn't have the benefit of *time*."

"No, we didn't. There were reasons, a lot of them." She realized how that might have sounded. "It's not like I'm pregnant, and we *had* to or anything, but there were reasons for the abbreviated courtship."

"As long as you've got each other, you'll figure it out."

"I hope so." She sighed. "He has asked me to do something I'm completely unfamiliar with."

"What's that? Is it something one of us can help with?"

Katrín wasn't sure what had possessed her to mention it at all, but it was the truth. "His mother's Social Media Manager has to take a leave of absence, and he's asked me to help her with it. But the truth is, I've never been on social media. I didn't even have a smart phone until after the wedding." She hated skirting the truth again, but the rest came too close to her reality.

"Then it might be good for you to learn." Katrín saw her new friend wince. "I hate to say it, but your husband needs to learn how to use social media to his advantage. He's no good at it or doesn't have anyone working for him who is, anyway."

"I don't think he has a social media person on staff," Katrín admitted.

"And you need to learn, too." Elise leaned forward. "You both need someone who can help you learn. We talked about the royal family yesterday. Princess Genevieve is helping the family's image with her public face, but this is the 21st century. I don't think the whole family needs to be public, especially not the younger children, but you, the king, the older ones, all need a public relations expert to help you."

"You're probably right." She gave Elise a half-smile. "I don't suppose you know anyone?"

Elise wrinkled her nose. "I promise this isn't why I said that, but I do a lot of freelance social media networking and public relations type stuff for several businessmen and women, and I've even worked with a couple of local politicians. I don't know that I could do everything you need, even if you wanted me to, but I can probably help you get started and steer you in the right direction until you can hire someone to handle it properly."

A weight lifted from Katrín's shoulders. At least Elise could help her figure it out and get Benjamin set up so that when she disappeared, he'd already be poised to handle it. "That would be wonderful. A huge blessing really. I have no idea what my authority is, if anything, to actually hire you, but I'll find out. Until then, would you help me get started?"

Elise smiled. "I would be honored. Do you have your phone, or better yet, a laptop or other computer, handy?"

She had her phone, but it was in the pocket of her uniform. "Tell you what? Why don't we start tomorrow? I didn't sleep well after all of the excitement last night." And what transpired later. "And I'm not in a position to absorb it all right now. I'll talk to Thor and Benjamin and see what we need to do. For all I know, they may have already created the accounts but not activated them. I remember hearing they do that sometimes. Then tomorrow, walk me through getting started?"

The door opened and Thor entered carrying several bags. Katrín gasped as she recognized them. "Are those from last night?"

Elise smiled. "I knew you'd want them. I called a friend who was working nearby. He'd seen them picked up and taken to lost and found."

Katrín stood and hugged her new friend. "Thank you."

Elise picked up her purse. "If we're going to get started tomorrow, I have some things I need to do tonight."

"I'll see you in the morning."

Katrín watched her leave then turned to Thor. "I need to talk to you."

"SHE DID WHAT?" Benjamin wasn't sure he'd heard Chamberlain right.

"She hired Elise to assist her with social media." The man's face was impossible to read.

"Why?"

"When did she get her first smart phone?"

"Last week? The week before?" Wasn't that right?

"Did she have a computer?"

"No."

Chamberlain just stared at him until the implications sunk into Benjamin's brain. "Katrín doesn't know anything about social media, does she?"

"No, sir."

Something he should have considered before volunteering her to work in that capacity for his mother. "What do we need to do get Elise hired at least temporarily until we can get someone permanent? I presume Elise knows what she's doing."

"According to Thor's preliminary background checks last night, yes. She does freelance social media management for a number of people. I do not know if she would be willing to work exclusively for the palace, even temporarily."

Benjamin managed to stifle his sigh. "Find out?"

"Yes, sir."

"And ask Katrín to come here, please."

Chamberlain hesitated then nodded with a slight smirk. "Yes, sir."

What could the smirk be about? He'd made similar requests many times a day, almost every day. What could be different about this time?

With an internal shrug, Benjamin went back to the paperwork on his desk. It all needed attention, and now.

His intercom buzzed, and he pressed the button, his attention still on the papers. "Yes?"

"Her Majesty, Queen Katrín to see you, sir."

That was fast. "Send her in." Benjamin pushed back from his desk and stood. Katrín entered and curtsied, much as she had earlier, but her face held less antagonism. He motioned to a sitting area near the window. "Have a seat?"

She hesitated then sat down, perched on the edge of the wingback chair. Benjamin sat in the chair next to hers.

"I owe you an apology," he started.

Her eyes narrowed, but she didn't respond.

"I should have asked you if you knew how to use social media effectively before volunteering you to help my mother. It didn't occur to me that you might not be familiar with it, though it makes sense, given that you didn't have a phone or computer. I'm sorry I didn't ask, and that I put you in a position that could have been quite awkward when you went to work for my mother."

She shifted backward slightly. "Apology accepted. I take it you heard about Elise?"

He relaxed a bit. "Chamberlain informed me." Benjamin stared out the window and at the ocean in the distance. "There is something we need to consider."

"We? No edict for the rest of us to go along with?"

Her sarcasm cut. "No."

With a release of her breath, Katrín slumped against the back of the chair. "That was uncalled for. I'm sorry."

"Forgotten. But we do need to consider your role as queen until such a time as you disappear." He'd sort of ignored it, but this social media thing made it impossible. In the back of his mind, he'd known it wouldn't work for things to go on as they had been the last several weeks, but asking Katrín to fully embrace the role of queen hadn't occurred to him until minutes earlier.

"What about my role? I stay in the background, do the minimum, the country mourns on your behalf but not for me which makes it very easy for your next wife to surpass me in popularity."

"No. I think you need to fill the role of queen as much as you feel you are able, just like you would if we were planning for you to stay forever." He folded his hands together. "That means assembling a staff for you. For now, Elise can handle social media and teach both of us about its use. I have accounts. I've never written a tweet in my life."

Her smirk reappeared. "That will shock absolutely no one."

"I don't think anyone uses it on my behalf except occasionally for events of great import. Congratulatory notes after elections, commemorating important holidays, things of that sort, using quotes from the official statements. It turns out that Marty is a web designer. He and Harry own an Internet marketing company where Marissa works as a graphic artist."

Her smirk softened. "Almost like someone knew what we needed before we did? Think maybe God might have arranged all of this?"

Benjamin didn't reply immediately as he thought it over. Finally, he answered. "I'm not sure. I think that might be pressing the issue a bit, but that God has a hand in our lives? Definitely."

"You think it's a coincidence that I need social media help, you need public relations and marketing help, and we just *happened* to sit at a table with people who can do all of it? *And* knew the Heimlich maneuver? If you hadn't choked, we all would have gone on our merry ways, and we wouldn't be positioned to learn from them."

She made an excellent point, and he told her so. Benjamin stood and so did Katrín. "I will have Chamberlain make arrangements for a meeting with the four of them as soon as possible."

"Just let me know." She curtsied again and turned to leave.

"Wait." It had bothered him some before because he knew it should bother him, but not because it actually did. Now, it bothered him.

"What?"

"Protocol only dictates that you curtsy the first time you see me on any given day." That sounded awkward even to his own ears.

Katrín crossed her arms. "So, this morning, I slip out of bed, curtsy and leave?"

The snark made him smile. "Well, maybe the first time when I'm awake."

"Duly noted. I won't curtsy every time I see you anymore then."

She started for the door as Benjamin went back to his desk. A yellow note caught his attention. "One other thing," he called as she started to pull the door open. "My mother's birthday party is coming up." And the only reason he hadn't suggested an even more extended vacation. "It's a very formal event, and we will be expected to attend together. There will be dancing."

A look he couldn't define crossed her face before she came back to sit across from his desk. "Then we may have a problem."

20

Katrín couldn't believe this.

"What kind of problem?" Benjamin asked, sitting in what was surely a very expensive, custom made chair.

"I don't know how to dance."

Benjamin seemed to consider her words. "I don't have time to work with you, but I will have Chamberlain see to it that someone does."

"Thanks." She stood again. "I appreciate it." She also appreciated not needing to curtsy every time she entered or left a room with him in it.

When she reached the door again, his voice stopped her. Again.

"Are we going to discuss last night?"

Katrín didn't turn around. "What is there to discuss? You had a near death experience. Emotions were running high. Things happened." Things seared into her mind. Things she wouldn't soon forget.

She still didn't turn but waited for him to respond. Finally, he said, "Excellent points. I must get back to work."

Katrín let herself out and headed for her suite. At least the coat provided by Thor meant she didn't have to go the long way. Despite only working half a day, she was ready for a soak in the sunken tub in her bathroom followed by a nap.

She did just that, awakening to a knock on the door to the lady in waiting's room where she slept.

"What?" she called, her arm flung over her eyes.

"We have dinner plans."

Benjamin's voice shocked Katrín, and she sat up fast enough to give herself a head rush. "We do?"

"Yes. Both couples were able to come to dinner tonight. We'll be meeting with them. You will also need an assistant and a stylist, though Elise may be able to fill the assistant's role temporarily, and Rosalie will be your stylist until you decide if you'd rather have another one or not."

"You were a busy beaver while I slept, weren't you?"

All she could see was his backlit form in the doorway. "Pardon?"

"I took a nap. You arranged dinner and for me to have staff members."

"No. I asked Chamberlain to take care of it. I doubt he even did it all himself, but rather made some calls."

"How long do I have until they arrive?"

"About an hour."

"And we're meeting where?" She didn't know her way around most of the palace, but surely she could ask someone or call Thor.

"Meet me outside our suites in an hour, and we'll go together."

"Thanks." That helped. "I'll be ready."

She didn't need a shower, but she did need to do her hair and make-up. Fortunately, by the time she climbed all the way out of bed, Benjamin had left.

All of her clothes were in the main closet, so that's where Katrín headed. Slacks and a nice blouse seemed safe enough.

Benjamin hadn't said anything about how formal it would be. Surely he would have if it required anything nicer than that.

After spending longer than expected on her hair and carefully applying make-up, Katrín dressed quickly and left her suite. Benjamin already waited in the lounge area.

He looked her up and down, and she waited to be found wanting. "You look nice," he finally said. "Ready?"

"Yes." She let him take the lead, staying close, but still a bit behind.

He reached back and took her hand as they walked into a small dining area. The skin-to-skin contact sent an electric vibe roiling through her. Was he as aware of her presence as she was of his?

If so, her husband seemed surprisingly unaffected.

The other two couples waited for them. They all stood and bowed or curtsied. Benjamin acknowledged them with a tilt of his head. Katrín wasn't sure if she was supposed to or not, so she didn't.

"Can you tell us what all this is about, sir?" Harry asked. "Elise told us a little about her discussion with the queen earlier, but we're not sure how it relates to the rest of us."

"It doesn't directly," Benjamin told him. "But in your background checks, your occupations came to the attention of my security team. When we discussed Elise's new role, even if it turns out to be temporary, the rest of your professions suddenly became relevant."

"How so?"

Benjamin motioned to a table set up nearby. "Why don't we discuss this over dinner?"

Katrín found herself on the far end of the table with a server holding her seat for her as Benjamin seated himself on the other end. Salads appeared in front of each of them.

"As we discussed yesterday, my family needs help in the area of public relations. I'm told our websites and social media presences are incredibly out of date, with the possible exception of Genevieve's. We would like to hire your firm to do an assessment of what we need to do and perhaps help us do it."

Looks were exchanged between the four of their guests.

"Elise, Katrín already discussed some of the social media with you."

Elise nodded. "I started to clear some things off my plate so I could devote most of my time to this starting tomorrow, but with this dinner, I'm afraid I won't really be able to start until next week. I'll spend most of tomorrow finishing up and handing some of it off to a friend who works for me when I'm out of town and such."

"That's acceptable. What about the rest of you?"

Marty and Harry exchanged a look.

Harry didn't look straight at Benjamin. "It's actually a topic we've discussed a number of times before." He sighed. "A few of us got together to see who could design the best website for your family. Winner got to be kings for a day. It was just for fun, but the competition was serious, not to see who came up with the biggest spoof or something. We won. We'd be happy to show you what we came up with, and if it's not the direction you'd like to go, we can come up with something new."

Benjamin nodded. "I would like to see it. Yesterday, the four of you carried on a lively discussion on what the royal family could do to improve our image. If you are willing to work with us and we can come to terms, I would like to see an official proposal that focuses on what those of us over the age of eighteen can do."

Katrín listened far more than she spoke during dinner. The four of them knew what they were talking about. Benjamin was willing to admit he needed guidance and listened intently, asking pointed and insightful questions as the meal went on.

She didn't know enough to know what she didn't know, so she'd do what seemed to be her new job. Sit quietly out of the way and let the others figure it out.

By the time dinner ended, Benjamin was more convinced than ever that these four were the answer to a prayer he wasn't sure he'd ever felt the need to pray.

But he'd noticed Katrín remained very quiet throughout, only speaking if someone asked her a direct question. She likely absorbed it all, despite her silence.

He returned to his office to make some notes while they were fresh in his mind. After a quick shower, he stared at the rosettes on the wall of his bathroom. Did he want to see her again?

The answer was a resounding yes, but given the direction his thoughts were drifting, it probably wouldn't be the best idea. Something made him think Katrín wouldn't feel right telling him "no" even if she wanted to, not after the night before.

Neither one of them said no then. He was absolutely convinced of that.

But he did want to know her thoughts on what had been discussed at dinner. Finally, he decided just to send for her in the morning, have her come to his office and discuss it then.

With that decided, he went to bed and slept fitfully.

In the morning, he was greeted with a surprise that would keep him from meeting with Katrín longer than expected.

His family had returned a day early.

"Good morning, darling." His mother breezed into his office five minutes after he arrived.

Benjamin stood and walked around his desk. "Mother! When did you get here?"

"We landed about half an hour ago. I asked them not to tell you, but I didn't want to stay away any longer, even if it did give you and Katrín a bit of a honeymoon staying here alone, such as it were." She extended her cheek for him to kiss.

"I missed you." It almost surprised him to realize how much.

"And I missed you, but more so than that, I missed being able to get to know my new daughter-in-law."

They walked toward the grouping of chairs near the windows. "Then you'll be happy to know that Katrín will be working on your social media team. We have a new young woman hired to help her learn to use social media and teach the rest of us as well. I know you have Clari, but she's unavailable for the moment."

"Good. But Katrín doesn't know how to use social media?"

"Not effectively for what we need to do." He motioned for her to sit in the seat Katrín had occupied the night before. Rather than sitting, Benjamin leaned against the window near her. "We did something a bit unorthodox the other night." He told her how they managed to spend some time at the Festival unnoticed and what he'd learned.

"I don't want to hurt you, Mother, but the truth is, when Father died, the family did as well, at least as an entity visible and relatable to the public. We all need to change that."

"Genevieve has been saying that for years," his mother told him. "And I know much of it is my fault. I didn't know how to breathe without your father. By the time I'd pulled myself together, I had an infant and far less influence over you. I certainly didn't have any desire to be in the public eye after a year of grieving so deeply, I almost wished I'd died as well."

"I, for one, am quite glad you didn't."

She reached out and grasped his hand. "I know. I am, too, really, but it took a long time for me to reach that point. I am interested in seeing the proposal they put together. I have some ideas of my own. That was one thing I realized during this trip away. I miss being with my peo... with your people."

A wry grin crossed his face. "I'm fairly certain you're far more popular with the people than I am. They still see themselves as your people, despite the coronation when I turned eighteen."

"Will Katrín have a coronation?" She dropped his hand and folded hers primly in front of her.

"I don't see why. She's not the regent." In truth it hadn't occurred to him if she should or not. "If we were already married when I was officially crowned, then she would have been crowned at the same time. Weren't you crowned with Father?"

"I was. How does she feel about that?"

Benjamin gave the only answer he could. "I have no idea. We haven't discussed it, but it would surprise me if she expected one. I can barely get her to stop curtsying every time she sees me."

His mother smiled, but it faded quickly, though she didn't say anything else. Something likely went through her head, but she wouldn't say what it was until she was ready.

"Now, is everything on schedule for your birthday party?" A change of subject seemed just the ticket.

She shook herself out of it. "I believe so. I did adjust the guest list to include your new in-laws."

Benjamin merely nodded. Why hadn't that occurred to him? When was the last time Katrín had spent any real time with her family? Given what she'd told him about her indenture, likely it had been quite some time. He'd put Chamberlain to making arrangements for them to come visit. He also needed to see about making sure they were financially comfortable.

His mother stood. "I am sure you have plenty of other things to be doing, so I will leave you to them."

After a long hug, she left and Benjamin called Chamberlain in. "In a moment, could you have Katrín come at her earliest convenience, but before you do that, I have something else I'd like you to see if you can arrange." He outlined his plan.

Chamberlain nodded. "I will see that it's arranged as soon as possible, perhaps even this afternoon?"

Benjamin nodded. "I would like to be there as well, if at all possible, but if that can't be arranged easily with the rest of the schedules involved, make it happen anyway."

"Yes, sir." Chamberlain took his leave and promised he'd send for Katrín.

Certain he'd done the right thing for once, Benjamin went back to work feeling lighter than he had in quite some time.

21

"Where exactly am I going?" Katrín stood at a fork in the corridor.

"I have no idea." Elise had surprised her by showing up around noon, saying she'd managed to get everything wrapped up for the time being. "I went to a conference in the States once. This hotel had an app that would tell you where you were and give you step by step directions on how to get where you wanted to go. You'd think a place this size would have something similar."

"It would be handy," Katrín admitted. "But how many people are left to wander around without an escort? At least those who don't know their way around anyway."

"Good point. It would still be nice. Maybe there's a basic floor plan or map that Thor could get us. Nothing over classified, just enough to figure out how to get where we need to go."

Elise tapped on her phone. "They've already set me up with a palace email. The email was copied to me." She held out the screen for Katrín to look at. "Is that the room where we were the other day? With the piano?"

Katrín nearly melted in relief. "It is. I know how to get there."

In an effort to be less late than she would be otherwise, Katrín hurried forward, leaving Elise to catch up.

"There you are."

She looked up to see Benjamin waiting for her to arrive. Had she already seen him? Did she need to curtsy? Out of the corner of her eye, she noticed Elise do so.

He leaned down and kissed Katrín on the cheek. That was new. She wasn't sure how to react. She settled on, "Good afternoon. What's going on?"

Benjamin looked like a he was about to burst. "A surprise."

"My very own red grand piano?"

To her shock, he actually chuckled. "Actually, I think you might like this better."

She blinked. "Okay."

He motioned for her to go ahead of him. "Go on."

Puzzled, she pushed the door open then stopped, her jaw hanging open. "Mama? Allen? Nína?" With a gasp, she bolted across the room, clinging tightly to her mother for a long few minutes, then hugged her sister, before kneeling next to her brother's chair and holding onto him like her life depended on it. "I am so glad to see you, brother."

"Me too, sis. Is he treating you well?" Allen eyed his new brother-in-law. "I can roll over him and say my chair developed a mind of its own."

That made Katrín laugh as she pulled away. "There's no need." She stood and introduced her family to Benjamin. It hit her that Elise would have expected them to already know each other, but then she realized the other woman wasn't in the room.

Benjamin made certain it was just the five of them. She needed to thank him later.

"As much as I hate to say hello and leave, I must do just that." He clasped his hands behind his back. "Unfortunately, I have a phone call with Queen Adeline that has already been postponed more than once. I do hope you'll join my family for dinner this evening."

"Your family's back?" She hadn't seen or heard them.

"They arrived this morning. My mother is looking forward to this dinner." He smiled. "I will see you this evening, if you're able to stay."

"We would be honored," her mother answered. "Nína, can you stay?"

Nína hesitated. "Actually, I can't stay long. My flight leaves this evening. I'm joining the prince and princess and their family in Serenity Landing for a few days."

"Give them my regards," Benjamin told her then nodded to the group. "Until then." He turned and left.

Before she knew what was happening, Katrín found herself seated next to her mother and with her brother close enough she could hold his hand.

"How are you?" her mother asked.

"I miss you guys, but overall I'm doing good. I don't miss working all the time, of course, but I miss seeing both of you."

"We miss you," Allen told her squeezing her hand. "You got our letters?"

"Every one." As far as she knew. "I didn't always have a chance to read them and get back to you right away. That's why it didn't always seem like I saw them before I wrote you back. I wrote when I could even if I hadn't had time to read your later letters yet." No sense in them knowing she didn't always get them promptly.

"We figured as much." Her mother clasped her hand gently. "I know what life here can be like. It's so busy you can't think straight sometimes. Even worse depending on where you're working." She gave Katrín the look only a mother could. "Don't think I didn't notice you never told us where you were working. I guess you probably weren't on the serving staff."

Katrín shook her head. "No. I washed dishes in one of the kitchens."

"Oh, sweetheart."

Katrín heard her mother's tears before she turned and saw them. "It's okay, Mama." She reached out and wiped them off. "I didn't mind."

Her mother took both of Katrín's hands in her own and turned them over. "The callouses are still there."

"We haven't been married long. I worked in the kitchen right up until the wedding." She shook her head. "I don't want to talk about that. I want to hear all about you two and how you're doing."

For over an hour, Katrín listened as her mother and brother regaled her with tales from the outside world. Her brother had started university the year before and wanted to be a lawyer, specializing in helping those like him with disabilities who were discriminated against or taken advantage of because of their condition.

Her mother had been working at a local café for years but finally took a job that required her to be on her feet less. Katrín wondered when Benjamin would make good on his promise to make sure they were taken care of.

Elise entered the room nearly ninety minutes after Katrín had. "Pardon me, ma'am, but there are a few matters that need your attention before dinner." She smiled at all of them. "It won't be long. It will take you more time to get to dinner due to the route your chair must take, sir." She nodded at Allen. "Someone will be here momentarily to show you both the way."

Katrín hugged her brother and then her mother again. "Don't you dare leave," she whispered.

She could almost hear the smile in her mother's voice. "I wouldn't dream of it."

THE INDENTURED QUEEN

BENJAMIN HAD no idea who decided on the seating arrangements for such events, but someone had. Probably his mother, if she'd known about their guests in advance.

Normally, his mother sat at the foot of the table. Now Katrín would often occupy that spot at a family meal. Instead, Benjamin was at the head, Katrín to his right with Mother in the second seat. To his left was his new mother-in-law and then his brother-in-law. With Darius absent, there was an odd number of people, and no one at the foot of the table.

He took his seat and the rest of the table started to follow suit.

"Oh, dear." The mutter came from his left.

"What is it?" his mother asked.

"I'm afraid the way Allen's chair sits, he needs to be on the end." Katrín's mother glanced at him. "I trust that won't be a problem, sir?"

Benjamin shook his head. "Of course not. I look forward to talking with him, and this will make it easier." That might have been a bit of a stretch, but he was curious why Thor thought he could learn much from the younger man.

Two of the stewards rushed over to help make the switch. It didn't take long.

After his mother said grace, the first course was served, and Benjamin focused on listening for the time being. He was learning that it was often better to listen than talk and certainly better than not paying attention at all.

"You look familiar," his mother told Katrín's. "Have we ever met before?"

"Yes, ma'am." Mrs. Jónsson shifted slightly in her seat. "I used to work in the palace."

"In what capacity?"

Katrín's mother held her head high. "I was the king's server, ma'am."

"For my husband?" his mother clarified.

"Yes, and briefly for your son."

Benjamin didn't remember her ever serving him food, but did remember her standing in front of him facing the accusations.

"May I ask why you left?"

His mother-in-law's gaze flitted to Katrín briefly. "I was accused of stealing something from the palace. I could not prove my innocence."

"Did you steal it?"

"No."

Benjamin jumped in. "You were caught before you could leave, if I remember correctly."

She held his gaze. "That was the accusation. Mine was the first accusation of that nature that you handled as king."

"I remember. You offered no defense. You stood there silently until I decided the penalty. Even then you said nothing." Why were they reliving this?

"What penalty?" his mother asked.

Benjamin glanced down the table to find his siblings ignoring the five of them. "A fine commensurate with the fine imposed if convicted in a criminal cases. The amount and terms vary based on the value of the object in question."

"That had to be quite a sum." His mother's eyes had widened but she covered her feelings quite well.

"It was. Your son took pity on me, though. Princess Louise made certain he knew about my three children at home, Allen's challenges, and that I was a single parent. He arranged to have a small portion of my wages garnished until the fine was repaid."

Was she going to leave it at that?

"Katrín took over the payments." Allen jumped in. "That's why she worked here."

His mother turned to look at Katrín. "Why would you do that?"

Katrín shrugged. "My mother needed to be home more, helping Allen. I had no real job or schooling prospects, so I petitioned Benjamin to allow me to take over under much different terms. I could put as much of my wages toward the debt as I wanted, though there was a minimum amount required. When the debt was paid, I could leave the service of the palace."

"When would that be?"

"Not for some time." Katrín smiled sweetly at him, though he sensed something else lurking behind the smile. "But since I officially met Benjamin, and he proposed, the terms of the contract have changed quite a bit. You could almost say the new ones are *to die for*."

His mother laughed. "I wouldn't go quite that far, I'm sure." She asked Allen about his schooling.

Allen grew quite animated as he told her about his dream but when she asked him why he so passionately wanted to help those taken advantage of, he grew silent.

Katrín's mother reached over and rested a hand on his shoulder. "About five-and-a-half years ago, Allen was in a rehab facility after a particularly nasty bout of pneumonia. He's paralyzed from the waist down and confined to bed or his chair for his entire life. At this facility, they weren't nearly diligent enough in helping him move. Given his weakened state, he couldn't maneuver himself as much as normal, and they were no help. He's always struggled with bedsores, but this one was the worst, by far."

Allen seemed to straighten his shoulders. His upper body bulk was impressive, though clearly not muscle tone. If he were as tall as he should have been while retaining his size, he would have been a formidable man.

"It wasn't entirely their fault," he told them. "Some of them could have been better, but that wasn't unusual in a place like that. Most of them cared deeply, but they were perpetually under-staffed and the management kept them that way. They didn't have time."

Benjamin found himself curious. "So why would you sue them? Who would you try to hold accountable and how?"

"The management. They knew they were understaffed and

couldn't properly care for the number of patients they housed. I would have also sued for them to cover medical bills and lost pay, especially for my mother as my primary medical aide, as a result of the bedsores."

"Lost pay?" Benjamin's mother asked.

"That was when I left the palace employ," Mrs. Jónsson said. "My new job was much more flexible with hours, but far less lucrative financially."

Benjamin's mother turned to Katrín. "So you volunteered to take her place?"

Katrín nodded but didn't say anything.

"You know, it wasn't all bad." Allen's face lit up. "I spent an extra month in another facility after that, but that meant I had the chance to witness to a bunch of others. I earned my nickname during that time, and at least three people changed their lives through a relationship with Christ."

"What nickname?" Benjamin asked.

Allen's smile grew. "The Wheelchair Preacher."

22

Katrín changed into her pajamas but wasn't quite ready for bed. It had been a big day, one full of emotion. She wasn't sure sleep would come easily.

A knock on the wall caught her attention. "Come," she called.

The panel swung open to reveal Benjamin. She tried not to let her gaze linger on his bare chest, but instead noticed his pajama pants. Dark maroon like his shirt had been at the wedding and covered with the royal crest. "Nice jammies."

He looked down and grinned. "Thanks. They're really quite comfortable."

"I can't imagine you wearing something that wasn't, Benji."

Benjamin walked all the way into the room and let the door close behind him. "Something has bothered me for years."

She didn't want to know what. "Why InGen keeps making dinosaurs?"

He blinked twice. "What?"

"So we clearly need to add the Jurassic movies to our watch list. But really. Who thinks taking a T-Rex to a big city is a *good* idea?"

"Sure. We can watch them too."

He barely acknowledged her comment, but something else occurred to Katrín. "You're the king. Can you get new releases for the theater downstairs? The next *Jurassic World* movie comes out in June." The first *Jurassic World* was one movie she'd managed to see, though not in the theater downstairs.

"Maybe. I've never tried."

He was clearly preoccupied, so she didn't follow up. Yet.

Benjamin sat near her. "I remember your mother being brought to my office. I'd been king for a couple months, at most. The accusations were made. I asked her what the truth was. I gave her several opportunities to defend herself."

Katrín's head fell as she turned away, but she didn't speak.

"But she never said a word." His hands were warm on her shoulders, even through the thin material of her pajama shirt. "I always wondered why. Something tells me you know."

"What makes you think that?" She couldn't keep the tears from her eyes or the crack from her voice.

"Because you know why, don't you?"

She didn't want to tell him. Didn't want him or anyone else to know why she'd worked her fingers to the bone for several years.

"I won't make you tell me." His hands slid down her arms and he pulled her backwards into an embrace. "I could order you to, but I won't."

Katrín felt warm, safe, despite the burden she carried. "I can't," she whispered.

His hold tightened. "Whenever you're ready, whenever you trust me enough, I'm here."

"And if I'm never ready?" Fear gripped her. Would he force the secret from her?

"Then you're never ready."

They stood there, in the consort's sitting room. The weight continued to lift from Katrín's shoulders.

"Thank you for today." She leaned her head back against his chest. "I've missed my family."

"When was the last time you saw them?"

"The day before I moved to the palace."

"That's a long time."

"There were reasons." She'd lived with it because she felt she had to.

"I know." Benjamin let his arms drop before he grabbed one of hers and led her to a large chair. He sat down and pulled her next to him with one arm pulling her close. His nearness unsettled her.

"I have a proposal for you."

"Didn't you already do that?" He hadn't, not really. No king of Eyjania would get on one knee before anyone.

"A different kind of proposal. There's a groundskeeper's cottage on the property. No one is living there at the moment. I would like to offer it to your family. There's room for both of them and it will need minimal modifications to be accessible for your brother's chair. I'll make sure he has whatever assistance he needs. A home nurse or aide or whatever."

Katrín didn't know what her mother would think. It would be a relief in some ways, but it would also mean a loss of independence to a degree. "Would you charge her rent?"

"Of course not!"

Katrín had never heard such indignation from Benjamin before.

"That would be ridiculous."

"Would my mother be required to work in the palace in exchange for room and board?"

"No, but if she would like a job in the palace again, I'll see that she has one."

But what kind of job would it be?

"A good job," he continued. "Whatever job she wants that has an opening and she's qualified for. I won't fire or demote or move someone who doesn't want to just so she can have a position or give her something she's not qualified for."

"She wouldn't expect you to."

"Would you like to speak with her or would you like me to?"

"Can they come over for dinner again tomorrow and we can tell them together?"

"I don't see why not." She felt him stiffen next to her as his hold on her shoulders tightened. "No. I'm sorry, but I have a meeting to prepare for a dinner with some members of Parliament that I have coming up. In fact, it would be good if you were at the dinner in a couple weeks. I'm sorry. But we could do a movie after dinner, if you wanted to."

She didn't know how she felt about it, but she couldn't say no. "That sounds good."

Benjamin chuckled. "No one is *happy* to have dinner with members of Parliament. Not usually. Maybe your family could come for lunch after church on Sunday."

"That would be nice."

He kissed the side of her head, a move that shocked Katrín. "I need to get some sleep. I'll talk with you tomorrow and make sure Chamberlain tells whoever he needs to that you'll be accompanying me to the dinner."

He stood and left, leaving Katrín to stare after him as he walked away.

Katrín pulled a blanket off the back of the chair and covered up with it, trying to retain the warmth of having him so close. What she didn't want to do, but knew she could easily fall prey to, was wondering if what transpired between the two of them was why he'd done something nice for her.

No. She chose to accept that he'd done something nice because he could be nice. He wasn't always the grump everyone thought he was.

Was he close to his siblings? He was seen in public with his twin sisters regularly, but she hadn't seen him spend time with either one in the last couple months. She reminded herself they'd been gone with the rest of his family for several weeks. How could he have seen them?

Katrín finally heaved the blanket off in a quick motion. Otherwise, she wouldn't want to move and would sleep in the chair all night. That wouldn't be good for her neck or quality of sleep, so she headed for the room she used.

As she did, Katrín passed the main bedroom, paused as she stared at the rosettes on the wall. With a shake of her head, she continued to the lady-in-waiting's room and curled up under the blanket to wait for sleep to claim her.

As BENJAMIN FLIPPED the page over the top of the file he was reading, he noticed Katrín sit awkwardly in the chair next to him.

"Where are we going?" she asked.

"Montevaro."

"You didn't think to mention this last night? While we watched *Back to the Future*, you couldn't be bothered to tell me I'd be woken at the crack of dawn to fly out of town? You know, sometime *before* you kissed me then ran off?" *Princess Bride* had been postponed in favor of the time traveling flick.

"No. I didn't." He knew he was distracted, but something wasn't working right. "It wasn't the crack of dawn. Did you not want me to kiss you?" The memory had stayed with him all night. "Did you want me to stay again?" He'd wanted to, but common sense told him to leave.

She ignored him. "I suppose the time off wasn't cleared with my boss either, since I'm still working in the kitchen and all, and he'll add a couple more months to my indenture."

"I gave Chamberlain instructions to take care of it. You'll be shopping with Evangeline tomorrow and will have time to do some sightseeing if you want."

"Where will you be? Meetings?"

Benjamin still didn't look up but frowned as the numbers didn't seem to add up in his head. "Genevieve will be accompanying me to former King Jedidiah's birthday party tomorrow." Where was his phone? He needed to check these numbers with a calculator.

"King Jedidiah?" Katrín's incredulous tone caught Benjamin off-guard. "Like the guy who fell while skiing with the American First Family a few years ago?"

"Yes."

"Of course."

He dug around in his satchel for his phone then opened the calculator app.

"Am I going to be meeting any of them?"

He frowned again as he hit the wrong number. "I don't see why you would."

The sound he heard seemed to be a stifled sigh. "What am I supposed to be shopping for?"

"Anything you want." Then he remembered an offhand comment from Chamberlain. "The only restriction is that you don't even look at anything baby related." They wouldn't want anyone to get the wrong idea, even if it was technically a possibility after the encounter they'd had. He should have thought a little more clearly that night in her quarters.

"Of course not. Wouldn't want anyone to think King Benji might be a daddy in a few months."

Her sarcasm finally made him put his file down. It *had* to be completed in the next few days, but not in the next few minutes. "What?"

She shrugged. "Nothing. I'm just not sure what my purpose is on this trip. Everyone's going to be so focused on the wedding that no one is going to have any idea what I go shopping for. If anyone does notice, they'll wonder why you're at the wedding with your sister and not your wife."

He started to say something, but she held up a hand to stop him.

"If I did shop for baby things, and someone asked me about it, I could mention that my sister's employers are having a baby. I could know lots of people who are having babies that aren't you and me."

Benjamin turned back to his file. "I'm not trying to be rude, but I do have to have this ready for dinner with Parliamentary leaders next week, and something just isn't right. The math isn't adding up."

"Fine. Is there anything else I need to know about this trip besides I don't actually need to be here except so people don't think you left your wife behind."

He hadn't thought this through. Maybe he could send the plane home and tell everyone she wasn't feeling well. When he'd proposed this marriage to her, things like this hadn't occurred to him. "There's a dinner tonight with a number of other royal families from Europe and the Atlantic. You'll be expected to attend. A dress has already been chosen for you, or so I'm told."

The fifteenth scan of the page in front of him finally showed him the typo in the numbers. "If you'll excuse me, I need to work on this."

At least he knew what was wrong, but the whole thing was giving him a headache.

Katrín didn't say anything but swiveled her seat to stare out the window.

Now that he knew what the problem was, he could move on to the next part of the report. By the time they landed, he'd finished going through that section. The flight simply hadn't been long enough for him to begin the next one.

They disembarked the plane in a protected section of the airport. No one would see that he rode in an SUV with Chamberlain rather than the limo with his wife and sisters. The conversation centered around the budget proposal until they reached the

Lydia House near the lake housing the island where Montevaro's castle was situated. He and Chamberlain were already upstairs before his sisters and Katrín arrived.

His sisters were sharing a suite across the hall from the one he would share with Katrín. He saw her enter, but didn't see her again until time to go downstairs for the dinner with the representatives from the other countries.

"Are you ready?" he asked looking down to button his tuxedo jacket. At least he wouldn't have to wear this coat again for the wedding.

"As ready as I'm going to be." She sounded doubtful.

Benjamin looked up and stopped in his tracks. Shimmering red fabric hung from Katrín's shoulders and molded itself to her curves before landing in a small puddle on the floor. "You look..." He swallowed. "...very nice." It was the best he could come up with, but inadequate.

Katrín gave him a tight smile. "I'm glad you think so. I think I look like a kid playing dress-up."

"No one else will think that." Benjamin took another step closer until he could reach out and brush back the curl framing her face. "You look lovely."

She gave him a half-smile. "And you look very kingly."

He offered her his arm, and she slid her hand inside.

Chamberlain let him know his sisters weren't quite ready and would meet them downstairs. A Lydia House staff member led them down two flights of stairs until they reached the ground floor. A member of local security bowed his head slightly as Thor moved into position in front of them. The large foyer was lined with doors on either side.

From their left, he heard laughter and children's squeals. From the right, nothing. Hopefully, the noise from the left wouldn't spill through the foyer into their dinner.

When they reached the doors, Thor turned to the left and opened the door.

Puzzled, Benjamin stopped in his tracks.

"They're waiting for you, sir, ma'am." Thor held the door.

Were they going to be announced? He usually was at things like this.

Katrín's grip on his elbow tightened as they turned to walk in. Once inside, Benjamin stopped again as he looked around.

This was most definitely not what he'd planned for.

23

The scene inside the room made Katrín's stomach drop. Her grip on Benjamin's arm tightened as a woman looked up at them from her spot on the floor and smiled.

"Benjamin!" She made sure someone took over care of her baby before standing. "It's good to see you again!" Not a strand of her blond hair was out of place.

"Christiana." Benjamin shifted so Katrín's hand slid out of the crease of his arm. He took the woman's hands in his and kissed her cheek. "A pleasure."

The blond turned to Katrín. "And you must be the queen who stole the stoic king's heart." She held out a hand. "I'm Christiana from Ravenzario."

Katrín's mind scrambled to catch up. "Queen Christiana?" She tucked one foot behind and dipped at the knees.

Christiana rolled her eyes. "None of that is necessary in here. If we curtsied to every monarch or queen consort in this room, we wouldn't do anything else."

Katrín looked around and felt even more conspicuously out of place. Except for herself and Benjamin, the fanciest outfit consisted of khaki pants and a collared shirt. Christiana wore jeans with a blouse tucked into them.

The rest of the room was filled with at least two or even three dozen people of all ages. She recognized several of them, though she couldn't quite put her finger on who they were, but this clearly wasn't what Benjamin had expected. This was more family reunion than formal dinner.

"Katrín, why don't I introduce you around? Benjamin already knows almost everyone." Christiana linked her elbow with Katrín's. "If you'd rather go back upstairs and change first, that would be okay." Her voice had softened. "Someone didn't get the memo that this is a casual get together. All of us brought our families. Even my brother-in-law is going to be here with his family, and another family that many of us are friends with."

"All of Benjamin's family isn't here, though. Only his twin sisters even traveled with us."

Christiana shrugged. "Everyone was invited, though I know not everyone is attending tomorrow's party. That's likely why not everyone came."

Before Christiana could introduce her to anyone, an announcement was made that dinner would be served in just a moment.

Everyone scrambled to find seats. That's how Katrín found herself sitting at a table with Benjamin, the Crown Prince of Auverignon and his date, Prince Nicklaus of Ravenzario and his wife Princess Yvette of Mevendia, and Princess Jacqueline Grace and Prince Harrison of San Majoria.

As everyone sat down, Katrín noticed her sisters-in-law entered, but had obviously been told what kind of attire to wear.

The whole day had been exhausting. Katrín knew if she went upstairs to change, she wouldn't return. From Benjamin's distraction on the flight to several hours of solitude while he worked until time for dinner, combined with the stress that just came from living at the moment, Katrín wanted nothing more than to sleep. To settle into the plush bedding waiting for Benjamin in the bedroom they were supposed to share. Instead, she'd likely end up sleeping somewhere else, much like she had on their first trip.

She focused solely on her food, only answering questions when they were directed specifically at her.

The door opened and two more families spilled in. One of the men looked just like the one seated at Christiana's side. He carried a car seat in each hand as the woman with him urged two children, a boy and a girl of different ages, toward a table to the side. Behind them came another man Katrín knew she should recognize, along with a five- or six-year-old girl and a tired looking woman carrying a tiny infant.

Prince Richard and his wife sat at the table behind Katrín, and she smacked her husband's arm. "You didn't tell me Jonathan was coming. I haven't had a chance to hold that baby yet."

Who was Jonathan?

"You can hold that baby later," Prince Richard told her.

The conversational level died back down to a dull roar. From her seat Katrín could see most of the room. She counted at least thirty adults and, with the recent additions, at least twenty children ranging in age from the newborn who entered last to a teenage girl.

Dinner eventually ended, and Katrín found herself seated at the table alone until two men sat on either side of her.

One held out his hand. "I'm Charlie. I'm married to Queen Adeline of Montevaro."

Katrín shook it and asked hesitantly. "We're in Montevaro, right?"

Charlie grinned. "Yes. My daughter and I moved here about three years ago when I married Addie." He pointed to the teen. "She adored Addie before I even met her."

Katrín blinked. "Oh. I'm Katrín, Benjamin's wife."

"We figured." The man on the other side shook her hand as well. "Alexander. My wife is queen of Ravenzario. We figured we might be able to commiserate better than anyone about what it's like stepping into the limelight as the spouse of a monarch."

Katrín shook her head. "There hasn't been much limelight at this point. Mostly, I lead a pretty quiet life."

Alexander nodded as though he understood. "So did I. So did Charlie. He was a single dad working at a home improvement store in the States when he rear ended the prettiest woman he'd ever seen. She turned out to be the Crown Princess and held her coronation just days after their wedding. I was a teen television star who went back to living a private life then fell in love with a queen. It happens. Before long, you will be front and center in Eyjania." He handed her a business card. "If you ever need someone to talk to, I'm here. So's Charlie."

Charlie handed over another card. "If you're more comfortable talking to another female, I'm sure we can round one or two of those up, too, though none are currently married to monarchs. My mother-in-law used to be until Jed abdicated because of his Parkinson's. Alicia, the queen of Mevendia, would probably be a good one to talk to. We've got a couple of years of experience, but they have decades."

Alexander grinned. "Or your own mother-in-law. Her reputation from her time as queen consort is that she was an excellent one."

Katrín just nodded. "I'll take that under advisement." That didn't mean she'd actually take them up on it.

A whistle split the air. Princess Yvette hugged her husband's arm. "Thank you, Nicky. Everyone, we need a big group picture. We can all post the same one on social media, and it will accompany any official statements about this gathering. Some more candid shots will be taken and sent to the appropriate publicity teams for approval."

Their new additions to the public relations team would like that.

Once again, Katrín found herself alone at the table as the rest of those in the room sought to organize themselves by country, family, and relative importance. At least that was the best she could figure it out. Her husband was right in the center.

Fortunately, her seat was a bit back, out of the line of sight of those setting up the shot. She should stay out of it.

Benjamin's forever wife would prefer it that way.

AS HE GLANCED AROUND, Benjamin realized he was the only one without his spouse. Where was Katrín?

He looked around the room and found her sitting in her seat from dinner. When the pictures went public people would point out that his spouse is the only one not there. He wouldn't be able to make some glib remark about how she hadn't felt well or another excuse for where she'd been because everyone else knew she'd been there.

"Katrín!" Before he could say anything, Queen Adeline of Montevaro called to her. "You need to be in here, too."

Katrín hesitated, then pushed back from the table, holding the bottom of her dress up as she walked toward the group. Everyone around Benjamin rearranged themselves so Katrín could squeeze in beside him.

The photographer, one of the assistants who'd been helping keep an eye on the children, told everyone to squeeze in a little closer. Benjamin's hand settled on Katrín's hip, his awareness of her sharpened by their shared experience the week before.

Without making a conscious decision to do so, he slid his arm around her waist and pulled her a bit closer as everyone pressed in around them.

The instruction came for them to smile, but Benjamin felt weird trying to smile the way they wanted him to. He just didn't smile like that, certainly not very often. So he didn't smile. What was it Katrín had called his look? His resting grumpy face?

That's what they were going to get in this picture. No one here, except his sisters, knew him well enough to give him a hard time over it, and they wouldn't mention it. They didn't have those kinds of conversations with him.

In fact, outside if his almost weekly phone calls with Darius and occasional homework with Alfred, he didn't have idle chit chat with any of his siblings.

Maybe he needed to change that.

Based on what he was observing of the other couples in the room, he probably needed to talk to Katrín more as well. They needed to be able to put on a good facade when in front of the public.

She leaned back slightly into him as his arm tightened around her. At least the picture should look like things were going well in the Eyjanian royal family. He needed to look more like an actual human. Wasn't that what Katrín told him after the pictures of their dinner together came out?

"I think I got one with at least one phone from each family," the assistant told them. "You can share from there. Did I miss anyone's?"

"We can share further if we need to." Queen Adeline took charge. "Thank you."

The assorted nannies and assistants came to gather the children, one announcing that it was bedtime for little ones.

Genevieve grabbed Katrín's hand pulling her out of Benjamin's embrace. "Come on. We're going to let you change into something more comfortable."

Benjamin started to say something but turned when Evangeline linked her arm through his. "They'll be back," she told him. "That's why Genevieve took her instead of me. If I did, we'd both hide out the rest of the night."

The group around them had mostly disbursed to other parts of the room. "I thought you liked hanging out with the people in this group."

Evangeline shrugged as they walked slowly toward an empty table. "I don't mind it, but I had a long day yesterday and didn't sleep well last night."

"You get to shop tomorrow. You like that."

"It'll be fun getting to know Katrín better, but I still think you should take her to the party tomorrow." He held a chair for her to sit down.

"When we were notified of the party months ago, it was indicated that I was invited along with one of my sisters as my guest." A glass of water was set in front of him by a waiter who also asked if he'd like anything else. Benjamin waved him off.

Evangeline smiled and asked for a glass of wine, thanking the waiter for the water he also set in front of her. When he moved away, she turned back to Benjamin. "You weren't even publicly engaged to Katrín at the time. No one knew you had a significant other until the engagement announcement was made. Thanks for the heads up, by the way. Mother was devastated she didn't know first."

He sipped his water as the waiter returned with the glass of wine. "It's a long story. I didn't set out to hurt anyone. The press release was sent out without my consent."

"We wondered if you hadn't given the go-ahead yet, and it was sent before you had a chance to introduce all of us to Katrín. It would have been nice if Darius and Esther could have been there, though."

"It would have been a distraction." He took another sip. "He told me Esther didn't return home when Kensington's daughter was abducted because she knew she would become the story rather than the little girl."

"Still." She swirled her wine in the glass. "You should go visit when the babies are born. The doctor said any day now."

"I thought she wasn't due until the end of the month."

"She's having twins. They tend to come earlier."

"Who's having twins?" One of the princes from Belles

Montagnes took a seat at the table. Malachi? Except for William, Benjamin had never been able to keep them straight, but he'd never really tried. He probably should.

"Someone we know." Evangeline turned a smile toward the other man. "How are you, Malachi? It's been a while."

"We're doing well. Jessabelle hasn't been sleeping well, so she already went upstairs, but other than that, things are good. The baby is still taking a toll on her, even though she's well into her second trimester."

"We'll keep her in our prayers," Evangeline promised.

Malachi turned to Benjamin. "Congratulations are in order. We wanted to attend your wedding, but had a previous engagement with one of the charities we support and the date simply could not be changed."

Benjamin nodded and sipped his water. "I understand. I was unable to attend your brother's wedding to Princess Margaret due to an unavoidable conflict." Christmas in the States with his brother and his brother's in-laws.

Where King Edward had lectured him on the awful job he was doing as king, told him he wasn't living up to his father's legacy.

Confirming the worst things Benjamin regularly thought about himself.

Where was that waiter?

He needed something stronger than water to drink if he was going to make it through the rest of this night.

24

Using a trip to the bathroom as an excuse to stay in her suite didn't work for Katrín. Genevieve wasn't going to let her get out of going back downstairs.

Back in the room, now filled solely with adults, Katrín wanted to slink to a corner and stay there.

"Keep your chin up," Genevieve whispered. "I'm sure a group like this can be intimidating for someone who didn't grow up attending events with these people. Remember, though, not only are you a queen yourself, you are a child of the King of Kings, and that's what really matters."

Katrín nodded, knowing she would likely never be comfortable in this kind of gathering while also knowing it would be less than a year before they would all believe her to be dead.

"You don't even have to sit with my beast of a brother."

"He's not a beast," Katrín replied, automatically.

Genevieve linked her arm with Katrín's and walked toward a table with several women seated at it. "I know you're in love with him and all, but he can be a beast. Like this party tomorrow.

When we were first told to save the date, no one knew he had a girlfriend, much less that he'd be married. I'm not going, just so you know. I've already told your stylist that you'll be attending with him."

Katrín shook her head. "I wasn't the one invited."

"I don't care. I'm not going with my brother to one of the biggest events of the year when his wife is in town. If you were sick or pregnant and dealing with hyperemesis gravidium like Catherine does, that would be different."

"Catherine?"

"The Duchess of Cambridge. She's lovely. You may get to meet her tomorrow, but I'm not certain they're coming so soon after the birth of Louis. I'm sure every woman wishes she could bounce back as the Duchess does after giving birth."

Katrín wouldn't have to worry about that. She wouldn't have Benjamin's child before disappearing and wouldn't be able to remarry someday. Not when she knew the truth.

She looked over to see Benjamin had taken off the tuxedo jacket and removed his tie allowing him to undo the top couple of buttons and roll his sleeves up.

The muscles in his forearms held her attention as he lifted a glass of something amber-colored so he could take a sip. The arm that held her close to him while they took the group pictures. The arm that wrapped around her and the hand that splayed on her lower back as he kissed her in the consort's quarters just a few days earlier. The muscles she'd secretively admired as a member of the staff, but now had a more intimate knowledge of than anyone else, save perhaps his trainer.

With a shake of her head to clear the thoughts from it, she took the seat next to Genevieve, determined to not join the conversation and confirm to all that she really didn't belong with this group of women. She searched her mind to remember who they all were.

Two queens. Two crown princesses. The wife of a crown prince. A princess married to a prince who should have been king. A princess engaged to a prince who would be king.

"Do you know everyone, Katrín?" Katrín thought the woman was Queen Adeline. "I'm Addie. I'm from here in Montevaro. I believe you talked with my husband, Charlie, earlier."

Katrín nodded.

The woman next to Queen Adeline - Katrín couldn't even make herself think the name Addie - smiled. "I'm Christiana from Ravenzario. We met for a second before dinner. I think my husband was talking to you about the same time Addie's was. Probably telling horror stories about being a consort." She rolled her eyes.

Katrín shook her head. "They were both very kind, but did offer to commiserate about the role of consort should I ever want to." She still wouldn't.

"I'm Yvette." The next young woman jumped in. "I'm from Mevendia, but my husband is Christiana's brother."

Right. The prince who wasn't dead, though everyone had believed it for many years.

"Alexandra," the next woman said, "but everyone calls me Alex. I'm Litian by birth, but I'm married to Theo from Valdoria. We met briefly at your wedding."

Katrín nodded. "I remember. Thank you for coming. I appreciate it."

"I'm Maggie from Mevendia," the woman seated to Queen Adeline's other side told her. "We were actually married in Eyjania several years ago. William and I hoped Benjamin would be able to attend the ceremony at Christmas, but understand he had another engagement. It was kind of last minute like yours was."

"Esme, from Islas del Sargasso." The woman next to Maggie told her. "I'm told you'll be visiting us next month for a conference. I'd love to do lunch."

Katrín's mouth went dry, and she reached for the water a

waiter had dropped off. After a sip, she nodded. "I believe so, but I'm not certain of my schedule just yet."

"I'll have my assistant get with yours. It needs to happen. Perhaps Benjamin could join you for a couple of days after the conference ends. I know you didn't have a wedding trip."

Katrín fought the pink that had to be coloring her cheeks, but knew she was unsuccessful when the table either tried to hide their giggles or shot her sympathetic glances.

"Benjamin sent the rest of the family away for a few weeks," Genevieve told them. "He couldn't get away, but didn't want to postpone the wedding either."

"And I'm Astrid." The last woman took the attention off Katrín for a moment anyway. "From San Majoria."

Katrín nodded. She'd known that.

"How did you and Benjamin meet?" Queen Adeline gave a gentle smile. "We're all romantics at heart. We love a good meet-cute."

Wasn't that how the first meeting of a hero and heroine was described in a couple of the blogs she'd read about the books Thor recommended?

The queen went on. "Charlie's car rear-ended mine when I abandoned my security team and went driving on an icy day in Serenity Landing while I was still in grad school."

Not only was the woman a queen, she held a Master's degree. Katrín had barely graduated high school.

But they were all watching her expectantly. "I've worked for the palace since not long after I turned eighteen." She stared at her fingertips as they rubbed lightly against the stem of her water glass. "But I love to play the piano. My old keyboard wasn't the same. I snuck into one of the reception rooms to play one night when I thought no one would be around. I didn't see Benjamin until I finished playing *King Alfred's Overture*." She shrugged. "He kissed me a few minutes later. The rest is history."

No need to mention the inappropriate proposition or the lack of any real relationship existing between them even still.

She sipped her water and wished she could ignore the calls for her to play for them. Just a few measures.

But Queen Adeline clasped her hands together, her eyes bright. "Would you, please, Katrín? Just a little bit?"

Katrín tried to hide her resignation with a smile. "Of course."

BENJAMIN CONTINUED to sip his drink occasionally as conversation flowed around him.

It wasn't until he realized the conversation halted that he turned to see what everyone else was staring at.

Katrín.

At the piano sitting to one side of the room where a small group of musicians had been playing during dinner.

The first song she played sounded familiar but he didn't place it until he heard many in the room singing the lyrics to an old hymn. The second was another hymn, though not one he recognized well.

"Will you play the *Overture?*" Adeline asked her. "I'm not sure I've ever heard it."

Katrín glanced at him.

Benjamin tried to give her a reassuring smile, but wasn't sure he succeeded.

Her voice drifted to him. "I don't think I'm quite warmed up enough, and it's been a while since I've played it. I may have to sort of edit a little bit in the more complicated parts."

"That's all right. Except for maybe Benjamin, Genevieve, and Evangeline, none of us will know the difference," Adeline assured her.

Katrín looked at him again. Did she want his permission?

Approval? Either way, he tried that reassuring smile again and nodded. "It will be amazing, love." He'd never used the word in this context before, and likely never would again, but he'd heard several of his counterparts say it to their spouses, and it seemed fitting.

She took a deep breath and stared at her hands. He could almost feel the tension radiating off her. Could everyone else?

The first notes were soft, much like the first time.

He took another sip of his drink as the music built, ebbed and flowed, until it reached a crescendo several minutes later.

Yet, every hair remained in place as Katrín's fingers flew across the keys. Looking at her, she seemed to remain calm and collected, but Benjamin suspected she trembled inside.

Had she even played since the wedding? Since the night they met?

He'd been told her keyboard was returned to her, but between working so hard and her few duties as queen, he doubted she'd had much time for piano playing.

As the last note died away, the tapestry of King Alfred the First, complete in his suit of armor with his Wulfrith dagger in his hand came to Benjamin's mind. He avoided that hall whenever possible, but he remembered the look on his ancestor's face. Stern. Impassive. Much like the face Katrín accused him of making regularly.

As everyone stood to applaud, Benjamin set his drink down and joined them. He let his face relax into a smile. Several of the women gathered around Katrín as she turned backward on the bench. He could see her face turn pink as she tried to accept their accolades graciously.

"She's going with you tomorrow."

Benjamin turned to see Genevieve sipping on her own glass of wine. "Pardon?"

"I'm not attending a party with you when your wife is in the same town and not indisposed." She smirked at him. "You might even find some tips on how to look more comfortable with the love of your life in public." With another sip of her wine, she sauntered away.

Benjamin made his way toward the piano as everyone went back to their knots of conversation.

Katrín smiled up at him, a nervous smile if he had to guess, the other women moving off. "So?"

"I think the night we met was a little better, but it was lovely. I do think I'm ready to retire, though. Would you prefer to stay a little longer?"

She shook her head. "No. I'm ready to go."

Several people stopped them as they walked out, congratulating them and complimenting Katrín on her music. A few minutes later, Thor led them into their suite.

Their one-bedroom suite.

With all the VIPs in town for the party, and most staying at the Lydia House, no one was able to get a larger suite.

"Will there be someone in the suite all night?" Katrín asked quietly as they walked toward the door separating the bedroom from the living area.

"Most likely." Was she planning to sleep in the living area if not? Did he want her sleeping with him?

"I see." She grabbed her pajamas, already laid out on the bed, and walked into the bathroom, closing the door behind her.

He took the opportunity to change into his own pajama pants and wished he could do the kind of workout he would at home. It just wasn't feasible when not at home.

For the next ten minutes, he skimmed through the news sites wondering if there was anything about his family. He stood and headed for the living area as the bathroom door opened.

"It's all yours," Katrín told him. "I'm done for the night."

Benjamin nodded his thanks but left the room. "Thor?"

Thor looked up from his paperwork. "How can I help you, sir?"

"Have you heard anything about Isaiah recently?" He sat across from Thor and set his tablet on the table.

The security man shook his head. "Nothing of consequence, sir. The last report I saw he was living quietly in San Majoria. We, along with the San Majorians, are keeping an eye on him."

"Keep me apprised of any new information?"

"Of course."

Benjamin settled back into his seat, pulling the folder for next week's budget meeting toward him. For nearly an hour, he went through it line by line.

As he was about to flip to the last page, something caught his eye, making him frown. Clicking his pen, he made a note. He would need to discuss it with Chamberlain at a more civilized hour, then possibly make a few calls - or have Chamberlain make some calls for him.

Closing the folder, he pushed back from the table. Thor did the same.

"Sleep well, sir. Someone will be out here all night."

"Thank you, Thor." Benjamin yawned and ran a hand down his face and over his beard. He needed rest before being in public all day.

He entered the bedroom to find the lights out except for one in the bathroom to let him see where he was going. After finishing his bedtime routine, he walked toward the bed, wondering which side Katrín had chosen.

When he realized neither side was being slept in, he looked around the room. A lump in a chair near the window told him where Katrín decided to sleep.

He crouched near the chair. "Katrín? You can't sleep over here." Gently, he shook her shoulder. "Katrín?"

She sat straight up, her forehead hitting his chin.

"Ow!" They spoke in unison.

He rubbed his chin as Katrín held a hand to her head. "Are you all right?"

Katrín winced but nodded. "I'll be fine. Just hope there's no bump or bruise there in the morning."

Benjamin lightly gripped her chin with his hand and tilted her head so he could see it better in the light from the street. "Let me look." It was dim, but good enough. "I think you'll be all right."

She moved her head just enough that he could look into her eyes, so dark they were nearly black.

Before he could think, he brushed his thumb across her lips. "May I?" he whispered.

Katrín gave a barely perceptible nod.

He replaced his thumb with his lips, kissing her softly, differently than he had the first few times. His hand slid around to the back her neck, his fingers tangling in her hair as she grasped the front of his t-shirt and kissed him back.

KATRÍN WOKE to light streaming in from behind the curtains on the window. The plush covers were tucked tightly around her. The cocoon-like warmth made it so she never wanted to leave.

"Thank you." Benjamin's voice was soft but carried from across the room just before he closed the door. A few seconds later, she felt him sit on her side of the bed. "Katrín?" His hand rested on her shoulder.

"I'm awake," she muttered, but didn't open her eyes again.

"You have about twenty minutes before your stylist arrives to help you get ready for the party."

She rolled onto her back but kept her eyes closed. "So I'm your plus one after all?"

"Yes. I've been told clothes were sent for you, just in case something changed."

"And Genevieve doesn't want to go? She isn't friends with Queen Adeline?"

"I don't believe so. We've never really run in the same crowds, as it were, not like the families from Belles Montagnes do, or us with the other Quad-Countries to a lesser extent."

"I see."

His fingertips brushed hair back off her forehead. "I'm going to go into the other room to discuss some security details with Thor. You probably need to go ahead and take a shower or whatever else you need to do before your stylist arrives. She'll work with you in the other room or in my sisters' room. It won't take me near as long to get ready."

Katrín nodded, her heart skipping a beat as he placed a soft kiss on her brow. When the door closed behind him, she sat up and swung her legs over the side of the bed. She stared at the hem of his shirt, the one she wore.

Part of her wanted to regret what happened the night before, but she couldn't.

As much as she wanted to protect herself, protect her heart, she had a feeling she could very easily fall for her husband.

Not for the man he was, the man he showed the world, but the man he *could* be, the man she believed he *wanted* to be.

The man he was deep inside.

With a heavy sigh, she pushed up from the bed and went to get ready for the day. No matter what she thought about who she really was, the world knew her as the queen of Eyjania. She couldn't curl up in the chair where Benjamin found her the night before and take a nap or read a book.

Katrín knew she'd probably have to wear a tiara, if past parties were any indication. Her picture would show up on best or worst dressed lists around the world. She doubted she'd have any more say in the dress she was to wear than she had for her own wedding.

She took a shower and washed her hair, dressing in a shirt that wouldn't require lifting over her head after her hair was finished.

With a towel wrapped around her head, she wondered about exiting into the main portion of the suite. Before she could decide the door opened. Benjamin entered, pushing a cart with a silver-domed tray on it.

"Thor had breakfast sent up. Nothing too heavy, he said."

"Thank you."

A small table to the side gave them a place to sit and eat without going out into the main room.

"How did you sleep?" Benjamin sat in the chair across from her.

She shrugged as she took the dome off the tray and stashed it in the bottom of the cart. "Fine, I guess. I didn't get to bed as early as I would have liked. I didn't work hard like I usually do, which can make it hard to get to sleep." Did she want to go on? "And I'm not at all used to having someone in the bed with me, which made it a bit more difficult to get back to sleep when I did wake up. You?"

He gave her a half-smile that she recognized as an attempt to humanize himself. "I can't say that I remember waking up at all until about ten minutes before I spoke with you."

"I'm glad."

"There is something I wanted to discuss with you. There's a dinner with several members of Parliament next week." He broke off a piece of the pastry he'd selected. "I'd like you to attend."

Katrín tried to contain her rapid blinking. "Me? With Parliament?"

"Some of the leaders, not the whole group. It will be a fairly formal meal, followed by cocktails and mingling for a short while, then a meeting at which you are not allowed, I'm afraid. It is tradition for the consort to attend the dinner, but more than that, I would like you to be there."

She tried to take it all in. "Sure. I guess. If it's something I'm supposed to do, I'll be there. What kind of meeting is it?"

"Budget proposals for next year. That's what I've been working on finalizing the last few days." He popped a bit of pastry in his mouth. "By law, I'm required to submit them next week."

"I didn't realize you set the budget." She took a bite of the bagel she'd selected.

Benjamin gave her a real smile as he chuckled. "I don't. I make suggestions. The different parts of the government send me their budgetary proposals. Usually, they've already been discussed with Parliament. I take them, make changes I feel necessary both to increase or decrease funding. Parliament is then free to do what they want with the money, though there are some limited situations where I can overrule them."

Katrín swallowed her bite. "I had no idea."

"I doubt most people do."

A knock on the door interrupted whatever thought she was having. Katrín found herself whisked away, into her sisters-in-law's suite where her make-up was done, her nails polished, and her hair arranged just so before she slipped into a dress she prayed was appropriate. Surely the stylists knew what kind of attire was expected, even if it was still more suited for her mother-in-law.

Back in her own suite, she waited for Benjamin to emerge from the bedroom. This time he wore a morning coat that looked both more formal and less uncomfortable, at least to Katrín's untrained eyes.

He gave her another real smile and offered her his elbow. "You look lovely. Shall we?"

Katrín slid her gloved hand into his arm and took a deep breath. Her first real appearance on the world stage, and she was wearing stilettos.

Too bad she didn't convince the stylist to let her trade for silver Converse. At least in those she knew she probably wouldn't trip.

They would emerge out the front of the building in full view of anyone waiting outside for a glimpse of the royals from around the world in town for the former king's birthday celebration.

Katrín took another deep breath as the doors opened. She could do this.

She had to.

25

"Can we get it delivered tonight while the Parliamentary leaders are here for dinner?" Benjamin tapped his pen on the notepad in front of him.

"Unlikely." Chamberlain swiped the screen of his tablet. "If you want a custom one, it will take quite some time."

Benjamin thought about that. "What's the best brand we can get today? Is it worth it as a temporary substitution for a custom one? If so, make it happen. If all we can get is something cheap then perhaps one can be moved temporarily."

"I will see what I can do. The queen is joining you for the dinner tonight?"

"Yes. She needs someone to go over who everyone is and proper protocol. I simply don't have time today."

"If I may make a suggestion, sir." It wasn't a question. It never was.

Benjamin motioned for him to go ahead.

"Take a few days off and take your wife with you. Go somewhere else. Perhaps a secluded cottage somewhere. It would be good for you to take a real vacation, as much as you are able."

"I'll take that under advisement."

"I mean it, sir. You need a break. You'll wear out just like anyone else."

"You know what my schedule is like. It won't be anytime soon, but keep an eye out for several light days over the summer and perhaps we can go to San Majoria or Ravenzario for a few days." It shocked him to realize he would enjoy a couple of relatively uninterrupted days with Katrín, getting to know her. Maybe she'd trust him with the secret about the circumstances around her indenture to the palace, why she took over for her mother. There was more to it than just her brother's ongoing care.

"I'll make sure she's briefed on what to expect this evening." Chamberlain stood. "I will also see what I can find out about the other thing."

"Thank you."

After Chamberlain left, Benjamin turned back to the papers he needed to go over - again - before the dinner in a few hours.

When he'd gone over them all several times, he went back to his suite, changed into a suit and went to the outer sitting area to wait for Katrín. He skimmed another document.

"Are you sure you need me to go? I might throw up on someone important."

Benjamin looked up to see Katrín looking a bit queasy. "I'm sure you'll be fine." He closed the cover on his tablet. "Ready?"

She took a deep breath and blew it out slowly. "No. I'm really not."

He walked over until he stood in front of her. "Why not?"

"It's the top four or five members of Parliament. I've never met important people. I tend to make a fool of myself." It surprised him to see she really looked nervous.

"You basically told me off the first time we met." Something he needed to apologize for some time soon. Sincerely.

"That's different."

A smirk crossed his face. "You do know I'm the king, right? Kind of the definition of an important person around here."

"But you were being a jerk. It was easy not to get nervous." She smoothed her hands over her stomach. "I don't think I can do this."

He cupped her shoulder with one hand. "You'll be fine. If you really feel like you're going to puke, signal me."

That drew a small smile from her. "You've never said puke in your life, have you?"

This time he gave her a full-fledged smile. "No." His hand slid down until it captured hers. "And you look nice."

"I look like your mother."

Benjamin stilled. "What's wrong with my mother?"

"Nothing. She's classy and elegant, and everyone should want to look like her."

He sensed more to it. "But?"

"I spent quite a while with your mother this afternoon, and I think she's wonderful, but she's a long-time widow in her late-40s. I'm a newlywed in her early-20s."

Comprehension began to dawn. "And my mother's style, while impeccable, isn't yours."

"Exactly. I found a few things in what someone bought for me that I like for me, and I've been able to make do, but most of them are like this dress. It's nice, classy, elegant, but not *me*."

"Why didn't you say something sooner?"

She dropped his hand and crossed her arms across her chest. "Like what? 'Sorry, Benji, I don't like any of the probably thousands of dollars of clothes someone bought me. Get me new ones because I'm broke.' That would have gone over so well."

"Probably not, but you have a stylist. Did you talk to her?"

"I like Rosalie, but she takes orders from your mother's stylist and doesn't dare try to step out of the box." She let her arms fall to her side. "Let's just do this. We can talk about it later."

She started for the door, not waiting to fall in next to or

behind him. It startled Benjamin to realize it didn't bother him, though he knew protocol would be followed once they were around others. He liked that she was comfortable enough with him to ignore protocol.

By the time they reached the dining hall, she'd fallen back and slid her hand into his offered elbow. They stopped before the two giant doors with doormen waiting on either side. He nodded to them.

"You've got this," he whispered to her.

"I'm glad you believe in me," she whispered back.

The doors opened before them as a voice boomed, "Their Majesties, King Benjamin and Queen Katrín of Eyjania!"

Chairs scraped back from around the table as those already assembled stood.

"I'll seat you," he whispered to her. "Just be pleasant to those near you, and you'll be fine."

"If you insist."

Her seat wasn't far, so in just a few steps, he held it for her as she sat down, before going to his seat on the other end. As he sat down, everyone else did, too.

Dinner was served as chatter began to fill the room. This time was more for unofficial posturing and networking. After dinner would come the official political discussions regarding his proposed changes to the budget. As king, he had no real authority to do anything but propose changes. Parliament would take his suggestions, toss them out with the bath water, and do what they wanted, but there was one item in particular that caused him great concern.

There was a reason why he'd invited his mother-in-law and brother-in-law to the beginning of the reception after dinner.

They wouldn't know what hit them.

KATRÍN MADE it through dinner without losing any of it. She didn't taste any of it either. The Queen Mother had walked her through what was going to happen and who everyone was. She did her best to be polite and diplomatic, brushing off questions deemed too personal.

All too soon, Benjamin stood at the other end of the table. Everyone else joined him, though she'd been told to remain seated until he reached her side. A moment later, he was there and she managed not to let her shoulders slump in relief.

They walked out a different door into a reception hall of some sort. Not as big as she feared it would be, it was still too big for the dozen or so people in attendance.

"Ladies and gentlemen, I don't believe my wife has officially been introduced. May I present to you, Her Majesty Queen Katrín of Eyjania, Duchess of Schmansk, Countess of Húskavník, and Lady of the Auroras."

She had all those titles? Katrín tried not to let her shock show, but nodded slightly as everyone in attendance bowed or curtsied.

Talk about surreal.

"I've invited a couple other people to join us," he told them, turning to the side. "My wife's mother and brother have some unique insight into at least one of the items on the agenda later tonight."

Katrín turned to see them enter. A smile crossed her face and her heart skipped a beat. Her brother looked so handsome. Had she ever seen him in a suit before?

Benjamin dropped his arm to give her mother a kiss on the cheek then shake hands with Allen. Katrín followed in his footsteps to give her mother a hug and clasp Allen's hand. What was this all about?

Servers circulated with glasses of wine and small desserts. Katrín took a glass when it was offered, but didn't do more than sip.

"Your Majesty."

She looked up to see the Prime Minister staring intently at her. "Good evening, Mr. Prime Minister. I hope you enjoyed your dinner."

"It was delicious, but then every meal I've ever had here has been."

"That's wonderful to hear."

He moved to stand to her side, using his glass to point at her mother and brother on the other side of the room. "Why exactly are they here?"

"I'm afraid you'd have to ask my husband about that."

"He didn't tell you?"

Katrín gave him a polite smile that she prayed didn't look fake. "Is that what I said? I didn't mean to imply he didn't tell me. I merely meant that it's not my place to interpret my husband's actions for others when he's chosen to keep his reasons to himself for the time being." She wished she knew what the reason was so she could obfuscate better.

Benjamin stood next to her brother, talking with the Minority Leader and one of the leading members of a smaller party.

Her brother sat as he always did, tilted heavily to the left side of his chair. His legs had never fully developed, with his feet barely hanging over the edge of the chair. His upper body more than made up for it. Allen would never be the solid mass of muscle Benjamin had turned himself into.

Yet... In a room filled with a king and national leaders, her brother outshone them all.

His face lit the whole place. He motioned with his hands, as animated and passionate as she'd ever seen him. The more he talked, the more of the group gathered around them.

Her mother stood off to the side with the second most powerful member of the majority party. Katrín drifted to her side.

"What's he talking about?" she asked quietly when it was just the two of them.

"What do you think?" Her mother slipped an arm around Katrín's waist.

"Conditions in some of the facilities."

"Got it in one. They're talking budget cuts, you know."

And that was why Benjamin had invited them.

"My mother used to work for the king." Allen's voice drifted back toward them. "She quit to take a job where she would have more flexibility to care for me when I was so neglected. It wasn't the nurses or aides. They couldn't take care of everyone like they should. Things haven't improved."

"Not me," Benjamin interjected. "Or not in the same role for long anyway. She was my father's meal server for many years and performed admirably, but with any change in administration, there's often changes that trickle down. She had more flexibility in her new position, but not what she needed when Allen required more care. She was greatly missed."

Like he would know that. He obfuscated well. She'd learned that word a few days earlier and it stuck with her. To bewilder or stupefy. Benjamin did that well, all without lying.

Conversation drifted to other topics, until Katrín heard the Prime Minister challenge her brother.

"What kind of future can someone like you have?"

Katrín saw red and lunged forward, but her mother's hand gripping her arm stopped her.

Allen just laughed, causing the Prime Minister to frown. The question hadn't been asked out of genuine curiosity, but with derision. "Someone like me? Really? What exactly can you do that I can't besides get tired walking from place to place?"

The Prime Minister's mouth opened and closed twice.

"For instance, what exactly would disqualify me from being Prime Minister?" Allen stared at him, his ubiquitous smile suddenly gone. "The requirements are fairly simple and straightforward. Subject of the Eyjanian crown, willing to swear allegiance to the same and the Eyjanian Documents of Governance, and at least thirty-seven years old. That is, literally, the only thing that keeps me from being eligible, at least for a few more years."

"You're in a wheelchair, clearly disabled."

Allen actually laughed. "And the fact that my legs don't work precludes me from understanding government? From intelligence? From setting my sights on your job someday? I kind of hate to tell you this, but walking doesn't exactly make you uniquely qualified for anything. Pretty much anyone can do it."

Katrín glanced over to see Benjamin hiding a smirk behind his wine glass as he took a sip.

Then he winked at her.

26

Benjamin didn't know what he'd expected when he invited Allen and Mrs. Jónsson. All he'd wanted to do was make sure Allen and those who struggled similarly were fresh in the minds of the leaders in Parliament when they discussed budget cuts. He'd known the Prime Minister wasn't particularly inclined toward keeping that line item in the budget, but hadn't expected him to confront Allen about his abilities.

"It's nice that you've found your passion in helping those like you..." the Prime Minister started.

"You presume an awful lot, sir. Yes, I'm passionate about helping those who don't have other resources, but that's not what I'm most passionate about. Tell me, Mr. Prime Minister, how is your relationship with Christ?"

The Prime Minister sputtered.

Benjamin wanted to hear the discussion, but Chamberlain approached to tell him the other project had been completed. He took another sip of his wine and smiled. Good.

"Ladies and gentlemen." Benjamin spoke up. "I believe it's time for us to adjourn to the Council Chambers. Since my wife has not yet been approved as a member of the Council, it's time for us to take our leave of my bride and her family." He motioned toward another door. "I believe you all know the way."

Allen and Mrs. Jónsson were already being ushered away by Chamberlain. Benjamin called for him to wait as he reached Katrín's side. "Why don't you take them to the cottage and let them look around? A temporary ramp was added today. It won't be completely accessible, but enough to get an idea of what it's like."

"Thank you." She stood on her tiptoes and brushed a kiss against his cheek, stumbling into his chest. His arm wrapped around her waist to keep her from falling.

Her dark eyes swam with unshed tears. Why? Because he'd made arrangements for her family to live close? Just because they were there? Did she know about the proposed cuts and understand why he'd invited her family?

The moment between them ended when Chamberlain cleared his throat.

"I'll talk to you later," she whispered. "Or tomorrow."

"Most likely tomorrow. This meeting will last a while longer." He didn't understand why it was held on a Saturday night, but he couldn't change the custom.

She stepped back and spoke with Chamberlain who nodded and held the door for them before returning to Benjamin's side.

"A masterful stroke, sir."

"We'll see." He turned to join the members of Parliament in the Council Chambers. "See what we need to do to get Katrín on the Council. If I remember correctly, it's generally a formality to have the consort added."

"It is. Parliament is presented with the proposal on the first business day of the month. If they do nothing, she's added the first business day of the next month. They can take a vote of no confidence. At this point, it would take a 2/3 majority. If, in the future, they chose to remove her, it would take a 4/5 majority."

Neither were likely to happen, but the refresher was good.

Benjamin took a deep breath. "Let's do this and inform them of my intention to add Katrín at the next opportunity."

Chamberlain followed him into the Council Chambers, where he was announced again. Everyone was already standing by their seats waiting on him.

"Ladies and gentlemen, let's get down to business. The budget changes I propose are, of course, just suggestions, but I do hope you'll take them seriously."

For an hour he went over the suggestions in the proposal. There were a few questions, but this meeting went as most budget proposal meetings did. When they got back to Parliament in a few days, they'd argue it out, ignore most of what he said, and do what they wanted.

A few more minutes of mingling, and he went back to his quarters. By the time he reached his closet, his tie and jacket were off and his shirt was halfway unbuttoned. As soon as he could get into workout clothes, he went to his workout room. His trainer wouldn't be there, but he could still get a good workout in. He just needed to push himself rather than only doing it because his trainer yelled.

Mountain climbers. Planks. High knees. Oblique crunches.

Not a workout his trainer had designed to target a specific area, but things Benjamin mostly enjoyed.

He picked up both of the ropes and lifted them up and down in unison. They were far heavier than they looked after everything else he'd done.

Sweat dripped off of him as switched to alternating arms. When he'd finally worked off the meeting with Parliament, he put his equipment away and went back to his suite. After a hot shower, it would be time for bed.

Katrín clasped her hands in front of her as she tried to keep her excitement from spilling over as they left the reception with the members of Parliament. "Benjamin and I discussed something, and he asked me to go ahead and talk it over with you." She started down the hall. "Come on. I'll just show you."

One nice thing about the wide hallways of the palace was that they could walk - or roll - three abreast until they had to go a back way to get to the elevator and a side door that exited at ground level. Her mother-in-law had told her how to get there earlier and showed her the path through the gardens.

"Where are we going?" Allen asked.

"You'll see." A few minutes later, the building appeared as they rounded the turn.

Her mother stopped in her tracks. "Is that a wheelchair ramp?"

"A temporary one. This house is available to you, rent free, for as long as you want it. Some renovations will need to be made, but they've already made temporary ones so Allen can get inside and look around. Not all of the house will be accessible to him. They don't want to put an elevator in because the building is insanely old, but Mom, you could live upstairs. There's plenty of room for Allen downstairs." Katrín started for the building, but stopped when she realized her mother didn't follow.

"Free?" her mother whispered.

Katrín nodded. "Come inside, and I'll tell you the rest of the details."

A minute later, they were inside. Katrín stood in the entry as the two of them explored the first floor. Her mother exclaimed over everything. Allen called back every few seconds with something he'd discovered the other direction.

"Go on upstairs, Mama," Katrín called. "I think you'll love it." At least based on what her mother-in-law had told her about it.

After ten minutes of exploring, they met back in the sitting room.

"We can really live here?" her mother confirmed again.

"Yes."

Her mother glanced at Allen. "Did you tell him..." She didn't finish her sentence, but Katrín knew what she meant.

"No. He asked, but I didn't tell him."

Allen jumped in. "Tell him what?"

"Nothing," their mother answered. "King Benjamin is serious about letting us live here, though?"

"Absolutely. He also said he'll provide anything Allen needs forever. A nurse or aide to help with all the medical stuff and whatever equipment he needs."

"His bed is on its last legs," her mother admitted. "I looked online to see what it would cost to get a new one." The last one had been a gift from a group that helped kids with medical needs - and used at that. "The kind we need, if we bought it in the States, would cost something like $70,000 new."

Katrín blinked. She knew her new family was worth a boatload of money, but that was far more than the drop in the bucket Benjamin likely expected. "I'll talk to him. And your chair is looking a little worn, too."

"It's seen better days," Allen admitted. "So has the van."

"I'll talk to Benjamin about all of it." She knew the kind of vehicle they needed to handle Allen's chair wasn't cheap either.

"So I'd just have to work enough to buy food and clothes, things like that?"

Katrín turned back to her mother. "Not even that if you don't want to, especially if you're helping Allen. Benjamin did say he would be happy to get you a job in the palace. Any job you want as long as it's an open position and you're qualified. As many or as few hours as you want."

Her mother slumped backward. "It seems too good to be true."

One of the biggest smiles ever crossed Katrín's face. "It's not.

Even before the wedding, Benjamin promised me he'd make sure you were both taken care of forever."

"Spoken like a true man in love."

Katrín laughed again and changed the subject. By the time they left, she was certain she knew what her mother's decision would be. "Just let me know whenever you decide." Katrín clung tightly to her mother as they prepared to leave.

"I think you know what we'll decide, but give me a few days to pray about it."

"I'll tell them to get ready to remodel, but not to start then."

"Can we redecorate?" Allen asked as she hugged him. "It's kind of girlie."

Katrín laughed. "I'm sure you can, but I'm also sure that there's going to be some restrictions about what you can and can't do to the actual building or the furniture and that stuff."

"Most likely."

After another minute of discussion, they left. Katrín went up to her suite, but before entering she stopped and stared at the door to Benjamin's. She knocked and waited. He answered in his pajama pants and no shirt, his hair still wet from his shower. Did he ever wear a shirt when he was alone in his suite?

Benjamin stepped to the side to let her in. "Are you just getting back?"

"Yes. They just left. I haven't even been to my room yet."

Something she couldn't quite put her finger on crossed his face. "How did it go?" he asked.

"Fine. I'm almost positive they'll move in." She tried not to wring her hands. "But there's something else."

"What?"

"Allen needs probably $150,000 US dollars in new equipment." The words came out in a rush. "I don't think most of it is stuff that's generally available here because it's so specialized, so Mama found everything in the States."

He shrugged. "Okay. Have her find exactly what he needs, not the cheaper version because it's cheaper, but the whatever they dream of for Allen. She can email an itemized list to Chamberlain, along with links. He'll figure out the best place to get it."

Katrín rested her hand on Benjamin's bare chest and tried to ignore the warmth and the feel of his heartbeat. She stood as tall as she could on her tiptoes and pressed a kiss against his cheek. She could barely get the whisper out over her tears. "Thank you."

27

Benjamin headed toward his bed, more than a little disappointed that Katrín hadn't found the surprise he'd arranged, but he was both mentally exhausted after the meeting and physically weary after his workout.

He sank onto the bed and, after pulling his blanket over his shoulders, let sleep claim him.

Despite that, he knew it hadn't been long when his covers flipped back.

"What did you do?" His sleep addled mind noted that Katrín sounded angry.

"What?" he asked, sitting up and reaching for the blanket. "I'm sleeping."

"Not until you explain." She pulled the blanket back.

"Explain what?"

"The giant piano sitting in the middle of the consort's bedroom."

He pushed himself upright. "Pretty sure it's a piano for you to play whenever you want."

"Why?"

"Why is there a piano in your suite?" It was too late and he was too foggy for this argument, especially when he had no idea where it was coming from.

"Yes."

"Because you like to play the piano." He ran a hand through his hair as he yawned. "Can I go back to sleep now?"

She kept hold of his blankets. "Where did it come from? Is it one of the ones from another part of the palace? Because I don't remember it, and I'm pretty sure I tried to play every piano around here at least once."

"No. It's new." He tugged on the covers, but she didn't let go. Benjamin raised a brow at her. "If I pull much harder, you'll be in the bed with me, but I'm going to have my blankets back."

Katrín dropped them like they were on fire. "Never mind." She turned and practically ran back toward his bathroom and the passage between the suites.

With a sigh, Benjamin swung his feet over the side of the bed and followed her through the rooms, down the hall and stopped the door to the consort's bedroom from swinging shut in his face.

She stood in the middle of the room, her back to him, shoulders shaking as she stared at the piano.

"Why can't I get you a piano?"

No answer.

"I'm waiting," he told her after a minute. "Don't make me pull rank."

Katrín spun on one heel. "Because it's too much. You're already going to spend exorbitant amounts of money on my family for the equipment my brother needs, to renovate the building, and the assistance he needs. I'm going to 'die' in about ten months, or everyone will believe I did, so why would you spend this kind of money on a piano that won't be used long, and your second wife surely won't want to keep around."

Benjamin took a couple more steps toward her. "Because I wanted to. I thought you would like having access to a good piano whenever you wanted, but in private, because I know you don't particularly like to play in front of people. I have the money to do that, so I did."

"I day dreamed about these pianos one time. You could feed a small country for what it cost."

"That's probably pushing it."

"You know what I mean."

Benjamin took another step toward her, moving slowly so he wouldn't scare her off. When he stopped in front of her, he rested his hands on her shoulders. "Look at me, Katrín." He spoke softly.

Her eyes glittered in the dim lighting, and he could see the shine off the tear tracks on her cheeks. "I got it because I wanted to, because I thought you would like it, and I wanted to do something nice for you. Period."

She sniffled. "If you want to do something nice for me, make me dinner. Buy me a CD. Maybe a puppy. But a grand piano? And not just any piano, a Bösendorfer Imperial Grand piano."

"I have no idea what that means."

That shook her out of the tears. With a roll of her eyes, she turned and walked toward the piano. Benjamin followed her. "See those?"

Some of the keys on the far left were black. "Is it supposed to be like that?"

"Yes. It's a 97 key piano instead of the usual 88."

"And this is good?"

"The keys are rarely used, but it doubles the price of an already very good piano." She tapped the farthest left key and it sent out a low, resounding tone.

"I told Chamberlain to find you the best." His tone remained soft. "I just wanted to do something nice, that's all. I had no idea it would be a whole thing."

"Is this because of what happened in here the other night? In Montevaro?"

Benjamin wanted to reflexively tell her no, but he took a few seconds to consider the idea. "No," he answered. "It has nothing to do with what happened between us." He motioned toward the bench. "Would you play something for me? Anything."

She stared at him then nodded once, turning to slide onto the bench. Her fingers ran lightly over the keys, not pressing them down but just getting a feel for them. Her fingertips settled into place.

First one note, then another filled the room until her fingers flew across the keys.

He'd expected the *King Alfred Overture*, but instead got something he didn't recognize. As the last note died out, he spoke. "What was that? I don't think I've ever heard it."

"That's because I wrote it."

His wife was extremely talented. "It's beautiful."

She started playing again, softly and tenderly this time. He knew this song. *It is Well*. The hymn seemed to bring peace to her troubled brow.

Without asking, he slid onto the edge of the bench and just watched her play. This time when she finished, she dropped her hands to her lap. Benjamin turned to sit fully facing the piano.

"Think you could teach me to play *Chopsticks*?"

Katrín laughed, exactly as he'd hoped. "This piano is far too fine for *Chopsticks*."

"But I made you smile." He leaned his shoulder against hers. "That's all I wanted to do."

"A nice bowl of gelato would have accomplished the same goal."

"Noted." With one hand, he found himself brushing the hair back at her temple. In the low lighting, her hair looked even blacker than usual. "Is this your natural hair color?" he asked softly. "It's so dark."

"It is."

His fingers pushed through the silky strands. "I like it."

"That's good, because I'm not dyeing it for you."

"I'm not asking." With his other hand, he used a finger to turn her chin toward him. "I would like to kiss you again though."

Her eyes searched his, though he wasn't sure what for. "Last time it didn't stop at kissing. It didn't the time before that either."

"So?" He bent forward and pressed his lips against her forehead before doing the same to each eyelid. "You're my wife, aren't you?" he asked softly. "It's okay if we do more than kiss."

"I know."

When her hand brushed against his side and went around his back, he knew he had her permission.

"Is this one of those times I'm supposed to curtsy while you're asleep and will never know?"

Katrín glared at Benjamin's bare back, covered only to a few inches above his waist.

He pushed up onto his elbows and looked over at her, his hair tousled and completely adorable. "What?"

"I only have to curtsy the first time I see you right? I needed to go to the bathroom too badly a few minutes ago, so I thought I'd wait."

Benjamin rolled over, keeping the covers blessedly in place. "You really don't have to curtsy at all unless we're in public. Then you only need to if it's a protocol thing for everyone to or if anyone around would expect it's the first time you've seen me that day, like if I've been out of town but don't see you before an event or something."

"Awesome." She started for the door. "I'm told your whole family is attending church together this morning, so I'd bet you need to go get ready, too."

"Wait."

She didn't stop.

"Katrín." This time his voice held a command. He'd gotten

good at that sometime in the last thirteen years since he'd become king, though it was only since he tried to imitate King Edward that he'd had any real success with it.

Good enough that she stopped in her tracks. "What?"

"We need to talk about last night and after the Festival, and Montevaro."

"Why? Like you said, we're married, we both wanted more, end of story."

His sigh followed her as she left the room. In less than an hour, she'd be making her first official church debut as a member of the royal family. For one reason or another, they hadn't attended since the wedding. Streaming services came in handy on those days.

He pulled on his pajama pants as his phone rang, causing him to turn away from her retreat. Darius? It was the middle of the night in the States.

"Hello?"

"Hey." His brother seemed out of breath.

"Is everything all right? Esther? The babies?" Had he even told Katrín why his brother missed their wedding?

"We're at the hospital. The babies should be here later today."

"Have you told Mother?"

"No." Darius's voice went quieter than expected. "You're my brother and my king. I thought you should be the first to know. I'll call her in a minute."

How things had changed. Where he initially scheduled ten minutes for his weekly conversation with Darius, Benjamin now set aside at least an hour, though the calls seldom lasted that long. "Thank you. Esther will be in our prayers."

"We'd love to have you come visit, even briefly, once things settle down. I haven't met your wife yet."

"We'll see what we can arrange. Call Mother. I imagine she and at least one of the girls will want to fly out immediately."

"Why?" Benjamin looked up to see Katrín in the doorway

wearing something more appropriate for church than the robe she'd been in before.

He held up his hand. "Keep me posted, Darius." He hesitated. "And the thing we don't ever talk about? If I found out you'd fixed it somewhere else before the year is up, and I can fix it on this end, I wouldn't take any official action."

As much as he wanted to, Benjamin couldn't tell his brother he'd ignore the statute requiring him to exile Darius, but he could hint around it.

"Then I won't tell you that it's been fixed so you don't have to decide whether to take any official action or not. It was fixed the first week in January."

As he'd suspected. "I'll talk to you soon." Darius hung up before he could.

"Where are your mother and sisters going?" Katrín sat in a chair on the other side of the room.

Benjamin sat against the headboard. "I haven't told you where Darius is, have I?"

She shook her head. "I overheard a conversation that may have told me more than I was supposed to know at the time."

He sighed. "Last March, he went on vacation to Sargasso, met a young woman, and spent some... quality time with her. She didn't know who he was. He didn't know who she was. A month later, he stood in my office and married Princess Esther of San Majoria after her father threatened to kick my family off the throne."

Katrín blinked. "How could he do that?"

"A treaty from three hundred years ago or so. Esther was pregnant. If Darius didn't accept responsibility by marrying her, Edward could take the throne and give it to someone of his choosing, likely Esther. They married and moved to the States."

"So you're an uncle?"

He shook his head. "Not yet. She miscarried, but is now in labor with their twin girls." His head rested against the headboard as he looked toward the canopy covering it. "I was his first call. Until Christmas, I don't remember the last real conversation I had with any of my siblings. Something not superficial or related to business. It's gotten better since then."

"No one was here in the days leading up to Christmas. Speculation was rampant where all of you were. Visiting Darius, wherever he is, was one of the top contenders."

"They invited all of us and the San Majorian royal family." He stared down at his hands. "Edward called me out on a few things, told me if I wasn't careful, my heirs wouldn't have a good example to look up to. Not just as the monarch, but as a father, a husband, and a man. Not like I did."

Benjamin blew out a breath. "He wasn't wrong. He told me whenever I had a decision to make I should ask myself what King Alfred would have done - either my father or King Alfred the First. That's why I was in the Rainbow sitting room that night. Alfred's Wulfrith dagger is kept in there. I always wanted to know I was worthy of it. Not in the sword fighting sense, of course, but is my character worthy of being knighted by the famed Wulfrith family?"

"And are you?"

2 8

Katrín didn't know what possessed her to ask the question. She hoped he wouldn't be mad at her for it.

"No. I'm not. Not yet, but I like to think I'm somewhat better than I was at Christmas. I don't know that I ever will be." He looked up at her, the most honest look she'd seen from him on his face. "This time last year, I was looking forward to the anniversary celebration later this year because I'd finally get to handle the dagger that was my birthright. Now, I'm intimidated at the thought of those who earned one and what they would think of me."

"Your sister told me something when we got back to the party in Montevaro. She said it doesn't matter that I'm married to a king, that as far as anyone knew I was the beloved wife of the king of my country. What mattered then was that I was a child of the King of Kings. The same is true for you. Despite the crown or the responsibility you carry on your shoulders, that's what really matters."

Before he could respond, his phone rang. "My mother," he told her as he swiped across. Maybe he'd at least consider what she'd said. Katrín knew she needed to remember it much more often.

She left him to his conversation and stared out the windows over the city of Akushla.

"We won't be attending church after all. Several members of the family are leaving almost immediately. They're hoping to arrive before the babies do."

She turned to see him looking at her.

"If you'd like to go with them, you could."

Katrín shook her head. "I'll stay." His family had been nothing but kind to her, but she wasn't comfortable enough with them for this kind of trip just yet.

Benjamin seemed to hesitate before he spoke again. "Would you like to have lunch with me this afternoon? Just the two of us?"

She gave him a small smile. "I'd like that."

Another call came in for him, so she left him to it and went to change into something a little more comfortable. She likely wouldn't leave her quarters.

Instead, she curled up with a book on her ereader, then swallowed her disappointment when a text from Benjamin canceled lunch. Something came up.

She barely saw him for days. She continued the lessons on etiquette and other things she'd need to know for her mother-in-law's birthday party.

That was the next time she saw Benjamin for more than a few minutes. The sleek navy gown was much more her style, and made her feel wonderful, though the slit up the side was a little higher than she'd normally prefer. The tiara was practically stitched into her hair and the silver heels were also a bit too high.

Who was she kidding? Any heels were too high.

This time she beat Benjamin into the outer portion of their apartments. She studied a painting of his parents' wedding day. They looked so in love. Since marrying Benjamin, she came to realize she'd likely never have that, but more recently - after the

Festival, after London, even after he bought her that amazing piano - she found herself longing for him to look at her that way.

Eventually she'd come to terms with it, but not until she'd been "dead" for a very long time.

"Ready?"

She looked to see Benjamin wearing his tuxedo with a sash that matched her dress. Was that the same color as he always wore or chosen specifically so they would match? Or had her dress been chosen to match his sash? "Yes." She tilted her head to look from Benjamin to the painting and back. "You look a little like your father."

He stopped next to her. "I'd rather be like him, I think."

"You'll get there. He likely wasn't the man everyone remembers when he was twenty-five, and he hadn't been king for twelve years already."

"Twenty-six." Benjamin continued to stare at the tapestry. "I know that on one level, but at the same time..."

"I didn't realize I missed you'd had a birthday."

"A few days before we met."

"Speaking of birthdays, I haven't heard how your brother's babies are doing." Katrín slipped her hand through his elbow as they exited the room.

"I talked to Darius earlier today. He said they're still very little, but doing fine."

"Of course they're little. They're babies."

"Even I know that."

Katrín glanced up at him, her lips clamped tightly together as she tried to hide a grin. "Was that a joke?"

His mouth twitched into a half smile. "It might have been. But what he meant is that they were both just over five pounds when they were born. They have another doctor's appointment Monday to see how they're doing. Mother said they reminded her of me. I was born just over a month early. Darius did wish he could be here for the party, but it's just not really an option."

"I didn't know you were a preemie."

"Most people don't. I was small but healthy."

"You overcame your preemie status, and I'm sure they will, too, but you never told me why they haven't gone public with their relationship."

He sighed. "That's a discussion for another time."

"Have they named the girls?"

Benjamin stopped mid-stride and pulled out his phone. "Yes, but I don't remember their names. Let me see if I can find the text." He scrolled back. "Alexis Susanna Eliana Grace is the older one."

"Very elegant."

"Victoria Amelía Miriam Louise is eight minutes younger."

"Also very nice. I'm kind of surprised they didn't use like Benjamina or Alfreda." She slid her arm back through his as they started walking down the hall.

He actually chuckled. "Unlikely it even crossed their minds. Darius did say they thought about Akushla after the first Alfred's wife, but ultimately dismissed it."

"Probably for the best."

Benjamin stopped again, turning to face a tapestry hanging there. "This is Alfred, from his days as a knight." He pointed to his left hand. "That's the dagger from the Rainbow Reception Room. A Wulfrith dagger. He trained at Wulfen Castle in England and was knighted there."

She tried to remember what he'd told her about the knight tapestries. "Is this one of the ones you mentioned to me when you told me about the rosettes?"

His face returned to its normal look. "Yes. It is."

Clearly something that bothered him. He started back toward the ballroom where they were going.

A shuddering boom stopped him in his tracks seconds before a loud clanging sound filled the palace.

Benjamin froze for a split-second then grabbed her arm.

"Let's go."

Katrín tried to wrench her arm from Benjamin's grasp, but he held firm as he dragged her behind King Alfred's tapestry.

There was no light once it whispered back into place behind them, but she could hear Benjamin muttering to himself.

"There it is," he said a little louder.

"What's going on?" She tugged her arm against his grip.

"Sh."

She could hear the series of clicks that meant the wall would be opening. After they were through it, he loosened his grip slightly and turned on his phone's flashlight. Their footsteps echoed throughout the corridor.

The spiked heel caught in a crack pitching her forward into Benjamin's back, her nose connecting with his shoulder blade.

"Come on." His urgency didn't diminish but he did slow a bit.

An alcove appeared on the right. He pushed her in ahead of him, blocking the corridor from her with his body. "Open it. Down on the bottom."

She took his phone and found the small stones about knee level. A few seconds later, the door swung toward the inside. When it closed behind them, Katrín breathed a sigh of relief, though she still didn't know why.

"Care to tell me why we're here?"

In the glow from his phone's light, she saw him turning on a lantern. "I don't know why we're here." He turned, his eyes going wide. "Are you all right?"

"What?"

He started looking around. "Your nose."

Katrín reached up to find the skin below it sticky, her fingertip red when she pulled it away. "You gave me a bloody nose."

"I didn't."

"Your back did because you were practically dragging me down the corridor, and I tripped."

He pulled the pocket square out of his breast pocket. "Here. Use this. There's supposed to be all kinds of supplies in here, but I'm not finding napkins easily."

Whatever adrenaline that had kept her from realizing she'd hurt herself began to wear off. "Do you have any pain relievers in here?"

"I don't know." He ran a hand through his hair as Katrín looked around for a place to sit down. A cabinet, probably filled with those supplies, stood on one wall and a giant trunk on another. She walked to it and sat down as Benjamin began to pace.

She checked his phone. "So palace wifi doesn't penetrate through this many stone walls?"

"I don't know."

Much like he had weeks earlier in the elevator, he walked in squares, mumbling to himself.

"Why are we here?" she asked again.

"I have no idea. The alarm goes off, you get to a secure location as soon as you can. Period."

"And this is a secure location?" She needed to get him talking again.

"Supposedly. You have to know where to find the secret doors and how to open them. Then you have to know the alcove has a door to this room."

She looked at the handkerchief. The bleeding seemed to slow already. Good. "This isn't your first time in a bugout room, is it?"

"No."

With her head leaning back against the wall, Katrín closed her eyes. "I bet Thor does drills, doesn't he?"

"Yes. I don't participate. Not fully. I'll go in the corridor, stay near the door for a few minutes, then use the tunnels to get as close to my quarters as possible. Once I make it there, I let him know and stay put."

"You don't think he's doing a drill and just didn't tell you to make sure you respond appropriately?"

"No."

The single word, bit off at the end, told her something. He'd been in a room, much like this one, and it scared him. Something happened to him in one of those rooms. If Thor didn't run surprise drills, at least not surprises to Benjamin, there was a very, very good reason for it.

"You're going to make yourself sick if you don't chill. We could be here a while until they clear up whatever the situation is."

"You think I don't know that?"

She managed not to sigh and glare at him. "That we're going to be here a while or you're going to make yourself sick?"

"Both. Whatever is going on must be something really bad for them to sound the general alarm and not text me immediately that there's no real danger. My stomach is in knots, and I'm glad I haven't eaten anything."

He was going to wear a deep path into the stone. "Benjamin!"

Snapping at him worked for a few seconds until he went back into his annoyed state. Then he glared and kept walking.

What he'd said the last time they were stuck. "When we were getting off the elevator, you told me no one knew you were claustrophobic."

"No one does."

"Then why does Thor always tell you about the drills? Why doesn't he surprise you like everyone else?"

"Because he knows I absolutely will not stand for it. He does not know why."

"You don't think he suspects?"

"I have no idea what he thinks." Benjamin let out a frustrated growl. "This room isn't big enough to pace in."

"Then sit down."

"No."

"Then make yourself sick. See if I care. I'm warning you, though, if you start gagging, I probably will, too."

"Is your nose okay?"

"I think so. No permanent damage done."

"Good. I'm glad."

Keep him talking. "How many of these bugout rooms are there?"

"I don't know."

That was helpful. "Do you know where they all are?"

"I think so."

He needed a distraction. "Then count them."

"There's this one."

Katrín couldn't help but roll her eyes. "I'm proud of you for noticing."

That brought him to a halt. "Seriously?"

"Seriously what?"

"You're going to give me a hard time."

"If it gets you to stop pacing I will."

With that he started again, ticking the safe rooms off on his fingers. "A dozen? Maybe a couple more I'm forgetting."

"But you're still pacing."

He stopped, but jumped up and down in place a few times. "I won't sit still until we're out of here."

Time to pull out the big guns. "What if I told you I was pregnant?"

29

That stopped Benjamin in his tracks. His knees gave way beneath him. Fortunately, he was near enough the other trunk to sit on it. "What?"

She stared him straight in the eye, her face as expressionless as he'd ever seen it. "I said, 'what if I told you I was pregnant?' Would that get you to stop pacing?"

He managed to calm himself enough to really hear what she said. "Are you pregnant?"

Katrín didn't wilt under his gaze. "No. I'm not."

"Could you still get pregnant?"

She arched one neatly groomed eyebrow at him. "Are you planning to do any of the sorts of things that people do to get pregnant with me?"

"No."

"Then I can't *get* pregnant."

"We didn't plan the other times either."

Her face softened some. "No. We didn't."

"Could you already *be* pregnant and not know it yet?"

Her eyes closed, and she seemed to be counting, at least if the twitching of her fingers was any indication. "It's possible, but I don't think it's likely. The timing wasn't right."

That particular knot in his gut began to loosen. "If you're wrong, you'll tell me as soon as you know?"

"Because you want to know if my anticipated death will leave you both an allegedly grieving widower and a very real single father?" Her tone was far softer than the words would imply.

"Yes."

No.

He didn't know anymore.

She'd begun to sneak her way under his skin. When he'd proposed the deal to her, he hadn't expected to get to know her. If pressed, he would have said he didn't expect their lives to change much at all, though looking back that seemed incredibly naive.

"You wouldn't really be a single father, you know. Not if you didn't want to be one." Her voice cut through his thoughts.

"What's that supposed to mean?"

"I know your mother has been a very hands-on parent, and your father was, too, but you don't have to be. Lots of monarchs aren't. Find a good nanny or two. Trot the kid out on big occasions. Make sure he or she knows how to be a good king or queen eventually. But you don't have to start that training until the teen years are nearly over."

Did she really think that little of him? Most of his people probably thought the same thing, though. If what their newest employees said was truly accurate. He shoved the thought to the side. "I was king when I was thirteen."

"And odds are, you'll be king until your heir is much, much older than that. Look at Queen Elizabeth. I'm pretty sure they conducted some experiment on her and Prince Philip during World War II and made them both invincible like Captain America. I think they're both immortal. Prince Charles has been in waiting since he was like three or four. He's almost *seventy*. Your kid could be waiting until, literally, the next century."

Benjamin let his head fall back against the wall behind him. "You really think that's likely?"

She gave the half-laugh/half-snort thing she did from time to time. "No. Of course not. But I doubt your child will become queen or king at thirteen like you did."

His eyes closed. "I sincerely hope not."

"Hey. Look at me."

She'd leaned forward, her navy gown shifting with her as she did. "I really don't think you're going to be that kind of dad. You grew up quickly without one. I can't imagine you doing the same thing to your children when you're still here to be with them. In fact, I think you'll even let them show up for breakfast in their pajamas sometimes, even after they turn five."

He managed a half-smile. "I might." Something she'd said before they were married came back to him. "I might even do the pajamas on Christmas thing."

"You should. At least until you do any official stuff that day. I wouldn't show up wearing reindeer pants if you go to that soup kitchen like your mother sometimes does."

That pulled a small laugh from him. "It might boost my popularity." He stared at the ceiling until he realized she was walking across the small room.

Katrín sat next to him and rested her head on his shoulder as she took his hand. "It really bothers you, doesn't it?"

"Being in here?" It wasn't as bad as it had been a few minutes earlier.

"No. The popularity thing. It bothers you that the people don't like you."

Benjamin started to give his standard, glib answer. It didn't really matter how many people liked him. No one was liked by everyone. But she would see right through him.

How did she do that?

"Not so much popularity as *approval*." He needed to change the subject, though. "Have you lost someone close to you?" he asked, avoiding the question.

"My father left us when my brother was tiny. They told us he wouldn't survive his first week after birth. My father would have preferred that. When the going got tough, he took off. I have no idea where he is, except he's probably not in Eyjania. For all I know, he's dead. Or remarried with five kids and twelve grandkids."

"Really?"

"Probably not the grandkids. It hasn't been quite twenty years yet."

Benjamin let go of her hand and wrapped an arm around her shoulders, pulling her closer. "You know that hole inside that never quite goes away?"

She nodded against the front of his shoulder.

"That's how the popularity thing is. I want Eyjanians to like me, to think I'm doing a good job, to approve of the job I'm doing. I'm doing the best I know how, but I'll never be the man my father was."

"You don't need to be. Your father did the public persona thing incredibly well. From what I've read, he never made a public misstep, though it's possible those he did make have faded in the wake of his untimely death. You'll never be him, but hiding here, in your palace, only showing up when you have to and looking cranky the whole time, isn't the way to make the public fall in love with *Benjamin*. They want to, but they don't know you."

He leaned his head to the side, her tiara catching on his beard and causing him to shift his head a bit further back. "How do I do that?"

"I don't know." Her hand rested on his thigh, just above his knee, and her forefinger began tapping. "I've done a lot of research on some of the other royal families, particularly of smaller countries recently, particularly the ones represented at the party in Montevaro. What if you found a reporter you could trust? Let him or her into the palace to see how hard you work, see you with your siblings. I know you help Alfred with his homework sometimes. I've seen you with all of them. You feel like you have to be their father figure, even though that's not your job. Let your people see you working out with your trainer. Maybe even show them this room. Tell them what it's like to be stuck in here when you have no idea what's going on in the outside world."

The tension flooded back, and he stood, almost not caring that she nearly fell to the side. "No. No one comes in here."

Catching herself before she hit the corner of the trunk, Katrín pushed back upright. "Touched a soft spot, did I?"

He glared.

She kicked off her shoes. They hurt. Standing in front of him as he paced, she reached out and put her hands on his chest. "Listen to me." Using her most soothing tone, she tried to get him to focus. "Take a deep breath in and hold it until I tell you to let it out."

His nostrils flared as he continued to nearly hyperventilate.

"Don't make me have to find a paper bag in this place." Her tone sharpened. "Deep breath in."

She saw him suck in air and hold it. After counting to five, she spoke again. "Slowly breathe out through your mouth. In through your nose, ten count, out through your mouth."

His blue eyes snapped, but he didn't say anything.

"Do it," she ordered.

A minute later, his shoulders began to relax.

"Now, you're going to have a seat over on the trunk. I'm going to look through the cabinet."

Benjamin followed her instructions, taking his seat again, though this time he tugged at his tie until it came loose and he'd unbuttoned the top of his shirt.

Katrín turned the handle on the metal cabinet that looked surprisingly modern, but had to have come from the 1980s or so. Inside, she found a case of water bottles. Looking for a use by date, she realized it had been restocked in the last year. But it was water. It would have been okay anyway, wouldn't it?

She poked her thumb through the plastic and tore it open until she could get two bottles out. Holding one out to Benjamin, she waited for him to take it. "I wouldn't drink too much too fast. You don't want to have to go to the bathroom down here."

That brought another half-smile from him. "No. I'd rather not." But he twisted the cap off and took a sip. She did the same then turned back to the cabinet.

"What else is in here?"

"Should be some snacks, enough to get us through a couple of days if needed."

"And if whatever this is drags on longer than that?"

"We stay here until we, literally, cannot stay any longer. Then we leave and go to the actual shelter unless we've received instructions otherwise."

That made her turn and glare at him. "There's another shelter? One that probably has real furniture and food?"

"It does. Thor never told you where it was?"

She glared at him. "Does this look like the face of someone who knows these things?"

He glanced her way. "No. But the rules are you get to one of these shelters. If there's no all clear or no one comes for you, and you're out of supplies, then you go to the main shelter. The only exception is if you're already close to the main shelter."

"Where is it?"

He looked over at her, mild shock on his face. "You really don't know?"

She glared again and shook her head. "I really don't."

"Your room? The one you lived in for the last few years?"

"I remember it well." Too well. She hated it.

"Most of that side of the hallway is really a secret hideout. Even behind your room is part of the complex. There's a secret door between your room and the shelter."

Her jaw dropped. "You're kidding."

His brows pulled together. "Why would I joke about that?"

"I don't know, but I can't believe I never knew that."

"Most people don't." He didn't even smirk. "If they did, it would void the whole concept of a secret shelter."

"Good point." Something else occurred to her. She'd meant to ask earlier when she told him about her father, but had been sidetracked. "What about my family?"

"What about them?"

"Where do they hide out?"

He took another sip of his water, and leaned forward with his elbows on his thighs as he undid another button on his shirt. "I honestly don't know. I'm sure they're fine. They haven't even moved in yet, have they?"

"Not until next week, but they were here today going over what they wanted to keep in the cottage. My sister, Nína, officially still works for the Crown Prince of Mevendia's wife, but they're taking a breather right now, so she's here until they go back to Mevendia. She redid their house earlier this year, so she's working with Mama and the people here."

"Good."

"So where will they go?" She pressed for an answer.

"I don't know, but I'm sure the security teams are on it."

He took another sip of water, prompting her to as well. "What about your family?"

"They're probably all in rooms like this."

He grew silent after that statement, and she turned to the cabinet. "There's some games in here to help pass the time." Pulling a deck of cards off the shelf, she turned and held them up. "Poker?"

"What do we have to bet with?"

"There's a box of chips, but that's a good point. There's no real stakes." An idea popped, fully formed, into her mind. "Unless we play a version of Truth or Dare at the same time."

He looked up from the water bottle he'd been studying intently. "What?"

She waved her hand to dismiss his question. "Never mind. I know how we're going to do this. Push the two trunks together over there, would you?" After pointing to where she wanted them, Katrín pulled the chips out as well.

Setting them on the trunks, she hiked up her skirt and sat on the floor with her back to the wall. Picking up the cards, she pointed to the other side. "Have a seat. Give us each a single set of chips while I deal? One color each, don't divide them out."

"You really think playing for pieces of plastic is enough incentive for this?"

"Nope. I do think bragging rights could come into play. I also think you won't want to lose."

"Of course I don't want to lose."

She dealt the cards. "It's more than that. Don't bet more chips than you can afford to lose. Because every time I collect ten of your chips, you have to answer a question and answer it honestly. Same the other way around."

He didn't look convinced.

Time to sweeten the pot. "I promise I won't ask why you're freaked out and claustrophobic."

Benjamin gave a wary nod. "Fine."

Hopefully her smile hid her true intentions. She wouldn't ask, but Katrín had every intention of figuring out why so she could help him through it.

"FOLD." Benjamin tossed his hand down, even though he was almost certain it would have won. Without absolute certainty, he wouldn't play.

Katrín was cute when she was annoyed. "You haven't played one hand yet."

"So? I'm not going to bet a bunch of chips when I don't think I can win." It was bad enough she'd insisted both of them had to toss a chip in every hand. Eight hands in and he had none of her chips, but she was closing in on being able to ask him anything she wanted.

The tenth hand came before he knew it. As much as he didn't want to play it, the hand was too good.

Her mouth dropped open when he tossed four more chips on the pile. "You're playing it? Really?"

"Call or raise?"

"Call." She put four chips in and turned her cards over. "Two pair. Aces and eights."

A smile crept across his face as he turned his. "Full house. Queens over Aces."

Katrín groaned but pushed the chips toward him. "You live another round, Benji."

And another round was all he lived. She won, somehow managing to end up with fifteen total chips.

Counting out ten, she handed them over. "Which of your siblings is your favorite?"

Not what he expected. He'd thought she'd try for something deep and personal. Instead, he had to actually think about it rather than just refusing. "I don't know. Genevieve, I guess. We go to the most events together, or we did. For identical twins, she and Evangeline have very different personalities. Half the time, when Evangeline was supposed to join me for something, she'd cancel and Genevieve would come instead."

"Well, neither one of them have to worry about being your official date again for a while." She tossed some more cards in front of him. "Ante up."

Ten minutes later, she asked him another question. "What happened the night we met?"

Benjamin blinked. "You were there."

She waved her hand. "I mean at the Mevendian dinner. No one seems to know."

Right. That. "I stood up to my uncle for the first time when he almost hit Princess Margaret. I grabbed his arm as he went to backhand her."

She looked as shocked as he'd been when it happened. "Wow."

"That doesn't go any further than this," he warned. "As far as I know, no one else knows, except the four of us that were there." No, that couldn't be right. "I'm sure William told his family. They were all there that evening when Margaret passed out."

"She passed out? Is she okay?"

He'd gotten a report from his family physician, though not all the details. "Apparently, she'd been working too hard, not taking care of herself, and was newly pregnant. She didn't actually pass out, but came close. I was dancing with her when she collapsed, and I carried her to their room." He tried to give her his best king look. "She's a lot like someone else I know."

Katrín just rolled her eyes. He didn't really think they were too much alike in that sense, though they both worked hard. He suspected Katrín knew when she needed to say enough was enough and was willing to do so more than Margaret had been.

"What happened between her and Prince Isaiah?"

Benjamin wasn't sure how much to say without making his uncle look worse than necessary. "He RSVPd that he wouldn't be there, showed up an hour late, and made a scene. When she refused to give him a seat at the head table, he became enraged. When I stepped in, he tried to pull rank on me. He went so far as to tell me I had to respect him because he's my uncle. I reminded him I was his king. Then I told him he had three days to get out of the palace."

Realization crossed her face. "That's what was going on at the other end of the palace. I thought I could get away with playing the piano that night because everyone was preoccupied with all that."

He pointed to the cards. "I think you got more than your ten coins worth."

She shuffled again. He asked her a question, though he couldn't come up with anything really good.

A few minutes later, it was her turn again. "How many other women have you ever told to meet you in your quarters? Or your office or anywhere else?"

If he'd known what she was going to ask, he would have expected her to avoid looking at him, but instead her dark eyes held his gaze without flinching. He had to be honest. "None."

"Then why did you think you could tell me to?"

Benjamin thought about reminding her she hadn't earned another question, but had the impression this question was more important than he realized. He couldn't tell her about the men in his family, how they knew who they'd marry the first time they met a woman. Not when he'd only just starting admitting to himself it might actually be the case. "You intrigued me. I wanted to get to know you."

"You didn't think to ask me to dinner? Instead you thought propositioning me was the way to go?"

Benjamin pulled his knees up until he could rest his forearms on them. "Isaiah always told me I could expect any woman I wanted to jump at the chance to sleep with me. I didn't really expect anything to happen." No, he had to be completely honest. "I don't think. I really don't know what I expected."

"You put up a good front," she told him softly. "You talk a good game, but deep down you're just like the rest of us. Scared of failure. Of being found wanting. Not being enough. But for you, the stakes are much higher than they are for most people."

"I'm afraid." The words were out before he could stop them.

"Of what?"

"Of everything you said. Failing my country. Failing my father.

Failing myself." He stared at the door. "Of being trapped somewhere like this and never getting out alive." He knew what her next question would be.

"Why would you be afraid of that?"

He closed his eyes and tried not to remember. "Because when I was six, I was trapped in this very room for eighteen hours and thought my whole family was dead."

30

With her breath caught in her throat, Katrín stared at the side of Benjamin's head. "What?" she whispered. Was he actually going to trust her with the story?

"The alarms sounded throughout the palace. I knew what to do. I ran and hid. In here."

She just watched as he took another swig of his water.

"For over eighteen hours."

She couldn't stifle her gasp. "Eighteen hours? In here, by yourself? What happened to keep you here that long?"

He sighed. "Miscommunication."

"Wait. If you were six, your father was already king, right?"

A single nod.

"Then you're telling me that for the better part of a day, no one knew where the Crown Prince was?"

"They all thought I was with someone else. I should have been in school already. We had tutors who came here, but I was late because there was a new foal at the stables, and I'd run out there to see him first. When the alarm sounded, my parents and my nanny thought I was at school. The tutor thought I was still with one of them. Apparently, everyone else knew it was a false alarm within minutes. No one else ever even made it to a safe room."

He lifted the bottle of water to his lips and took a sip. "The cabinet was locked. So were the trunks. Or at least, my six-year-old self couldn't open them."

"Eighteen hours with no food or water and no clue what was going on in the outside world?"

"Yep. I was the only kid working with the tutor at the time so he thought my parents decided to keep me 'home' after the false alarm. My parents and nanny thought I was with him. My parents had an event later that evening. In the shuffle, everyone thought I was with someone else until my parents got home about ten. I forget where they went, but it was something I'd attended with them before. They'd talked about me going but decided I wouldn't."

He let out a deep breath. "The nanny had been busy with my younger siblings and thought I'd gone with them. My parents thought I was with the rest of the family. It wasn't until they got home and the nanny asked where I was that they realized I was gone. Several more hours passed before they finally found me."

She couldn't begin to fathom it. "I was lost at a market for like ten minutes once. I know how freaked out I was that I'd never see my mother or sister again. I can't imagine being somewhere like this for that long without knowing what was going on."

"Imagine is the right word. My imagination worked overtime. In my six-year-old head, I knew there were dangers that could come after me but had no clue what they were. I was absolutely convinced I was the only survivor of whatever it was that set the alarms off. I'd leave the room, eventually, and everything would be gone. Just me and this room still standing."

"But they came for you?"

"Not exactly. I was so hungry. I hadn't eaten breakfast in my rush to get to the stables. Finally, I decided I had to risk it. I went out the way we came in and for a few minutes peeked out from behind the tapestry. There was no one in the hallways. So at least the building was standing, but all the people were gone. I was headed for the main kitchen when an employee found me. I don't know who it was or where she came from, but she gasped and hugged me for all she was worth, said my parents had been so worried about me. I said I was hungry. She took my hand and rushed me to the kitchen then called security to let them know where I was."

"Did you get in trouble?"

"Only for not telling them where I was going that morning. I wasn't really in trouble, not like I would have been if there hadn't been that false alarm, but I did get a stern talking to and asking why I hadn't emerged when the all clear sounded."

"Why didn't you?"

"I never heard it." He pointed to a box mounted high on a wall. "That speaker should make announcements, but it didn't."

Katrín stood and walked around the trunks until she could sit on the floor next to Benjamin. She slid her hand between his arm and his body and rested her head on his shoulder. Her other hand gripped his elbow. "That had to be petrifying. It's no wonder you don't like small spaces."

"I had the office redone as soon as I was old enough to make them do it while keeping the look of the original architecture."

"You added windows?"

He nodded. "I could literally not have lived in your room. I would have gone stark raving mad. I'm kind of surprised I'm not right now. How long have we been in here?"

Katrín checked her watch. "A couple hours. They won't let it go nearly so long without verifying your location once it's safe, you know that, right?"

Another nod.

She looked up at his profile. How had she not noticed the tear tracks in the space between his eyes and his beard? "Can we get to the safe apartment place near my old room from here? Without leaving the tunnels?"

"Yeah. But we're not supposed to leave here until we get the signal, or we can't stay."

She used his shoulder to push herself back up. "We can't stay. I need to go to the bathroom, and you're going to go crazy. We don't have to go out into the outer world, so I say we sneak down to this other place. We'll leave a cryptic note here and if they throw a fit about it..." She gave a shrug. "You're the king, and your mental health required the move. Your wife said so."

He finished off his bottle of water. "Grab a couple of bottles, just in case, and let's go."

As KATRÍN WROTE a note she said would be cryptic enough some random bad guy wouldn't know what it meant but Thor would understand, Benjamin stood next to the door.

Get out.

He needed out.

She understood that, despite his relative calm since she started that card game.

"All done. Let's go." Katrín gripped his upper arm as she put her shoes back on. "But if you could go a little slower this time, I'd appreciate it."

Benjamin picked up the lantern. "As long as I think it's safe to do so."

"Fine."

He turned the lantern down as far as it would go and still give off light before he opened the door, just in case. The corridor was dark and quiet. "Let's go." He turned the light up a little then reached back and took her hand. Just that bit of contact calmed him.

They'd come from the left, but this time they went right. Katrín remained quiet as they walked the tunnel, went down the steep spiral stairs, and eventually came to another door. Last time, he'd had Katrín open it, putting himself between her and whatever danger might lurk behind. This time, he opened it, unsure of what they would find on the other side.

His entire family lounging like it was no big deal? Assassins with guns? Nothing?

The latter was most likely, but until he knew... He pushed Katrín behind him as he opened the door. As it swung open, relief flooded him. Only emergency lights. No assassins. No family members wondering why he'd freaked out. Just dim lighting until he turned everything on.

Because in about two minutes, every light in the place would be burning.

He wouldn't sleep in the dark for weeks.

Walking through, he flipped a switch and bathed the sitting room in the florescent glow.

"This is nice," Katrín said, walking in and letting the door shut behind her.

"It could be worse." But he still didn't like it.

With the indication that someone was there, the rest of the room began to come to life. There were no windows for obvious reasons, but picture frames with outdoor scenes lit up.

"I don't supposed there's clothes I can change into?" Katrín set her handbag down on a side table, and used it to balance as she took her shoes off.

How did women walk on those things? Spikes held her heels several inches off the floor. Benjamin found himself grateful for men's more practical footwear.

"There should be." He pointed down the hall. "There's no separate quarters here. The monarch gets his or her own room. Everyone else bunks up. Clothes for you should be with mine."

He watched her walk down the hall and wondered what this day would have been like if she hadn't been with him.

Still climbing the walls in the safe room, most likely. Or curled into a fetal ball of quivering mess.

After following her down the hall, Benjamin closed and locked the bedroom door behind him.

"You really think someone's about to walk in on us doing what exactly?" she asked, tossing her shoes into a corner.

"Another layer for someone to get through if they show up here."

She just nodded and headed for the closet. "So where exactly are we in the palace?"

It took him a minute to get the mental map in place, then he pointed at a wall. "Your old room is right through there." Were those stones what he thought they were? "Looks like there might even be a door into it."

"So the monarch's room has an extra way in and out. Makes sense," she called as she went into the small closet. "I don't have any clothes in here. Can I borrow something of yours for now?"

"Sure. I think my sisters have clothes down here somewhere though." It had been a very long time since he'd given this hideout anything more than a passing glance.

"I'll look later. I just want to get out of this dress. I can use a t-shirt and a pair of shorts that probably don't fit you anymore but have a drawstring."

Benjamin took his jacket off and threw it on a nearby chair. "Go for it."

He heard a frustrated groan from the closet. "I'm sorry to ask, but I need some help. I can't get this stupid thing undone."

"Just a minute." He took his cuff links off and set them in the tray on the side table, then rolled his sleeves as he walked through the small room.

Even in his mind, he knew it wasn't small. Katrín's old quarters on the other side of the wall were maybe a third of the size, possibly even less. But he'd spent most of his life avoiding rooms with no windows and preferred rooms as big as he could find.

Katrín walked out of the closet as he neared it. She'd already removed the tiara and taken her hair down. She turned her back to him and swept her hair to the side. "I undid the top few hooks, but I can't reach all of them on the top."

It looked like six or so inches of the two sides of navy blue lace were connected with little hooks as close together as they could get. Her back was bare until close to her waist.

Had he ever noticed how smooth the skin of her back looked? "Just undo the hooks on top?" he asked.

"Please."

His fingers fumbled with the small metal hooks, the tips brushing against the skin of her neck and back.

By the time the last one came free, he wasn't sure he remembered how to breathe. Taking a giant step back, he blew out slowly. "There you go."

Her arms twisted around to reach the hooks on the bottom part of the dress. "Thanks."

Katrín disappeared into the closet. "Do you want something to change into?"

"I'll wait until you're done."

A minute later, she emerged in an old Eyjanian Olympic shirt and a pair of sweatpants with bare feet. She stopped in front of him. "I'm proud of you."

"For what?"

"Facing your fears. Letting me in."

"Running away." That thought had been plaguing him since they left the other room.

"Running to a safe place both physically and emotionally." She reached a hand out and rested it on his midsection. "Acknowledging that you need a change of scenery or to get out of a situation where you're uncomfortable is okay, good for you even."

Katrín stretched up, likely on her tiptoes until her face was closer to his.

Benjamin reached out to rest his hands on her waist and help her balance.

"I'm proud of you," she said again, her dark eyes earnest. Then she brushed a kiss against his lips, and time stopped.

31

"Benjamin? Katrín?"

Katrín blinked as she heard a key scraping in the door.

"Don't get up," Benjamin whispered, tugging the blanket further over her shoulders. He sat up, blocking her from whoever's view, but he didn't seem concerned.

"There you are." Was that the Queen Mother's voice? Katrín heard footsteps that stopped far too quickly. "Oh." Shock? Surprise? "I didn't realize we were interrupting something." Amusement.

"You're not," Benjamin told her. "We both decided it was time to rest for a bit since we had no idea what was going on. We'll be out in a minute."

"Of course we didn't." Definitely amusement.

The door closed.

"I'll get dressed, and you can follow me out in a few minutes."

Katrín buried her head in the pillow. "Please don't leave without me."

"Why?"

"I'm never going to be able to face your mother again. Or Thor. Or whoever else came in with her."

"Just Thor, I think."

"So I'll never be able to face either one of them again."

"Why exactly?"

She pushed up on her elbows. "Because the whole palace is on lock down because of a threat, and we have no idea what it was, but hey, let's go to the monarch's secret lair and..." Her face fell forward until it was buried again as she groaned.

"I promise you, my mother is ecstatic to find us together."

"So? That she has any reason to think anything about it at all is mortifying."

If she didn't know better, he was probably stifling a chuckle. Come to think of it, did she know better?

"Then why don't you go get dressed in the closet? I'll get dressed out here, and we can leave together."

"Thank you." She pulled the top blanket off and wrapped it around her before hurrying to the closet. A minute later she sighed in frustration. "I'm still going to have to wear your clothes, because all I have is that dress."

"I'll wear something very casual too then."

At least he seemed to care about not embarrassing her by dressing far more nicely than she would be able to. The bathroom mirror let her fix her hair into a ponytail. Better than nothing.

"I'm ready when you are," he called softly.

She stared at her reflection in the mirror, wiping a bit of dried blood she'd missed earlier from under her nose. "I'm going to live in here forever."

"No, you're not. You're too strong to let something like this keep you from living life. So come out here, and we'll face them together."

Walking out of the closet, she refused to looked directly at Benjamin.

"It won't be that bad."

Katrín didn't think she believed him, but took his hand as they walked out of the room and down the hall.

Benjamin stopped before reaching the sitting room, and she nearly ran into his back again. This time she peeked around to see Thor and Queen Mother Eliana standing close to each other but looking at the ground, and somewhat guilty.

"Care to tell us what's going on?" Benjamin asked.

"Nothing," his mother answered quickly. Too quickly.

"There was a breech at the front gate." Thor motioned for them to sit on the sofa. "Until we knew more about what happened and why, we wanted all of you somewhere safe."

"What happened?"

"The investigation won't be complete for some time, but early indications all point the same way." He held a file folder toward Benjamin who took it. "A man was driving a moving truck. He had a stroke less than a quarter mile away from the front gate, hit the gas, and went straight through at high speed until the retractable bollards stopped him near the building."

"Retractable bollards?" Katrín asked.

"Barriers that pop up when the gate is breached," Benjamin explained. "They're designed to stop the vehicle before it actually reaches the building, but there's a minimum distance to allow enough time from breach to full protection. It's closer to the building than we'd like, but with current technology this is the farthest from the building they can be. There's not nearly as much room between the gate and the building as there would be if it were built today."

"So guy has a stroke, happens to be directly lined up with the gate, rams it, stopped by the bollards?" Benjamin leaned forward with his elbows on his knees as he looked through the paperwork. "There wasn't any evidence of foul play or explosives or anything that would indicate there was more to it?"

Katrín watched her husband carefully. She hadn't seen this side of him before, the businessman she knew he was.

THE INDENTURED QUEEN

"Nothing at this time, sir." Thor leaned forward to point at a note on the page. "This wasn't his first stroke, but we didn't want to give the all clear until we had the bomb squad and dogs check it out. It took a while to get everything cleared."

"How long as it been?" Benjamin asked.

"About four and a half hours."

"What about the man? What's his status?"

"We didn't approach the vehicle immediately, because we didn't know what might be in the back. Instead we focused on evacuating areas near the truck." Thor hesitated. "He was deceased by the time we got to him. We think he was gone before he hit the gate, but we won't have definitive answers for a while."

Benjamin blew out a breath. "As much as I hate that, is it possible his family could come after the palace legally or publicly for allowing him to die by not attending to him right away?"

"Probably not."

They continued talking for another twenty minutes. Every time Katrín didn't think she could be more impressed by Benjamin and his insightful questions, competence, and all-around acumen.

This was the Benjamin the people needed to know existed. The one who knew his job, did it well, and cared about others.

He tossed the folder on the table. "Why did it take four hours to give the all clear? What threat is there that I don't know about?"

"THE REST of us got it an hour ago," his mother told Benjamin gently. "You probably would have, too, if you'd been awake. It should have sounded in here."

"Wouldn't it have woken us up?" Katrín asked. "We weren't that sound asleep."

"It's not nearly as loud and obnoxious as the other one," he told her. "So three hours. That's a long time for a guy in a truck who had a stroke." He gave Thor his best "I'm the boss" look. "What threat am I unaware of?"

Thor leaned forward and stared at his clasped hands. "Your uncle was seen talking to some rather unsavory characters. Until today, we had no reason to believe it was anything more than incidental contact. As it looks now, that is still likely the case, but until we cleared the scene, we couldn't be certain."

The knot in the pit of his stomach grew. "So Isaiah may or may not be looking for a way to get back at the family, specifically me, but this wasn't it?"

"Correct."

"And why wasn't I told about this sooner?"

Thor shared a look with his mother. Benjamin needed to talk to Thor about what exactly he'd seen when he and Katrín came into the sitting area.

"Because it's nothing definitive," his mother told him.

"But you know?"

"I was discussing another concern with Thor when he got the first call. He told me about it."

"And you didn't think I should know?" He glared at her.

She glared right back. "You may be the king, but I am still your mother."

He gave her a slight nod.

"There was no reason to tell you. The source is reliable, but uncertain about exactly what he saw. It could have just been two men having lunch in the same restaurant and making polite conversation."

"Do you really think that?"

Thor shook his head. "No, but it's all we have right now. We were finally able to get information off his computer that he set up the email to send the press release on his way back from the Mevendian house. Even if you'd called right away and had his access revoked, it would have been too late."

Benjamin looked back and forth between the two. "What else aren't you telling me?"

Thor exchanged a look with Benjamin's mother. "San Majorian police were called to the house where Isaiah had been living. They found blood everywhere, enough to kill a man from exsanguination. That was two weeks ago. The tests came back yesterday. Every spot of blood they tested was Isaiah's, but no body has been found."

"So he's dead?" Guilt poured over Benjamin. He shouldn't be relieved his uncle had likely been murdered.

Thor shook his head. "There's no way to know for sure without the body. We're cautiously... optimistic isn't the right word, but I don't have a better one, that he's no longer a threat, but we can't be certain."

Benjamin blew out a breath. "I presume the authorities are still looking?"

"They are, but they don't have much to go on. He lived on the water with a dock. There are reports of a boat being heard the night before the blood was found. If someone killed him then loaded him on a boat and went out to sea..."

Realization dawned. "If they weighed his body down, he's at the bottom of the Sargasso Sea and will never be found."

"Correct. However, we did find one of his safe houses here in Akushla earlier today. There's a ton of paperwork in there. We've just started going through it."

"Okay. So we table discussion of Isaiah until there's more information. But where do we go from here? The ball has clearly been postponed. What's been told to the press?"

"Not much. That the premises are secure, and there will be a press conference in the morning."

Benjamin stood. "Then we need to get to work on what we'll say." He glanced around. This wasn't nearly as bad as the safe room, but he needed windows. "Let's get out of here."

"Actually, it's already being taken care of." Thor and his mother both stood. "If you'd like to get some sleep, that would probably be best. We'll go over the findings with you then, but there's really nothing more for you to do tonight. I'll see that your clothes from the party this evening are collected and brought to your rooms."

"Thank you."

His mother and Thor left through the main entrance, but Benjamin stopped Katrín with a hand on her arm until after they'd left.

"What is it?" He could hear the concern in her voice.

"Can you get into the room across the hall?"

"I have the key in my pocketbook."

"We can get upstairs from there, right?"

"It's a long, narrow, winding staircase, but yes."

"Let's do that. If it's okay with you. I'd rather not go anywhere we might see people, even family."

"Sure. It goes straight to our suites."

He picked her pocketbook up off the side table. "Then let's go."

In a couple of minutes, he began to wish they'd gone the other way. This would be quicker, much more discreet, but she hadn't been kidding about a narrow staircase. He could feel beads of sweat forming on his forehead.

As though she read his mind, Katrín reached out and wrapped her forefinger around his pinky. They were too far apart to do any more than that. "It's not too much further."

He managed a chuckle. "I'm pretty sure you're lying to me."

"Compared to how far it is to the moon, it's pretty close."

That made him smile again. "Thanks." They reached a landing. "All the way to the top?"

"Yes. I have no idea where any of the other exits go."

"That's fine. I don't want to go anywhere but my quarters." And he wasn't even sure about that. Once he got there, he'd be alone again. Even with the windows and the lights, he wasn't sure how he'd deal with it.

They kept climbing past two more landings. "That's the last one," Katrín told him. "The next one is the top."

Relief settled over him. "Good."

They reached the next landing, and Katrín let go of his finger. "Your door is to the left." She turned to the right. "I'll see you tomorrow."

With the flashlight he'd brought from the bunker, he found the correct stones. Katrín was already pressing them on her side.

"Wait." He surprised even himself.

She turned, curiosity written all over her face. "Yes?"

"Would you do something for me?" Fear reared its ugly head. This time, fear of rejection.

"I won't tell anyone what you told me."

He shook his head. "It's not that."

She simply waited for him to speak.

Benjamin had to dig deep to find courage he didn't know he had, the courage to be vulnerable. "I know we're whatever we are, and you sleep in your quarters and I sleep in mine, but would you sleep in my quarters tonight?"

A smile crossed her face. "Of course. I don't particularly relish being alone either."

His shoulders slumped in relief when she didn't want an explanation, but he felt he owed her one anyway. "It's not just that."

"You're afraid of nightmares." She moved past him and opened the door into a room he seldom used. "I don't blame you. I may have one myself."

"I won't be able to turn the lights off," he warned.

She shrugged. "That's okay. I know how to close my eyes."

KATRÍN WASN'T sure what part of Benjamin's quarters this was, but the door to the hallway from this room stood open. She did know the two suites weren't mirror images, so it wasn't as simple as going backwards, but she made no missteps into his bedroom. Visual cues for the win.

"I think I'm going to take a shower." Benjamin started for the bathroom.

"Then I'm going to run back to my quarters for just a minute and change into clothes of my own." She started for the main door. Going back the way they came and across the secret passage would be the fastest way to her pajamas.

Benjamin turned as he reached the door. "I kind of like that look on you."

She looked down. "I'm a mess, and your clothes are way too big."

His mouth quirked into a half-smile. "I still like how you look in my clothes, even if they are too big for you and too small for me."

Katrín didn't quite know what to do with that.

"But if you want to change, you won't upset me."

She nodded and turned. Once in her room, she decided to take a quick shower and put on her most comfortable pajamas, which also had the benefit of being not very revealing.

When she returned to Benjamin's room, she could still hear the water running. Going to bed seemed awkward, so instead she stood and stared out the window. Given how close it was to summer, the sun still hadn't quite set.

She gazed out at the twilight and whispered a prayer, really a continuation of the prayers she'd been praying since the alarm first blared and Benjamin grabbed her arm. For his peace. For a clear mind to make the decisions necessary. For the safety of those involved in their protection.

Behind her, she could hear the shower turn off and a minute later, movement. She didn't jump when Benjamin slid his arms around her waist and pulled her back toward him, but it did surprise her. He'd never shown any kind of affection when they were alone together, not really. Except a couple of times, but this clearly wasn't one of those.

"Thank you." His hold tightened.

"For what?"

"Keeping me calm. If you hadn't been there, I don't know what I would have done."

"You would have managed."

"I doubt it, but I do know that I want to try to get some rest."

"Then let's get some sleep." It should bother her to be sleeping in this room. Just like it bothered her to sleep in the consort's bedroom with him, but this time seemed different.

It took them a couple of minutes to both find a comfortable sleeping position, but even with the lights on, Katrín found herself too drained to stay awake for long.

But she was woken up by Benjamin muttering in his sleep.

She reached over and rested a hand on his shoulder. Just that slight touch seemed to ease the lines on his brow a little. Rather than shaking him like she'd planned to do, Katrín moved closer, wrapped her arms around his shoulders and prayed her way back to sleep as his trembling ceased.

The next time she woke, she realized, even before opening her eyes, that she was alone in bed.

Pushing herself into a seated position, she saw Benjamin standing on the other side of the room staring out the window. "What time is it?"

"Almost seven. I'm usually awake by now. No one has set an alarm off for me yet, though."

"Set an alarm off?"

He turned and pointed to the clock by the side of the bed. "That can be remotely programmed. If I'm needed earlier than usual or if I've had a late night and plan to sleep in, it ensures I don't sleep too late."

Katrín patted his pillow. "Then why don't you get some more rest? They'll wake you when they need you."

With a shake of his head, he turned back around. "It's no use. I won't get any more sleep."

She flipped the covers back and turned sideways. "Then why don't we find something to eat?"

"There's an en suite kitchen. It doesn't have a full complement of food, but there's enough for you to find something."

"Not me. Us. We can find something to eat."

"I'm afraid my stomach is too twisted in knots about this whole thing to keep anything down."

Katrín walked across the room until she stood behind him. Wrapping her arms around his waist, she rested her cheek against the warmth of his back. His arms laid atop of hers. "How did you sleep?"

"Better than I expected," he said. "I think it's because you were here."

"Or because, while yesterday was no fun, the actual trauma of feeling trapped was a long time ago."

"I barely slept for days after the elevator," he admitted to her. "And a couple other times when I've found myself temporarily unable to leave a confined area, the same thing happened."

"Then I'm glad I'm here." Something else had occurred to her. "Will I be needed at the press conference today?"

"I don't see why you would. The head of security will answer some questions. I'll give a statement and maybe answer a question or two. Thor may, but he may not since he's not the head of security. I would imagine the chief of police will be there. Possibly someone to tell everyone the man was already deceased. I doubt they'll mention anything about Isaiah, just something vague about unspecified threats against the royal family."

"I'm kind of glad you don't need me there. I've not done anything like that before, and I'd rather not just yet." Or ever.

He shifted and turned in her arms until her head rested against his chest and they held each other. "I told you something yesterday, something intensely personal."

The way he said it made her wary. "Yes, you did."

"Will you trust me with your secret?"

For a long moment, she didn't move at all. "I'll be leaving in a few months. Then it will no longer matter. Can't we just leave it at that? Unless something changes and you *need* to know for some reason, and then I'll tell you."

His hold tightened around her as his hand ran up and down her back. "Fair enough."

"When do you need to be downstairs?" She started to move away, but he held her close.

"What if I don't want you to go?"

She kind of snorted. "You have to get ready, and I have things to do today."

"No. In a few months. What if I don't want you to go?"

Katrín pulled back and looked up to see his blue eyes as serious as she ever had. "You mean you want me to stay? Forever?"

His gaze flickered down to her lips then back to her eyes. "What if I do?"

32

As Katrín stared up at him with those big brown eyes, Benjamin knew he wanted her to stay.

"Because the nightmares didn't come as much last night?"

He reached up and brushed a stray hair off her face. "That's a small part of it, but I don't want you to go."

"Why?" she pressed.

Why did it matter? "Because I don't want you to go."

She sighed and closed her eyes. "Because you love me? Because you like kissing me? Because you hope I'm around whenever that blasted alarm goes off?"

"I do like kissing you. I do like having you around when I end up stuck in an elevator or in a safe room." He needed to be honest with her. "But I can't honestly say that I love you."

Her eyes narrowed. "Not yet or not ever?"

How was he supposed to know if he'd ever fall in love with her? "I want to have a marriage like my parents did. They adored each other. I don't know how to get from here to there, but I want to."

After searching his face for something he didn't understand, she gave a single nod and took a step back. "I think it's time for us to get moving."

She hadn't given him a yes, but she hadn't said no either.

His phone buzzed in his pocket. "Yes?"

"Sir, you're needed in your office in fifteen minutes."

That wasn't enough time. "I'll be there as soon as I can."

Turning off his phone, he went to his closet where his clothes for the day had been set out. He dressed as quickly as he could and still look put together before leaving for his office. He didn't know where Katrín had gone.

"What is it?" he asked Chamberlain as he walked into the outer office.

"The press conference is in an hour." Chamberlain handed him a folder. "It was moved up."

"Why?"

"Because it was."

Benjamin sat behind his desk and flipped through the paperwork Chamberlain handed him. "Fine. What specifically do I need to know?"

"Everything we have at this time is in there, though it hasn't changed much from what Thor told you last night."

For the next forty-five minutes, they went over the reports then walked to the garden where the press conference would be held. Benjamin waited just inside until it was time.

Once in front of the reporters, the head of security made a statement, followed by the chief of police. Then it was Benjamin's turn.

After introductory remarks, he moved on. "I would like to personally thank all of the members of the palace security staff, the local police, the bomb squad, and everyone else who worked so quickly to ensure the safety of my family, my staff, and the honored guests who had already arrived. My family and I extend our deepest condolences to the family and friends of Mr. Borgen, and wish them to know that our thoughts and prayers are with them during this difficult time."

He stepped back from the microphone and the head of public relations for the office stepped in, informing the reporters that they would take questions.

Question after question flooded in.

Was Mr. Borgen still alive when the crash occurred?

Would he have survived if medical aid was given immediately?

Where did the royal family go during the crisis?

How long did they remain in their secure locations?

On and on.

Benjamin wanted to leave, to find Katrín and talk more with her about his desire for her to stay.

As the press conference began to wind down, more and more reporters seemed distracted, checking their phones and reading rather than listening.

Finally, when the head of public relations asked if there were any more questions, a reporter stood. The woman had a well-deserved reputation as something of a pit bull, but always fair and in search of the truth.

"I have a question for King Benjamin," she called.

He moved closer to the microphones. "Yes?"

"What is your response to the story sent out anonymously a few moments ago?"

Benjamin glanced at the PR gentleman, who clearly had no idea either. "I have not had a chance to look at any press release or recent story. Whatever it is, it did not come from my office."

"I'm sure it didn't," she assured him. "But anonymous sources in the palace claim that you had never met the queen prior to the announcement of your engagement, and the press release was actually sent by a disgruntled former employee in an effort to embarrass the royal family."

The PR official started to say something but was cut off by the reporter. "I would like to hear from the king. I'm sure everyone would."

Benjamin looked through the crowd for a friendly face and found none. He took a step to the microphones. "As I said, I have not seen the report." Time to face the music though. There was no sense in denying it or waiting for someone else to put their own spin on it. "However, there is some truth to it."

The gasps and muttering among assembled reporters grew louder.

"I had met Katrín prior to the announcement, but we were not in a romantic relationship. If you look back at all other communications from my office, you will notice very careful wording so that we - I - never actually lied to the people."

He took a deep breath and gripped the sides of the podium. "When my office became aware of the news, I sent for Katrín. We spent some time together, and I discovered that I quite liked her. She reminded me, in many ways, of my mother, not in her mannerisms, but in her utter devotion to those she loves. The more I learned about Katrín, the more I wanted to know. The decision was made, mutually, to go forward with the wedding and do the rest of our getting to know each other afterward."

Benjamin hesitated for a second. "The men in my family often tell stories about how they knew the moment they met their future wives. It was no different with Katrín." He could finally admit that to himself.

Shouted questions threatened to overwhelm him, but Benjamin stopped them with a raised hand.

"Katrín is a beautiful woman, but beyond that, she is kind and compassionate. Her heart breaks when she sees injustice and wants to right it." He gave a half smile. "And, to be quite frank, she knows how and when to tell me to stick it."

That actually generated a laugh.

"She has been instrumental in what many of you have commented on in recent days." Time for more truth. "After the death of my father, my mother and I both found ourselves rudderless. For her, she was able to find her own way back, but for a young man, barely a teenager when he became king, it was a bit more difficult. As a result, I shut myself off from those closest to me, and from my people. As the years went by, it became easier and easier to do, until what Katrín calls my 'resting grumpy face' became my every day face."

The reporters, and hopefully the country beyond the cameras, waited in silence for his next words. "I love my God, my family, and my country and her people with everything I am. I have never quite known how to convey that to any of them. Katrín is helping me learn how." He pulled out his phone. "These photos will be made available to all of you momentarily." He quickly sent them to the PR office who put them on the screen, beginning with a selfie Katrín took of the two of them not long after they arrived at the Festival.

"My wife and I went to the Festival recently and spent time with some new friends who are now members of my staff." A selfie of the six of them appeared on the screen. Benjamin knew the picture well. He and Katrín looked very much in love, though that wasn't the sole reason he chose it. "They did not know who we were and spoke frankly with us about the reasons why the family isn't nearly as loved as it was when my father lived. With their help, with *Katrín's* help, I want to show all of you that I am the kind of man my father would have been proud of. It's something I have to work toward daily, but I can assure all of you that it is my heart's desire to spend the rest of my life taking care of and loving my God, my wife, my family, and my country and her people, to the best of my ability."

With that he turned and walked back toward the palace, ignoring the shouted questions, and praying it would be enough.

"You could have told me."

Katrín looked up from the desk in the office she'd been given to use. She suspected it wasn't the usual queen's office and that her mother-in-law still occupied that one.

Now the Queen Mother stood in the doorway with an a look Katrín couldn't decipher.

"Pardon?" Should she stand and curtsy? That seemed like the thing to do, but the other woman had come into Katrín's office, not the other way around.

"That the two of you weren't in a relationship when the announcement was made by an anonymous, disgruntled, former employee."

The former queen swept into the office and perched on the edge of one of the chairs.

Katrín just stared at her. "What are you talking about?"

"The story broke during the press conference. A disgruntled former employee managed a press release that looked authentic announcing your engagement. Benjamin told the press that the two of you had met but were not in a relationship at the time. You could have told me."

Katrín managed to control her surprise. "That would be a discussion you should have with your son. He controlled those discussions. I was just along for the ride."

"Oh, I will be having a long talk with my son. I've known for a while that Isaiah had something to do with it, but I thought the announcement was simply premature." Her hands remained folded in her lap and her entire being was the picture of poise. "What I would like to know is why you went along with it."

Katrín wasn't sure how to answer that question. She decided on a version of the truth. "He promised to take care of my family, especially my brother, for the rest of their lives."

The look on the queen's face softened. "I can understand the appeal in that offer." Tears filled her eyes. "My brother also had spina bifida. Not as severe as your brother's - he used arm crutches not a wheelchair - but he was in and out of hospitals his whole life." She smiled sadly. "He passed not long after Alfred and I married. His name was Ben."

Katrín didn't say anything else. She didn't know what she could say that wouldn't end up poorly for herself, Benjamin, or even his mother.

Before either one could say anything else, Benjamin walked in. "Katrín, we need to talk abou..." He stopped when he caught sight of them. "Good morning, Mother."

"I think all three of us need to talk about the press conference." The Queen Mother tilted her cheek to accept the kiss from her son. "Have a seat."

Katrín jumped up. "You can have this one."

Benjamin shook his head. "That's your seat. Or we can go upstairs, which might be a better option."

His mother nodded, then stood. "I agree."

Katrín waited for them to leave the office first, planning to follow in their wake. Instead, once in the outer office, Benjamin let her catch up then rested his hand on the small of her back.

It disconcerted her, the way the warmth spread from the point of contact all the way to her extremities. They walked through the outer doors into the main sitting area leading to the family's quarters. From there, they went into the smaller one and through the doors to Benjamin's quarters.

Their quarters?

If she was staying, did she live here with him?

Had she ever actually committed to staying?

"Did either of you see the press conference?" he asked as they all sat down.

Katrín shook her head as his mother told him she'd seen part of it.

Benjamin clicked the remote causing a screen to come out of the ceiling. After a couple more clicks, Benjamin appeared on it.

She watched as he gave a statement, then a few minutes later took a question.

Knowing what she knew, Katrín could hear the subtle undertones and slightly more than half-truths. He never lied.

She gasped when the pictures from the Festival showed up. At least he'd used ones where they weren't wearing their hats. The rest of his words began to seep in.

"I do wish you would have discussed this with me." His mother stood and gave Benjamin a kiss on the cheek. "But for now, I think the two of you need to discuss where you go from here." She hesitated. "For the record, your father and I were always proud of you. He still would be."

Benjamin shook his head. "I know you believe that, but there's a lot Father wouldn't be proud of. I'm working on it, though."

"I know you are." She squeezed his forearm then glided out of the room.

Then it was just the two of them.

Benjamin clicked the remote and the screen vanished back into the ceiling. "I hope I didn't presume too much in my statement."

Katrín leaned back in the chair. "Even if you did, the plan was always for the country to believe that we were the real deal and that you truly mourned me when I was presumed dead. What you said today doesn't change any of that."

He rested his forearms on his knees. "I meant what I said earlier. I want to spend the rest of my life taking care of and loving you to the best of my ability."

She wanted to believe him. "What exactly does that look like?"

He shrugged. "It looks like you're my wife, and I'm your husband, and we have a real marriage."

It sounded good. Benjamin was saying all the right things. "But I barely know you."

His blue eyes conveyed a vulnerability she'd never seen. "On the contrary. You know me better than anyone. I've never talked with anyone else about being afraid of failing my father, or why I'm insanely claustrophobic, or that I have to sleep with the lights on for days after an incident like the elevator and probably weeks after yesterday." He reached over and rested his hand on her knee. "You're the only one who's ever made me look... what was it you said? Like an actual human, I think you said."

"Any date night with your wife would have had the same effect."

With a shake of his head, he moved his hand. "No. Most of the women I'd looked at as potential marriage partners were nothing but socialites and gold-diggers. They'd have looked the part, but wouldn't have cared one bit about me. Most of them would have been freaking out worse than I was last night." He tilted his head. "About the only exception would probably be Anabelle Gregorson. She married Prince Kensington of San Majoria because she loved him and couldn't stand the idea of being married to me."

There had been other women? "How many other women did you talk marriage with?"

33

Benjamin wasn't sure what he'd said to upset Katrín, but he clearly had. "Other women? There was never anyone else." He'd already told her that more than once.

"How many other women did you discuss marriage with?"

Oh. That. "There was Anabelle. I'm not quite sure why Isaiah thought it was a good match, though her grandfather turned out to be a criminal, so maybe there was something to that. He also talked extensively with the family of the Duchess of Cantor, but as far as I know, there was never any sort of deal struck."

"So the thought of marrying someone you didn't love was always part of your life?"

Benjamin hadn't thought about it like that. "I suppose. I always knew my parents shared something extra special. It was difficult for me to fathom that I could have the same thing. It still is."

Katrín wasn't looking at him and didn't say anything.

"I don't know what it looks like," he told her softly. "I just know I want you in my life. I want to be more like you."

She leaned forward and started to say something, but his

phone buzzed before she could. Benjamin groaned and pulled it out of his pocket. At least it was a text and not a phone call.

"The new team is here to meet with us and the PR staff to go over some of the plans to make the country fall in love with the royal family again."

Katrín bounced out of her chair like it had an ejection seat. "Then we should go."

Benjamin blinked and watched her move off, realizing how rare it was for her to walk away without him when they were going to the same place. He trotted to catch up with her, and she fell in step slightly behind him as he did.

It had never bothered him before. When his mother started doing it not long after his father's death, it bothered him some, but he'd grown used to it over the years.

The longer he'd been married to Katrín, the more it bothered him that she did the same thing, especially since it wasn't a situation like Queen Elizabeth with Prince Philip who towered over her and would block the view of anyone trying to glimpse the monarch.

Before he could decide if he wanted to discuss it with her, they reached the conference room filled with about a dozen people. On one side of the table sat their new friends. Chairs on the other side were filled with members of the public relations team. They didn't look happy about the arrangement.

Benjamin didn't particularly care. He knew the public relations office wasn't entirely to blame for the approval and popularity ratings. In fact, they likely weren't even mostly to blame, but over the years they'd become complacent, just like he had. It was time to shake things up.

"Good afternoon," he said as he walked into the room, and everyone started to rise. "Stay seated." He took his seat at the head of the table then realized there wasn't an obvious seat for Katrín, except the foot - where the presentation would be projected onto a screen. He looked at Marty and his team. "If all of you would move down a seat, my wife needs to be closer to me than is currently possible."

It wasn't a request, and wasn't worded as one. He could have made the palace team move, but he didn't like the optics of Katrín against the new team.

A moment later, they'd all resituated themselves with Katrín at his right side. He turned to the right. "Marty, Harry, Marissa, and Elise, would you show us what you've put together?"

The lights dimmed as the screen lit up. Marty spoke first. "We've put together a comprehensive plan for getting the monarchy back on solid footing with regards to approval rating and popularity. It starts with a cohesive online and social media presence and continues with an increase in personal appearances by the older members of the family at events chosen for their appeal to the public as a whole and in keeping with the family's corporate purpose."

Benjamin frowned. "We are not a corporation."

"Not in the traditional sense, no," Elise answered. "But corporate can also mean a large group or, in this case, an entity even if it's not a company."

He glanced at Katrín. "I'm not sure we have a corporate purpose."

Harry spoke up. "If I may be so bold, sir, you do, even if it's never been spelled out as such." He clicked a button and the slide changed. "In fact, it's the very first thing we need to discuss. We took the liberty of coming up with what we believe is the family's purpose, though we are, of course, open to having it amended as you see fit, sir."

At least two people on the PR side of the table muttered something Benjamin couldn't understand, but he put a stop to it with a glare.

After another click the words "Corporate Purpose" were joined by several more lines.

To advance the well-being of the Eyjanian people as well as use personal and corporate philanthropy, public relations efforts, and personal appearances in an effort to bring public awareness and an increase in funding through other avenues when appropriate to causes the family is passionate about.

Benjamin nodded. "It may need some reworking, but for our purposes today, it will suffice." He'd never thought about articulating what the family's purpose was, but that was a good start.

Relief showed on all four faces. Marissa took over. "With that in mind, the first thing many people will see is the online presence of the family. We recommend cohesive visuals and layouts, while still allowing for personal expression of each family member." She went through a sample website, Facebook page, Twitter, and Instagram.

Elise jumped in. "One thing we'd like to do is make sure each page has the same basic layout. As an outsider looking for information, few things are more frustrating than knowing the information exists and not being able to find it in the same place every time. For instance, Your Majesty..." She clicked a button. "This is your website." After another click an arrow appeared. "This is where a visitor can find your public schedule." Another click showed a picture of Genevieve. "This is the page for Princess Evangeline."

"That's Genevieve," he interrupted.

Elise smiled at him. "I know, but this isn't her website."

Benjamin gave a single nod Elise's direction. She knew her princesses.

Another click and another arrow, nowhere near the one on his page. "This arrow leads to a drop down menu where, after three more clicks, you can find Princess Evangeline's schedule. We recommend working with each family member to create websites that are unique to the individual but standardized in their layout and overall look."

"And have the right pictures?" Benjamin asked with a smirk.

Elise glanced across the table at the fuming head of public relations. "Exactly."

KATRÍN DIDN'T SAY anything as the presentation continued, but she could tell the group of four had impressed Benjamin and infuriated the PR team.

Because they were right about almost everything. The things they got wrong, they didn't get very wrong, and could easily be adjusted.

The presentation ended and the lights came back up. Benjamin spoke to her. "What do you think, Katrín?"

She looked up, shocked that he'd ask in front of the others. "Pardon?"

That made him frown. "What are your thoughts about the presentation?"

Right. "Overall, I think it was excellent. There are a few minor things I'd change, but nothing of great consequence. For instance, I agree that the family should have a unified list of causes they support as a whole, but I think each person, or possibly couple or small subsection, should also have a list of their personal causes."

Her husband appeared to be listening intently. "For instance?"

"The family as a whole may be interested in supporting research into childhood diseases in general, but, for me personally, the Wheels and Walkers to Wings Foundation is something I support in greater measure than the family likely would. In fact, I'm scheduled to attend their annual get-together tomorrow. I attended for many years until I came to work here, and my schedule conflicted."

"What is it?"

"It's the annual party for all of those in Akushla, and Eyjania as a whole, with spina bifida and their families to get together."

He simply nodded, then turned to Harry. "Your thoughts?"

"We agree with the queen," Harry told them. "However, we felt this was a good place to start. Though the family has monetarily supported many organizations over the years, when it comes to personal appearances, we thought it best to start smaller with a list of organizations the family as a whole already supports then branch out later as each individual or smaller subset chooses and vets organizations to support personally."

Benjamin asked several more questions, once again impressing Katrín with his attention to detail and insight. As the meeting wrapped up, he pushed back to stand. Everyone else did as well.

"I think this is a great start." He turned to the head of public relations. "I would like you to work with them to get the information they need to get the final, official versions put together. I want to see all of it before it's approved and goes live."

The head of PR bowed slightly. "Of course, sir." He clearly didn't relish following the instructions, but didn't dare do otherwise.

Benjamin thanked his newest employees for their time, then turned to leave. Katrín, unsure of what she was actually supposed to do, followed in his wake. After rounding a couple of corners, he slowed to allow her to catch up.

"What did you really think?" he asked as he turned again, this time toward his office.

Katrín shrugged. "Just what I said. They did a good job. And Elise was right. It's very annoying when you're looking for the same information on related websites and it's all in different places."

"I can't say that I've ever noticed, but I don't do much searching online." He pushed open the door to his office, and she followed him in. "What is this Wheels and Wings thing?"

"Wheels and Walkers to Wings," she corrected him. "Many people with spina bifida can't walk unassisted, and many, including my brother, can't walk at all so use wheelchairs exclusively. Your Uncle Ben used arm crutches."

Uncle Ben? His mother's brother? She hadn't talked about him in a very long time. He had spina bifida?

"Wings refers to death," Katrín went on. "Some will live a long, full life, but many won't." She took a seat across his desk from him. "They help with acquiring assistive devices as well as end of life expenses when the time comes, especially for families of children."

Benjamin leaned back in his chair. "I can see why this particular cause is important to you."

She took a deep breath. "Would you like to come?"

He blinked a couple of times. "You want me to?"

"I think you'd enjoy yourself." And it would be good for him to see some of the other side of things.

"When is it?"

"Tomorrow night."

He flipped the page on his calendar. "Looks like I'm free. I would love to join you." A slow smile crossed his face. "Perhaps we can have dinner here first?"

Katrín felt her face color. "I would like that, but they do serve dinner."

His smile widened to a full-fledged grin. "It's a date."

The phone on his desk rang, preventing her from responding. Benjamin glanced at the display. "I need to take this privately. I'll talk to you later?"

With a nod, Katrín left his office and returned to her suite. Rosalie would be there in a few minutes to go over her wardrobe for the trip to Islas del Sargasso the next week. Before the Queen Mother arrived earlier, Katrín had learned she'd be attending a summit for children's causes among the four countries.

Alone.

Well, not alone, but the only member of the royal family in attendance.

Rosalie spent nearly an hour going over her options. Katrín still wasn't completely satisfied, feeling that much of her wardrobe would still be better suited for the Queen Mother, but it was improving.

"You'll be staying with Princess Astrid and Prince Jordan. You were supposed to stay with Prince Kensington and his wife, Princess Anabelle, who is Eyjanian by birth," Rosalie told her.

"Even though it's in Islas del Sargasso?"

"Yes. I'm not sure who made the arrangements, but that is what I've been told. Prince Kensington and Princess Annabelle decided not to attend given the recent birth of their son."

Wasn't Princess Anabelle the one Benjamin had sort of proposed to? She had a baby?

Rosalie left without answering the silent questions, but Katrín had nowhere else she needed to be. After finding some food in the kitchenette, she snuggled into a chair with her ereader and phone. A quick search showed that Princess Annabelle gave birth to a boy named Prince Jacob Clarence Edward a couple months earlier. picked a book at random. *Short Straw Bride* by Karen Witemeyer took place in Texas and was the story of a marriage of convenience, something Katrín felt hit a little too close to home.

Without any word from Benjamin, she decided to get ready for bed. Slipping under the covers, she pulled them close around her and willed herself to sleep.

34

Benjamin wasn't sure where Katrín had gone to and hadn't seen her since his phone rang in his office hours earlier. She didn't answer his calls, though he knew she hadn't left the premises. Maybe she'd just gone to bed early. It had been a long couple of days, and if she was half as weary as Benjamin, she'd succumbed a while earlier.

A half-smile crossed his face as he entered his quarters. He found the idea of slipping into his bed next to her quite appealing.

But first he needed food and maybe a workout. The kitchen held some easy to prepare meals for nights like this when he needed something quick and simple.

No. Workout first. He didn't do nearly as much as normal, but his mind and body weren't capable of a full workout. He grabbed something light from the kitchen, using the passages to avoid his bedroom so he wouldn't disturb his, presumably sleeping, wife.

Nearly ninety minutes after first arriving in his quarters, he used the passages again to get to his bathroom. The warm water of the shower soothed him to the point he didn't want to get out, but eventually he did. Dressed in a pair of pajama pants, he crawled into what he guessed would be his side of the bed from then on.

When he reached for Katrín, though, Benjamin found the other side empty. He wanted to go find her, but found it too difficult to leave when his mind and body both said it was time for sleep.

Despite his exhaustion, sleep came only in fits and spurts, punctuated by nightmares of being trapped and emerging to find a post-apocalyptic world void of his family, his few friends, and his wife.

By 4:30 he was wide awake and sitting in one of the chairs staring out the window looking over the city. Why hadn't Katrín slept in here with him? Had he not made it clear that was his preference? Or did she not feel the same way?

Would he, if it weren't for the anticipation of nightmares?

Finally, he sent for breakfast, though he wasn't sure he'd eat much of it. By quarter to seven, he was in his office, looking over paperwork for a meeting with the Prime Minister later in the morning.

A little after eight, his mother breezed through the door connecting his office to hers.

"It's past time, darling."

He looked up to see her actually slouch in one of the chairs across from him. "Time for what?"

"That I move out of that fussy office and into one more suited for the Dowager Queen. Your wife needs that office."

"I doubt Katrín wants it."

His mother dismissed the thought. "No matter. It's already been set in motion. Did I tell you I hired someone to cover for Clari while she's on leave?"

Benjamin didn't believe that for a minute. "You hired someone?"

"Fine. My chief of staff hired someone." She shrugged and sat up, once more resembling the aristocrat he'd always known. "Katrín does not need to concern herself with it."

"I'll make sure she knows."

His mother leaned forward and rested her arms on his desk. "You didn't sleep well."

It wasn't a question, but when the former queen wanted an answer, you gave it anyway - even if you were the king. "No. I didn't."

"Is that why Katrín's not down yet? You kept her awake with your tossing and turning?"

His chair nearly tipped over as he leaned all the way back. "I didn't keep her up. She slept in the consort's quarters last night. At least, I presume that's where she was."

Her frown deepened. "I know you two weren't quite ready for marriage, but I thought things were better."

"They were. They *are*, at least as far as I know. I avoided my bedroom so I wouldn't bother her when I returned to my quarters last night. By the time I went to bed, I was exhausted. When I realized she wasn't there, I didn't have the energy to look for her."

She pointed at him, something his mother rarely did. "You make the energy. I know there are two quarters for a reason, but the reality is you need to live with your wife. Even if you choose to sleep apart from time to time, or even often, it needs to be a choice you two make together. I slept in one of the other rooms when all of you were little, because your father worked so much harder than I did, and I refused to let nannies do the overnight shifts most of the time. I could get up with you, do all the things that need doing in the middle of the night, and go back to sleep without ever bothering your father. When he was sick, he snored like a freight train, so I would sleep in another room. But not just because."

His mother rose from her seat. "Talk to her, Benji. She's exactly what you need, and that means the two of you need to act married."

With that she left the office as suddenly as she came.

Benjamin reached for his personal cell phone and called Katrín. She didn't answer, but did text a moment later to say she was in a meeting. His brows pulled together as he checked her calendar for the day.

No meeting scheduled.

He had an hour before the Prime Minister arrived. Deciding to use that time to find Katrín and see if they could get some resolution, he left his office and asked Chamberlain if he knew where she was.

Chamberlain knew without looking that she was in the gardens, at the cottage her mother and brother would be moving into in a matter of days.

It wouldn't take him long to get there, so he hurried, as much as a king ever does when it's not an emergency, toward the outer door.

Time to find his wife and see if she would be honest with him about where they stood.

Katrín looked up from the blueprints laid out on the table. "Hi." She curtsied, sort of. More of a barely-there dip of her hips to pretend she was following protocol. Besides, no one in the cottage should know she hadn't seen him yet today.

"Hello." Benjamin smiled at her, but it didn't reach his eyes.

When had she gotten to know him well enough to know his smile was even capable of reaching his eyes? Everyone she'd ever known thought he was perpetually grumpy.

She turned back to the contractor who was overseeing the renovations and making sure as much of the house as possible was accessible to her brother. After pointing out one more thing, Katrín turned and walked toward Benjamin.

He offered her his arm, but she clasped her hands in front of her as they walked down the steps.

"I missed you last night," he said quietly.

"You missed me or you had nightmares and think you wouldn't have if I'd been there?" She tried to make it sound like an actual question without the hints of snark she wanted to inject it with.

He hesitated, and she gave him credit for at least pretending to think it over. "Both, if I'm being honest. I like having you there with me, and not just because the nightmares seemed less intense."

"Fair enough."

"There's something else you need to know. I figured that, given your response to your quarters being moved, I'd let you know about this one ahead of time."

She stopped and tried to control the anger building. "Are you moving all of my things into your quarters?"

He shook his head. "I *could* have them moved, but I wouldn't do it myself anyway. Even if I planned to, I wouldn't without discussing it with you first. This is something my mother put into motion. She's leaving the queen's office and having your office moved there. Her orders."

"Understood."

"You don't mind?"

"It doesn't matter if I mind." At least he'd told her ahead of time so she wouldn't be arrested.

"No," he said slowly as they started up the stairs to the palace itself. "But I would like for you to be comfortable with it."

"I'll be fine." Katrín knew she had to be, at least for a while longer, but this whole thing had gotten way too real in the last couple of weeks. She took a deep breath as he opened the door for her. Why didn't this side have a doorman? Because it only went to the garden? "We'll need to leave about six tonight, unless you want to be one of the first ones there."

"Why would we want to arrive early? Usually I get somewhere as the event begins."

Of course he did. "Because this event isn't about you. It's about the kids, mostly, but also the adults with spina bifida. If we get there early, we can wait inside and greet everyone as they arrive. They would think that's pretty awesome to have the king waiting for them."

She glanced up to see a thoughtful look on his face. "What time would we need to be there?"

"Probably 5:30 to be safe. Doors open at 5:45 and the event officially kicks off at 6:30." Would he go for it?

"Let me check my schedule. I'm not sure I can be gone that early." He looked at his watch. "I have a meeting in ten minutes, but wanted to talk to you first, at least briefly."

Katrín gave him a tight smile. "Go on. I have some things I need to do, too. Let me know about later."

He nodded as he walked backward toward his office. "I'll have Chamberlain let your assistant know." With a small wave, he walked away.

Her assistant? She had one? It had been mentioned before but Rosalie was the closest she'd come. Or did he mean Elise?

The rest of the day was spent learning more queen-ish things. Elise let her know Benjamin expected to be able to leave in time to be the first ones there.

Katrín walked out of the dressing room, ready to go, though she knew Benjamin wouldn't be for another ten or fifteen minutes.

The piano caught her eye. It had been ages since she played, even with the gorgeous instrument available to her whenever she wanted.

Sitting on the bench, she tucked one foot slightly back under it and reached the other toward the petals as she lifted the lid.

First one note, then another, followed by a third. She deliberately chose a slow song that wouldn't require her to be too warmed up or well-practiced. When she finished, another song came to her. She played a hymn her grandmother loved, followed by Allen's favorite.

Softly and tenderly Jesus is calling
Calling for you and for me
See on the portals He's waiting and watching
Watching for you and for me

She played the whole thing, every verse, singing softly each time she reached the refrain.

Come home, come ho-ome
Ye who are weary come ho-o-ome
Earnestly, tenderly, Jesus is calling
Calling "oh, sinner, come home."

"That's gorgeous."

Startled, Katrín clanged on the keys and turned to see Benjamin watching her from the doorway. "You scared me."

He pushed off and walked toward her. "I didn't mean to. I just wanted to listen for a few minutes. I had no idea you had such a lovely singing voice, too."

"It's okay. Allen's is better. He may sing something tonight."

Benjamin held out a hand to help her up. "Then I look forward to hearing him."

She took his hand and stood. "Are you ready?"

He tucked her hand into his elbow. "I am. I'm looking forward to this."

"Me, too." She always did. This year, conflicting emotions filled her. The event itself excited her but being the king's wife meant she'd be treated differently, even if he wasn't coming with her or planning to greet every guest.

In less than twenty minutes, they pulled up outside a decent hotel, but likely one Benjamin had never been to before. It was a nice venue, but not royalty nice.

A member of the security team opened the car door for them. Benjamin climbed out then turned to help her. Only a few members of the media waited. They both smiled and waved. Benjamin made a comment about how the night wasn't about him, but about the guests on their way.

Katrín took a deep breath as the doors slid open in front of them. Whatever happened, this was sure to be a night to remember.

35

Had he ever been to an event so full of happy people? Benjamin knew he probably had, but he didn't remember. About half of those who entered needed some sort of mobility aid - either forearm crutches or wheelchairs. The other half were parents or guests.

He and Katrín stood near the entrance to the ballroom where the event was being held, greeting each person as they walked in. Usually, he had an aide of some kind standing next to him feeding him names, but not this time. Everyone did wear name tags, which helped immensely.

Katrín didn't know everyone who walked through the door, but she did know quite a few of them. Many of them greeted her with a big smile and hug, then saw him, remembered who she'd married, and things got awkward as they'd try to bow or curtsy. Maybe coming early wasn't the best idea after all.

He greeted everyone who walked by, but his greetings were stiff and uncomfortable, nothing like he'd seen members of other royal families do, including his own family, especially Genevieve. Maybe it was something that came with practice.

Finally, it seemed that the last guest had arrived.

"If you'd come with me, sir." One of the organizers, but not the main one, spoke quietly as someone else went to the front to start the event.

Benjamin found himself seated in the back, a most unusual circumstance he didn't quite know what to make of.

"This isn't about you," Katrín reminded him quietly.

"I know."

"I don't think you do."

They were the only ones seated at the table for eight, though he thought Katrín's mother and brother were supposed to have joined them, but they were seated on the other side of the room with friends. "I completely understand this isn't about me," he reiterated. "I just don't think I've ever sat in the back of a dinner and it's a bit disconcerting, that's all."

"Suck it up and deal."

A waiter set a plate in front of him then one in front of Katrín. Benjamin decided not to say anything else. She wouldn't sympathize with him, so better to keep it to himself.

Dinner was fine, but nothing to brag about. He ate slowly, knowing that usually when he finished, everyone else had to be done as well.

"Don't be pretentious." Katrín's quiet voice held hints of exasperation. "The food is fine, and no one cares when you finish tonight."

Benjamin took another bite but didn't say anything. He knew this event was important to Katrín, but at the moment everything just seemed... off, including his relationship with his wife. "What happens after dinner?" Seemed like a safe enough question.

"There will be some awards and a memorial for those who've passed in the last year. Then we'll all head into the next room to mingle for a while."

He nodded and took another bite then pushed his plate back a bit. Everyone else seemed to be having a great time talking with each other. Katrín seemed quiet, though he wasn't sure why. Because it was only the two of them?

After a little while the awards started. They seemed to be mostly in fun - like most blinged out forearm crutches at a non-formal event. Pictures had apparently been submitted and votes taken online.

Benjamin found himself smiling and clapping along.

"See? You can enjoy yourself." Katrín gave him a genuine smile.

He looped his arm around the back of her chair. "I know I can, and I am."

"Next up," the MC spoke into the microphone. "...most likely to run over a VIP's foot."

Everyone laughed.

"Given his new brother-in-law, there's only one person this award could go to."

Benjamin was a bit uncomfortable when everyone turned to look at him.

"Allen Jønsson!"

Cheers filled the room as Allen maneuvered his wheelchair onto the stage and took the statue from a red haired woman wearing a sequined dress. The announcer held the microphone for him.

"I always wanted to win one of these awards. I just thought it would be for the 50-meter wheel."

Laughter filled the room as Benjamin smiled.

"In all seriousness, I suppose I can admit, just to this group of friends, that I told my sister I'd run her husband over if he didn't treat her right. But in that house, you can't turn around without rolling over the toes of someone important. Fortunately, I can blame faulty wiring in my chair."

As everyone laughed some more, he waved and went back to his table.

The next fifteen minutes were filled with awards for graduates, musicians, and others who had achieved something special in the last year. As one of them played her flute, he found himself wishing he could play an instrument. Maybe Thor had been right about learning something from Allen.

As they were wrapping up, one of Benjamin's bodyguards for the evening leaned in close. "I need you to come with me, sir."

Benjamin moved back from the table and reached for Katrín.

"She can stay, sir."

Benjamin nodded and followed the guard out of the building. Chamberlain waited for him, his face grim.

"What is it?"

"A story has been leaked to the press. You need to come with me."

"Katrín doesn't need to come, too?" Surely Chamberlain wouldn't leave her behind to face whatever it was on her own.

Chamberlain hesitated in a way that concerned Benjamin but went on before the king could say anything. "She'll be taken care of by another team."

A sense of foreboding swept over Benjamin.

Whatever it was, it wasn't good.

WHERE WAS HE GOING? Katrín didn't know, but knew when security said to go, he had no choice. It couldn't be too serious, not if she was being left behind. Likely just something that needed his attention.

But it left her completely alone at the table in the back.

Her mother and Allen had planned to join them, but when Allen's childhood best friend had unexpectedly shown up with too many people in tow to fit at the table, she'd urged them to sit elsewhere. Both of them would appreciate catching up with the other family.

A few minutes after Benjamin left, Katrín slipped out of the ballroom and into the reception room. She wanted to greet everyone again as they came in. Maybe without Benjamin at her side, everyone wouldn't be so awkward. Many of them she'd known since they started coming when Allen was little.

Her suspicion was right. Without Benjamin, everyone was a little more relaxed. The hugs lasted a little longer, the talk was a little more animated. Maybe if they came again every year, and got involved on a more regular basis, some of the celebrity shock would wear off. Maybe he'd continue even after she left. The community would welcome him with open arms as a grieving widower.

This group knew all too much about loss.

She should tell him it was one condition of upholding her end of the bargain.

Except he wanted to adjust that bargain.

He wanted her to stay.

Did he really mean it?

She didn't delve too far into the alternatives.

After everyone entered, Katrín circulated through the group, just as she normally would have, though with far more sneaky and not-so-sneaky phone pictures taken of her, along with selfies galore.

Nearly an hour after the mingling started, her bodyguard, a man she'd never met before leaving the palace, stood at her side. "It's time to leave, Your Majesty."

Katrín nodded. "Let me say goodbye to my family."

"I'm afraid not. My orders are for you to leave quickly and quietly."

She nodded and walked with him to the door. In fifteen minutes, the car glided to a stop underneath the functional, but not rebuilt, portico.

Inside, the few people she passed averted their eyes and hurried away from her. What was going on?

When she reached the family's private portion of the palace, the guard standing there was the same one who had been there the day she'd been detained.

"You're to go straight to the king's office, ma'am."

Katrín started past him. "I'll go down in a minute. I'd like to change first."

He blocked her path. "My apologies, ma'am, but my instructions are for you to go straight to the king's office."

She crossed her arms and narrowed her gaze. "Why didn't they tell me before I got out of the car? I would have been there by now."

"I have no idea, ma'am, but I am not to let you pass until I have word that you've talked to the king." Though his expression remained impassive, she knew he meant what he said.

"Very well."

Spinning on her heel, she made her way to Benjamin's office. Thor waited in front of the door, looking very security guard-ish. He didn't smile, but just nodded politely as he opened the door, taking a spot on the inside as the door closed.

Odd.

Katrín walked into the office to find Benjamin with both arms braced on the conference table as he read something on the tablet that lay there.

"Have a seat."

His tone took her aback. It sounded grim and authoritative, asserting his authority as the king in a way she'd never quite heard from him.

Arguing was out of the question.

She perched on the edge of one of the wingback chairs across from his desk and watched as he and Chamberlain discussed whatever it was. They were intense, but quiet, and only the occasional sentence carried.

"And there's nothing we can do to stop them from running with it, even if we categorically deny the allegations?" Benjamin asked Chamberlain.

"We don't even know if we can deny them, but no," Chamberlain told him.

Benjamin's sigh carried as he turned. His face had basically the same expression as the first guard's and Thor's. He sat in his desk chair, with Chamberlain standing behind him.

Katrín felt like she'd been called into the headmaster's office.

He leaned back in his chair and stared at her, but didn't say anything.

"What?" she finally asked. "What's going on? What news story are you worried about, and what does it have to do with me?"

Benjamin stared for another minute before speaking. If he wanted to make her uncomfortable, to make her squirm, it was working. Finally, he said, "Your indenture."

The one that still hadn't actually been paid off. "What about it?"

"You took over paying your mother's fine, correct?"

He already knew that. "Yes."

"She was accused of attempting to steal..." He looked at a paper on his desk. "...a priceless hand mirror. She mounted no defense whatsoever. Based on my aunt's recommendation, I approved a ten percent wage garnishment and perpetual service until the fine was paid. A few years later, I approved you taking over the payments, though I don't recall actually doing it."

Katrín's fingers twisted together. "Yes."

"Why?"

"Why what?"

"Why did you take over the payments for your mother?"

Was he going to make her explain everything? "You know this. My brother was having more severe medical issues than normal, and my mother needed more flexibility in her job."

He shook his head. "That's the reason you both gave everyone, but I want the truth. I need to know."

Katrín's gaze shifted to Chamberlain. "Does he?"

"Yes." The steely glint in Benjamin's eyes told her he wouldn't brook no arguments.

"Fine." She looked down, staring at her hands until Benjamin cleared his throat in warning. "The reason my mother didn't defend herself is the same reason why I took over the indenture as soon as I could and used my brother's health as my excuse."

Going on took too much courage, something she found herself lacking at the moment.

"Katrín." The sharply spoken rebuke did its job.

Tears swam in her eyes. "My mother wasn't trying to steal the mirror. She was bringing it back." Her heart broke as she spoke. "I stole it."

36

Benjamin didn't let his surprise show on his face. Instead, he sat and waited for her to go on.

He could see the tears streaking down her cheeks, but she made no move to wipe them away.

"Allen needed surgery and a new bed, a specific kind of hospital type bed that would enable my mother and Nína to help him in and out of it much easier. Me too when I was a little bigger. It wasn't cheap. It's the same one as the one my mother sent information about to Chamberlain last week."

Torn between anger and feeling sorry for the girl she'd been, Benjamin decided to keep waiting for the rest of the story.

"I was here with my class for a tour, and my mother took the day off to go with us. When everyone else left, I stayed with her, and she took me to the kitchen and a couple other places that weren't on the official tour. Someone gave her permission to take me though."

He watched as she finally swiped at her cheeks, but still said nothing.

"When she wasn't looking, I took the mirror and put it in my backpack. I thought I could sell it and get the money we needed. When we got home, she found it. I never heard her yell like that before or after. She was *furious*. The next day, she planned to tell her boss what happened, but she was caught with it before she could."

Katrín finally looked up at him, anguish in her eyes and written all over her face. "She didn't say anything because she refused to lie to you, but she also refused to throw me under the bus. I knew her job changed after that, but I didn't understand about paying off the fine until I was sixteen. I used Allen's medical situation to convince her to let me take her spot. My terms were much more stringent than hers, but I don't know why. I don't get time off. My hours are more intense. I have a minimum of twenty-five percent withheld from my earnings. It does mean it would get paid off that much sooner than my mother would have."

Benjamin wasn't quite sure what he should say to her or what he was expected to do. Finally, he nodded. "Very well. Thor will see you are allowed into your quarters."

"Will you tell me what's going on?"

He shook his head. "If I need anything further from you, I'll let you know."

Thor held the door for her as she left, then sent a text. He turned to look at Benjamin, his face as unreadable as Benjamin hoped his had been.

"Permission to speak freely, sir?"

Quite a question given the moment Benjamin had seen between Thor and the former queen. He gave a single nod.

"You, sir, are a moron."

That made Benjamin blink. He glanced up at Chamberlain who seemed to purposely be looking elsewhere, and trying to contain a smirk.

Benjamin waved a hand toward Thor. "Please, elaborate."

"I know you and your wife didn't start a relationship under the best circumstances, but I believed you had begun to genuinely care for her."

Benjamin gave another single nod.

"You knew, or at least suspected, from the beginning there was a deeper reason behind taking over the payments from her mother. So when she sat here and bared her soul to you, you might have considered a different response than sending her to her room."

"I didn't send her to her room."

Thor simply raised a single eyebrow at him.

Benjamin sighed. "I suppose the implication was there."

"What exactly is the news story and when is it expected to break?"

He leaned forward and picked up a pen, more as something to fiddle with than use. "The essentials are correct. The item taken is not. The dates are not. The other reason for taking over when she did hasn't been mentioned to my knowledge. But the gist appears to be accurate."

"Then how do you protect your wife?"

"Can I? Without lying to my people? They are my first responsibility," he pointed out.

"Are they?" Thor bowed and turned to leave.

"Stop." Benjamin waited for him to turn around. "What's that mean?"

"Just that. In certain circumstances, your people must come before your family, even your wife. In others, you are, sir, first and foremost a husband and, someday, a father. You will have to find a way to reconcile those two things when they conflict. Remember the night this all started?"

When did all of this start? It seemed an eternity. "The Mevendian Independence celebration?"

"You confronted your uncle, rightfully so, but what else happened that night?"

Benjamin searched his memory. "Princess Margaret collapsed. I carried her to their room and called my physician."

"Why did she collapse? It was all over the news until your wedding announcement pushed it off the front page."

He shook his head. "I don't remember." A half-truth at best.

Thor crossed his arms over his chest, looking as intimidating as the actor who played the character did in the movies. "She pushed herself to the point of utter exhaustion and collapsed. I think it might have happened a bit sooner because she was pregnant, but I believe it would have happened eventually anyway. Where are they now?"

He knew this. "The family home in the States." Near Darius and Esther, though Benjamin didn't think his brother knew that.

"Why?"

That he knew. Even without having discussed it. "Because William decided protecting his family, specifically his wife, meant more than continuing to work here on Mevendia's behalf."

"Good guess. I did talk with him before they left. He practically flogged himself for not realizing what a toll their lifestyle was taking on his wife. They're going to have to put together a plan that will allow her the rest she *needs*, even once he eventually becomes king. You, sir, need to find a way to take care of and protect your wife, while meeting the needs of your people. I don't know what that looks like at the moment, but you need to figure it out."

Benjamin nodded and Thor took that as a sign he was dismissed. "Your thoughts, Chamberlain?"

"I believe Thor covered it quite thoroughly. I'll leave you to your ponderings."

Once alone, Benjamin stood and looked out the windows at Akushla. Neither of them knew of his deal with Katrín. Maybe the time had already come for her to disappear, perhaps even cutting this story off all together. If she was gone, this story wouldn't matter.

Deep inside, he knew that wasn't what he wanted. He needed to find a way to make her want to stay, to face this together, to become the family he'd always craved.

But how?

WOULD Benjamin come looking for her?

Katrín debating sneaking into his quarters and waiting for him there, but that seemed too desperate. Instead, she sat on the bench of the piano and stared at the keys, unable to bring herself to play.

When he didn't come, didn't call, didn't text, Katrín finally let herself curl up on the big bed in the consort's bedroom. Once there, she let the tears fall again, one after another until the steady stream wet the pillow underneath. The whole thing was damp long before she fell asleep.

Waking to sunlight streaming in the windows didn't help the headache that came from the crying jag.

Katrín sat up and looked around, hoping against hope she'd find Benjamin asleep on the other side of the bed, all the while knowing he wasn't there.

Instead of getting dressed for whatever she was supposed to have going on, Katrín found her tablet and opened the browser. She didn't mean to go looking for stories about herself, but one popped up in the news feed of the home page.

The Indentured Queen the headline read. The story, currently unconfirmed by the palace, was essentially true, though a few of the minor details were wrong.

At least she knew why Benjamin wanted to know the truth about the incident.

She went to the home screen and pulled up his schedule. He would be out of the palace most of the day, the beginnings of the rebuilding of his reputation with the populace as a whole. The press would be crawling all over the appearances, shouting question after question.

Should she watch one of the live feeds? Surely there would be one. See what he was saying for herself.

That would just be inviting trouble, wouldn't it? She didn't need to see him distancing himself from her to know he would be.

Her phone buzzed. Security. With a sigh she answered. "Hello?" Was this where they'd kick her out?

"Your mother is here to see you, ma'am."

Katrín would rather be exiled than face her mother at the moment. "Send her to my quarters. I'll meet her in my sitting room in a few minutes."

There was no way to hide the remnants of the crying jag the night before, but she had to try. Quickly, she threw on a pair of jeans and old sweatshirt. After splashing water on her face, she decided it wouldn't get any better.

Her mother waited in the sitting room. When she turned around, Katrín could see she'd spent time crying as well.

"How are you, sweetie?" Her mother reached for her, and Katrín let herself be enveloped in her mother's embrace.

"I don't know how I am."

"I never told anyone." Her mother held on tighter.

Katrín laid her head against her mother's shoulder. "I know. I never told anyone until I told Benjamin, Chamberlain, and Thor last night. They already knew the story was coming out and wanted the details."

After a final squeeze, they sat down on one of the settees. "What was Benjamin's reaction?" The gentle question cut like a knife, though that couldn't have been the intention.

"Nothing, really. Just sort of stared at me then I was dismissed."

"When I saw the announcement about your wedding, I was afraid something like this would happen."

"I'm sorry I couldn't tell you." She leaned against her mother, the side of her head resting against her mother's shoulder.

"I know your time here was far different than mine, even after the incident. You didn't talk about it much in your letters, but the fact that you only wrote letters and we never saw you told me plenty."

"It wasn't awful." It could have been worse. "But no, it wasn't quite like the terms you had to pay off the fine. I would have been done much faster."

"Is it officially paid off or just sort of set aside?"

Katrín closed her eyes. "As far as I know, it's just sort of being ignored. Benjamin hasn't paid it off or forgiven it, and I don't have access to that kind of money."

"Oh, sweetie."

They sat there for several more minutes when Katrín's phone buzzed again. "I've got some things to do before lunch." She stood. "When are you and Allen moving?"

"Next week, if all goes according to plan. They said it could be a little longer."

Good. "I'll be out of town for a week or so. By the time I get back you should be settled." They walked to the door, and Katrín gave her mother one more hug, a long one where she didn't want to let go. Ever.

Soon enough, she was alone. Rather than go to the office next to Benjamin's, Katrín set up her laptop in the room she usually occupied. Sleeping in the consort's room had been a little too weird, and she had no plans to do it again.

The browser window automatically refreshed when she woke up the computer.

King Benjamin Disavows Knowledge of Queen's Theft

Against her better judgment, she skimmed the article. The video had automatically started playing, and Benjamin's voice came out of the speaker.

"No comment."

"Did you know about Katrín's stealing before you proposed?" one reporter asked.

"No comment."

"Is she still going to Islas del Sargasso on behalf of the crown?"

"Yes. Katrín's departure has been moved up to this evening."

That was news to her, but welcome news.

"When will she return?"

"I'm not certain of her return date at this time."

Something in the way he said it made Katrín wonder. Had he changed his mind about wanting her to stay permanently? And this was his way of letting her know?

Rosalie came in to finalize her clothing choices. Elise joined them for most of the afternoon, but the whole thing was strained and uncomfortable.

Shortly before dinnertime, Rosalie declared her job finished for the time being and left Katrín and Elise alone.

"I'm not going to ask if it's true," Elise told her as she closed her laptop. "But, I suspect if it wasn't, the palace would have issued a vigorous denial already. And if it is, I can only guess there was a very good reason."

"There would have been."

"Your flight leaves in about two hours. Rosalie and I will meet you down there in a couple days, before your first official engagement."

"Thank you."

Elise left and Katrín spent over an hour playing the piano in her room. One song after another, though she chose something else each time her fingers itched to play *King Alfred's Overture*. Too many memories with that one.

Twenty minutes before her car was set to leave, she changed clothes and put her hair up in a ponytail and applied a smattering of makeup - just enough that if anyone took her picture she wouldn't look too blotchy.

With just a few minutes left, she stood next to the piano. After running her fingers softly over the keys one more time, she closed the lid

Before she could change her mind, she slipped the engagement ring off her finger, laid it on the closed piano lid, turned, and walked away.

37

"What on earth have you done?"

Benjamin turned from where he stared out the window to see his mother giving him the look he'd hated as a child. "What are you talking about?"

"Where is your wife?"

He glanced at the clock. "On her way to the airport for her trip to Islas del Sargasso." Maybe. He wasn't certain what time she was actually leaving.

"Without you?"

"I was never planning to go."

"A major story just broke about your *wife*. Have you even talked to her since?"

"She stole from the palace."

"Over a decade ago! She was a child trying to help her little brother get medical care and equipment he needed!" She pointed a finger at him and poked his chest. "You never wanted for anything. You never wondered what it would be like to not have enough or how to provide something. When you wanted to do something nice for her, what did you do?"

He shrugged. "Had Chamberlain find a piano for her."

"How much did it cost?"

I've looked at these online before. They cost something like two hundred thousand US dollars. "A lot."

"And you didn't think twice about it, did you?"

He started to understand. "I didn't even ask how much it would cost."

"If a member of your family needed something that badly, and you had no access to funds, what would you do?"

Benjamin felt the conviction his mother intended for him. "Anything I could, I suppose."

"And exactly what did you tell the press today when they asked you about it?" The way she arched an eyebrow at him said he'd done something wrong.

"No comment."

"What should you have said?"

So she was on the same side as Thor. Somehow, that didn't surprise him for more than one reason. "I couldn't lie about it." He turned and walked back toward the window, running a hand over his beard. "How could I defend her without lying to the entire country?"

"You don't. You set up an interview with your wife and a trusted reporter, and explain everything. Katrín explains why she did what she did, how her mother took the blame rather than let it ruin Katrín's life, then Katrín took over as soon she was old enough, because she wanted to right the wrong as much as she could. You tell the whole story, and let the people decide for themselves."

He didn't reply.

"You're doing your best to be a good king, Benjamin." Her voice was softer. "But to be a good leader, you have to be a good servant. You have to stand up for those below you, including your wife. You have to serve them, even when it doesn't seem to be in your own best interests." She rested a hand on his shoulder. "I'll be praying for both of you to find your way back to each other."

Benjamin watched her in the mirrored surface of the window as she walked out of the office. What would his father do? What would King Alfred the First do? Both of them would be far better at this than he was.

With a sigh he walked out of his office and found himself wandering around the palace, until he came to a stop in a familiar location.

Benjamin found himself standing in front of that blasted dagger belonging to King Alfred.

Not worthy. Not enough. King, but not servant.

What did that even mean?

A vision of Christ washing the feet of his disciples flashed before him. To be a true leader, one needed to be willing to serve, to put others before oneself. To look out for those under one's command.

I get two half-days off a month.

How many full days?

None.

And yet he had never bothered to follow-up. To make certain all of the members of his staff, even those working in the industrial kitchen, were given adequate time off. Working off a debt to the royal family shouldn't be a virtual prison sentence.

Benjamin couldn't go back and change the past, but he could make sure things were better going forward. He spun on his heel, heading for his office to begin the memo that would make sure no one else worked themselves the way Katrín had.

Katrín.

His wife.

The queen of his country.

The way she continued to work, first in the kitchen, then for his family and their reputation. She could be annoying, frustrating, infuriating even when she decided she wasn't going to just take whatever he dished out, but he couldn't say that she wasn't a hard worker. That she wasn't determined. That she was just out to get an easy road in life because she'd lucked into a way to marry the king.

He started to turn left, to go to his office, but right drew him instead. The palace chapel, a small room filled with stained glass windows on three sides, was part of the original building. His steps slowed as he entered, reverent. Though there hadn't been a member of the clergy on staff in the building in over a century, the place was holy, consecrated as it had been for so many centuries.

At the front, he fell to his knees, like most kings down through the centuries had done.

Conviction swept over him, followed by resolve.

He needed forgiveness, not just from his Maker, but from the flesh and blood people surrounding him.

From his wife.

For not making sure the members of his household staff were adequately taken care of.

For not publicly taking his brother's side when their marriage license went missing.

For so many things.

He sought forgiveness and asked for strength to do what he needed to do. When Benjamin rose, he felt better than he had in ages, if ever.

Finding out where Katrín was would be easy. All he needed to do was ask Thor, but Benjamin wanted to find her himself.

He trotted up the stairs as quickly as he could and went straight into the consort's quarters. "Katrín?" But as soon as the door opened, he knew she was gone.

The sitting room was dark with only the light streaming in through the windows to guide him. Just to be sure, he went toward the consort's bedroom.

She wasn't there.

But as he turned a glint caught his eye.

There.

On the closed lid of the gift he'd sent someone else to obtain on his behalf, with little thought or attention of his own.

The ring she'd slid on her own finger.

Snatching it up, he pulled his phone out of his pocket and started making calls.

Time to find his wife and make things right.

KATRÍN no longer cared about keeping the tears at bay. Technically, she was still queen, and she'd learned staff would leave her alone if she gave off an unapproachable vibe.

Thanks to Benjamin sending her out of the country sooner than expected, she had an escape route. Not the one she'd planned, but one that would work.

Benjamin would be more believable as a grieving husband if he had no idea where she had gone. The plane would land in Islas del Sargasso, and Katrín would simply disappear. It happened all the time. She would "slip away" from her security and no clues to her whereabouts would ever be found.

Her hair would be short - and possibly purple - for the foreseeable future. Maybe rainbow.

The plane taxied toward the runway. The pilot made an announcement, but Katrín didn't pay any attention. She was buckled in. Her seat back was in its upright position.

What more mattered?

She pressed back into her seat as the plane picked up speed.

But then...

Deceleration?

No announcement was made. The plane came to a near stop and taxied back toward the hanger.

"Why did we stop?" she called, though no one was in sight. There was no answer.

They came to a stop and the door opened. She could hear someone climbing the stairs, but couldn't see who it was.

"Ma'am?" It didn't surprise her that Thor was the one who came through the door. It couldn't have been Benjamin.

Katrín unbuckled her seatbelt and stood. "Where are we going?" She couldn't hide the weariness in her voice, didn't even try.

"A car is waiting for you, ma'am."

A car to where? She didn't ask, and Thor didn't offer. Another man drove the car while Thor rode in the passenger seat.

Katrín closed her eyes and waited for the car to reach the palace, but after a while realized it must be going much further. She stared out the window and tried to place the passing terrain. They were headed north, more or less.

The cottage at Lake Akushla?

Benjamin had mentioned it several times. His parents had spent many happy times there, both alone and with their children. He'd talked about taking her someday, but someday had never come. Until now?

The drive lasted nearly two hours, but eventually they pulled through a gate and down a long, tree-lined lane. The car rolled to a stop in front of a dwelling that didn't quite deserve the name "cottage." Palace-by-the-lake maybe. Katrín had never even seen pictures of it before.

Thor opened her door but didn't say anything. Another member of the staff opened the front door to the cottage for her.

No one waited for her inside either. One small step after another, she worked her way through the long foyer. Off to her left, she could see through partially open doors. Windows showed the lake beyond, but none of the rooms called to her.

Finally, she reached a door near the end. Pushing it open, she saw a large ballroom with windows reaching two stories high and overlooking the lake on all sides. It must be situated on a bit of a peninsula to have so many lake views.

First one note filled the air, then another. Katrín turned to see where it was coming from, but no one sat at the instruments off to the side. By the time she turned back, she recognized the tune as *King Alfred's Overture*.

"May I have this dance?"

Benjamin's voice didn't surprise her, but she turned to see him bowed slightly at the waist and holding out a hand.

"Why should I?"

His blue eyes were soft, filled with regret. "Please?"

She took his hand and let him pull her close, though not as close as he wanted to. With his arm around her waist, Katrín felt herself beginning to relax.

"I'm sorry," he whispered as the music reached a crescendo.

"For what?"

"For not taking up for you, not coming up with a plan to present the whole story to the people. For not being your champion when you needed one."

Whatever she'd expected, that wasn't it. "Being sorry is fine, but what are you going to do now?"

He squeezed her hand. "We have an interview scheduled in a couple of days. A reporter is coming here for a wide-ranging conversation, including a frank discussion about how and why we got married, today's story, and our plan for the monarchy and the family as a whole going forward."

"We?"

"If you'll stay. You're not actually needed in Islas del Sargasso for a few more days."

Had he found the ring? Did he know she wasn't planning to return?

"Tonight, it's just the two of us and a few staff here. I'm hoping we can spend some time talking, being together. Tomorrow, there will be a number of others here, too. We'll go over everything with a few members of the publicity team, including Elise, Marty, Marissa, and Harry. Tomorrow night, I'm taking you out for dinner in town, if you want to go. Then the interview."

She'd found herself moving closer and closer to him as he talked. Despite everything, Katrín felt a connection to Benjamin, wanted to be his wife in truth and not just for appearances sake, wanted to stay.

Forever.

"Okay," she whispered.

"I want to make this work, love. I know I said that before, and I know I didn't act like it today. I need something from you though."

Her heart stuck in her throat. "What's that?"

"I need you to be the sassy, take-no-prisoners Katrín I met that night at the piano. Take me to task if you need to. Tell me what I need to do to be good at this husband thing, because I don't know how to do it. I need you to help me, and not be scared you're going to offend me or that I'm going to exile you or something."

Katrín leaned her forehead against his shoulder. "I can do that."

She felt him take another deep breath. "I need to ask you one more thing, something far more serious."

"What's that?"

"Can you promise me you'll never leave?"

BENJAMIN FOUND himself holding his breath as he waited for her response.

"I can do that."

His shoulders slumped in relief. "You'll stay?"

"Yes."

The music drifted to an end. "You have no idea how happy that makes me."

"To be honest, I'm not sure how I'm feeling about it just yet."

"I can understand that." He stopped moving and stepped back. With her hand still snug in his, he led her to the door to outside. The balcony overlooked the lake and one of the tables held a simple meal of sandwiches and salad.

Benjamin held Katrín's chair for her then sat next to her. He reached for her hand again. "I'll say grace." After thanking God for the meal and those who made it, he let go. "I've never asked you about your life. Tell me about your favorite teacher?"

For two hours they talked about everything and nothing, moving from the table to a porch swing. Katrín's head dipped then rested more heavily against his shoulder, and he knew she'd fallen asleep.

After considering his options, Benjamin decided on the one he liked best. Katrín in his arms felt right. Once in his quarters, Benjamin laid her on the turned down bed and watched as she curled onto her side. He changed into pajamas and slid under the covers on the other side. As much as he wanted to pull her into his arms as they slept, he didn't. He wasn't sure how she'd feel about it.

Despite the long summer days, the room was dark when he woke up, thanks to the heavy curtains over the windows.

Without thinking about it, he reached across the bed to find it empty.

"I had to go to the bathroom." Katrín's voice carried across the room as a door closed behind her. The bed dipped as she sat back down. "Thank you for letting me sleep."

"The staff have instructions not to bother us until noon unless we decide to talk to them sooner." He didn't hold back his yawn. "Then we have those meetings."

"Is it bad that I wish we could stay here all day?" She sat against the headboard.

"No. I wish we could, too. I know I've promised several times, but I mean it. I will bring you up here soon when we have no other plans." He pushed himself up into a sitting position next to her. "Have someone bring us breakfast in bed, lunch in bed, dinner in bed, if we want. Or even just a day with nothing on the schedule."

"I like that plan better. As nice as all those meals in bed sound, I don't like the idea of all those crumbs."

Benjamin chuckled. "All right. There's a table over there where we could eat if we didn't want to leave the room. Or we could just tell everyone we want to be left alone except for meals."

She leaned her head against his shoulder. "It would be a bit of a relief not to have to see anyone or do anything for a whole day. I don't think either one of us have ever done that in our adult lives."

He tilted his head sideways until his cheek made contact with her hair. "I'm not sure I've ever had a day where I had nothing on the schedule. Certainly not since my father passed."

Katrín slid her hand down his arm until their fingers linked. "I don't think I ever knew. How did he pass?"

His fingers tightened around hers. "A heart attack, sort of. Not your usual kind. He had a blood clot that got caught on the buildup in his artery. It caused a heart attack. The doctors said he had a little more build up than they would have expected from a man his age, but not enough to actually cause the heart attack. Odds are, if it the clot hadn't gotten caught there, he would have died of an embolism, either in his lungs or in his brain. There was nothing anyone could have done."

"I'm so sorry. Growing up without your father couldn't have been easy, much less with a crown to deal with."

"I had plenty of people around me to help. I wish I'd listened to some of them a little better a little sooner. Then Isaiah wouldn't have been so entrenched."

Katrín seemed to be thinking something over, though she didn't say anything until he asked her. "Is it awful of me to admit

I'm still afraid your uncle is going to come back and cause trouble?"

His thumb rubbed along hers. "I am, too. More tests confirmed all of the blood found in his house was his, but the body still hasn't been found. So maybe he could be back someday, though, but for now, we have nothing to worry about."

"Thank goodness."

They talked for a little bit longer, until his stomach grumbled. He kissed the top of her head. "I think it's time for that breakfast." A tap on the button of his phone told him it was after ten. "I'll have it sent up, then we'll need to start our day."

Reluctantly, he let go of her hand and stood up, moving one of the curtains aside just enough to let some light in.

"This room's a lot smaller than I expected for the monarch, even at the lake cottage."

He held out a hand and she scooted across the bed to stand up next to him. "That's because this isn't the monarch's room. It's mine. It has been since my father became king. I never wanted to take over the monarch's room here, and refused to let my mother make me. I actually pulled rank on her, though she doesn't use it either. Someday, I'm sure we'll use it, but maybe we won't. Maybe, eventually, our oldest child will use it when he or she becomes monarch."

They moved to the window and stared out over the lake. "Our child," Katrín said softly.

Benjamin turned to face her. "Yes. Our child. We're expected to have at least two or three, you know."

A smile crossed her face. "I know. I'm looking forward to it. Eventually. Not just yet."

He chuckled. "I'm okay with that." With one finger, he pushed her morning hair off her forehead and behind her ear. "Can I kiss you?"

Katrín reached up and laced her fingers behind his neck. "I wish you would."

A first soft brush of his lips on hers wasn't enough, would never be enough, but Benjamin knew it was too soon to get carried away. After several soft kisses, he moved back and just held Katrín in his arms.

They might have had a rough start, but he had a feeling they were going to be just fine.

EPILOGUE

The kiss from Benjamin surpassed her memory of all the others. Grateful no one was around to see their reunion, Katrín framed his face with her hands as he easily lifted her off the ground with arms tight around her waist.

"I missed you," he murmured between kisses.

"I missed you, too."

"Three days was too long."

For some reason, that struck Katrín has much funnier than it should have. Giggles escaped until they overwhelmed the kisses.

Benjamin chuckled and set her feet back on the floor. "I'm glad I can make you laugh."

"I hope you always do."

He looped an arm around her shoulders and she slid hers around his waist as they walked toward the door to his quarters.

Their quarters.

Her things had been moved in while she was in Islas del Sargasso.

"Do I want to watch the report?" It had aired while she was overseas, and Katrín had done her best to avoid it.

EPILOGUE

"I haven't watched yet either. Mother did, though, and said it was a good piece." He pulled the door open and let her walk through. "She didn't include the question about Darius."

"How'd you get her to do that?"

"I promised her the exclusive when the time came. When I told Edward about it, I also asked him to be my mentor. Thor and Chamberlain are already doing the best they can, but it would be nice to talk to someone who's actually been a monarch, you know?"

"I'm so glad he's willing to help you."

"He was there when my parents met. So was Thor. My father and Edward were roommates at university in Auverignon. Thor was young enough to be in my father's classes with him. Edward met Miriam about the same time. In fact, they're my unofficial godparents." His thumb rubbed up and down her arm.

"Unofficial?"

"Because Edward was going to be monarch in another country, legally he couldn't be my godfather."

"So he still feels responsible."

"I think he always has, he just wasn't able to help like he wanted to, not until Darius got Esther pregnant. He was able to use the situation and the Treaty of 1703 to insinuate himself into my life and eventually begin to use the connection to begin to override Isaiah's influence." He pulled her a little tighter. "It worked."

"I'm so glad."

"Oh!"

She looked up to see his face light up. It made her smile.

"And as Thor's men were going through Isaiah's things, they found the original marriage license for Darius and Esther. I can't overturn the resolution until fall, but it doesn't matter. They're legally married in Eyjania, and it's effective before the resolution was enacted."

EPILOGUE

"That's wonderful. Will they be coming for a visit soon then?"

He shrugged as he sat on the sofa. "I haven't even had a chance to tell them yet. I found out about the time your plane landed."

She curled into his side as he pressed play on the recorded program. "I hope I can meet them soon."

"I hope so, too." He hesitated. "I also had a conversation with Laurie."

Katrín closed her eyes and blew out a breath. "I knew you were going to."

"She did let most of the story slip to someone she didn't know was a reporter. The guy had picked her to date in hopes of picking up some palace gossip. He picked the right person."

"And her consequences?"

He rubbed his hand up and down her arm. "Ten percent garnishment until she pays the fine for violating her nondisclosure agreement. She keeps her promotion to assistant pastry chef."

Laurie had won that part of the competition on the show. Katrín had been happy for her.

"However, she's not allowed to work on food prepared for the family. At least not for the foreseeable future."

Because that was a privilege not given to someone who had betrayed them, even unintentionally.

"Even Thor and Chamberlain pushed for a demotion, but it's their job to look for the threats, physical and otherwise, but I thought your idea for mercy fit this particular situation better. She knows she won't get another chance."

"Thank you." Katrín snuggled in closer. "I appreciate that."

He kissed the top of her head. "Shh. It's starting." Another kiss let her know he wasn't upset.

"King Benjamin knows as well as anyone that his family, and the monarchy in general, isn't nearly as popular as it was during his father's reign. He also knows the recent stories about his relationship with Queen Katrín haven't helped matters any." The reporter stood in front of

EPILOGUE

the lakeside cottage. *"Here, at the royal family's Lake Akushla residence, I sat down with the king and queen to discuss both of the recent news stories with them, as well as a wide range of other subjects with the king."*

The picture changed to the two of them seated on the couch. Katrín couldn't help but contrast the slightly awkward looking couple on the screen with others she'd seen - like Prince Harry and Meghan Markle when they announced their engagement or at their wedding. They were clearly in love and loved being around each other. Would she and Benjamin ever be so comfortable together?

For fifteen minutes, she watched as they told their story, every detail, except the plan for her to disappear and Benjamin's claustrophobia. Katrín was proud of herself for managing to avoid devolving into a blubbery mess as they'd talked to the reporter. She'd been in tears, but not nearly as bad as she'd feared.

The next twenty minutes were spent in the palace with Benjamin the day after Katrín left, talking about all manner of topics.

"There are a couple of priorities inside my own walls," Benjamin on the screen told the reporter. *"One thing I learned from Katrín was that some of the staff members aren't given adequate time off. It was written in her contract, one I approved five years ago, but clearly didn't read carefully enough, that she only got two half-days off a month. That's completely unacceptable. I realize her situation was a bit different than most of those who work for the palace, but all of the contracts need to be looked over again. I've appointed Katrín's mother, Mrs. Jónsson, to go through all of those, outside of the executive staff, to make sure there aren't any others that need to be renegotiated."*

"Why Mrs. Jónsson?"

"Prior to the incident we discussed yesterday, she was my father's server. He trusted her implicitly, and she's proven again that she's trustworthy. She and Allen, my brother-in-law, are moving onto the property

EPILOGUE

to be closer to Katrín which necessitates a job change for her anyway. I offered her this one, and she seems especially suited it."

Katrín found tears spilling down her cheeks. "You didn't tell me that."

"It wasn't definite when you left. I meant to tell you when you returned, but we kind of got sidetracked kissing."

The program started to wind down, but the reporter stood in front of the palace with a sly grin. *"There's one other thing. With the way their relationship started, there was one thing King Benjamin never did. He didn't tell me why he had the engagement ring first worn by the Queen Mother, since Queen Katrín has worn it since before the wedding."*

The picture changed to Benjamin and Katrín walking on the dock. Katrín knew what was coming, but she felt her heart in her throat anyway.

Benjamin-on-the-screen dropped to one knee and held up the ring. Katrín saw herself gasp and nod, knowing she'd said yes several times. He'd slid the ring back on her finger and picked her up and swung her in a circle. The video changed back to the reporter before Benjamin kissed her.

"And there you have it. King Benjamin on one knee asking Katrín to be his queen, our queen, for life." The reporter smiled. *"The headlines last week called her the indentured queen, but the truth is she's become a chosen marriage partner, and eventually, the mother of our next monarch."* The picture changed again to the two of them on the dock after the kiss ended. *"Seeing the two of them together, I can tell you, whatever their beginnings, they are the real deal. A match the late King Alfred could be and the Queen Mother will be quite proud of."*

Benjamin turned the television off and reached for something on the side table. "I have something else for you. First, the piano has been moved into *our* room. If you'd like it somewhere else, just let me know, and I'll see it gets moved." He handed the paper to Katrín. "Second, this."

EPILOGUE

She opened it and read the legalese, trying to make sense of it. After a few seconds, it sank in. "My contract?"

"It's been paid off."

Katrín twisted until she could give Benjamin a kiss. "Thank you. I didn't realize until just now how much this was hanging over my head."

"I realized something the night you almost left."

"What's that?"

"I stood in front of King Alfred's dagger and realized I'll never be worthy."

She started to interrupt him, but he stopped her with a finger to her lips.

"And I thought about what you said about him at my age, how he probably wasn't the person history has made him out to be, not yet. I realized the truth is that none of us are worthy. The men knighted at Wulfen Castle passed every test the Wulfriths could give them, but even they needed a Savior. I'm sure if we dug deeply enough into their lives, we'd find out they failed, maybe even failed often. But they didn't stop striving to be worthy." He kissed the side of her head. "And that's all I can do."

Katrín turned his words over in her head. "That makes sense. It's all any of us can do. We all need mercy and grace, from God and from each other. We're all works in progress."

"I know, but I should have done that a long time ago. We both know I never should have offered you that stupid deal, but my first priority should have been to take care of this legally. Can you forgive me for taking so long?"

She smiled softly at him. "It's already forgotten."

Benjamin's fingers threaded through her hair as he kissed her again. "She was right you know."

"Who?"

"The reporter. Indentured queen might have been accurate at first, but given the choice, I'd choose you. Every time."

"And I'd choose you."

EPILOGUE

He kissed her again. As Benjamin stood and picked her up, carrying her across the threshold to the room they'd share for the rest of their lives, Katrín knew what it was like to be wanted, to be chosen. From lowest in the palace to queen of her country, chosen by the king to be his partner.

And she'd never felt so at home.

LETTER TO READERS

Dear Reader,

Thank you for joining Benjamin and Katrín in *The Indentured Queen*! I appreciate you and hope you enjoyed it! This is the fourth book in the *Crowns & Courtships* series!

I've mentioned before that the *Crowns & Courtships* stories have been divided into two separate series - the main one with the novels, and the novellas. As currently envisioned, the novellas will be shorter (clearly ;)) and come in between or around the novels and won't NEED to be read. Rather, they'll enhance your understanding of the stories. The blurb section of Amazon's product page will have a list of the combined order in case you'd like to make sure you've read them all :).

In fact, *Love for the Ages* is available free as a thank you to newsletter subscribers! It's the story of Alfred and Eliana when they first meet. (Ah! The early 90s… ;))

Next up is Jacqueline Grace's story - and hopefully we'll find out whether Isaiah is really gone for good or not.

Her story will release this fall! Swipe through for a preview!

Allen

LETTER TO READERS

If you read dedications, you noticed this story is dedicated to my cousin. If you follow any of my Facebook stuff, you've likely seen me talk about him. Technically, Allen was my second cousin, but what's a few degrees of separation ;)?

Last November, I was all set to write *The Inadvertent Princess* for my 2017 National Novel Writing Month project. Instead, I felt an urgency to write *The Indentured Queen* (then titled *In Concert with the King*). I had already talked to Allen about basing a character loosely on him, and he loved the idea.

I saw him last September, during his last hospital stay. In October, he was sent home and told it was simply a matter of time.

In January, he heard the words he'd longed his whole life to hear - *well done, my good and faithful servant.*

But in December, I was able to send him the first, very early and very rough, copy of *The Indentured Queen*. I don't know that he was able to finish it, but I know he read some.

My reaction when Benjamin first thinks unflattering thoughts about his brother-in-law was actually quite visceral It was all I could do to type his (realistic) thoughts that I knew in no way reflected my feelings toward Allen. There were tears, and even anger at a fictional character of my own creation.

But in the end, we all know the truth.

Allen was a beloved gift from God.

My life, along with so many others, was changed by knowing him.

The Wulfriths & Valdorians

Some of you may have recognized some familiar characters! The Wulfriths of Wulfen Castle who knighted King Alfred the First and gave him the Wulfrith Dagger come from the amazing imagination of Tamara Leigh! Her Age of Faith series is AMAZING, and if you haven't read it yet, you totally should! It's knights and ladies and sword fights and swoony heroes (#TeamGarr!) and everything amazing! And her covers! They're so gorgeous, I had to have paper copies ;). Seriously, check her out! I am SO VERY HONORED she allowed me to use the Wulfriths in Benjamin's story. No, there's no plans for either of us to write King Alfred's story, but we can imagine it for ourselves! Here's her Amazon page!

Tamara is not only an incredible writer (seriously!), but an amazing person! Thank you so much for letting me use your world, Tamara!

Special thanks also to Julia Keanini for letting me use Prince Theo of Valdoria and Princess Alex, now of Valdoria but previously of Litiania! If you haven't read her royal books (the Princes of Valdoria series as well as *A Royal (Fake) Engagement)*, you should check them out! Here's her Amazon page.

HEA-TV

Once again, this is still a work in progress, but it's being worked on (and hopefully, by the time this releases, all of the Crowns & Courtships books will be done).

It's found at www.hea-tv.com (that's the name of the Hallmark type channel in this universe, remember?) you'll find "Everything You Ever Wanted To Know About Carol Moncado's Fictional Universe... & More"! There's a "universe" timeline where you can see how everything fits together. Each book will have (or already has) it's own timeline. There's book wikis with character and location/business lists (what was that restaurant again?! ;)) with each entry as a glossary term so you can hover over it to find out more about that character/place, along with summaries of what that book was about. Hello, SPOILERS! :D

There aren't any character or location/business wikis - yet. But eventually. Once we get the book wikis caught up, we'll work on the others.

Previews

Next up you'll find that preview for Book 5 in Crowns & Courtships along with more information about it.

After that, you'll find a preview of *Love for the Ages*. You can find it on Amazon, but if you'd like a free copy, simply sign up for my newsletter, and a link will be sent to you as a thank you.

Serenity Landing Book Club

What is that?! It's the Facebook reader group that started last summer! I'd love to have you there! It's easier for you to see what's posted than on a Facebook page and we do fun stuff! There will be discussion questions after the release of a book, sneak peeks of the next one, general discussion, and chances to win copies of books and other goodies! I'd love to have you there!

Other Stuff

I see a meme floating around Facebook from time to time that tells readers what they can do to help their favorite authors. Buying their next book or giving a copy away is kind of a no-brainer, but the biggest thing you can do is write a review. If you enjoyed *A Royally Beautiful Mess* would you consider doing just that?

I would LOVE to hear from you! My email address is books@candidpublications.com. To stay up-to-date on releases, you can sign up for my newsletter (there's fun stuff - like a chance to get *free* novellas from time to time)! You'll also get notices of sales, including special preorder pricing! And I won't spam!) or there's always my website :). You can find my website and blog at www.carolmoncado.com. I blog about once a month at www.InspyRomance.com. And, of course, there's Facebook and my Facebook page, Carol Moncado Books. But... the way pages work, sometimes very few people (often 1-5% of "likes") will see anything posted. I keep trying to find the best way to get to know y'all and "spend time" together outside of your Kindle - at least for those of you who want to!

Thanks again!

ACKNOWLEDGMENTS

Writing can be very lonely, but the reality is no one walks alone. I can't begin to name all of those who've helped me along the way. My husband, Matt, who has always, *always* believed in me. All of the rest of my family and in-loves who never once looked at me like I was nuts for wanting to be a writer. Jan C. (my "other mother") has always believed in me and Stacy S. who has been my dearest friend for longer than I can remember.

Then there's my writer friends. Bethany Turner (have you read *The Secret Life of Sarah Hollenbeck* yet?!) and Mikal Dawn (AH! *Count Me In*!) have both been so wonderful the last few months keeping me laughing and my spirits up. #MiBeCaIsEternalYo

Ginger Solomon, author of *One Choice* and a bunch of other fantastic books (but *One Choice* is still my favorite!), has been invaluable with her proofreading services. Check her books out!

Then Jennifer Major, a Canadian no less ;), who does life with me and loves me anyway! There's my MozArks ACFW peeps who laugh with me, critique, and encourage to no end. Then there's the InspyRomance crew, the CIA, my Spicy peeps (you know who you are!), and all of the others who've helped me along on this journey.

HUGE thanks again to Tamara Leigh for the use of the

Wulfriths and Wulfrith Dagger! Big hugs, my friend! And to Julia Keanini for the use of Theo and Alex!

And Emily N., Ginger L., and Tory U. who are INVALUABLE to my writing process! I have NO IDEA what I'd do without the three of you!

I know I've forgotten many people and I hate that. But you, dear reader, would quickly get bored.

So THANK YOU to all of those who have helped me along the way. I couldn't have done this without you and you have my eternal gratitude. To the HUNDREDS of you (I'm gobsmacked!) who pre-ordered and encouraged me without knowing it as that little number continued to climb, you have my eternal gratitude. I hope you stick around for the next one!

And, of course, last but never, *ever*, least, to Jesus Christ, without whom none of this would be possible - or worth it.

ABOUT THE AUTHOR

When she's not writing about her imaginary friends, USA Today Bestselling Author Carol Moncado prefers binge watching pretty much anything to working out. She believes peanut butter M&Ms are the perfect food and Dr. Pepper should come in an IV. When not hanging out with her hubby, four kids, and two dogs who weigh less than most hard cover books, she's probably reading in her Southwest Missouri home.

Summers find her at the local aquatic center with her four fish, er, kids. Fall finds her doing the band mom thing. Winters find her snuggled into a blanket in front of a fire with the dogs. Spring finds her sneezing and recovering from the rest of the year.

She used to teach American Government at a community college, but her indie career, with over twenty titles released, has allowed her to write full time. She's a founding member and former President of MozArks ACFW, blogger at InspyRomance, and is represented by Tamela Hancock Murray of the Steve Laube Agency.

www.carolmoncado.com

books@candidpublications.com

facebook.com/AuthorCarolMoncado

twitter.com/CarolMoncado

amazon.com/author/carolmoncado

bookbub.com/authors/carol-moncado

The CANDID Romance Series

Finding Mr. Write
Finally Mr. Write
Falling for Mr. Write

The Monarchies of Belles Montagnes Series
(Previously titled The Montevaro Monarchy
and The Brides of Belles Montagnes series)

Good Enough for a Princess
Along Came a Prince
More than a Princess
Hand-Me-Down Princess
Winning the Queen's Heart
Protecting the Prince (Novella)
Prince from her Past

Serenity Landing Second Chances

Discovering Home
Glimpsing Hope
Reclaiming Hearts

Crowns & Courtships

Heart of a Prince
The Inadvertent Princess
A Royally Beautiful Mess
The Indentured Queen
Her Undercover Prince

Crowns & Courtships Novellas

Dare You
A Kaerasti for Clari
(currently available in the Out of the Blue Bouquet Collection)
Love for the Ages
(available as a thank you to newsletter subscribers - click here to join)

Serenity Landing Tuesdays of Grace
9/11 Tribute Series

Grace to Save

Serenity Landing Lifeguards
Summer Novellas

The Lifeguard, the New Guy, & Frozen Custard
(previously titled: *The Lifeguards, the Swim Team, & Frozen Custard*)
The Lifeguard, the Abandoned Heiress, & Frozen Custard

Serenity Landing Teachers
Christmas Novellas

Gifts of Love
Manuscripts & Mistletoe
Premieres & Paparazzi

Mallard Lake Township

Ballots, Bargains, & the Bakery (novella)

Timeline/Order for Crowns & Courtships and Novellas
1. *Love for the Ages*
2. *A Kaerasti for Clari*
3. *Dare You*

(the first three can be read in any order,
but technically this is the timeline)
3. *Heart of a Prince*
4. *The Inadvertent Princess*
5. *A Royally Beautiful Mess*
6. *The Indentured Queen*
7. *Her Undercover Prince*

Made in the USA
Columbia, SC
01 October 2023